PHANTASMA

The Awakening

A PHI ATHANATOI NOVEL

EFTHALIA

Phantasma: The Awakening (Rev. ed.) Previously published as Phantasma.

ISBN: 978-0-6487854-3-9

DEDICATION

To the three people in my life who I love unconditionally, Dimitrios, Leonidas and Kassandra. You are the center of my universe. *Sas agapo*.

AKNOWLEDGMENTS

To all my amazing friends in the writing community and family, thank you for all your encouragement and wisdom.

"It's not a myth if you believe it, embrace it, live it and have seen it."

EFTHALIA

ONE

"I do not know whether there are gods,
but there ought to be." ~ DIOGENES

Present Day, Charleston, South Carolina, USA

"*Gamoto*." The Greek profanity slid without effort from her lips. "Remind me to kick Tom's ass." Carissa Alkippes glanced at her partner, John Lopez, who nodded in agreement.

"I'd be glad to help." A sneer broke across his mouth. "The slime bag has misled us for, like, what ... the third time?"

"Closer to the trillionth, and I have better things to do than chase dead leads." She had her share of seedy Greeks, giving her false information. *I might pin his balls to the wall. Not that I want to see that part of him.* Grinning, she envisaged Tom's face when she shoved her gun up to his nostril and threatened him.

"Let's see if there's a party happening inside. Otherwise, I'll buy you a burger," Lopez said, pulling open the door to Jostlers warehouse.

The hinges creaked and echoed inside the dim, hollow abyss, breaking the fantasy playing out in her head. The minute she stepped into the warehouse, the cool darkness caressed the skin on her arms, sending goosebumps over her body.

"Something tells me we should ditch this and go for the burger. Besides, we're off duty."

"Does look like a waste of time," Lopez grumbled, moving in behind her.

"I'm salivating, thinking of the burger. Did you need to put that erotic image in my head?"

"Burgers are not erotic."

"Says you, but hell, my stomach and taste buds think they're orgasmic." A growl sounded from her belly.

Lopez's laugh reverberated in the dark space. "I think your stomach has just announced we're here."

"Let's get this search over with," she uttered, trying to mask her embarrassment. The lack of vehicles and lights clicked her awareness into top gear. Her skin stung and realization carved words in her brain, the type she didn't fancy. *This has all the makings of a setup.*

Light coruscated through the filthy windows and etched a path ahead as they walked further in and surveyed the bare space. Something locked her feet to the concrete. Sounds. She strained to listen between heavy breaths. *Fighting.* Nothing accelerated her heartbeat like a good dustup.

"You hear that?" she whispered to Lopez.

"Yup. I'm going to go check the other side."

"Be careful," she cautioned.

"Probably a couple of raccoons." He walked past her and turned his head to wink at her, then made his way to the other end of the warehouse.

Her reflexes snapped into action and her hand traveled to her gun side, springing the Glock free from its holster.

Fresh grunts echoed from further inside the warehouse. Her fingers tingled before they converted to steel on the gun, becoming one with it. Recognition spiked in her chest. "Raccoons my ass. Something is going down," she muttered.

A door slammed and disappointment bungee jumped into the pit of her stomach.

"Damn, I'm not going to get that burger," she whispered. Her hunger would have to wait. The first order of business was to find out who or what was making the noise.

She continued with small steps toward the middle of the warehouse. A movement to her right caught her eye. Surprise punched her lungs and spread down to her abdomen. A monstrous shape materialized from the darkened depths. Dark crimson skin covered bulging muscle on his body and bare head. He snarled, showing off his chalky, razor-sharp teeth. It wasn't the dental work, pointy ears, and pig-like nose that set her on edge. No. The reptilian yellow eyes alerted her gray matter to the fact he wasn't human. Fear fused its way back up to her heart, sending it into a wild gallop.

She tried to focus as bile climbed up her throat. Fear gripped the soles of her feet and held her rooted to the spot. The crimson figure stalked toward her, swinging a sword in his thick, talon-like hands.

"What are you?" she whispered to the cool, dark depths. "Maybe I should lay off the *baklava*. It's seriously causing sugar-induced hallucinations."

Her grip tightened around the weapon. She blew out a breath and hoped her religious practice at the shooting range paid off. An ear-piercing boom split through the warehouse. Shell casings dropped to her feet, one smacked her in the forehead. The bullets from her Glock met their target. The crimson beast flinched and looked down to where the bullets had torn through tissue. He closed the remaining distance with speed. His height towered above her. Reaching forward, he pulled the gun out of her hand and crushed it. It landed on the concrete with a dull clunk.

His yellow eyes met hers. A roar tore from the beast's throat and vibrated through her. The fine hair on her neck stood to attention, propelling her to retreat. *Move your ass, Carissa.* With measured steps, she backed away. But it was useless. The beast pointed his sword in her direction, making his intentions clear. Another deafening growl rumbled from his mouth.

"For something ugly, you sure move fast."

A sneer broke across her assailant's face, revealing his sharp teeth. He was in front of her again before she could inhale her next bit of moldy air.

"*Gamoto.*" She ducked and came up, throwing a kick to its midsection. It was unmovable and unstoppable. She pulled back fast. From the corner of her eye, she caught movement as something leaped in her direction.

"What the ... Is that a dog?" She squinted for better focus. Realization slammed into her—a wolf. "This is one epic nightmare."

She shook her head, trying to process the scene, but her mind was lethargic in response. *Impossible.*

The wolf tore into the crimson beast, but he broke free and made a beeline in her direction. The sight propelled her feet into action. She turned and ran, her heart pumping wildly as she surged forward. Speed failed to put distance between her and the gruesome creature hot on her tail. He pushed into her with enough force to knock her facedown. She scrambled to right herself, nails clawing at the concrete, tearing like paper. Her body coiled tight, ready to use every martial arts move she knew. Hell, she'd even make those stupid sounds they made in the movies if she had to.

The crimson antagonist fell dead in front of her.

How? The wolf? She looked around for the furry creature, only to find him tearing at another crimson figure.

She patted her pocket for the pepper spray, but a pair of vise-like hands seized her by the throat and halted her actions. Gasping for air, she struggled, kicking and elbowing against the unbreakable granite grip of her attacker. She had four minutes to break his front choke hold before she lost consciousness. She jabbed at his throat, but he didn't flinch. With each action she executed, her momentum waned. Her breath became labored and her last kick landed with an ineffective thump.

The fingers around her esophagus tightened. Pain slammed into her chest and lungs, squeezing out every drop of her life juice, her existence slowly slipping into the dark chasm of dissolution. She'd seen plenty of death as a police officer, and those moments shuffled through her brain like a deck of cards. They all brought her to one horrible thought—*game over*.

Fear gripped her. She let out a whimper. Anger rushed forth from her unconscious mind, and then she caught the light reflecting off metal. The sword sliced through the air, connecting with its target. Warm blood, thick and foul, splattered over her face, the beast's grip no longer a threat. She fell to the ground on her ass, her body like a heavy bag of grain.

The creature's head rolled beside her. She recoiled at the sight of its sharp teeth and open yellow eyes.

Air rushed to her lungs, causing her to cough. Twisting her body onto her hands and knees, she barked out another cough to dislodge the stab of discomfort that skewered her larynx. Slowly her erratic breathing stabilized, and a wave of adrenaline surged. Her stomach rolled and somersaulted. Bile rushed to her throat. She got it under control. Being sick wasn't an option.

Booted feet filled her vision.

Xen Lyson scrutinized the woman at his feet. When he had scented her fear from across the warehouse, a tidal wave of possession and protection raged through his body. He smirked at the ease with which he'd eliminated the creatures that threatened her. Spikes of power emanated from her, caressing his skin.

What are you?

He probed her mind, trying to access information that would tell him who she was. It was fruitless. A wall blocked his path. The only thing he lifted from her memory was her name—Carissa.

Intriguing, he thought. He would have to study her more closely, but first, he had to get her away from the demons. The skirmish was nowhere near over. His men were fighting all around him, two of whom had his back. He studied the woman who knelt in front of him on all fours and held out his hand to her.

She appeared reluctant to take it. Her eyes darted left to right. His keen sense picked up her rapid heartbeat. It didn't surprise him she sought a way to escape. The blood on his fangs would be a sight. He retracted them to assure her he wasn't the monster she should fear.

Her breath hitched at his action and clued him in to her uneasiness. Her hand traveled to her throat, clasping it. He watched her swallow hard and wince. Deep red threads had emerged where the demon had her in a choke hold. His anger rose as her discomfort played out before him. Desire to wrap her in his arms hit him with an unknown force. He wanted to decapitate every demon in the warehouse.

"Give me your hand. I'm not a threat." Emotion thickened his voice. He wanted to be her shield from the chaos that surrounded them.

He waited.

Her hand closed firmly around his. A smile broke on his lips as the coolness of her hand mingled with the heat of his own. He liked the brief connection. He hoisted her to her feet, and her body shook against him when he wrapped his arms around her to steady her.

A vibrating growl from the depths of the warehouse brought him out of his momentary daze, and the brief bond splintered.

He had a small window of time. He stepped close, placed his fingertips on either side of her head, and looked into her eyes. A low, commanding voice broke from his lips, this time penetrating to the dark recess of her mind. He had to be quick.

She shook her head beneath his grip, fighting him. Admiration flowed through him. *Never* had he had difficulty in using *hypnosi* to mesmerize and alter someone's memories telepathically. He'd been doing this for over two thousand years. The woman in front of him presented the first challenge to his abilities. Interest—and something more—wrapped its tendrils around his mind. He began his ancient Greek chant.

"*Charis*, you will forget the *aletheia* you have witnessed, and you will do me the *doxa,* and remember only me, *pantote.* Get your partner," he commanded.

"Yes—forgive you—forget the truth, honor you by remembering only you always, and get my partner," she repeated under his *hypnosi* spell.

"Run now," he yelled.

He pulled out his *xiphos* and spun around to carve an unrestricted path. The two men who had his back moved towards the new rush of demons entering the fight.

He hacked and sliced demons with his sword, clearing the way. He caught sight of her yanking the door to the warehouse open. The sheen of moonlight cocooned her body. Relief washed over him.

"*Eftychos*—fortunately, safe for now," he uttered.

Bones crunched in front of his fist while his blade ruptured flesh.

Carissa ran out of the warehouse. Her thoughts resembled muddy water. All she wanted to do was find Lopez.

"Where's the car? Lopez, you'd better not have driven off," she yelled into the night.

Patting the pocket of her jeans for her keys. She sure as hell didn't have them.

"How could he do that to me?" Adrenaline spurred her instincts and rushed through every nerve in her body. She needed to find Lopez. *Why am I out here?* She shook her head trying to get clarity.

Her legs moved and a single thought repeated in her mind. *Find Lopez, find Lopez.* The string of replaying words propelled her towards the rear entrance door. Pulling the handle, she yanked it open with force. Lopez's voice reached her ears.

"Asshole," he choked out.

She squinted, trying to adjust her sight to the darkness. When her eyes had adapted, she could see Lopez fighting. A glint of metal entered his stomach. Lopez dropped to the ground. She broke into a sprint toward him, but something hard obstructed her path. The impact catapulted her backward. With a clunk, her head connected with something solid.

Her vision blurred.

Detective Gelon Jones's face appeared beside her when her heavy eyelids blinked open, fluttered, then closed. She could hear an ambulance siren. *Some dream.* She cracked open one eyelid, then tried to take in her surroundings. Jones wore a mask of stone. His crystal-clear blue gaze was fixed on her. *He has the prettiest eyes.* Those blues were burning a hole in her head in some weird, bizarre, Superman kind of way. *Okay, he's pissed but why?*

She tried to move.

He leaned closer. She caught a light whiff of the aftershave he always wore.

"Carissa. Can you hear me?" His stone face disappeared, and concern shifted across his features.

"Argh." The only thing she could manage in her present state sounded very much like a wild animal.

"You were hurt. We're on the way to the hospital."

"*Skata,* I'm in an ambulance?"

"Yes."

Her mind raced, trying to stitch together what had happened, only to be met with flashes that made little sense. Her head spun and she swallowed hard.

"*Gamoto.*"

Gelon leaned closer. "I'd say it's pretty fucked, as you put it."

"Here, I thought this might help." Carissa's best friend, Ligi Achilles, shoved a paper cup of cocoa into her hands.

The steam beckoned her to take a sip, but it was the chocolate that lured her lips to the rim of the cup. Vending machine cocoa wasn't her favorite, but right now it seemed better than zilch. A sudden thought halted her hand before the cup reached her lips.

"Do you think I should drink this? Maybe I should wait till after they've given me the hepatitis shot." Her feet dangled as she sat there on the hospital bed in nothing but a white gown. She shivered. On the inside, she was cold, freezing. The type of chill that was arctic. Stuff like this didn't happen to her. *Pote*—never.

"You're probably right," Ligi said, taking the cup and placing it on the over-bed table.

"Thanks for coming and bringing me clothes."

"Don't be silly, girlfriend. Where else would I be? I'm the only family you've got." Ligi owned a little shop called *Siren Music* on King Street in Charleston. They had been best friends since college. Carissa had clumsily stepped on Ligi's flip-flop and sent her catapulting into the arms of the most popular quarterback. This scored Carissa a lifelong friendship and Ligi a date. Ligi had not been impressed with the quarterback's intellectual talent.

"Rubbing two rocks together gives off more of a spark than he does," Ligi had complained later. "It was like looking at a brick with eyes." She'd ranted for an hour and then swore never to date a football player again. So far, she hadn't. The plus for Ligi was that she was so knowledgeable about everything. Yes, she was clumsy, but boy did she rock in the intelligence department. Maybe that's why she went through men so quickly. She needed someone who would sizzle her brain.

The sound of the door being pulled open brought Carissa out of her musings.

"Officer Alkippes, I'm Doctor Curtz."

Startled, Ligi stood up and knocked the over-bed table, spilling cocoa all over the bed where Carissa sat.

The doctor eyed Ligi, amused. Carissa watched as her friend batted her eyelashes at him.

The flame-haired vixen easily put men under her spell just by looking at them—like now. Carissa stifled a laugh, then cleared her throat. "Ahem."

Pain sliced through her esophagus. Had someone tried to choke her? There were red and purple marks on her throat, the deep throb of the injury a constant reminder something had gripped her throat hard, yet she had no recollection of it.

"Ah yes, Officer Alkippes. How about I give you that shot so we can get on with the routine check?" His lips twitched.

From the corner of her eye, she watched Ligi retrieve some tissues from her bag. She'd spilled the cocoa and was now flapping around like a loon, trying to clean up the mess she'd made. Carissa turned her head at the same time as the doctor did, watching the spectacle unravel.

Dr. Curtz shook his head. Carissa caught the amusement that danced on his features. She beamed at her friend. Ligi and clumsiness were a marriage that couldn't be severed.

Ligi flashed one of her smiles.

"I'd like to get it over with," Carissa said. The spell the doctor was under broke.

He jabbed the needle in her leg. *Boy, he's heavy-handed.* She bit her lip to mask the discomfort. His fingers worked quickly, using a swab to stop the speck of blood after he removed the needle. "What about my partner, John Lopez? Can you tell me anything?

"He's in critical condition."

"Can I see him?"

"They wheeled him into surgery, again."

"Where?" She grabbed the doctor's arm and shook it hard. "Where?"

"You have two police officers outside your door. It doesn't appear that you're going anywhere." He gave her a smug look.

Her fist itched to plant a punch right on his nose. She clenched her hands. She lacked Ligi's magical charm.

"I get it."

"Good. You can see him after they've discharged you."

Asshole, she mentally shouted at his back when he exited the room.

"Let's go over this again." Detective Gelon Jones said, raising an eyebrow. He straightened his spine, parted his muscly thighs, and then crossed his arms across his wide chest. His t-shirt stretched over bulging muscles.

Uh oh, he's going all alpha on me. That's his "this is shit" stance.

Tension and annoyance rolled off him in waves and slapped her hard in the face. Suspicion had ugly tentacles when it wrapped itself around one's mind. A weighted sigh left his lips. He did not believe her. At this moment, their friendship meant nothing. This reflected his duty as a detective.

Her partner had been wounded and was fighting for his life. She'd act the same way if the tables were turned. Jones was doing his job.

"You proceeded into the dark warehouse with Lopez roughly at eight p.m. You both heard a noise and separated to investigate where it was coming from, and that's all you remember."

"Lame, but yes."

"You have no recollection of how you ended up at the back of the warehouse, passed out, with blood all over you. How your car was found dumped, upside down, two miles from the warehouse, or how Lopez was stabbed?" With each enunciation his razor-sharp words hit like bullets, lashing her fatigued body with the potency of his doubt.

The vein in his neck twitched. She watched the little anger party that danced inside him. She'd tell him one more time.

"I've told you, Jones, I can't remember." She cleared her throat, trying to soothe the dryness. There didn't appear to be any good reason to mention the tall, dark stranger with the sword. No, that little doozy had to stay close to her chest until she could connect the puzzle pieces of her fragmented memories. No point in sounding crazier, right?

"I wish I could tell you more, but I can't because it's not there. Tom gave us the tip-off that something was going down in the warehouse. We were going to do a routine check and call for backup if it looked suspicious, like a drug deal. When we got there, there was no movement, so we did the routine thing, and were contemplating getting a burger." Her stomach growled on cue. She caught Jones's quick smile and heat crept up her cheeks. "I can't remember anything after that. Not even how I hit my head or got these lovely bruises on my neck. You know more than me."

He let out a long breath that swam right over her, his jaw clenched, and his features hardened to stone. "You know they have declared you unfit for duty?" His lips tightened.

"I guessed as much." She wished with all her bruises and the aches in her bones that they'd never gone into that warehouse. A thickness formed in her throat. *It's your fault your partner's condition is critical.*

He stepped closer and whispered. "Your shell casings on the floor of the warehouse tell me you hit something, but the body is missing." He eased back and watched her with a raised eyebrow.

Her eyes widened. Nausea rolled in her stomach. "You think I killed someone," she bit out, hushed and through gritted teeth.

"I never said that."

"But you implied it."

"No. I didn't." He ran a hand through his dark hair. "It's suspicious, Carissa, and I'm trying hard to clear your ass."

"I'm sorry, Jones, but I don't remember jack. You have to believe me."

"I do, but if you remember anything, anything at all, you call me. I don't care where or what time it is, got it?"

"Got it." He gave her a tight hug. Sitting on the bed made her feel so small. His acceptance of her lack of memory made the world of difference. She fought the tears that threatened to break free behind her eyes. He pulled back and walked to the door.

"Hey!" she called out. "Do you think you could speed up the process so I can get out of here?"

"You've got to see the psych before you can go."

Drat, she'd forgotten about having to be shredded to pieces over her state of mind, which was already in ribbons.

"Okay. For what it's worth, thanks for finding me."

"Thank Lopez. He texted when you two separated."

The intensity with which he looked at her unnerved her. He held her gaze for a moment longer, then pulled the handle on the door and disappeared.

What was that about? She drew in a breath, then expelled it.

Naturally, he didn't really buy the bit about her not remembering anything further. She'd known Jones a long time. They'd joined the force together. He was family, and family knew when you weren't willing to share details.

The minutes tapped into hours at a sluggish pace. The psych evaluation lasted longer than Carissa would have liked. Jones's repetitive questioning did little but add a layer of exhaustion to her rickety nerves. Images of her comfortable bed soaked into her conscious mind. Ligi, bless her, assisted her to her beat-up VW. She opened the creaky door and tossed the rubbish on the floor into the back before helping Carissa into the seat. The cut-up vinyl stabbed her skin through the thin material of her trousers.

"You should get a new car."

"Girlfriend, I like my car, and you should stop riding that death trap of a bike."

Carissa loved bikes and rode hers whenever she could. "Okay, I so don't want to do the bike argument right now."

"I know you're not divulging all. What really happened?" Ligi asked, shoving the key into the ignition and bringing the old girl to life. She slammed her foot on the accelerator, maneuvering around the hospital parking lot like she was on an obstacle course.

She narrowly missed a few parked cars as she wove in and out among the gaps.

"Why can't you drive up and down the designated aisles like a normal person?"

"Because it makes me dizzy and I feel like I'm going around in circles."

Carissa rolled her eyes, then braced herself for the scene before her. An old man strolled into their path. Her gut dropped and her muscles tightened, waiting for the impact. Her silent scream died on her lips. To her sweaty relief, Ligi swerved in time.

"I seriously wonder how you keep your license."

"I have friends in high places."

"Oh no, no way will I wipe your tickets from the system. You're a menace to the population of Charleston."

"Don't go getting any ideas about having my license revoked. I can see those wheels in your head turning."

"Me? Never." Carissa put her hand to her chest for dramatic effect.

"You know, that's not very convincing. Now stop changing the subject and tell me what happened. And I want the entire story, not the condensed version."

She bit her lip. Time to rehash what she could remember. "How do I explain what happened without sounding like a patient who's escaped a mental institution? It's a little scratchy."

"Then hit me with what you've got, girlfriend."

"Remember, you asked."

"Will you get on with it? I'm about to burst a blood vessel here."

A long breath left Carissa's lips. "Do you recall the weird dreams I've had over the years?"

"Yes, the ones about the hot-ass Greek god?"

"Well, here's the thing, and I know I'm going to sound insane, but he was there. Like, *really* there." She dragged her hands through her hair, then exhaled loudly. "I know it sounds stupid and the whole dream-into-reality thing makes little sense." Her tone dropped a few octaves as she finished her bizarre word-regurgitation of the events that had transpired inside the warehouse. "He's real, not a dream. I swear it's the truth."

Ligi's mouth opened, then closed. She swerved and narrowly missed hitting a stray dog.

"So, let me get this straight. You don't remember much, but you *think*—and this is the key—that your dream man appeared in the flesh, while you were following a dodgy lead?" Ligi narrowed her eyes and pursed her lips.

Carissa noted her discombobulation. "Yes."

"Sounds to me like you hit that head of yours pretty darn hard."

Carissa laughed. "I did hit it hard. I told you that at the hospital." Absent-mindedly, she raised her hand to the back of her head. The golf ball-sized lump hurt when her fingers brushed over it.

"Yeah you did, and I'm just reminding you."

"It's surreal, Ligi."

"Listen, your dreams have been happening more frequently. Maybe that, plus the hit on your head, is what makes you think he was there."

"No. Ligi, you're not listening to me. He was there, and he had a damn sword in his hands. He saved me. I know he did."

"What does this mean?"

"It means that I remember jack shit about anything else that happened tonight, or last night if you want to be particular with time." She caught Ligi's amusement because her friend was a time Nazi. Ligi swerved sharply into the driveway, almost plastering Carissa's head to the passenger window. After tonight, stunt driving would take on new meaning. "You just missed the tree and the neighbor's cat."

"I did not."

"You need glasses."

"I do not."

Ligi killed the engine, and the car sat anything but straight in Carissa's wide driveway.

Carissa yanked her door open and staggered out of the car. Ligi fell out of her door. They looked at each other; their laughter echoed in the quiet street.

"You know, Ligi, I'm starting to think your clumsiness is catching."

"I'm not clumsy."

"Then what do you call it?"

"Uncoordinated."

"Ha, it's the same thing—clumsy."

"Gah, I will not win with you."

Carissa grinned and shook her head firmly. Ligi would not win this round because, on the inside, Carissa was torn, and the banter helped keep her sane and grounded.

They walked to the front door. "Do you need me to get you anything?" Ligi asked.

"No." Yeah, she needed a new brain, but, hey, those were scarce. "Thank you for all you've done. All I need is sleep, and badly." She pulled Ligi into a hug, savoring it. This sliver of a moment provided the relief her bone-weary body needed, and the fortification only friendship offered.

"Okay, you give me a buzz if you change your mind." Her friend headed towards her car.

"Goodnight," she whispered.

The events of the evening crept into her mind, taking it captive and smothering it in a haze of confusion. When Carissa lifted her hand to wave to her friend, she was already in her car, reversing out of the driveway. Ligi missed the trash can by a slick hairline.

Carissa unlocked her door and stepped over the welcoming threshold. Her home. Her sanctuary.

She closed the door and leaned her forehead against the hard surface. Turning, she placed her back on the cool wood and slid to the floor. *I'm so screwed. None of this could have happened. I just can't be off duty.* She glanced at her black and pink *Baby-G* watch. The past six hours had been phantasmagorical. It bothered her that her memories were scratchy, especially the bit about who carved up her friend.

When she had seen John Lopez in the intensive care ward, it wrenched her heart. All the equipment hooked up to his body had been her undoing. Avenging him would be her sole goal. Someone would pay for this. She didn't know how or who, but she knew she'd make them pay. *Orkizome—I swear it.* His wounds were deep, and it had been a sheer miracle he'd even made it out of surgery alive. Her eyes watered.

Pulling her knees up to her chest, she rested her chin on them. Her current lack of recollection proved a major problem.

A knot formed in her belly. How had they gotten blood all over them, and to whom did it belong? Detective Jones—a good friend—was one monumentally pissed man, and she couldn't work out why. Something was off, but she'd check it out at a more reasonable hour. Right now, she had to work out that one scene that kept replaying over and over in her mind.

Those black boots that had lined her vision when she'd glanced up into the face of her savior. The blood smeared across his cheeks. His appearance was beauty personified, but his demeanor—deadly, lethal, and chilling. Not to her, though—never to her. She didn't fear him. No, she recognized him instantly. She knew that chiseled image, those intense green eyes, and long brown hair. Her Greek god. A dream that had haunted her from the moment she'd turned sixteen. How was it possible for her *oneiro*—her dream—to exist?

"You're not real, you're only a dream."

She'd spoken the words aloud and brought herself out of the reverie. She was pulled back into the scene that kept repeating in her mind. Her dream man sheathed his sword and helped her to her feet. The atmosphere turned potent with the stench of blood. She'd taken a step back. Even now, she twitched her nose.

He'd stood there, sizing her up, his eyes devouring every inch of her before closing the small gap between them.

That was odd. Why did he look at me like I was dinner?

His hands had darted out to hold her head and when his gaze met hers with a jolt, her pulse raced and her heart had hammered at the contact.

Maybe it was the adrenaline?

His eyes widened, and his body had tensed right before his lips began to move.

Another nugget to file away.

Ancient words had left his lips, *charis ... aletheia ... doxa ... pantote*. They were melodic as his chant rose and echoed inside her head. A thousand pinpricks jabbed inside her mind and seized her brain. She'd shaken her head, but he'd held her still. His hands had traveled down her arms. Recalling it now made the moment seem almost intimate. A shiver ran through her. She tried to dismiss it.

His last words when he'd leaned in close to her ear were low, and they still rang in her ears. "RUN. NOW."

She scrunched up her nose in confusion. There were too many inconsistencies, and exhaustion had settled deeply into her bones, to make sense of it now.

Maybe a shower would help. Lifting herself from her position on the floor, she made her way up the stairs for a nice, warm shower to wash away the stickiness and fatigue that clung to her. *What an ordeal, and that dream man in the flesh. I'm losing it.*

When her right foot hit the top of the landing, she let out a deep sigh. The house was a present from her *yiayia*. Her grandmother had made her arrangements with a nursing home when she'd realized her health was declining.

I must see her soon. It's been weeks since I visited last.

Carissa padded over to the en suite. She slid her hands under her t-shirt and unclasped her bra, then removed it and her t-shirt in one fluid motion. Wiggling out of her jeans and underwear, she tossed them into the laundry hamper. The shower sang to her in an enticing lure. She opened the glass door, stepped in, and turned on the taps. The warm tranquil spray of water cascaded down her body, the welcome solace she'd yearned for back at the hospital.

As much as she enjoyed the steamy shower, she was dead on her feet. In a lethargic motion, she turned off the taps, stepped out, and towel-dried her body. She slid her feet into her slippers and put on her pink bathrobe. The luxurious feel of the bathrobe on her skin gave her a moment of enjoyment. *Silly that a piece of material can give comfort.*

Satisfied, clean, and warm, she headed downstairs to the kitchen for a quick bite of whatever leftovers were in the fridge. Her stomach growled at the thought of food. Hospital cocoa did not satisfy her hunger. Then again, she hadn't been able to think of food because of the mess she'd been in, and Lopez's condition had become her top priority at the hospital.

She pulled open the fridge door, armed with her fork, and scanned the neatly stacked takeaway containers, all with compliments of Aunt Irene, her regular supplier of Greek cuisine.

Eyeing her favorite *yemista*—stuffed tomatoes and peppers with rice—she pulled them out and dug in with gusto. She shivered as the cool rice hit her tongue. Replenishment came quickly to her hungry stomach. Satisfied, she discarded the remaining contents of the container and made her way back up to her bedroom.

Her bed sang in invitation. One she couldn't refuse. She dropped onto it, still wearing her bathrobe and not bothering to dry her hair. It would be wild and curly in the morning, but who cared?

Her thoughts lingered on the tall, dark, sexy dream man she'd seen today. *Phantasma*—the Greek word flitted through and etched itself in her mind. A dream began.

TWO

*"I see the state of all of us who live,
nothing more than phantoms or a weightless shadow."
~ Sophocles*

Xen Lyson's fingers moved to the pulse point of the woman lying at his feet. She did as he commanded. She came back for her partner. He'd have to leave her.

Take her. He jerked at the sudden possessiveness that demanded he acquire ownership. *She's yours.*

His hand moved to her hair as he pushed the strands back from her face. The pads of his fingers deliberately caressed her cheek. His nostrils flared when the scent of her exotic blood hit his nose. He examined her without delay. A large bump and cut graced the back of her skull. He lifted his fingers to his mouth and tasted her blood. Ambrosia danced over his tongue and warmth spread through every cell in his body.

Dikia mou—she's mine.

"Xen, we should move." Kane Hart, his right-hand man, brought him out of his strange musings and sudden infatuation.

"Bring the truck. Get the clean team. Stack the demon bodies."

His brow creased in contemplation of what would be the best course of action for the female and her partner. Taking her would risk exposing her to his world. He looked over her body again. *Take her.* He wanted to give in and do as his mind bid. "Leave these two untouched."

As the leader of the *Phi Athanatoi*, an ancient specialist group of vampires and werewolves, he was sworn to protect humankind. Right now, leaving the woman and her wounded partner would be an act of protecting them from the *Kakodaimones,* the demons that walked amongst man. Bringing them into his world would only paint them as moving targets.

He stood and sheathed his double-edged *xiphos.* His acute senses picked up the potent smell of demons. Before he could turn, one descended upon him, blade in hand. He braced himself. The impact was inescapable. Slamming into his back, the demon knocked him forward.

"*Vlaka,* " Xen yelled.

He found his footing quickly, speed and skill on his side.

Reaching for his sword, he readied himself for combat. The demon changed tactics when he saw Xen's weapon. He stopped on the spot, trying to avoid his opponent's blade.

Xen sneered and bared his fangs at the demon. A threat—one that other creatures would acknowledge as an indication of who held the power. The demon stood expressionless.

"Well, come and get me," Xen coaxed. The demon didn't move.

Statues ... thicker than Greek marble. Xen didn't need an invitation. His blade hissed through the air, cutting through the demon's neck and spinal cord, severing his existence. Blood splattered on the already sticky floor. The head thudded on the ground while the body teetered for a second before it, too, slumped to the concrete.

Kane laid his boot on the beast. "Nice cut, Xen. The bastard didn't have enough time to blink."

The *lykos* let out a growl of satisfaction. His demeanor changed, his nostrils expanded at the scent of another demon headed in their direction. He turned in time and swung his double sword, severing the demon's head, blood gushing over him.

"Damn." He let out a frustrated breath. "I just bought this jacket." He kicked the headless body to let out his frustration. It flew through the air and landed with a thud when it hit the wall on the right. "Dumbass. When will you demons get it?"

Xen smirked. His friend excelled at the combination of lethal and loyal.

"Let's move. The human police will be here within minutes." Time was running out. They needed to move fast. They shifted through the warehouse quickly, blurred images transferring demon bodies while another team assisted in cleaning the blood from the floor.

"Gives new meaning to speed cleaning."

"Save the jokes for later, Kane."

"Can't a *lykos* have a bit of fun?"

Xen's brow rose. "Are all the bodies taken care of?"

"We're ready to roll."

A siren sounded in the distance.

"Let's move," Xen ordered.

Kane jumped into Xen's Porsche just as he threw it into gear, a smile tugging at his lips.

"Jacket, Kane." Xen didn't want his seats stained.

Kane tore off his ruined jacket and bunched it in his lap. "I'm hungry. How about a *gyros*?"

Xen raised an eyebrow. Kane could eat two lambs on the spit without coming up for air. That his *lykos* friend was hungry was no surprise to him. He too was hungry, but he controlled his urges with more finesse. The tires on the Porsche screeched as the car sped out from the rear of the property. Another siren sounded.

"That was cutting it fine," Xen said, maneuvering the Porsche at breakneck speed.

Kane fiddled with the jacket in his lap, balling it up more. "Why on earth were those off-duty police officers there?"

"Off-duty?"

"I went through the man's pocket … Lopez. They were in civilian clothing, so one and one ..."

"Doesn't always make two," Xen cut in.

"But in this case, badge plus street clothing equals off-duty," Kane finished.

Xen turned his head in time to catch the smug look on Kane's face. He probed his mind.

"Stop that."

"Why? It would be faster."

"Yes, but it's invasive and a drain on me."

Xen let out a sigh. "Converse."

"You know, you could expand your sentence structure more, so that it sounds like conversation."

"I do. When necessary."

"Now would be ideal."

"Now we collate data." Xen caught Kane rolling his eyes and shifted in his seat. There was no point arguing about lengthy vocabulary. This was the after-skirmish info dump they often did.

"What were you able to glean from the girl?" Kane asked.

"First name and police officer. She slammed me out. Denied access to where I needed to lift information." He narrowed his eyes in irritation.

Kane let out a whistle. "Well, that's a first. Never thought I'd see the day. And a woman. Ha."

"It pleases me that you find humor in my inability to penetrate a human mind." He pressed his lips tightly against the sarcasm on his tongue. Abruptly, he changed the subject. "Someone is playing us."

"I think you're right, Xen. Whoever it is, they wanted the humans at a demon skirmish and intended that they'd get caught in the crossfire."

"Makes no sense. Even if they had both died, it means nothing to us. They would not have tipped the balance in the demon horde's favor."

Kane turned towards Xen. "Something is definitely not right. They've amped up the skirmishes and are obviously after something or someone. The question is, who or what?"

"They are becoming more than a thorn in our side. Their reckless actions pose a larger problem. We can't have humans exposed to our world." *I have to end these stupid games.* "I have an idea." He gave Kane a knowing grin. "But I will map it out a bit more before I share."

As a vampire, Xen's inclination had always been to keep delicate information to himself. "These fights are becoming more difficult and we could use more allies. Notice their numbers have increased?" He turned his head to gauge Kane's response. "We need more recruits," Xen said.

"More meat." The corners of Kane's mouth turned up.

Xen laughed. Kane loved nothing more than a good excuse to assemble recruits and kick ass. It was why Xen let him manage the newbies.

Gears shifted, and he accelerated. The car moved along the highway with engineered precision, swallowing up the worn road leading home. His face turned to steel as he crunched the statistical strategies to execute the best action.

Four hours after the *Phi* made their exit from Jostlers warehouse, Xen stood in the library of his house gazing out into the darkness. His eyes scanned the grounds. Even in pitch blackness, he could see what the human eye could not.

He'd placed a few men around the boundary of his estate. The *Kakodaimones* could not be trusted. How exactly they were being transported to the earthly plane from the depths of Hades was any-one's guess, and Xen did not like to speculate. His prime objective was to investigate who was aiding them and sever their access. The *Phi* team needed to be alert. He could not guarantee that the demons would not pop in on his territory. A stupid move if they dared, but of late it had become a strong possibility.

A vein pulsed in his neck. His fury had not settled. He braced his hands behind his back and dug his nails into his flesh. Warm blood trickled out to wet his fingertips.

The fighting had almost exposed the *Phi* to the off-duty police. What were those two officers doing there in the first place? Now, one was fighting for his life, and wiping the mind of the other did not bode well for her. The repercussions often left a stigma on the brain, like taping over a VHS tape too many times. Over time, the ribbons of the recording got scratchy.

And that luscious female police officer … logically, he should have removed the memory of himself from her mind. His body had dictated otherwise. Her scent had stirred something familiar. A pow-erful urge to protect her had seized him when he saw her in the de-mon's clutches from across the warehouse. Had he not been there to save her, she would've been eliminated.

Tonight's battle further proved they were fighting against the idiocies of demons and their reckless presumptions that they could defeat the *Phi*. The rules of the game had just gotten dirty. These fun-filled clashes were escalating. It was only a matter of time before things got out of control and a horde of unearthly beings joined forces with the demons. He had to show the card he didn't want to play. Something that could cost him and many *Phi* their lives. He understood exposure would mean a snowball of cataclysmic reactions.

Humankind was not ready to grasp the concept of their planet being shared with unearthly creatures. The *Phi* and the other unearthly ones had to remain invisible, as they had for many millennia.

Xen's mind drifted to the more delectable topic ... the woman at the warehouse. He'd been quick in racing through the matrix of her mind to remove the information he wanted, but something ancient had slammed into him when he'd tried to probe into her memories.

A sharp slap had connected with his mind. She'd fought him. The defense she'd used to seal her mind from his access was powerful and not easily broken. *Concrete.* It bore the marks of a masked power. One he didn't recall, and he'd come across a plethora of unearthly creatures. He had encountered nothing like her before. He'd have to explore it further. *Who is she? I have to find out.*

Certainly, her recollection of the demons and wolves would be nonexistent. On purpose he'd left her with one memory. One overshadowing most of the night—him. A grin spread across his face.

When their eyes met, his body had reacted. Intense burning, longing, and a desire to possess her in every way had seized him. A lustful and possessive sensation had coursed through him at that moment. Something unexpected. He didn't know it was possible to be filled by a woman's scent and be dizzy with the intoxication of it. It had taken all his willpower to keep focused on the task at hand.

What was she? When he'd placed his fingertips to her temples, his blood pulsed and rushed straight to his groin. He'd craved only to taste her, drink her, devour her. "I'd bet my money she'd be a delectable cocktail." His fangs elongated, but he retracted them quickly.

The questions about his unexpected and fierce attraction towards her turned around in his head like a dysfunctional merry-go-round. There was only one way to stop it. He needed information on the beauty that caused this unorthodox desire to spin out of control.

He pressed the preset number on his cell phone and dialed his *lykos* contact at Charleston's police force, Gelon Jones.

Jones's role was crucial to their cause, an inside man for the *Phi* and *lycanthrope*. An ally in the war against the demons. Making the call was complicated but safe. He would use Jones to gain an address. He waited for Jones to answer.

"Jones, a favor." His tone blunt, businesslike, and to the point.

"Been a while."

"I'd rather it was longer, but I must speak to you about last night."

"Nice to hear from you, too, Xen. Mind telling me why the *Phi* were there?"

"*Lykos*, the question is, why didn't you notify us that off-duty police officers would be snooping around?"

Xen heard the heavy release of Jones's breath down the phone.

"Because Carissa has a habit of digging around where she shouldn't. I didn't know, otherwise, you would have known. You didn't do a good job of protecting her and her partner."

Xen gritted his teeth. "I got her out of the way only to find she had raced back inside."

"Yeah, that fits Carissa alright."

"Enough. I need her address."

"Why?"

"The why of it is not your business and not your place to question, *lykos*." A growl rose from deep inside his belly.

"That's where you are wrong, Xen. Carissa is my business. She's family to me."

"I will not harm the girl."

"If you do, I'll stake you with pleasure."

"Your insolence will cost you." He gritted his teeth.

"And your arrogance will one day cost *you*," Jones bit back.

The young *lykos* was getting under his skin. Xen had more control than the wolf. He had to collect himself. He needed to obtain Carissa's address because she had been responsible for plaguing his thoughts and unleashing chaos on his control.

He hadn't considered a woman romantically in eons. A quarter of a century ago, a longing he couldn't describe had bubbled within him. He'd tried several times to assuage the ache with extreme sports at night. Even sex in many manners and forms had become unsatisfying. Instead, he'd thrown himself head-on into his work. But tonight at the warehouse, one glance at the woman and that longing, that raging urge to possess her, had escalated and forced its way to the surface. The inexplicable pull towards her was strong, wrapping its talons around him instantly.

Years ago, Kane had explained the mating for the *lycanthrope*. They mated with only one female. When she entered the life of the *lykos*—or, more to the point, when the *lykos* scented his mate—they desired no other. Xen had mocked it all. It seemed unimaginable to him. The gods would never gift him with such a thing. One woman to love him. What he secretly most craved.

His body's reaction baffled him. In his extensive years, he had never experienced anything of this magnitude. Sure, he had loved women, but this touched on something mystifying. He needed confirmation on whether it was blood lust or the result of an acute amount of adrenaline running its course through his body in action.

Good or bad, he had to investigate, because that adrenaline had only mildly subsided.

Jones's long silence told Xen he was stewing over whether he should give Carissa's address to him. Xen would never harm a human female. He was sworn to protect all humans. Jones knew this.

"I'm still waiting," he said after a long pause.

"You have the first name, surname is Alkippes. Lives at six-ze-ro-one Magnolia Street." A small breath escaped his lips. "And you won't be laying a finger on her. I left her at the hospital hours ago and her memory is quite scrambled."

"Jones, you mistake my intentions. I am merely following protocol. A further assessment is required. You understand, do you not?"

"I get it. As I said, she's like family to me."

"Your assistance, if somewhat unwilling, is appreciated." He hung up, not giving Jones any room for further barbs. Then he logged on to his computer. Yes, he had her name, but he needed the police file records. Typing his passcode, he logged into the Police Department database and punched in Carissa's full name to scan through the police officer's files.

Staring at the screen, he let out a lively laugh as he read, marital status.

Single.

How suitable. He wanted to beat his chest because that one word carved a pleasant path to her door. Xen didn't want to have to remove any boyfriend from the picture. He slammed the laptop closed and made a quick phone call to Kane.

Miss Alkippes had an interesting police file and quite an outstanding record and more than a bit of Greek fire in her blood. She'd be combustible in his arms. He knew it and felt it with every atom in his ancient body. He needed a fresh challenge. Women usually threw themselves at him. It would be a delightful change to be the predator that existed so close to his nature. It was time to hunt for his current addiction.

The digital clock in the car flicked to 4:00 a.m. as Xen pulled up outside Carissa's house. Conscious of time, he quickly checked all the windows and the back door. Everything was locked. *Good, I don't want anyone near what is mine.* He shook his head to dislodge his thoughts. What had gotten into him? His possessiveness had escalated. He didn't have time for long entanglements. Maybe seeing her would shake the current madness which had taken hold of him and threatened to consume him.

This brief excursion was a routine check to get into her mind and see if he had removed the finer details of the skirmish.

He picked the lock on the back door and entered her home. That garbage about having to invite vampires in always entertained him. The bonus of living for so long allowed him time to consider many ideas over the centuries. His cat burglar skills were alive and in stellar form tonight, a handy ability he'd gained to collect old artifacts he believed belonged in museums—his. Xen's collection was impressive. If any crazed collectors knew what his collection amounted to, they'd kill to obtain it. His face twisted at the thought. He'd eliminate any attempts before anyone had time to get close. If there was one thing he excelled at, it was killing.

He found Carissa by her scent and made his way up to her bedroom. Tuberose and jasmine assaulted his senses before he reached her door. *Tantalizing and delectable.*

A queen-sized bed sat in the center of the room, its headboard against the wall. The vision of her peaceful face as she lay asleep, with her hair mussed and curled around the white linen pillow, stirred a deep and dormant desire within him. His chest swelled as heat radiated throughout his body. His fingertips tingled with the need to touch her. Her scent all around him electrified his mind and body, something he'd never encountered before. Realization slammed into him like a forty-foot Freightliner on a collision course. She was his significant other.

His bride.

His mate.

The missing half of his *psyche*.

He ran a hand through his hair. His heart froze, then began a wild gallop as euphoria ran a rabid course through his body. Thinking back to the warehouse incident, she'd shown strength by preventing him further from access to her mind. His hypnosis failed to gain full admittance. He had suspected she had no inkling of what she was doing, or who or what she was. Quite frankly, neither did he. A small trickle of hope blossomed in his chest. All the more reason for him to claim her.

He leaned over and whispered, *"Eisai dikia mou,"* in her ear.

She stirred and mumbled, "I'm yours," then rolled over onto her side.

He glimpsed her bountiful cleavage. Wicked and dangerous images danced around in his head. The image of her beneath him and his mouth on her breasts became vivid.

Leaning forward, his fangs elongated.

THREE

"A thorn stings, even if small." ~ *Greek proverb*

Dawn's cozy rays tickled Carissa's eyelids. A low grunt escaped her lips, startling her aching and numb joints into action. She jerked upright, her head spinning. The events of last night filtered and flickered. Images began to reform and take residence in her mind. *Shit, shit, shit, this can't be real!*

Jumping out of bed, she headed for the bathroom but was assaulted by a wave of nausea that threatened its way up her esophagus. Her throat hurt and the dull ache that pounded in her head intensified with each step. Without warning, the hair on the back of her neck stood. Something wasn't right.

A distinct, faint smell lingered in her room. *Men's cologne?* She wiggled her nose and scrunched up her face at the ridiculous notion that someone had been in her room. *Odd.* Maybe the remnant effects of her overactive imagination were playing tricks on her.

Flicking on the light in the bathroom she turned on the faucet, splashing cool water on her face. She stared into the mirror long and hard. Light bruising marred her throat in pink hues. Turning her head to the right, she saw lesions under her jaw. Tiny red spots dotted her eyelids randomly. Somebody had tried to choke her; the evidence screamed at her from her reflection.

"I look like shit."

Her shaky hands reached for the string holding her robe to-gether, she untied it and let it fall from her body. She needed another shower to wash away the remnants of the ordeal, the pain and the notion that, psychologically, she was living in big mess territory. *Hello, loony bin.*

When the water turned cold, she took it as a sign to get out of the shower. She needed to write her thoughts down for clarity. Dressing quickly in jeans and a fitted t-shirt, she tied a scarf at her neck to conceal the bruising. She used heavy foundation and con-cealer on her face, then succumbed to her turbulent hunger and crav-ing for a cup of her favorite poison—coffee. She dug out a pair of flat shoes and then pounded her way down the stairs to the kitchen.

The warmth of the cup and the aroma of the dark brew gave her a mild comfort as she sat down to piece together the events of the previous evening.

Eyebrows furrowing, it became apparent that she'd have to make her own enquiries as to what happened last night. Clearly, she wasn't supposed to be anywhere near the warehouse or the police station, especially, since the pretty little words "unfit for duty" had been thrown in her face.

She took a sip of her hot coffee. The boiling liquid scalded her tongue. She pushed her shoulders back and sat perched on the edge of the kitchen chair. A pen and notepad stared up at her, enticing her to scribble on the stark white page. Grabbing the pen, she made points from the scattered information rattling around, consuming her scrambled brain. A ray of hope flickered in her chest. *Maybe I'll remember something more.*

Inhaling deeply, she feverishly scribbled all the details down. Line by line she wrote what little she could recall. The notepad and the pen took the brunt from her jerky hand movement. The deep indenting on the page increased along with her frustration at the lack of clarity. Sparse details looked back up at her. The words melded into images and replayed in her mind, the entry at Jostlers warehouse the most vivid. After that, her recollection faltered, bringing her to the only face and moment she could recall lucidly.

Recognition had speared her the second she'd caught his eye. He'd looked as though he'd seen a ghost. She had been certain her face had mirrored his, but why? *My dream phantasma is hot.* She'd dreamed of him for years. Now, she shook her head, ashamed that her thoughts had strayed when she should be working harder at trying to piece together what she couldn't remember.

Her pen scratched the surface of the paper. The list began to grow.
Blood.
Sword.
Dark.
Pain around my throat.
Sexy phantasma.
Stuff he mumbled.
Me running.
Blank.

She kept the frenzy of notes flowing even though portions of it sounded ridiculous, particularly when she read her ramblings out loud. A deep breath escaped her.

"Gamoto."

A small recollection flickered in the dark recess of her mind. It was fuzzy, like a pencil drawing that had been smudged. Her dream man had held her head and then yelled for her to get her ass out of the warehouse. She'd run hard and fast, that bit she recollected clearly. How had she ended up unconscious at the back of the warehouse? Something was missing. Those seconds when he'd looked her in the eyes, something powerful had happened. Her writing ceased. Her hands came up to touch her lips.

Comprehension dawned. He'd told her what to do. Her mind had blocked him. It had felt like a steel door crashed down, but he persisted and she refused to succumb to his will.

Slowly it came back to her, but parts seemed fragmented. *Oh shit!* He'd been trying to re-arrange her memory.

"Holy sweetness. Hypnosis? No way. Who can do that?" Holding her head with both hands she rubbed her temples, trying to release the building tension.

"Ridiculous. Can't happen."

But the more the scenes shuffled through her mind the more they became acceptable as possible truth. It appeared Mr. Tall Dark and Hotness had attempted a hocus-pocus trick, one that must have been unsuccessful because she remembered what he'd been trying to do. He wanted her to remember him and only him. The ancient words she'd recalled last night danced in her mind. Forgive. Truth. Honor. Forever.

"As if I could forget you." She'd been dreaming about him since she'd turned sixteen. As the years progressed, the dreams became more sexually intense. They became so graphic, she'd wake with her heart hammering against her chest and sweat pouring down her temples. She would sit in her bed shaking from the orgasmic dream. Her body throbbed, making it all seem real even though her mind knew it wasn't. "Well, up until last night, you were only a fantasy."

Now where could she locate her prime suspect? The man in question no longer fitted in the dream department. Real and in her town meant she needed to find him. Would he be a friend or a foe when she located him? Logically, she'd start with the police database and work back from there. Having his face tattooed in her brain would certainly help sift through the list of felons quickly.

Maybe Jones would be in a better mood and she could press him to give her details on the sweep of the warehouse. Maybe he had uncovered evidence that would help her recall some of the events. It amazed her how meticulous he was, when everyone else missed things. Exceptional and Jones seem to fit together perfectly. Always seeing what others didn't.

"I need to go back there and look around," she concluded.

Without further procrastination, she grabbed her keys and headed for her bike.

Parking at the back of Jostlers, she hid her bike in one of the old loading bays close to the back entrance. She couldn't help the dread that spread through her stomach as she dismounted and pulled off her helmet. Even the tiny hairs on her arms rose under her leather jacket, but she pushed the feeling aside and pulled the keys from the ignition and slid them into her jeans pocket.

She vowed she'd find out who hurt Lopez. The thought of him in his present state riled her. This was for him. She owed it to him because it was her stupid connection that led them to the warehouse in the first place. In her eyes, it made her responsible.

With each step, flashes replayed in her mind, jagged, with vital connecting pieces missing. If only something would trigger a bigger memory, then all the pieces of the puzzle would come rushing together.

She nudged the back door open. It creaked, voicing its age. Damp air assaulted her nostrils and something else … a cleaning product. *Funny, I didn't pick that up last night.* Moving inside, she closed the door carefully in case any police investigators were lurking around. She should have checked a little more thoroughly before entering the belly of the beast. *The worst they'll do is tell me to go home.*

Her eyes leisurely scanned the now daylit warehouse. Warm rays broke through from the windows above and gave the stillness inside an eerie glow. The old storehouse had been forensically swept. Taking small steps, she scanned where they had marked spots with numbers. She kept moving, further into the once thriving cotton distribution center.

Yep, the crime scene investigators had done a thorough job, but a niggling feeling in her gut told her to keep looking. In the middle of the warehouse was a staircase, inviting her curiosity to investigate. Concentrating all her weight on the balls of her feet, she executed each step lightly. The closer she got to the top landing, the more unease settled in the dark void of her stomach.

This is a bad idea. Maybe she should just turn around and go get that burger she and Lopez had missed out on last night. That thought slammed the oath she'd sworn for her partner back into position in her mind. Her chest tightened as guilt washed through her. She had to do this for him, to find out who stabbed him and put him in critical condition.

Clerical offices sat at the top landing. Looking down the walkway, she counted five in total. She walked into the first office and looked around. Nothing seemed to be amiss as she checked it and moved on to the next one. A foul smell assaulted her nasal passages. It became more potent as she neared the third office. She shoved at the door, but it was blocked by something. Ramming it with her shoulder, it budged.

She stepped in and glanced at the obstruction behind the door. It made her stumble back a step. Her heart shot into her throat to join the cry that wedged itself in her larynx. A scream bubbled and threatened to tear itself out. She forced everything back and composed herself. She shuffled forward for a closer look. The body was headless and black. *Why would anyone?*

"Don't get close, Carissa, it may be contaminated."

She screeched then, even though she knew the voice.

"Bloody hell, Jones. Don't you knock? I peed my blasted pants," she snapped at him.

He stepped closer and pulled her to him, hugging her tightly and planting a kiss on top of her head. The gesture stirred all the emotions of the previous night to the forefront. Tears pooled in her eyes, she sniffled.

"Hey, those better not be tears I see," he said pulling back and looking into her eyes.

"No, no. No tears here. Big girls don't cry," she choked out. Her words drew a hearty laugh deep from within Jones's belly. "I think I'm losing my mind."

His tone changed to one of authority. "You know you shouldn't be here."

"I do, but I need something, Jones. I need a speck of a lead to find who's responsible. It hurts too much to see Lopez in the condition he's in."

"We will find whoever is responsible. I'm on this case."

Her brain processed that information like watching a car in a tailspin before it did a one-eighty turn. Her brain was on full alert in that millisecond. "Then you can help me by giving me inside info. I can help you."

"No, Carissa."

"You can, you can ..."

"No, Carissa. You are not allowed anywhere near this. You shouldn't have come back here. What if someone else was here? The chief will fry your ass. It would be in your best interest to get away for a few days. You are still in shock and need time to process."

"I'm not in shock. I need answers."

"And I repeat, you are not authorized."

"You would do the same, Jones." Her eyes met his, willing him to understand.

"How about this: you lay low for a few days, then I'll see what I can do about getting you in on a little action. My ass is going to fry for this." The corners of his mouth turned up in a grin.

"Thank you, thank you, thank you, Jones." She grabbed him and peppered kisses on his cheek. "I'll do you the favor and go visit my aunt in Virginia. She's got some charity thing she wants me to attend. How's that?"

"Perfect, and it will give you time to think things through. If you remember anything that might help, you call me ASAP."

"I promise. I'll let you know, but I expect full disclosure."

"Full disclosure. Now get your pretty ass out of here."

"Before I go ... This guy ..." she said, pointing to the body. "What do you think happened? It looks like somebody poured something over him."

"Maybe the people he pissed off weren't satisfied with only his head."

"Who do you suspect?"

"Has the feel of organized crime."

She looked at it again. The image of a man shimmered into her mind. *Organized crime with swords.* "I better go."

"Good idea."

"Keep me in the loop, Jones."

"I gave you my word. It works two ways. I want to know the minute you remember anything."

A pang of guilt stabbed at her chest. She bit her lip, contemplating whether she should share the only detail she remembered, of the man with the sword. No, because that would only make her sound really crazy. Men don't carry swords in this day and age. She'd keep that nugget for a while longer.

She gave Jones another hug and took off down the stairs. At the bottom, she yelled back up.

"Bye."

It echoed and Jones didn't answer. She kept moving. The anxiety bubbling inside her dissipated when she nudged the door open and the bright southern rays touched her face.

Wasting no time, she jogged to her bike, jumped on, started the engine, put on her helmet, and headed home. Her mind raced as she glided effortlessly through the streets.

A few days away, that's all I need. Maybe then I'll be able to make sense of things and maybe Jones will have something for me to go with. She wasn't going to stand by and do nothing. The phone was ringing when she opened the back door. She bolted to it. "Hello."

"Hey, it's me. How are you this morning, fuzzy head?"

"Better, but still frazzled. I just know there is more, Ligi, and I'm dead certain that my dream is no longer a dream, but a reality."

"Stop it, Carissa, you're scaring me," Ligi teased. "If the real McCoy is as hunky as you described from your dreams, then you should be glad he's real. I know I would."

"I need thinking time, plus I've more or less been certified crazy by being labeled unfit for work." She let out a long breath.

"Then go clear your messed-up cranium, girl."

"That's exactly the plan, and Jones agreed to keep me in the loop." Warmth flooded her; Jones didn't appear as angry today, more like his usual self, and more like family.

"You didn't go back there?"

"Um ... yeah, I did. And I've decided to head up to my aunt's in Virginia Beach to clear my messed-up cranium, as you say. Sheesh, you could say head or brain like normal people."

Ligi let out a laugh. "That would be too easy, everyone uses the word head or brain. It's good to use a word everyone else does a double take on. Now, does my girlfriend need me to help her pack?"

"Ligi, everyone does a double take with you and you don't need to use words for that to happen. And no, I'm cool."

"Oh, flattery will get you everywhere. When will you leave?"

She could hear a hitch in Ligi's voice and knew she would worry. They were like this when one of them had to go out of town.

"Tomorrow morning. No point in hanging around. I can't do anything. You know the force is my life." She sighed. Without her work, she'd be lost.

"You could have fooled me."

"Takes more than little ole me to fool you, Ligi. Anyhow, my aunt has a charity thing the day after tomorrow which she invited me to and which I've been avoiding. It would be a nice change for me, and for her."

"Okay, sweet girl, you enjoy your thinking time and be sure to kick up those heels. I hear the men are like chocolate in Virginia."

She rolled her eyes. "Ligi, you say that about all men everywhere."

She let out a laugh. "Just be careful."

"Stop being such a worrywart. Gee, between you and Kelly, I'm being smothered." Exasperated, she shook her head. Her friends worried over everything she did and at times it had become a little overbearing.

"Speaking of Kelly, have you seen her?" Ligi asked.

"Actually, no, I haven't spoken to her for a while. Why?"

"Oh, nothing. I tried calling, but can't catch her. I'm sure she's just busy."

"She's probably snowed under with work or family. You know Kelly."

"Yeah, you're right. I've got to go, someone just walked into the shop. Talk to you when you get back. Bye."

"*Ta leme,* we'll speak. Bye."

Hanging up, she couldn't help the niggling sensation in her gut that something more bubbled in the background with Kelly. Ligi had not revealed all her assumptions. She might be withholding information because Kelly was known for vanishing without warning. She would wait two days and make a few calls.

Heading for the stairs, she climbed them two at a time. A sudden and urgent desperation to put miles between herself and Charleston dove into the recesses of her gut. A premonition formed behind her eyelids. She spaced out for a few seconds. *Her ghost in a suit, whirling her around at a ball.* She hated these glimpses of what might be. They popped into her head from time to time. Sometimes things manifested, other times not, but with Mister Sexy Pants she might be wishing for it. Virginia seemed like the perfect escape in order to regain control of her fractured and somewhat tangled mind. Her thoughts drifted back to the body over at the warehouse. It rattled her. She'd seen plenty of nasty stuff over the years, but that was sick and horrid. She'd have to exercise caution if and when she uncovered anything, but right now she had to pack. The long drive would help her mull things over.

She flung an overnight bag and a small suitcase onto her bed. A few extra combat essentials like her leather jeans, a leather jacket, knives and a gun with plenty of rounds would be needed.

Thinking about the charity event produced a small dilemma. What dress should she pack? She walked over to her closet and looked at the meager garments that hung there. They would not pass her aunt's scrutiny and approval because she loved going the extra mile with dressing up.

She shifted the coat hangers and her fingers ran over the prom dress that hung at the end. The recollection of that night rollicked behind her eyelids. There were a few bridesmaid dresses that brought back memories. Gods, how long had it been since she last had to dress up for an occasion? Then her fingers closed around a classic little black dress she'd bought on a spur-of-the-moment shopping trip with Ligi. It had hung there for the last two years. *Surely that will do? As if anyone will be looking at me anyway. It will be full of elderly people.*

She threw in some casual wear and a pair of black heels. She packed the toiletries last, throwing in a bottle of her favorite perfume. With her bags packed, she headed down the stairs to her garage. This trip required her Batmobile, not her bike.

A last sweep of the house ensured she had everything locked. As she tossed the suitcase and overnight bag into the car, images flashed through her head of the tall, sexy stranger—or more to the point, her dream man. Gods, to her utter embarrassment she wanted him the same way she always dreamed about him—horizontal and naked.

FOUR

"Where many die, there is no fear of death." ~ Greek Proverb

"Kane."

"Yeah," came the gravelly voice on the other end.

"Did I wake you?"

"It's of no relevance, pup. Tell me what you need."

"I've just done the second sweep of the warehouse. A body had been left behind. It's been discovered."

"Fuck! Who?"

"Carissa, the girl Xen had wiped last night."

"What was she doing there, pup?" Kane's deep tone penetrated right down the phone. The wolf in him rose to the surface.

"Carissa is not the type to sit around, especially after something's left her shaken. I found her upstairs standing over a headless demon."

"Headless?"

"Yes, odd that the decapitated body was upstairs. It's as if someone planted it there on purpose. Can you imagine if Carissa saw it without the *hypnosi*?"

"No, I can't." Kane digested the words. Something he didn't want to entertain, a human with memory of what went down. Although no one would believe her, it still didn't sit well with him. "Is the girl a threat or a problem?"

"No!" Jones yelled. "Don't touch her. I'll deal with it. And besides, Xen made it clear that he would take care of any memory issues. He said he'd ensure that he wiped any details of the event."

Kane pondered what Jones had relayed to him. If Xen hadn't completely wiped her memory, he'd have a reason for it. He would take it up with the man himself. But then again, no one really questioned Xen's motives, not unless they wanted their head detached from their body.

"Kane, are you there?"

"Yeah, still here, just thinking, pup." He let out a breath. "I'll let Xen know we fucked up with sweeping the place. He won't be happy. There was significant pressure in getting out of there, so I guess it's a miscalculation."

Still, he thought, it shouldn't have happened. They were slipping, too, the enormity of having to fight demons endlessly taking its toll. Jones's deduction had been right: the body shouldn't have been upstairs, primarily because there was a) no head, b) no blood, and c) no weapon. It had been planted. In truth, they had a mole.

"Have you disposed of it?"

"Yes, I did it as soon as I got Carissa out. I convinced her to take some chill time and get out of town for a few days until this thing blows over. It's for the best."

"Is that worry I detect in your voice, pup?"

"She's a close friend, Kane."

"Where will the little lady be heading?"

"Upstate, Virginia, to an aunt who has some charity event thing happening."

"Good. I'll pass it on to Xen."

Kane hung up and braced himself for Xen.

"Holy fuck," he yelled to the empty room. Missing bodies that could expose their world would not go down well with Xen. He took a sniff of the air and scented the man in question, the smell of power and fearlessness that he emanated was unmistakable. Xen was a total badass if you crossed him, but then, anyone with half a brain would tread lightly.

Kane made his way down to Xen's library. He lifted his knuckles to knock out of habit, but realized the pointlessness of the action because Xen would have picked up his scent. He could scent wolves the same way Kane could scent vampires and humans.

A stack of papers sat in front of Xen. The head of *Phi* and owner of Phi Industries, a company specializing in communication devices and technology, was knee-deep in work. To see him immersed in paperwork bordered on the highly unusual. The task of the day-to-day operations fell to Kane, since vampires were pulled into rejuvenation at this hour. Something serious or foul was stirring for Xen to be up. Kane stood in front of his desk.

"Couldn't sleep, boss?" he asked with a hint of sarcasm. He dropped his weight into the chair next to the table.

"I'm acutely exasperated, Kane. This demon situation is leading to a full-scale outburst, and one in which many innocents will die." He fiddled with his letter opener, which resembled a miniature sword, a weapon. The button on the side released poisonous mini darts, which were extremely lethal. "I'm going to use a little divine intervention."

Kane understood what he meant pretty darn quickly. Divine intervention always meant astronomical trouble.

"You haven't used the gods' help in over a thousand years. Why now?" He looked at Xen, surprised, but at the same time he realized the demon situation would inevitably escalate into a war of immense proportions. One they wanted to avoid at all costs.

Xen leaned back in his recliner and turned his gaze towards the covered window in the far corner of his office. Kane waited.

"I'm aware of many things, my friend, but last night's skirmish grazed too close for comfort. The demons have stepped up their craftiness by intentionally leading human police right into harm's way. It was a hairline short of cataclysmic exposure. We can't be placed in a situation like that again. I can't risk it. Can you imagine the hysteria it would cause?"

"I'm thinking the same thing, but involving the gods has consequences too, Xen. You know they don't do anything for nothing, and you also know there's always a catch, so mull it over, will you?"

"I've been mulling it over all night, that's why I'm still here rather than rejuvenating." He paused. "Sometimes a sacrifice of one man is of a lesser consequence in the brewing storm. It's unjust to let the innocent suffer when they are our essence. One life is naught in the face of millions. The demons will not show the humans mercy."

Despite being the predator that he was, his *Phi* leader held concern for the safety of humanity quite high on his list. It showed he cared a lot more than he let on. It wasn't merely about his food source. Ironically, they needed humanity as much as humanity required the *Phi* to keep them safe, even if they didn't know it.

Kane had learned much about vampires since meeting Xen. There remained even now a whole "us and them" thing that had been going on forever within their own little political structure. The two classes of vampires were the *Lamia Corinthia* and the *Lamiae*. The *Lamia Corinthia* or Corrs as they later decided to call themselves, understood the need to keep their world veiled from human eyes. A large number of Corrs had pledged themselves to Xen's cause as *Phi Athanatoi*, protectors of man.

Kane stretched his neck side to side, to clear his stray thoughts. Time to report the current findings.

"Jones called this morning."

Xen's head snapped in his direction. "And?"

"And ... a body had been dumped on the top floor. The police officer, Carissa, found it during an early morning snoop. Jones convinced her to take leave. She's heading to Virginia, to her aunt's, for some charity event." Kane exhaled, expecting his leader's wrath at their slipup. Instead, the corners of his mouth turned up. Kane stared in confusion. This couldn't be good, could it?

"I guess I have an interesting and challenging problem then, don't I?" Xen pronounced.

Kane rubbed his chin. This spoke weird loud and clear, even for Xen. Maybe he really did need his rejuvenation. "Why is it interesting? I thought you were handling that last night." Kane frowned.

"Right now, I can't give you the details."

"You're not thinking of keeping her as a toy?" Kane asked. "Jones got a bit cagey when I asked if she was a threat." He caught the immediate change in Xen's reaction.

"She is neither a threat nor a toy, and I don't keep playthings. I said I would attend to her myself." There was no mistaking the growl in his voice. It clearly highlighted the message. *Don't touch.*

"Whoa there, big fella. I didn't realize you had a vested interest." Kane put up his hands in surrender.

"I will be liable for her. Make sure no one interferes."

"No problem, Xen," he said, grinning to himself as he stood and left the office.

He knew Xen well enough to read what he was really saying—she's mine. He had just laid claim. The only downside—he hadn't spent time with her to develop something deeper, something more serious. Unless ... Yep, he didn't need to ask anything more. She was his fated and Xen's higher senses must have recognized this, just as his own kind did when they came in close contact with their mate.

Xen shuffled a pile of invitations stacked on his desk. The conversation with Kane had solidified one thing. He needed to pursue Carissa.

Picking up the phone, he made a few quick calls to the charity organizations he actively contributed to in Virginia and found what he wanted immediately. Punching the numbers on the phone, he mused about the delectable woman who would be placed in his proverbial court.

"*Kalimera* ... good morning, Mrs. Perdis. This is Xen Lyson."

"*Ti Kanis, Kyrios* Lyson. To what do I owe the pleasure?"

"I understand I haven't given you my RSVP to your charity event. I know it's late notice, but my diary is free for that evening. Since I'll be in the neighborhood ..."

"Oh, no need to explain. I would be delighted to have you here."

"Thank you. I look forward to it."

"Mr. Lyson ..." A heavy pause sounded down the phone. Xen waited, guessing she had more to ask. "A quick question before you go?"

"Yes, of course."

"Would you mind if I paired you up with one of my nieces? For the dinner only, of course."

"No problem at all." He had a crucial agenda and seating arrangements were not important to his end game.

"Oh, that's marvelous. Thank you."

"Enjoy your day." He hung up and stood to make his way towards his bedroom. His steps lagged, but not to the point where he couldn't speed up the stairs, lightning fast.

He lay down, thinking about Carissa's breasts. His earlier glimpse seared into his mind. He was hard in seconds. He shouldn't react this way, but the strong sexual urges told him otherwise.

He wanted to take matters into his own hand. Realization dawned that no satisfaction could be had, nor his hunger sated, unless he had her in the throes of passion beneath him ... naked. Rejuvenation pulled him under.

FIVE

"At the touch of love everyone becomes a poet." ~ Plato

"Carissa, I can't believe how long it's been." Her aunt Paula stood on the front porch, giddy and excited.

She dropped her bags and stepped into her aunt's squealing cries of happiness and warm embrace. She hadn't realized how much she'd missed her until the familiar scent of tuberose and gardenias tickled her nose. As a child, she'd spent the summers at her aunt's house. She and her cousin Chloe had got along famously, but Chloe married an Englishman, and moved to the U.K. *What was his name again? Garrison? Better not embarrass myself.*

"Too long, *Thitsa*." She used the Greek endearment and her aunt squeezed her harder. She couldn't help the joy that pounded behind her breastbone. They were both giving off blissful emotions—a euphoric moment that showed too much time had passed between seeing family.

"Come, let's get you settled, and tomorrow, we are going shopping," her aunt said, her face full of excitement.

Oh gods, she's planning something. She bit the inside of her lip. Carissa hoped it didn't involve another male. Her aunt had triumphantly introduced and arranged marriages for several of Carissa's cousins, earning her the title of Queen of Marital Hookups, or proxies as they called them in American-Greek.

"*Thitsa*, I hope you aren't concocting any of your whacky ideas and schemes."

"Me? No. Just a bit of dress shopping." But her aunt's expression told her that behind that word *no* there'd be a barrage of hidden plans.

"That's not very convincing, you know, and besides, I have a dress and I don't need another one." She frowned, never one to like it when people thought they knew best when it came to what she needed.

"I know, but since I haven't seen you in a long time, I thought it would be nice if I could do something nice for you." Her aunt gave her that megawatt smile and puppy-dog-eyes look that had always been her weakness. Hard to refuse anyone with that look.

"Okay, but I'm warning you, I have a gun. No funny business, okay?"

"No funny business, and I'll tell you what you can do with your gun," her aunt said, smiling.

She enjoyed her aunt's company and wit, although Carissa's gut warned her that her not-so-innocent aunt was up to something. Still, she'd wait and see. Date flops were her specialty, and if she knew her *thitsa,* this would be a Find-Carissa-a-Man mission and another date-flop notch to add onto the proverbial belt.

Aunt Paula led her to the spare room she used to sleep in when she visited as a kid. She stepped in, dropped her bags in the middle of the floor and closed her eyes for a moment, letting all her childhood memories assail her. A bigger bed now sat in the middle and the pretty pink wallpaper had been removed, but it still felt and smelled like the same old room. A huge grin spread over her face.

"I'll let you get settled, and I've got some *spanakopita* for you in the kitchen."

Not wasting any time, Carissa unpacked the bags she'd dumped in the center of the room.

When she entered the kitchen, her senses were assaulted with the decadent aromas of the Greek food on the table. A gorgeous spread lay perfectly before her eyes. Roast chicken with lemon potatoes, the promised spinach and cheese pie, salad with a huge slab of *Dodoni feta* piled on top, olives and bread. Her mouth watered—the kind of watering where you think you've been in the Sahara Desert without water or food for far too long. This feast would nourish and replenish her battered body and messed-up brain. *Eat and forget about tall warriors with swords and everything else.*

"Wow, this looks great. You shouldn't have gone to all the trouble, *Thitsa*." She pulled a chair out and dropped her weight into it.

"Don't be silly, it's nothing."

"It doesn't look like nothing to me. You've been cooking all day."

"This? No! Just a few hours. Besides, it's nice to have some family here. I miss my Chloe." Tears pooled in her eyes.

Carissa leaned over the table and gave her aunt's hand a squeeze for comfort, but her tears kept coming. Then she broke out with the same old sad story about the death of her husband, and Chloe leaving.

Carissa did what was needed ... she listened. *Honestly, we Greeks excel at tragedy.* When her aunt finally got it all under control, she said what she thought her aunt wanted to hear. "I have a hard time too, but you know what? We've still got each other and I promise I'll try and make a trip up every couple of months." She knew how it hurt to lose a loved one and how, at times, the loneliness became a huge weight on the heart.

"Oh, Carissa, I'm being selfish. I know it's harder for you." Aunt Paula wiped her eyes with a tissue and amazingly, her tears stopped. "Let's eat," she exclaimed with newfound gusto.

She didn't wait for her aunt to say it again. The burst of flavors on her tongue were divine. "Good idea," Carissa mumbled between bites of *spanakopita*.

The feeling that somehow she'd just played right into her aunt's hands jabbed deeply in her gut. Tears often did the job. Shrugging it off, she decided to enjoy the glorious food before her and the company of family that she loved.

Overfull, content, and dishes done, Carissa retired to the living room with her aunt. The conversation flowed, but Carissa's eyelids were shutters intent on closing for the night.

"I think you should get some rest, Carissa. You need sleep."

Her aunt's voice jolted her out of her dozing. For once, she listened to her body and her aunt.

"I'll see you in the morning, *Thitsa*. Thank you so much."

She stood and gave her a huge hug. Memories of her mother collided in that familiar embrace. Emptiness bubbled beneath the surface. Her job as a cop kept her busy, so it had been easier to push those desolate feelings aside, but right now they scratched and pawed their way back into the hollow fissure of her heart. Longing overwhelmed her and her eyes watered at the thought of her parents, and the need for love and security.

It took a bit of her willpower to finally break from her aunt's warm arms and make her way upstairs to the guest bedroom where recollections of her childhood danced in her mind as she pulled the covers down. She'd missed so many little things growing up without parents. The biggest had been not having them there when things got tough. Her grandmother, God bless her, had done her best to provide comfort, but there had always been a small chasm of emptiness in her heart.

The plush pillow summoned her. The moment her head landed on the soft feathers, images flickered and formed. His lips. His touch.

Challenge: a meager word when it came to Aunt Paula's idea of shopping, a vastly divergent idea from her own. *How do I get myself into these things?*

They walked through the doors of *Divine Dresses* and she began the tedious job of sifting through all the black dresses on the rack. Her aunt, however, had other things in mind.

Paula's no-nonsense voice broke the silence. "Carissa, you are not going to wear black to a charity event. You're young. Black is for mourning, not for young ladies," she said firmly.

Carissa rolled her eyes. *Greek mumbo jumbo.* "What do you suggest?" she asked, intrigued, knowing it would be a mistake to play games with her clever aunt.

"I think something vibrant and bright. Like a celebration of life." She waved the saleslady over.

She suppressed the laugh that bubbled in her chest. Her aunt was a ball of energy when she wanted something. And so it began, dress after uncomfortable dress.

"At this rate, I'm going to shoot holes in the dress." Sweat lined her forehead. The small stall did nothing for her overheating body. She needed water. No, something stronger—an ouzo.

"What was that, Carissa?"

"Nothing, I'm just mumbling."

"One more. This one should look divine on you." The saleslady handed the dress to her.

"That's what you said about the last one, which made me look like a giant version of Tweety Bird!"

"Carissa, that's not true. You looked ..." She trailed off, and laughed.

"Like a yellow cab with frills! See, you're laughing. Awful is too nice a word for it."

The bubble of laughter she'd bit down on earlier broke to the surface. Her aunt and the sales assistant laughed from the other side of the curtain.

She put on the last dress and smoothed her hands over the sensuous fabric. It paraded more flesh than she'd ever want to expose to anyone, and it fit like it was made just for her. The bruises around her neck were beginning to fade. It had been an uncanny thing for her, no bruising had ever last long. She seemed to heal faster than usual.

"Well?" her aunt called impatiently from outside the change room.

She pursed her lips as she stepped out and watched her aunt's face light up like a Christmas tree.

"Oh my, you're as pretty as a peach."

Yep, done deal written all over her aunt's face. "You like it."

"Like is an understatement. Hurry up, let's get moving, we've still got shoes to buy. Oh, and don't worry about your hair and make-up. I've got someone coming over to do it all."

"Gee *Thitsa*, you are going to a lot of trouble."

"It's no trouble, Carissa. I just want you to look and feel as gorgeous as you are. You should get out more."

That last line was loaded, and it confirmed her hunch: her aunt, the proxy queen, was up to something. Flashes of all the previous setups her aunt had prepared for her daughter Chloe burst and danced in her mind. No one was safe. She beamed, fully aware of the conspiracy that would manifest. *She is so setting me up.* She'd have to keep an eye out. Knowing full well how the grand master schemer worked, she'd have to watch out for the guy who stuck out the most, because, guaranteed one hundred percent, that's who her aunt would set her up with.

"Okay, I'm going to put these dresses back and make a few calls."

"*Entaxei,* Carissa *mou.*"

She stepped away and tapped Ligi's contact number on her cell phone.

"Hey."

"Hey yourself. How was the drive to Virginia?"

"Pretty smooth actually, but a long six and a bit hours."

"And how is that marriage broker aunt of yours?"

"I hate to say this, but she's in fine form. Expect another flop date."

"It can't be as bad as the guy who turned up with the suit smelling like mothballs, and who drank too much and puked on your shoes."

"Thanks for the vivid reminder."

"Doesn't she ever get tired of it?"

"Ligi, that's a silly question. Her mission in life is to see all the girls in the family wed."

"At least it keeps life interesting."

"Interesting? Don't you mean demented?"

"Greek crazy is the new black." Ligi laughed.

"You're not wrong, considering my life at the moment."

"Don't you turn sour on me, it's not what I meant."

"I'm not turning all vinegary on you. I'm just contemplating."

"Girlfriend, there is no room for thinking. Just get out and have some fun. You're a good cop and you'll work things out."

Ligi made sense. It's why they'd stuck together through thick and thin. Which brought the next question to Carissa's lips. "Have you heard from Kelly?"

The long pause told her the answer before Ligi even uttered it.
"No."

"Did you check all the usual spots?"

"I did. It's like she's just vanished."

"Let's give her another day. Then we can try that cousin of hers who lives in Washington."

"Yes, he usually knows where she's at."

"Exactly."

"Have fun checking out the eye candy."

"Ligi, there won't be any. It's mostly old people."

"And you know this how?"

"Oh forget it."

"Steer clear of mothball cologne."

Carissa laughed then. "Now there's an idea for men's after-shave. Not."

"Later, girl."

"Bye, Ligi."

Carissa ended the call and walked back to her aunt who had thrown shoes and other items into the mix of purchases. She raised an eyebrow at her.

"What? You need shoes with that dress."

"I have shoes."

"What, black ones?" her aunt shot back as she moved over to look at the lingerie sets.

"Oh, no." Carissa eyed the selection she held.

"Really, you can't have a panty line showing in that dress."

"It's going to be a long day and night," she mumbled.

At 6:00 p.m., a tingling sensation swept over her body as she slid into her dress. Butterflies exploded in her stomach and left her vibrating on the inside. Both righteousness and gloom pressed heavily on her chest. She placed her Beretta Pico 380, a small, deadly handgun, in her silver bag that matched her new shoes. Even with its compact size, it would be too big to sit holstered on the inside of her thigh. She made her way downstairs to wait for her aunt.

Standing in the foyer, Carissa looked up at the rustle of material descending the stairs. Her aunt looked elegant in her deep green gown. At the last step, Aunt Paula stopped and eyed her in the same manner.

"Carissa, you look like a goddess." Sheer joy spiced her voice. Her pleasure at the whole ensemble was palpable.

A car horn blared.

"Sounds like our ride is here, *Thitsa*."

"Showtime," her aunt said, taking the last step.

They made their way to the car, but unease had taken up permanent residence in the tight pit of her stomach. A light breeze blew across her skin and the hair on her nape rose. Quickly she scanned the street, but saw nothing conspicuous. *Doesn't mean something is not out there.* For once she had to agree with her omphalic muse.

When she entered Lesner Hall, a sharp breath left her lips. She had not been expecting the opulence. No expense had been spared. Obviously the charity her aunt belonged to had some major players involved.

Heads turned and gazes quickly swept from head to toe in an approving manner. Before Carissa could move another foot, several people were making their way over. Aunt Paula had magically turned into a well-oiled social machine. Within ten minutes, Carissa had met twelve guests.

Thirty minutes later, tolerating the acquaintance of more people would take monumental strength on her behalf. Her throat was dry, she needed something stronger than the champagne and wine the waiters eagerly distributed among the guests.

"Pardon me, but I need to use the ladies' room." She excused herself and headed not for the restroom, but for the temporary bar that stood out like a beacon, tempting her with the shot of spirits and the escape she needed.

The moment she reached the bar, she fired out her order. "Double shot of vodka with a shot of butterscotch schnapps."

The poor barman looked startled. "Sure." He dragged out the word.

Carissa eyed him. "Got a name?"

"Bill."

She nodded, accepting his name. She didn't offer hers and he didn't ask.

He picked up a clean glass and almost dropped it, then made a mess of the ice. Clearly his mind drifted from the job. For a split second she considered pulling out her gun.

No, behave, she warned herself. *Girl orders drink, bartender mixes drink, bartender serves drink.* What did Bill find hard about her order? In the mirror behind the bar, she could see displeasure mar her features. She also made it obvious by staring. The Greek evil eye seemed like a good idea.

Yes, Greek mumbo jumbo. Curse you, bartender. Hurry up with my drink.

He must have sensed something because he sped up, then practically slammed the drink down in front of her. She stifled a laugh.

Maybe the Greek stuff does work.

She thanked him then brought the glass to her lips and took a steady sip, letting the vodka and butterscotch burn down her throat. Its flaming path warmed her inside and out, and gave her a sense of calm.

Two drinks later, the alcohol had softened her brain to mush, still she asked for one more. She lost her balance for a moment when she placed the glass down.

"I don't think that's a good idea," Bill hinted.

"The gun and badge in my purse don't agree with your deduction," she concluded.

Bill eagerly went about his business and satisfaction surged through her. She turned to make her way back to Aunt Paula, but shock speared through her body, pinning her to the floor. Her legs froze into useless sticks. Her mind spun from the alcohol and at the same time, it screamed. Next to her aunt stood a tall man—her *phantasia* in the flesh. Scrumptious. Lethal.

A tiny sliver of undeniable reality punched her brain. He was real. Even in her slightly muddled state, there'd be no escaping the man who stood smiling and nodding at her aunt. The key to the answers lay through that man. *Hallelujah, the Fates must be on my side. Telika—finally.*

Carissa watched as women vied for her fantasy man's attention. She narrowed her eyes, scrutinizing the scene building around him. He could wield a sword with ease, yet these women would not be privy to that slice of information. The image, though, was seared into her brain. Vivid details of blood on his hands flashed in her mind.

The cluster of women thickened as she looked on. An unexpected thought seized her mind. She needed to go to his aid. A contradiction. The women needed rescuing, and so did he. The question was, who needed it more?

Her feet obliged and she moved to the center of the women. She closed her eyes and took a deep breath, exhaling slowly. *Move along, ladies. Move along*, she projected through her mind. Inaudibly, she parted the females around her like Moses did the sea.

"Dinner is about to start." She ushered the last few in the direction of the tables and away from her target. It sent a spike of joy through her to see the silent mantra work.

The crowd thinned, though for a moment it reminded her of Greek Easter at church— all those little old ladies barging ahead to get communion. Worse than lining up for a rock concert. Carissa had been poked more times by bags and umbrellas at church than anywhere else. She'd also had her hair set on fire, but the recollection of that story dissipated as her feet moved in the direction of her target. *The most handsome and lethal man.* Her tongue darted out to moisten her bottom lip. Standing close to him, she knew she had been right; he needed saving. The faces those women wore were not genuine. They'd jump him as soon as they got the chance. Obvious and transparent they were, and it had nothing to do with the drop-dead gorgeous factor either. No. He exuded power and wealth. Up close, you could almost stroke the invisible vibrations coming from him.

"Carissa!' Aunt Paula exclaimed. "I'd like you to meet Xen Lyson." Her aunt flashed her one-hundred-megawatt smile.

Yep, you are up to no good.

Her eyes locked with Xen's and her heart hammered wildly in her chest. She held out her hand, but a tremble ricocheted all the way down to her fingertips as nervousness settled in. Hell, this was her *phantasia* in the flesh. The knowledge that she was about to touch him in her waking state, not her dream one, made the whole situation surreal.

He took her outstretched hand and closed his fingers around it. A shiver ran through her at the warm connection. He raised her quivering fingers to his lips. Her eyes were riveted to where he placed a featherlight kiss on her hand, sending tiny ripples throughout her body, the gesture sweet and charming.

Something shifted inside her. *You need to get out more, girl. The words filtered to her mind.*

A giggle rose in her throat, but she took control of it and buried it back where it came from. She would not let his charms get the better of her. *I'm tougher than this fluff of emotions. Plus, I need to question him about Lopez.* Sadness pierced her heart at the thought of her partner.

"Your aunt was just speaking about you. It is indeed a pleasure to meet you, Carissa." The huskiness of his deep voice lingered on her name. Stroking it. Teasing.

A jolt lanced through her when she heard him clear his throat. She should pay more attention, especially to that grin he had spread on his face. *I could lick that grin off his face.*

"Something amusing?" she asked.

"Yes, as a matter of fact."

"Well then, share."

"Unfortunately, it's a private joke. Entertaining things pop into my head often."

She gave him a quizzical look and decided to catalogue that moment for replay later.

"I hope I haven't caused you offense."

"No. No offense. It's not a crime to laugh at our own internal musings."

Her eyes began a seductive dance up and down the length of his body. Unfortunately, sizing him up had notched up her attention to his overall masculinity, something she more than liked. Her heart began to pound with ferocity, jabbing against her breast. How would she deal with him and the situation? Her partner's injuries were fresh in her mind. Somebody had to be held accountable, but those green eyes looked straight into her soul and all sense of logic absconded to another realm.

One of her dreams had crashed into her faculties. Her breath hitched. His eyes followed every minuscule movement she made. Amusement twinkled in his eyes, but they turned hungry as his gaze cruised over her body.

Her aunt cleared her throat, bringing them out of the intense staring match they were locked in.

Okay, that was the horizontal mambo, only standing and with clothes on.

Xen cleared his throat too.

"Would you like to move over to the tables now? We are just about to start. Oh, by the way I took the liberty and seated you next to Xen. Table five." Her aunt grinned.

Could you be any more obvious? Aunt Paula had just pulled one of her typical setups, one that Carissa didn't mind. Really, who was she kidding? The man next to her could have any woman. Greek god didn't describe him adequately. From his perfect lips to the hard line of his jaw—perfection. The overgrown stubble gave him that hard edge.

"Carissa." A small shiver travelled up her spine, spreading a light spray of goosebumps on her hyperaware skin. Her body awoke from its sexless slumber. His proximity sent scorching tangled positions racing through her mind. Heat flamed low in her belly. Her breathing constricted, making her fitted dress two sizes too small.

What's wrong with me? she mumbled under her breath, cursing the intense reaction to him. It only amplified when he placed his hand on her lower back and guided her to their seats. Heat spread from her lower back through her body like a cocoon, warming it everywhere.

"This way." His voice lingered in her ear. Visions of him naked ran their assault in her overactive grey matter. *Get your head out of the gutter, girl, you have a job to do!*

From her peripheral view, she caught the grin on his face.

They reached their seats. Xen gracefully held out her chair for her while his glance flickered over her again. In that moment she felt naked. Bare.

"Thank you," she choked out.

"Always a pleasure to seat a siren."

She had never in her life failed to speak when needed, but around this man it became clear it would not be easy to focus. He had just referred to her as a siren, something mythical and exotic. Who said he needed a gun or any other weapon to render her helpless? He seemed to be doing a dandy job with words alone.

He was a connection to a large piece of the puzzle of what went down at the warehouse. Out of sheer dumb luck, here he sat. If you believed the Greek mumbo jumbo then it would be the Fates that deposited him right at her side. Her rational mind, though, appeared to be packing bags for that long overdue vacation.

What is it about him that's got me all tongue-tied and crazy? She answered her own question. I'll tell you what it is, you've spent all your adult life dreaming about him and now he is here, all real and oh so sexy, her muse teased.

He poured water into her glass. The action brought her out of her rumination.

"Carissa, I won't lie. We've met before, under unusual circumstances."

"Is that what you call it? I guess we weren't drinking sweet tea together."

"No." He paused and dropped his voice to a low whisper. "You don't strike me as a silly woman, and you know what I'm implying. So, let's drop the sarcasm."

"Fine, but understand one thing and one thing only, you will give me the truth of what happened at Jostlers and why it is that I remember only you there."

"And why should you trust anything I say?" he challenged.

"I don't, but my aunt seems to like you, and she's got some Greek mumbo jumbo instinct, so I'm going to go with that."

He lifted an eyebrow. "And what does your instinct say?"

"Now Mr. Lyson, telling you what I'm thinking goes against my principles."

"Then let us leave the business talk for later," he countered.

He had some nerve to dismiss the discussion without giving her enough to satisfy her muddled marbles. Irritation foamed and bubbled up her throat, blocking her vocal cords. She swallowed hard and pushed sharp words through gritted teeth.

"My partner is fighting for his life. I can't shake the feeling you had something to do with it."

"I'm sorry about your partner, and you are very mistaken. I did not have anything to do with his current condition. There is more at play here than you can possibly understand."

Guilt stabbed her in the chest at his words. It had been her stupid fault for listening to that scumbag Tom. Whatever Xen's connection had been, she'd have to give him the grace of presuming him innocent until proven guilty. "I'm sorry, that was uncalled for."

"No need to apologize. This is a discussion for later, away from prying eyes and ears. Let's enjoy the evening and our dinner." He leaned into her ear and lowered his voice. "By the way, you look stunning."

Heat crept up her throat and face, warming her cheeks. She blew out an exasperated breath, hating that she'd be at his mercy for information and disliking that he could flick all her switches with mere words. She was an explosive combination of warm and smoldering to volcanic in his presence. The need to cool down stifled her. *Rein it in, girl.*

"I'm holding you to it. I seek answers and I believe you have them. I will follow you relentlessly until I gain all I need."

The corners of his mouth turned up. "You have my word, *koukla*."

She shook her head at his endearment.

He winked.

"Do women line up to hear you call them doll?"

"Carissa, I do not go around professing fond compliments to women. However, when I am interested, I make it clear."

Heat burned her cheeks. Why did she think every time men paid her a compliment they were poking fun at her? Her outburst was uncalled for and rude.

"I ... I shouldn't have said that. I don't know what has come over me. I probably need to eat." Her dream had collided with reality and she had been drinking on an empty stomach. She needed to stabilize her rabid thoughts and stop her juvenile reactions to him.

"There's no need to apologize. You are probably trying to resolve too many things at once."

A waiter placed a mouthwatering *filet mignon* in front of her. Her stomach growled on cue.

"I guess you were right. You need to eat." Laughter danced in his voice.

Damn. This night had turned into an epic farce. She dove into the meat with as much aplomb as she could muster. Secretly she craved a rewind button to start the evening all over again.

"This is delicious," she said between bites.

"I've had better." Xen moved his food around his plate then stopped to pour champagne into their glass flutes.

She lifted the glass to her lips and took a small swallow. The bubbles slid down her throat in an easy glide. *Take it easy, Carissa. You had too much before and acted like an idiot. Don't embarrass yourself further.*

"Aren't you hungry?" She pointed to his plate.

"I indulged a little too much earlier," he admitted. "But feel free to have anything from mine if you like." He pushed his dish closer.

Yes, he exuded all the traits of a gentleman, but his attitude appeared devil-may-care. She made a mental note, warning herself of how easily she could be a victim of his charms.

"Thank you. I might steal one of your potatoes."

He pinned one from his plate and held it out to her so that she could take a bite. Without thinking, she wrapped her hand around his wrist to steady it before she leaned in and took a mouthful of her favorite starch, chewing and moaning her satisfaction.

His green eyes were fixed on hers. A spell began to weave. Time froze and the occupants of the room disappeared, only the two of them remained. Heat burned low and slow in her belly, her heart began a four-hundred-meter sprint, drumming fast in her chest.

Harnessing control proved insurmountable. *Okay, Carissa, compartmentalize.* Just when she thought she had it all in order, he leaned close to her ear again.

"It would please me if you would dance with me."

She turned her head and her lips brushed his cheek accidently. His aftershave teased her nose—sandalwood, vanilla and bergamot. On instinct she drew a deep breath, taking in his provocative scent. Not a good sign when she didn't want to be derailed from her true motive—answers to what went down at Jostlers.

"I ... I haven't danced in a long time, and these shoes weren't meant for dancing." She turned in her chair and brought out her foot, but the split in her gown opened, revealing her naked leg to her thigh.

"See." She fumbled to cover her exposure.

"Oh, I do see," he said with a wolfish grin.

Good going, Carissa. Might as well as offer yourself in the process.

"I'll lead. Don't worry yourself, *koukla*."

He stood. Her fingers charged to life when they settled in the hand he offered. The music started to play. He led her out to the dance floor with a fluidness and gracefulness that uttered sheer confidence, as if he'd done this many times before. Once positioned, his arms closed around her, pulling her intimately against his body. *Great, he's going to short circuit my brain.* The feel of his hard thighs against hers sent a spark of tingles racing through her in excitement. Rational thought eluded her and her knees turned liquid.

"Beautiful song." Stupid thing to say, Carissa.

"It is, *koukla* ... " He looked into her eyes. "Because the act of which it speaks is beautiful." His face took on a look of pure mischief.

"The act?" she asked, tilting her head to one side and pursing her lips. She'd lost track of their conversation during her distraction.

The heat from his body engulfed her in warm flames that licked her skin. She was on fire and needed to get some air. His lips brushed her earlobe, and in a husky tone, he whispered, "The act is making deep and sensual love." The words reverberated all the way down her spine, raising goosebumps on her skin. Her body tingled with awareness.

Oh boy. I'm in trouble. Her muscles relaxed, allowing her body to melt into his. Her heart rate danced and warmth pooled between her legs. *Stop, stop! Stupid brain, listen.* Too late. *Benedict Arnold body.* She cursed herself. Here she danced in the arms of a man, enjoying herself while her partner lay in hospital in critical condition. She should be retrieving information, not enjoying herself with a possible suspect.

His inhalation at her neck had her pulling back to meet his piercing green gaze. It dipped to her lips, speaking of a man not interested in the *Zorba*, but a more sensual horizontal dance.

Bang! Bang! Wake up, you twit! She snapped to her senses, as if someone had slammed a griddle pan upside her skull. Her over-indulgence in alcohol had blurred her rationality. On cue the music changed, transporting her out of her temporary enamored haze. Clearing her throat, she managed a few coherent words.

"Thank you for dancing with me."

The dryness in her mouth only added to the intensity of her desire for this powerful man. It scared her how her body and mind wove freely with his. Maybe the dreams had amplified her reaction. *It shouldn't be this easy. I shouldn't want him this much. I don't know him, only the dream.* She let out a breath. What was she thinking? *Remember, you are a police officer, Carissa.* The logical side of her brain told her that she had a job to do.

"Excuse me. I need air."

Pulling away from his embrace, she headed outside. Her sixth sense, which had been floating in obscurity, told her not to look back, because more than likely he had followed. The hair on her neck stood to attention, confirming her instinct. She pushed the door open and stepped out to the deck. Lights flickered in the distance across the Lynnhaven River and Chesapeake Bay. The saltiness of the water caused her nostrils to flare. Eyes shut, she took several long breaths to calm her overzealous hormones.

"Are you all right?" His voice sent goosebumps skittering down her back and along her arms.

"I am. I'm sorry if I gave you the wrong impression or led you on." She turned to face him. "I don't sleep with guys I meet at charity events."

Right or wrong, she had to make herself clear. She didn't want to give off any more mixed signals. She knew nothing about the real Xen. The dream version had, up until now, been just that, a dream, a wild fantasy like those alpha heroes in romance novels. Everything about this man screamed scrumptious sex. Six four with a killer body, long dark hair that touched his shoulders. Yes, he rocked the sword look. The word lethal bounced around in her head, a fact that clearly told her to be on her guard. Business first. Gears turned and locked into place, her muscles tightened to steel.

"I really need you to answer some questions for me."

"I will, but not here. Would you have dinner with me tomorrow night ... at my place?"

"Why? There's no one out here."

"As I said before, you never know who may be listening."

Her nails cut into the flesh of her palms. "Why are you making this difficult?

"Have dinner with me ... tomorrow night." Before she could form a reply he had a card out and scrawled an address on the back.

"What makes you think that I would agree?"

"I don't. I'm just hoping you will."

"That's taking a big gamble, don't you think?"

He lifted his eyes from where he'd been writing and pinned his gaze directly at her. Her breath caught. *Stop it, Carissa.* A simple look into his eyes and she'd turned weak at the knees. *Fight it a little.*

"Not at all. There's nothing wrong with wanting to have dinner with a beautiful woman." The corners of his lips turned upwards, showcasing his perfect teeth, but his dimples could slay a woman. Infectious didn't cover it. His smile had its own religion and zip code.

She shook her head. Surely he knew the power of his magnetism.

"Seven thirty p.m." He held out the card. "My place."

"If I agree—and I haven't yet—I get to ask questions first."

"You may ask at your leisure. I won't deny you the answers, just not here. It's not safe, *entaxei?* Okay?"

She raised an eyebrow pondering his last words about safety. "*Entaxei,*" she agreed. "I'm going to let my aunt know I've had enough for one evening." Getting away from Xen would be ideal.

Her body and mind needed time to build up some resistance—or, more like, a fortress with a moat.

He stepped aside to let her lead the way, following behind. Glancing over her shoulder, she caught Xen looking at her ass and close to salivating. His eyes flicked up to meet hers. She could not mistake the desire that danced in those green depths.

I can't believe it, she scoffed. He didn't even have the audacity to look embarrassed at being caught.

"Men ..."

"Did you say something?" he quizzed.

She ignored him and kept walking towards her aunt, reaching her just before she jetted off again to mingle with her charity donors. "*Thitsa.*"

"Carissa, Xen," she said, greeting them with a huge this-was-my-idea smile.

"I'm going to go. I'm a little tired," Carissa lied.

"I insist on giving you a ride home," Xen commanded.

"No, no, I don't need a ride. I've made arrangements." She held her hands up, palms out to stop the words that were about to come from both of them. She wanted to use her own means—a cab. Thank goodness they didn't push it. She leaned in to give her aunt a peck on the cheeks, and then turned to Xen.

Flares of pleasure skimmed down her spine as he took her hands in his, drawing her smoothly towards him. Her head tilted upwards towards his, her nose caught his ambrosial scent. *Gods he smells so good.* She brushed her lips softly against his cheek; desire ignited in her all over again. The temptation to linger was almost overpowering, but she managed to school her thoughts and pulled back. Her gaze locked with his.

"Tomorrow, seven thirty p.m.," she breathed, trying not to fall victim to the green depths of his eyes.

"Precisely, *koukla*." A small grin tugged at his lips. He let go of her hand and turned to leave. The flames ceased, along with the butterflies running riot in her stomach.

As soon as his long, graceful strides took him out of earshot, Carissa's aunt flew at her like a flighty bird. "Oh, Carissa, I just knew it. He is perfect for you. You would make a wonderful couple."

"Relax, *Thitsa.*" She rolled her eyes at her aunt's excitement. *Oh brother!* How in the name of Aphrodite would she deal with this? If Aunt Paula had her way, she'd be having babies by tomorrow morning and they'd be moving on to real estate acquisitions.

Right now, getting out of there had hit her top priority list. "I'll see you in the morning. No need to rush home because of me." She pulled her aunt in for a hug then turned to leave.

"Carissa."

She paused at the stairs leading to the ground floor.

"Be careful."

"Always, *Thitsa.*" She winked then did a quick jog down the stairs and outside. She pulled her smart phone from her bag and used the app to book a cab. Her phone beeped with a message.

"Twenty minutes," she whispered,

A chill ran through her, causing the hair on her scalp to prickle when she'd stepped closer to the curb of the parking lot. She scanned the lit area, looking for what might have caused her hackles to rise. Nothing looked out of place, no suspicious characters loitering around the function center.

It occurred to her that it bordered on stupid to agree to meet Xen for dinner at his house. She should've picked a public place, but desperation for answers made her do crazy and irrational things. *Like share dinner with a gorgeous stranger at his place. You're an idiot.* The rock that sat heavily in her stomach told her why she'd acted the way she had. She could not resist him, and secretly she craved to fulfill those dreams.

"Where is that cab?"

She fumed as she walked through the parking lot to the main street entrance of Lesner Hall, her heels clicking on the concrete. That same frosty bite returned, amplifying her unease. The darkness wove a camouflage blanket. The hairs on her nape and arms rose and her sixth sense screamed for her to get out of there. Her muscles tightened but she decided to keep her feet moving by pacing. Her cop instinct told her what she already knew—someone was watching.

SIX

"Pay attention to your enemies,
for they are the first to find out your faults." ~ Antisthenes

Behind the steering wheel of his SUV, Xen's lips curved up in gratification. The evening had gone better than he'd planned. His part had been so easy to play and he hadn't been required to amp up his charms to win her over. His *koukla* couldn't hold her alcohol, and it had been beyond amusing watching her and picking up some of her random thoughts. He hadn't envisaged she would drink and render her mind-shield down, a morsel of information he locked into the forefront of his mind. He'd have to give her a drink when he wanted her to be putty in his hands.

Some of the random thoughts he caught from her when he'd tuned in almost slayed him—entertaining and sexually needy. Gods, it had been difficult to keep his arousal down from her mere reaction to him alone. Her thoughts had only added fuel to his already out-of-control fire. Her scent on the dance floor had stirred his lust. He'd fought the beast within him. He'd acknowledged his lack of resistance to her and her maddening scent only escalated his rapidly increasing need.

It had been a calling. One he could not fail to answer. He had found her immediately when he'd walked through the entrance of the charity function. The sweet smell of tuberose and jasmine assaulted his nose. The turquoise dress she wore—his new favorite color—clung to her luscious curves, stunning in the way it accentuated the contours of the dips and swells of her figure. A vision danced behind his eyes. He could see his hands leisurely peeling it from her body to reveal the glorious prize that waited beneath ... a soft and sensuous woman.

The tires of his SUV screeched as he pulled up abruptly in the driveway of his Virginia Beach residence. He owned one of the many hotels in city but preferred the privacy of the house he kept here. Plus it would not be ideal to have his *Phi* walking through the lobby armed to the teeth with swords.

He pushed the gear stick into park, but before he killed the engine a deep foreboding settled into the pit of his stomach causing his muscles to tighten. What if some other man tried to hit on her in that dress? *I should not have left her there.* With precision, he swiftly shifted the gears and reversed, heading back towards Carissa.

His thoughts turned proprietorial and his foot pushed the accelerator hard, driving like a man possessed.

Carissa's steps were measured, her heels clacked on the asphalt. The twenty minutes the cab company had texted became thirty-five. She stopped her OCD strides and fished her phone out of her purse.

A gush of cool wind skipped over her flesh causing goosebumps to rise. A shiver ran through her, making her uncomfortable. *Come on! What's taking so long!* She touched the app on her smartphone and called the number of the cab company.

A usual greeting welcomed her. "Yellow Cabs."

"Good evening, I booked a cab over half an hour ago and it's yet to arrive. Can you tell me if you've dispatched the cab?"

"What's your location and destination."

"Location is Lesner Inn, 3319 Shore Drive, going to 912 Watsons Drive, Virginia Beach." Carissa fired back her answers, urgency laced in her voice.

"Can you hold?"

"Yes."

Music filled the line for a few minutes, then with a click the Yellow Cab lady spoke. "Okay, he's on his way. Said he got held up because of an accident. Should be fifteen minutes."

"Alright. Thank you."

She pressed end to finish the call and tried to shake some of her uneasiness. The parking lot was rather quiet, not many guests had left. In fact, only two couples had driven out in the thirty-five minutes she'd stood there.

Moments of the evening replayed in her mind and she tried desperately not to smile like a dork at the thought of Xen. *Now that's one hot man!* One she could not touch. *Work first. Yeah, like that's going to help, Carissa.*

The looks from Xen as he'd scanned her attire from head to toe, told her he liked what he saw. Warmth crept up her cheeks as she recalled his raking gaze.

She sighed and opened her purse to place her phone in it. The squeal of tires had her head snapping up. A black Range Rover with the license plate PHITECH1 came to a sudden halt next to the sidewalk. The passenger window of the car was down and behind the steering wheel sat none other than her dream god.

"Xen?" She dropped her jaw in surprise and held her palms out in confusion.

"Let me drive you home." His mouth twitched.

"Why?"

"Because you need a ride, and if I'm not wrong, you've been standing out here for far too long."

How odd. "But—"

"I realized I should have insisted on giving you a ride."

"You know, it seems a little weird that you turned back—" A loud squeal of rubber cut the words from her mouth.

"Run now!" Xen's voice penetrated through her mind and all the way down her body as an SUV rammed his Range Rover from the rear. Metal clanged against metal. The impact propelled Xen's car forward.

Déjà vu ricocheted in her brain. Carissa's dress tangled above her knees. Her fingers made quick work of hiking it up and into the elastic of her underwear. Her legs moved into a run in seconds. Gods, when had she strayed this far down the street?

The entrance to the parking lot lay ahead. Her feet, in the stupid heels, decided at that moment to make her see the pavement up close and personal. One hand stung at the graze, the other held her purse which took the impact of the fall. Her knees were another story, and the tearing sound told her that her gown would not live past tonight—just her luck.

A grunt alerted her to a presence. Turning she scrambled on the ground to face the source. Pain sharp and merciless stabbed her in the chest at the sight of a creature with a sword standing a foot away from her. She fumbled with her purse, pulling her gun from it. Her fingers wrapped around it, she pointed and fired.

Shell casings fell beside her but the creature wouldn't go down. *Shit, I'll be sliced ham soon.*

The bullets only seemed to aggravate him. He lurched, swinging his sword. She rolled out of the way and scrambled to her feet. *Ready.* He swung his sword. Her martial arts training allowed her to duck and expertly bring a heeled foot to his midsection.

A loud growl ripped through the night air. He flung his sword-less arm out and backhanded her out of the way. Pain shot up her spine and her vision clouded. Pushing herself up, she tried to stand. A head rolled onto the ground and stopped at her feet, a bloody trail lighting the way to where it had been attached.

Behind the falling headless body stood Xen, sword in his hand. *Where the hell did he get that?* He sped to her, a blur she couldn't clearly see moving. *How is that possible?* She shook her head.

"*Koukla*, give me your hand we need to get out of here now. It's not safe."

Doors slammed as another Range Rover pulled up next to Xen's. She noticed the similar plates: PHITECH2.

He barked out orders in Greek.

Adrenaline pumped through her veins, but the clarity of what had happened wasn't there. *What was that thing?*

"Xen, you need to talk to me."

He ushered her into his smashed-up but drivable car. "Let me get you to my place first, and I promise you'll have answers."

She watched as he shifted gears and burned rubber into the night. "Why? I mean—what was that thing doing here?"

"This is going to sound cliché, but it's because of me," he said.

"You must have really pissed someone off if they're coming at you with swords. Speaking of which, you had one too. How?" Dizziness threatened to overwhelm her, her body turned to liquid as she tried to fathom what had played out. "And why attack me?"

"Well, you were with me. They must think you are tied to me somehow."

"Who are *they*?" she croaked. None of the conversation made any sense.

"My enemies have only one prime objective—to kill," he explained. "You are, in their eyes, a mere obstacle."

She gulped hard at his words. She'd be dead if it were not for him. Raising her shaky hand, she wiped away the small beads of sweat that formed on her forehead. Her fingers tightened around the passenger door handle, turning her knuckles white from her iron grip. It helped to ground her muddled state. Her fear changed track to deal with the hand she'd been dealt.

"And here I was thinking it was the turquoise dress." Maybe she really was deranged.

A deep and throaty laugh left Xen's lips. "*Koukla,* if you don't mind me saying ... that dress can not only stop traffic, it could cause a pileup." A ravishing smile graced his lips.

She recalled her previous thoughts about his smile—its own religion and zip code, yes it definitely had that. He had his statement all back to front. She'd bet her bottom dollar he'd cause a pileup if he walked out on the street and flashed his pearly whites.

Her silly internal musings were short-lived, and her questions returned with full force. "What was that about?" she demanded. "I couldn't see my attacker's face clearly."

She shifted through her thoughts, replaying all that had happened. She couldn't remember the face. It was an odd thing. A bit like the warehouse incident where she couldn't recall what happened.

"Why is that?"

"Carissa, let's get you in the house first, then we'll talk. I promise to answer your questions."

"Why do I get the feeling you're hiding something?"

"Not hiding. You could say, protecting."

"Protecting what and whom?" she bit out. "Are you part of a mob?"

His laugh echoed around the interior of the car. "No, Carissa. Not a mob."

Her scalp prickled. Okay, if he didn't belong to some mafia group, what crazed fanatical group *did* he belong to? She might have bitten off more than she could chew.

They'd barely stepped into the house when a knock sounded at the door. Through it came a man as tall as Xen, but wider and more muscled.

Wonder if all his friends are this hot. Carissa shook her head, rejecting the trail of thoughts and the direction they wanted to take. She should be focusing on getting answers on what in Hades had just happened and why, not drooling over men.

Warmth rose to her cheeks as the man's eyes raked over every inch of her. It had never occurred to her that she might have looked cheap. "Nice dress," he said with a smirk.

That's it. I'm throwing this out when I get home.

Xen eyed her suspiciously for a moment before he introduced her to the large, imposing male. "Kane, this is Carissa."

He nodded in greeting.

A response lodged in her throat. She glanced at them for a split second and could have sworn she saw auras around them, like small sparks of electricity. She shook her head. She really needed to lie down, or eat something.

"Carissa, we will talk in a moment. I need to speak with Kane urgently. He works with me at my company, Phi Technologies."

"*Phi Technologies?*" Wheels turned and information spooled. "Don't tell me you own it?"

"Okay, I won't," he said with a wink.

She swallowed hard at the news, a little surprised at not having put it together when her aunty had introduced her. Xen Lyson was *the* Xenocrates Lysandros. Every Greek knew him. The man had billions. The Greeks even made jokes he could bail Greece out of debt.

Idiot, Carissa. The alcohol she'd consumed had obviously affected her rationality and ability to process simple data. *Way to go, Carissa. Your dream god is a living legend.* The man was shrouded in mystery and very little was known about him. No hits on any search engines, no photos online, nothing, *zip, zilch, nada.* Other than the rumors the Greek community made up because no journalist had ever been victorious in gaining an interview. Her mouth went dry and her mind spun in overdrive.

"Are you okay? You look like you're going to be sick." Xen moved closer to her.

"No, I'm okay. Just need some water."

He left the room to fetch it for her.

"Follow me." Kane motioned and guided her to the living room. "Take a seat."

"Thanks," she croaked.

"No problem."

All the insecurities she'd buried years ago shot to the surface and her self-esteem took that moment to plunge into a dark abyss. The only thing she could think of was how she must look to Xen, an enigma on his own—cheap trash vying for his attention in a discounted turquoise dress.

Xen stepped into the room, breaking her thoughts of self-loathing. He handed her a glass and leaned over to her ear. His breath teased. "Don't ever put yourself down, *koukla.* You look delectable and I will tell you much later—when I'm finished with your questions—what I would like to do to you in and out of that dress."

He lifted her hand, a smile curving his kissable lips. Slowly, he brushed them lightly against her skin. Tingles broke out through her body. Her cheeks warmed and heat pooled in her belly.

"I'll wait here." Her words were barely audible because a thief had stolen her breath without exerting himself at all.

"Thank you." He rose from his position and headed through another door to speak with Kane.

Her hands quickly descended to her strappy heels, removing them and casting them aside. She pushed her toes into the thick rug and let out a sigh.

Big, lovely books adorned the coffee table. *Tuscan Villas*. Her fingers touched the glossy cover, compelled to turn the pages. She flicked them over one by one, and pondered on how he'd known she was thinking about the dress.

Maybe I said something out loud.

"Care to tell me what went down?" Kane queried as he walked into Xen's office and stood near one of the chairs. Xen read his stance.

"You already know my movements ..." Xen paused, his body tensed and the muscles in his jaw quivered. He stamped his anger into submission. He needed a cool head to work out what game the demons were playing. That thought was briskly sliced in two—had he not returned in time, Carissa would be dead.

"You veered off your schedule. What if there were more demons lying in wait for you?"

"There weren't, and you know as well as I do I can take on a fair few."

"A risk you should not have taken, regardless," Kane challenged.

"We take that gamble every time we strap on our swords." Xen's words echoed in the room, cleaving the tension.

"Why the girl?" Kane fired.

"They are likely tracking my movements." It seemed too much of coincidence for the demon to have turned up when he did. No, they were waiting to strike.

"Still doesn't explain why they would try to kill the girl."

He agreed with Kane. It did not add up. "We're missing something." He clenched his fists.

"This thing smells bad, Xen. I can understand if the demon attacked only you, but he didn't. It's almost as if he rear-ended you to get you out of the way to go after the girl."

"I'm aware of that. See what you can dig up from our human connections back in Charleston. Anything further on why Carissa might have been coaxed into the middle of one of our skirmishes."

Kane nodded at his instruction. "So this girl isn't a passing fad?" he asked.

A growl escaped Xen's lips. Carissa belonged to him. "Firstly, she has a name—use it. I think you know me well enough to know what she may become to me."

"Whoa!" Kane's hands came up in defense.

It took Xen a minute to cage his possessiveness. It was time to share the most startling revelation of the evening, which had more to do with the delectable woman sitting in the living room and less to do with fighting demons.

"There's also something you might want to know." He paused, thinking of the best way to divulge his theory. "Carissa doesn't realize yet that she has the power of *Anagke*—force, through compulsion. I saw her move a whole crowd of women just to get to me." Amusement tugged at his lips as he recalled a small piece of information he had lifted from her mind this evening. Her guard had been down, allowing him access. "She basically compelled the women to do her bidding, thus moving them away from me."

"No shit." Kane's rise in tone highlighted his surprise. "Then she could become interesting enough for others to want to have her on their team, to manipulate her powers to their advantage."

"Yes." Xen let out a breath. She belonged with him now, even if she didn't know it yet.

"Any idea what she is?" Kane asked. "Obviously she's other."

"Actually, I think she's a demi-god, but something is suppressing her power. I can sense it like it's trapped and can't break through the surface. I doubt she knows." He paused before adding, "I suspect whoever bound her power did it to stop her being detected. The question is, why?"

Kane whistled. "Shit, a demi-god and clueless. That's a potent mix."

"Potent is too weak a word for it, Kane. If the power I sensed becomes unbound then I think we will have sparks that may draw the attention of the demons. We will need to help her develop it so she can protect herself."

"Wow." Kane ran a hand through his short brown hair. "If any other Unearthly discovers her talent by accident, they'll have her for breakfast."

"I fear they may already have." His expression turned grim as the recollection of the demon standing over Carissa filtered through to his consciousness.

"How will we train her if we don't even know the full extent of her power?" Kane asked.

Xen caught the conflict in his voice. "I'm sure we have details of a demi-god in our Unearthly database that has the power of *Anagke*. Run the search, Kane. Let's see what comes up."

"Sure thing."

"Oh, and Kane, just so that you understand my position, Carissa is mine."

SEVEN

"My tongue swore, but my mind's unsworn." ~ Euripides

In Xen's absence, ideas and misconceptions swirled around Carissa's mind. Time seemed lethargic as she sat there. He'd been gone for over thirty minutes. Irritated, she narrowed her eyes at the door and folded her arms across her chest.

Why couldn't he have told her about Phi Technologies and his involvement—or, correction—ownership? *Because you didn't ask him, you dimwit.* The voice in her head spoke the truth, but she flicked it the Greek version of the bird—five fingers.

The empty glass in her hand needed refilling. Taking the initiative to find the kitchen, she walked out of the living room and down a corridor, past the room that held Xen captive in discussion with Kane. Light spilled out onto the corridor ahead. Her feet stopped, her mouth falling open at the sight of the kitchen.

"Now this is a kitchen," she said to the expansive space. She traipsed over to the breakfast bar and ran a hand over the smooth marble. "This is definitely a cook's orgasm."

She breathed before strolling over to the kitchen sink. Large double windows looked out over an illuminated backyard. To her right, a floor-to-ceiling glass door led out to a manicured garden. She caught sight of movement beyond the trees. Doing a double take, her eyes zeroed in on something running towards the glass door. A loud grunt sounded from outside just before the door came smashing down. A scream ripped from her throat. The glass fell from her hands onto the marble floor. Shards flew and imbedded themselves into her toes.

Strong, muscled arms banded around her body as she met with the hard floor. Heavy weight pushed down on her as she gasped for air. Furniture crashed against the marble floor, the sound ringing in her ears, but what made her body shake was the unmistakable clash of metal against metal.

A loud growl reached her ears, followed by a swish through the air.

Silence.

Her brain slowly unfroze, recognizing that the weight belonged to Xen—positioned perfectly on top of her and shielding her from danger.

"Are you okay, *koukla*?" came his smooth, velvety voice against her ear.

She slowly found hers. "Yes," she said, her reply breathy.

"Are you hurt?"

She didn't have a chance to answer. Kane walked through the door that was now a shattered opening.

Gods, what happened?

"We have a problem, Xen. We'll need to get out of here *pronto*. We've eliminated four demons but my guess is we can expect saturation shortly. We need to move."

Carissa wriggled to get Xen's attention. He hadn't moved and it didn't feel like he had any intention to, despite Kane's revelation. If he didn't move soon her body would explode with desire from the contact. Already she crackled and sizzled beneath him, desire awoken as never before. She cleared her throat.

"Sorry, *koukla*." He got up and held out his hand to help her up.

Thank goodness her face was flushed from exertion. Otherwise, he would have noticed her embarrassment from their horizontal connection. He pulled her up as if she weighed nothing. *Wonder what he looks like naked? Bet he's glorious. Oh stop, stupid brain!*

She caught Xen's smirk and her brain backpedaled to what Kane had said.

"What does he mean by demons?"

She winced from the small cuts on the top of her feet.

"You're hurt and bleeding." Concern laced his words.

"I'm okay. It's just a little blood."

"It's not okay." His nostrils flared.

Kane moved around the kitchen quickly. "We need to clean you up, Carissa."

He walked over to her with an armful of first-aid items. "I've got this, Xen. Go get the men ready."

Xen backed out of the kitchen with his eyes on her and a tortured look on his face.

"Is he okay?"

"Yeah, he's fine. Blood does funny things to him."

Kane worked quickly, pulling the shards of glass from her feet.

The antiseptic stung as he sealed the cuts with adhesive bandages.

"Good as new." He stood to face her, sealing the swabs he'd used in a ziplock bag in his hands.

"Thank you, Kane. I could have managed it myself, you know."

"We need to move."

Xen appeared at the door. "We're ready."

Carissa caught the look Xen gave Kane, a silent communication, one that aggravated her. Anger sped through her body, heating it and making her heart pound.

"Xen, you need to explain what the hell is going on." She clenched and unclenched her fists, trying to curb her rising fury.

"Hell has a lot to do with it."

"This is crazy, and I'm deranged for even thinking I'd get a straight answer out of you. You've avoided the topic of what happened at Jostlers every time I've asked. And here I stand, bloodied feet and clueless." She crossed her arms, silently praying he'd acknowledge her irritation. "I want to go back to my aunt's house—*now*."

"I promise all answers will be granted to you, but first, relocation for your safety is of the essence." Urgency wove into his voice.

"No, I leave now." She tried to push past Xen—who was a wall in front of her.

Kane moved, blocking her retreat. "No can do. These things are targeting you as much as they are targeting Xen. You've been seen with him, there's no going back now. You're in the thick of it whether you like it or not. We have to move and you're moving with us!"

Her eyes widened at Kane's firm voice and she snapped her gaze to his. "I can't ... I can't be a target. I have to get back to my aunt, she'll be worried. Trust me when I tell you, she's quite a spitfire." She dropped her arms to her sides.

"You go back, *koukla,* and you'll be putting her in danger too," Xen added.

The scene at the charity event replayed slowly in her head as logic kicked in. She'd fired her gun and the target had failed to go down. How could she protect herself or those she loved if her gun failed to stop the attackers? She would have died tonight if Xen hadn't been there. Kane was right. *I really need one of those swords.*

Comprehension slammed into her rattled mind. Her chances were better with Xen, and risking her aunt's safety would be foolish. The problem would be telling her aunt what had happened. She'd sound like a loon. Aunt Paula would never buy that philanthropic Xen Lyson was really a slayer.

"Okay, I get it. We need cover, but I want answers as soon as we are secured." Her fingers itched to grab the lapels of his suit and shake him. "Convincing my aunt that nothing's going on will be difficult. She'll sniff you out in seconds. We need something conceivable—like helping you uncover some fraud."

"You have my word, Carissa. It will be believable." He reached out, captured her hand, and bought it to his lips, then clasped that tenderly kissed hand in his and proceeded towards the front door.

She let the breath she had been holding go. "Where are we headed?"

"To safety."

"You really don't answer in long sentences, do you?"

Kane let out a laugh, then stifled it quickly when Xen turned with a raised eyebrow.

Xen led her outside to one of the waiting SUVs. A team of men dressed in black gear resembling a SWAT team dispersed to different vehicles. His security team, or whatever they were, acted with the speed of light.

"Wait! My shoes," she yelled when her foot landed into what appeared to be water.

"You won't need them." In one swift movement, he had her in his arms. A squeal almost escaped her lips. Her nostrils scented his masculinity. Without thinking, she took a deep breath. Her heart sped up.

"Put me down," she insisted, trying to break the spell she was under.

"Your feet are cut. I won't have you walking barefoot."

"If you'd let me get my shoes, I'd have something to walk in."

"Not happening, *koukla*." In a few short strides he was at the SUV and placing her in the back seat.

"Nice dress." A man sitting in the front seat waggled his eyebrows.

Carissa rolled her eyes and Xen growled. Kane thumped the man hard in the left arm as he slid into the driver's seat.

"Carissa, this is Adam."

"Pleasure," he said and winked.

Xen growled again and Kane took one hand off the steering wheel to jab Adam again.

She would have laughed, but she wanted an explanation for all the weird things happening around her.

Kane started the car and they were moving. Surely Xen could brief her a little, bring her up to speed as to which gang or group seemed the likely threat. "Xen, I want you to explain, and the best place to start would be at the warehouse where this damn nightmare began." She closed her eyes and took a deep breath, waiting for him to answer, to hear his deep voice spell out the truth of the situation. Her eyes darted open at the heavy silence in the car. Turning her head, she zeroed in on Xen. He sat with his lips pressed tightly together. He pinched the bridge of this nose and closed his eyes.

"Xen," she said softly. Maybe she'd crossed some invisible line. *Maybe it is all a crazy dream and I've really lost the plot.*

Then he spoke. "Carissa, there is no easy way to explain without sounding ridiculous or far-fetched. None of what I tell you will sound like the truth." He turned in the seat. His eyes met hers. "I need you to trust me. Be open-minded, because what you hear tonight will change everything about the world as you know it." He shifted his body in the car so that his hands cupped her cheeks. "I need your trust, *koukla*."

"From where I'm sitting, it's a little hard to trust someone you've just met, someone who has yet to tell me anything significant." She lifted her hand and placed it over his. "Trust has to be earned before it's given." She dropped her hand and he did too. As she faced forward, she caught Kane and Adam looking at each other.

"Alright. I'll take what limited faith you can offer."

Xen picked up on Kane's and Adam's thoughts—they approved of Carissa. It pleased him because something deep within him wanted to keep her for as long as the gods would allow, but these thoughts would have to wait. Now his most vexing problem would be to convince her of their co-existence. His words would either make her run screaming or pique her curiosity so that she could learn more about his world and the unearthly creatures roaming the night.

How did one broach this topic without her thinking him a liar? No, he did not want that. He wanted to establish closer ties. Carissa wanted the truth and answers, so he'd give her the short version. Judging by her acceptance, he would proceed to fill in the gaps later.

He cleared his throat.

"There is no easy way to tell you this, but the most important fact is that we are on the side of good. We do not harm innocent people." He hoped that would soften the blow.

"Okay, so you and Kane are the good guys."

"And me!" piped up Adam.

"Correct." Xen said, frowning at Adam's intrusion.

"The night of the attack at Jostlers, the things you saw but don't clearly recall—and don't see clearly now—are *Kakodaimones* or demons." He turned, watching for any reaction. He reached out with his vampiric telepathy and found her guard down.

Great. That straightjacket will look better on him than me. Demons—is he kidding?

"I don't kid." He grimaced.

Surprise laced her features. "How did you ... oh, never mind." She ran a hand through her hair. "Why is my recollection obscured?"

He took a sharp inhalation of breath. How to answer this without sounding like a fraud? Maybe hard and fast would be better. "Because I used *hypnosi* on you so that you'd forget what you had seen, but your will was too strong. I couldn't completely harness a section of your memories to alter them. You pushed me out, rendering me incapable of completely erasing your memory of the skirmish." He shifted in his seat, expecting an onslaught from Carissa.

"I thought I was out of my mind, but I knew you'd done something hypnotic. I thought you guys were drug lords or part of some mafia organization. I thought ..."

Xen held up a hand to stop her onslaught of assumptions as to the *Phi's* real purpose. "Carissa, there is no mafia involved. It's an age-old war between unearthly creatures and human protectors."

"Unearthly creatures?"

"Let me tell you the rest before you jump to conclusions."

"I'm not jumping to anything. If you were in my shoes, you'd be reacting the same way."

He looked at her. She was right. "True, but I did ask you to trust me."

"Okay, I'll listen."

"Many years ago, I pledged myself to a secret order to protect mankind from the evil things that walk the earth." She scrunched up her face, and he thought she looked adorable. "Let me lift my *hypnosi* so you can see what I'm talking about." He turned to face her and placed his hands on the sides of her head. In a low, deep voice, he chanted the ancient Greek word *mnemoneuo* three times.

Xen watched as she sat unmoving. The veil he'd lifted froze her features. It appeared she'd gone into momentary shock. Her eyes widened, he heard her heart rate pick up and saw her body tense. He waited for the scream to come.

Three, two, one.

Nothing.

They rode for ten minutes in silence before he poked into her mind. This time he met a concrete wall. He ran a hand through his hair and exhaled when a tear ran down her cheek.

Tears streamed down her face—for Lopez, for her, for everyone who meant something. The images flickering through her memory shocked her to her core. *My God, how could any of this be real?* The only demons that existed were the human criminal kind. Not the ones she now saw crystal clear in her mind. No, those were found in horror movies, not real life. Yet the logical side of her brain knew it to be the truth, but still she had a hard time accepting it. Panic the size of a golf ball lodged in her throat, rendering her speechless. She sniffed.

Strong arms pulled her closer and a white hanky appeared in front of her face. *Luckily the mascara's waterproof.* She tried hard to recompose herself, clearing her throat.

"So what does that make you? If you and your men fight demons, you must be something else?" Her voice quaked.

"I'm a vampire, Carissa. A very, very old one," he confessed.

"I'm too numb to feel the full effects of fear right now. Although I should." A shiver ran through her body.

"Koukla ..."

"I mean, of course, you're a vampire." A stunned laugh escaped her lips. "If there are demons then it's obvious that you'd exist." The words coming from her mouth sounded foreign. *I'll wake up tomorrow and realize none of this happened—that it's been a bad dream.*

His arms tightened around her. Images replayed through her mind again and snippets of random observations she'd made during the evening suddenly made sense.

Her bloody feet.

His reaction.

Vampire.

She repressed the bile that threatened to rise up her esophagus.

She had to ask the inevitable. "As in sharp fangs and drinking blood?"

He didn't answer.

Her mouth dried, causing her uneasiness to notch up a bit. *Damn, what is wrong with the man?* "Xen, yes or no? Do you drink blood?"

"Yes, but not in the gory way you might think. Feeding is actually pleasurable to both parties."

She nodded her head, swirling the information around.

"You're taking this better than I thought," he admitted.

"You mean, I'm mentally a thousand hues of deranged. You've just obliterated the world I knew. I've been hunting criminals while you've been killing something beyond human understanding. The way I see it, you'd have to be strong to defeat those ghastly demons. A vampire is good enough for me. As long as I'm not your source of nourishment and you don't see me as a giant hot dog, we're okay." She spat the words out without taking a breath.

"*Koukla*, you would be more than food to me. You would be the most delectable and sweet dessert." He leaned close to her ear, his breath hot as he spoke. "I can't wait to taste you."

A laugh escaped Kane and Adam, whom Carissa had forgotten were in the front and could hear everything. Heat rose to her cheeks. Xen placed a hand on her cheek and rubbed his thumb over her bottom lip. Shivers danced all over her body, masking her prior nerves.

The SUV came to a stop.

Adam punched some numbers on the modified dashboard of the car and a colossal gate slid open. They drove straight into an underground garage. Carissa estimated that the ride had lasted about fifty minutes, tops.

Xen got out and came around to open her door.

"Would you like me to carry you?"

"No, I'm fine."

"This house is heavily secured so we shouldn't have a demon problem here. It's temporary, until we can work out why they targeted you."

"I understand." Her feet touched the cool concrete in the garage.

Xen motioned her to follow Kane and Adam. She followed behind, not liking the height difference without her heels.

Kane pressed some buttons on a keypad near a heavy metal door. It opened and they stepped into a dimly lit corridor. She followed behind Kane with Xen behind her. Adam came last, and closed the door. Her face hit a solid wall as Kane stopped in front of her.

"Kane," she moaned, holding her nose.

He let out a laugh but she didn't share his humor. "Sorry." The man was as solid as the steel door they'd come through. "One more door." Kane said.

Xen wasn't kidding when he said the place would be secure. *Sheesh.*

After they crossed the threshold of the last door, light encased them. A set of stairs in front of them rose steeply upward. *Just how far underground are we?* They started the ascent. *What is this place, Fort Knox?*

As they climbed the stairs the hair at her nape stood; the notion that a pair of green eyes were watching every step she made had her turning her head to confirm her assumption.

"Like what you see?" Their gazes collided. She faltered on the step but righted herself.

"I think you know the answer to that." His mouth twitched.

"You look like you're going to bite it. Don't tell me you draw blood from butts as well as necks?" she joked over her shoulder.

"She's onto you, boss," Adam said from behind him.

Don't turn around, don't look at him. Compulsion gave in and she turned her head to look at Xen again.

Undeniable heat flared in those deep green eyes.

Oh heck, he can draw blood from there and I've just made a fool of myself. "O-kay," she muttered.

At the top of the stairs, Kane opened the last door. They stepped through into a large foyer. To her left were double doors, which led to the main entrance of the house. They walked through to a large living room. Carissa blinked. She didn't know where to look first. Everything screamed lavish, from the French Louis XV couch and armchairs to the exquisite antique coffee table.

Kane and Adam walked to the far end and through another door.

"Call me if you need anything, Xen," Kane said. He and Adam beamed like mischievous school boys. "'Night," he shouted.

Xen turned, ignoring them as they left and closed the door behind them. "I should get you settled in one of the guest bedrooms."

"My aunt ..." A wave of concern crashed over her. She'd been too preoccupied with everything and had forgotten her again. "I have to call her and let her know where I am. She'll be worried sick." Her chest tightened.

Xen faced her and stepped closer. His hands brushed lightly over her arms.

"Don't concern yourself. I will make the call. It's better if it comes from me. You can talk to her tomorrow."

Her voice shook. "I should speak to her."

"Shhh." He lifted his hand to her cheek and ran his thumb over her bottom lip.

"Trust me, leave it for tomorrow."

What was it about him that made her give in so easily? "Okay."

"Feel free to take a look around. Your room is at the top of the stairs, third on the right. I'll make the call and be right up." His eyes flickered with something primal then he disappeared to the other side of the staircase to make the call.

EIGHT

"I have found power in the mysteries of thought." ~ Euripides

Curiosity—a tempting beast in a house like Xen's. She heeded his invitation to roam freely. "It's like giving me a search warrant." She padded around the mega-mansion taking inventory of materials used in the rooms: hardwood in the corridors, marble in the foyer and kitchen. The staircase invited her up for further exploration. At the top, she didn't follow Xen's instructions to the guest room because the one in the far-right corner with the door open and the soft glow of light filtering into the corridor beckoned to her. When she stood in the doorway, her breath hitched. "Oh gods, majestic doesn't cover it."

Her feet moved of their own accord, heading to the enormous walk-in closet that led through to the bathroom. Her eyes widened at the size of the Jacuzzi and shower. Images of herself and Xen danced before her eyes. Soft movement startled her from her fantasy.

"See something you like?" came his thick, smoldering voice. The use of her words from earlier did not escape her notice. She turned and her gaze locked with his. He leaned against the entry with a devilish grin on his face, bare skin teasing her eyes. He had removed his shirt. She gulped and absorbed inch by inch his male perfection. Her body stirred, and excitement pulsed in her veins.

Heat pooled between her legs. The tattoo on his right bicep did nothing to cool the temperature, sending a heated rush up to her breasts and neck.

He looks good enough to eat.

Her eyes met his for a brief moment; something dark and deep reflected in his eyes, something primal that declared lust. She shook her head to dislodge her wayward thoughts.

You need to start dating and having sex when you get back to Charleston.

Her voice found its way through her vocal chords. "From what I've seen, I think your house is divine, but I don't understand why on earth you would need a shower that big?"

"I like to overindulge." A wicked gleam shone in the green depths of his eyes.

Her breath hitched as he closed the distance between them. He took her hand in his. The pad of his thumb caressed the back of her hand. Goosebumps broke out over her body. She watched him as he brought her hand up to his mouth and placed a light kiss on it. *I like that.*

He leaned in closer, placed his arm around her waist, and pulled her to him. Their bodies connected. The contact of her breasts against his hard chest sent an ache to her core. Her lips met his, soft, sensual and teasing. He licked and suckled seductively, pulling back, tasting the kiss they shared with the swipe of his tongue across his top lip. She mimicked his action and a deep groan escaped his lips.

"I'm going to kiss you hard. There won't be anything soft about it this time." His words were thick with promise.

She barely managed to nod her head in agreement.

His mouth descended on hers, capturing it with the hungry urgency he'd vowed. A swift coax of his tongue and she granted him passage, the invasion heady as he plundered her mouth in ecstasy. Mindless with pleasure she snaked her arms around his neck to deepen the contact. *None of my dreams compare to kissing him for real.*

He stopped the kiss and pulled back.

Carissa met his fiery gaze. *I want you.*

In one swift move, he picked her up, her legs wrapping around his waist. His mouth crashed against hers in a long and drugging kiss. She moaned her satisfaction and his grip tightened. She was lost in his taste and scent. Fire coursed through her body. He backed her up towards the vanity table and sat her down, keeping the intimate position. Her dress inched up, leaving her thighs exposed. Her panties were wet, and the pressure of his rigid arousal did nothing to assuage the ache building between her legs. *Oh gods, that's big.*

Soft whimpers escaped her lips. His hand moved to her breast, teasing the peak between his finger and thumb. It puckered to attention through the material of her dress. Delicately, he trailed his hand down from her breast, past her abs, to her thigh. His fingers found what they were looking for, past her lace panties.

He expertly moved them aside to gain direct access, while his tongue continued its assault on her mouth. A swipe of his fingers and she almost came undone. He groaned into her mouth. The sound danced through her and licked the flames where his fingers stroked her into a slow frenzy. His lips left her mouth and moved to her ear.

"So wet, *koukla.*"

"You ..." Her breath hitched. It was all her fogged brain could manage with her heart rate in overdrive. *More.*

His mouth found hers again. A sweet pressure built as he continued his ministrations between her legs. She spiraled towards that blissful moment and everything around her added to it, the opulence of his house, his wealth, his irresistible looks. Heck, here she was lost in the heat of the moment with Xen Lyson.

Gold digger. You haven't done this before. Too fast.

Abruptly she pulled away, severing the sweet delirium she didn't reach, a loss she would mourn later.

"What's wrong, *koukla*?" His voice was husky and heady. There was no denying that their lip-locking session had affected him too.

She placed her hands on his chest. Her fingers itched to run along the hard contours of his muscles. Looking up, she met his searching gaze.

"I don't usually jump at men I've just met." She wiggled, trying to get off the vanity to stand. He lifted her as if she weighed nothing and put her back on her feet.

"I'm sorry, I didn't mean to take advantage of you."

"No, no, you didn't. Trust me. Regardless of all that has happened this evening—and as much as it is to take it all in—I enjoyed what we just did way too much. I think I need a little time out." She sidestepped him to walk back into the bedroom. Not wanting to run off and ruin what they'd just shared, she sat on the edge of his bed.

He gave her a moment before he walked out of the bathroom to the bedroom. He wasn't finished with her yet. The rhythmic beat of her heart and breathing told him she had not fled his bedroom. She sat on the edge of his bed. Images erupted in his mind—her naked body spread before him. He was hard. Her words brought him out of his temporary fantasy.

"I don't want you to think I'm some gold digger."

"Whatever gave you that impression, *koukla*?"

"Well, here I am with you and all this." She waved her arms around the room.

A corner of his mouth lifted. He understood immediately. "*Koukla*, I understand you being overwhelmed by many things this evening—me being a vampire for one, or the fact demons are targeting you, yet you seem to be fixated on me thinking you might want me for my money."

He closed the distance and crouched down to where she sat at the edge of the bed.

"It sounds silly when you say it."

"Because it is. I kissed you. I initiated it. I wanted it and I want a whole lot more." Heat crept into her cheeks. The corners of his eyes crinkled.

Slowly, she met his gaze. "I don't want you to think I'm some cheap floozy who wants into your bed and into your pants. Besides, I've never been with a man in *that* way." A deep shade of red colored her cheeks.

His jaw almost hit the floor. At her admission, explosive need and possession slammed into him. A single thought filtered through his mind. *So this isn't about her thinking she's a gold digger. She's scared.*

"I will not push you to do something you are not comfortable in doing. Trust me when I tell you, *koukla,* that you want me as much as I want you. It's mutual. There's a connection."

"This is going to sound crazy. I used to dream ..." She slapped a hand over her mouth.

"You used to dream what, *koukla*?"

"Oh, nothing. Forget I said that."

Still crouching in front of her, he searched her eyes. Then recalled a thought he'd picked up when he'd kissed her, *better than in my dreams*. Elation spread through him in a heated rush.

"You dreamed about me?" He wanted to ask, *when*?

Her face paled. "No, I don't think I want to continue this conversation."

"Oh no, *koukla*. You've piqued my curiosity." He traced his hand up her leg.

"You're not going to leave this alone, are you?"

"I think you know the answer to that."

"I've been dreaming about you for years, before I ever laid eyes on you in the flesh at the warehouse." She held her hands up. "I know it sounds demented, but with all that was going on that night, coming face to face with you was quite a revelation."

It felt like the floor opened up and catapulted him to the level below, as he did a quick scan through his memories of the first night he'd approached her. *You're only a dream*. He'd not given it much thought then, but now it made sense that she'd reacted the way she had.

A sharp spike of desire pierced him straight to the groin. Her confession added another layer to his pursuit and confirmed without a doubt that this had all the markings of the gods' intervention.

"I believe we are destined to be together."

She rolled her eyes. "You do realize that sounds like Greek mumbo jumbo, the stuff my aunties are always talking about. *Tyche*—fate, it was fate, he was fated, she was fated, they were fated. That's all I ever hear."

He let out a laugh. "Believe what you like, *koukla*, but know one thing, you and I, we will happen." He eyed the sensual glide of her tongue on her upper lip and groaned internally. "And don't mock the Fates. There are things we can't explain."

"I'm sure there are. I'm looking at one of those things I can't explain."

His mouth curved in amusement at her reference. "It takes time to adjust to new knowledge. It would be fair to warn you that you will have to make adjustments to your life. You can't resume that which you knew, or pick up where you left off. You've gained new knowledge. That changes things."

"What are you saying? Are you saying I can't go back?"

"No, you can, but there will be adjustments."

"Adjustments?"

"You will need protection. You've been targeted twice in one night. There is no doubt in my mind now, especially since a demon came at you in my kitchen. I can't trust that they won't follow you home and try to harm you." He paused and took her hands in his. "Kane and his men will keep an eye on you during the daylight hours when I'm in rejuvenation."

"Rejuvenation?" She scrunched up her face in thought. "Oh, yes, vampire. That's definitely new knowledge."

He beamed at how easily she accepted what he was and the urge to spread her out on that bed harpooned right through him, setting him aflame with renewed desire. "Let's continue this conversation later."

"I should get some rest."

"Actually, I'd like to taste your lips again." With lightning reflexes, he tugged her from his crouching position and she fell right into his arms. His lips crashed to hers, not giving her time to protest.

The hunger she'd seen in Xen's eyes was unmistakable. He wanted her and he was making it *very* clear as to how much. Still, uncertainty lingered in her thoughts, but she pushed the negativity aside and crushed her lips to his, slipping her tongue inside his mouth, hungry to explore more of his oral talents.

Goosebumps fanned out over her body as his hand trailed down the side of her leg, finding the split on her dress. Expertly, he pulled and tugged until her buttocks met with cool air. His hand closed and squeezed an exposed cheek. She moaned, loving the fire he ignited with his touch. He rolled her over then slid to the side so his weight wasn't on her. His hands moved so fast she didn't have time to catch her breath. Her thong was eased from her body and his long, thick fingers slid up and down the lips of her hungry, wet core. He set the pace in slow, circular motions. His tongue danced expertly with hers, never missing a beat. At this rate, she would not last under his skilled ministrations.

He broke the kiss and moved his head over her breast, nipping with his teeth. Her nipple puckered and he sucked it into his mouth under the satin material of her dress.

Lost in the building euphoria, she didn't realize he'd freed the breast he suckled on. The contact amplified her rising need.

"Xen," she whispered his name.

His fingers sped up the same moment as he bit down on her nipple. White light ruptured behind her eyelids and a scream tore from her chest, her panting wild and erratic.

"Beautiful," he whispered in her ear. "I'm only getting started."

He lifted her and took a few steps towards the bed then placed her in the middle. With one hand, he tore the dress from her body. She gasped at his action.

"Pity, I did like that dress on you."

"I think you did it a favor," she said, panting.

"How so?"

"It looked tacky."

"That is where you are wrong, *koukla*. It looked sexy as hell, but not as seductive as you do right now. I need to taste you."

As far as she was concerned, he had it all wrong. Nothing looked as tantalizing as he did, standing there half naked. The glide of her tongue on her bottom lip only reminded her she wouldn't mind tasting him too. *I'd like to lick you all over.*

His lips curved as he dropped his pants. His naked body emanated power and sex. The hard contours of muscle were utter perfection. *A Greek god.* Seeing his long and thick arousal only amplified her need to have him where she ached.

He moved like a predator about to devour his prey. He parted her legs and nestled his head between them. Anticipation drummed in her chest. His green eyes collided with hers and he did not shift his gaze as he bent his head to take a taste of her core. Her body shuddered at the long swipe of his tongue on her folds.

Heat burned through her body at the leisurely pace he set. Her panting increased as she held his gaze. Never had she experienced anything more erotic than his tongue on her folds and the refusal of his hungry eyes to break from hers. His building speed flamed her body and tremors began with every lick and swipe of his tongue. The rapturous moment she craved seized her and she came with a primitive, animalistic cry of his name.

He waited for her to calm down. "You are delicious, *koukla*."

Her breathing came in erratic bursts. "That was mind-blowingly phenomenal." She barely managed the words, trying to revive from her orgasmic bliss.

He moved up the bed and positioned himself over her, holding most of his weight on his hands. His lips crashed to hers and she tasted herself on his tongue. Passion exploded through her again.

How can you make me want you so much?

He stilled then broke the kiss. "I want you just as much, and right now, all I want is to bury myself inside you."

He balanced his weight on one hand and grabbed his long, thick length with the other. He pumped the thick hardness a few times and then slid it up and down her sheath. Her eyes rolled back in her head and a moan escaped her lips.

"Do you want this, *koukla*?"

A breathy *yes* left her lips.

"It might hurt."

"I know, but I still want you."

He pushed at her entrance with the engorged head.

"Wait—don't we need a condom?"

"I cannot impregnate you, even if I wanted to."

She nodded in understanding.

He slid in with excruciatingly slow speed, inch by inch, until he was almost all the way.

A sharp pain pierced her womb. She bit her bottom lip. "Give it a moment. Don't move."

As the bite of pain passed, she moved her hips the only way she could to soothe her discomfort. Xen followed her lead, sliding in and out at a gentle pace, but all too soon it turned frantic as he pumped into her hot slick sheath with skilled strokes and speed. The crescendo came coursing and crashing through her like lightning, tearing her in two. Xen's climax ripped through him and into her, filling her with his essence. Their primitive groans and breathlessness echoed in the room. Xen collapsed next to her.

"You are mine. There's no going back. I won't let you go. I don't want you doubting this. I want you." He pulled her into a spooning position.

"A bit possessive, aren't you?"

"That's putting it mildly."

She giggled at his response. "Besides, you just had me."

"And I will have you again and again," he breathed into her ear.

Her sex clenched. She'd never had a man want her and be that transparent about it. It was at that moment her police-trained mind decided to rear its head.

"I can't help but feel that, several times this evening, you knew what I was thinking."

"It's simple. I can read the thoughts of others," he said as he placed soft kisses near her ear.

She turned around to face him, eyes wide at his declaration and ability. "You what?"

"Read minds." He waggled his eyebrows.

"Oh my. Have you been doing that from the moment I met you?"

"Yes and no. You are harder to read. Sometimes you put up walls and I can't get in. It's one of the reasons I couldn't *hypnosi* you at the warehouse." He paused. "You seem to have a gift of blocking when you don't want the intrusion."

Her chest tightened as she did a mental rewind. "So how much tuning in have you done?"

He lifted a brow before grinning from ear to ear. "Enough to know all your dirty little thoughts. You project them very loudly."

"Oh gods, may the earth open up and swallow me whole." She buried her head in the pillow.

Xen's deep laugh coaxed her head up. "Don't be embarrassed. It is gratifying to know you desire me as much as I crave you." He swooped in and seized her lips. She had no problem surrendering to his appetite.

NINE

*"He is richest who is content with the least,
for content is the wealth of nature." ~ Socrates*

Carissa woke to muffled voices coming from the other side of the bedroom door and to a naked Xen spooning her. In a slow move she tried to rise without disturbing him, but the movement caused him to stir.

A light whisper left her lips. "Are you awake?" she probed.

"I won't be for much longer. My body calls for rejuvenation."

"What happens when you are in rejuvenation?"

"I'm dead to the world."

"As in heavy sleep?"

"No, pretty much as in you could dance the *Zorba* on my stomach and I wouldn't flinch."

A giggle bubbled up in her throat. "Oh ... that dead."

"Yes, *that* dead." With meager energy, he leaned over and turned her face so he could kiss her. His lips were sweet and gentle. Arousal flared instantly and raced in every direction. She could have easily slipped into more, but he pulled away.

"Stay with me till I'm out, *koukla*."

"Okay." She couldn't deny him his one request. A blush heated her face at the thought of the pleasure he'd given her last night.

It wasn't long before his body stilled completely.

Not wanting to lie there any longer than necessary, she got up and headed for the luxurious bathroom, with the sole purpose of investigating the dual showerheads. Experimentation was necessary and protocol required every officer investigate situations for possible threats. Her lips turned up at the corners. The biggest threat was lying on the bed, out cold.

After she almost drowned from the pressure and amount of water, the fluffy towel was a definite comfort.

"That shower is lethal," she voiced, while wrapping a towel around her head.

She headed for Xen's walk-in closet to cover her nakedness. Never had she seen so many drawers full of t-shirts. She found one that looked like it might fit. It said, "I Bite Everywhere." The other choice was "Will Bite Upon Request."

How convenient—a vampire with a sense of humor. The odd thing that nagged at her was that she couldn't see Xen wearing any of these t-shirts. From her profiling, he just didn't fit the picture. It revealed another layer to the man, another nugget to add to the list for later.

Finding a pair of bottoms proved difficult. She went through everything and finally found a pair of black shorts with a drawstring, ones she could tug to keep up. They were big but would have to do. All his shoes and slippers were huge. She grabbed a pair of sport socks to keep her feet warm and completed the ensemble. She giggled.

"God, I look awful." Then she pulled the socks off.

Padding back to the bed, she threw a sheet over Xen's naked body. A thousand emotions rampaged through her. The attraction—definitely two-way. The fact he was more than an average human—clearly enticing and at the same time a little scary. The fact that whatever she was tangled in was way bigger than anything she'd ever worked on as a police officer—without question investigating it. And the fact that Lopez lay on a hospital bed—she explicitly wanted the head of the demon responsible. She bent and kissed his cheek before heading downstairs for some liquid energy ... caffeine.

At the bottom of the stairs, Kane stood there with a box in his hands. She looked at him, a question in her eyes.

"From Xen. He ordered these last night." She caught him eyeing her up and down, and his smirk said it all.

"I think Xen would like the t-shirt, not sure about the shorts."

"And what is so wrong with the shorts?' she said defiantly.

"They look like you're swimming in them." Entertainment bounced over his face.

"Okay I get it, don't be such a smart-ass." Carissa snatched the box from his hands, almost dropped it, righted herself and headed toward the living room in a huff.

Laughter thick and rich sounded from behind her. "Oh by the way, I am smart and I have a great ass." He winked at her.

"That is not what I said or intended." Mortification swept up her chest in tones of red as she turned to face him.

"Listen, I'm just toying with you. I've got some coffee and breakfast ready, if you want."

"Coffee. The magic word." *Kane, you are officially my friend.* She left the huge box on the table and followed him to the kitchen.

She slid easily onto the bar stool. Kane brought over a hot cup of coffee and warm plate of eggs, bacon, mushrooms, tomato and two pieces of thick toast with butter. *Breakfast heaven.*

"Oh, and just in case you don't go for the American breakfast, here are some *tiropites.*

"Thanks, this looks delicious. I'm hungry, and those cheese pastries will go down well with the rest of it."

"Big appetite, huh?" The corners of his mouth turned up.

"Uh-huh."

"Well, that's not surprising since you and Xen were up most of the night."

Yep, he'd heard her. She blushed.

He cleared his throat. "You know, the demons and all."

Sweet. He was covering for embarrassing her and that made her all the more embarrassed. Her hand came up midair to stop him. "It's okay. No harm done."

She gobbled down a mouthful of food while she tried to process the facts. What could she ask him that would be beneficial to her understanding the supernatural world? She also wanted Kane's take on what he thought about her being a target. She finished her breakfast and took a sip of coffee. *Bliss.* She closed her eyes savoring it. *Divine.*

"You enjoying your coffee?"

She was startled out of her thoughts. *Don't tell me he can read thoughts too! Oh no. This would be very bad.* The idea of more than one man reading her thoughts didn't sit well.

"Do you do the mind-reading thing too?"

"Xen's talent. No, but I can read people's emotions and reactions pretty accurately, and I also have heightened senses. For instance, I scented you from the top of the stairs and the clothes you are wearing have Xen's distinct personality on them."

"So, you're obviously not like Xen since you're standing here with me and not rejuvenating."

"Good deduction. I'm a wolf."

She gulped. "As in sharp teeth and lots of hair?"

He let out a laugh. "Pretty much."

Lucky she was sitting down. Her mind spun. "You were at the warehouse that night with Xen."

He leaned on the breakfast bar counter and flashed her a wolf-ish grin. "Spot on."

"You ..." Her words stuck to her throat. She swallowed hard.

"Pushed you over and ripped the demon's throat out."

Her eyes went wide as she recalled with clarity the scene. She gasped and her stomach clenched.

"That was you?" Her posture stiffened.

"You must admit, I do have a good coat of hair."

A deep belly laugh escaped her throat. Her relaxed demeanor returned.

"Okay, that's definitely more to take in." Wow, she did expect something, but not his admission to being a wolf. No, that just wove other patterns of fear and curiosity in her consciousness. She got up and took her plate to the sink, rinsed it and put it in the dishwasher. The mundane task helped keep her tension in check, which was not easy.

She cleared her throat. "Thanks. I'll go sift through the box," she said, walking back to the bench to grab her coffee. Kane's hand landed on her arm and stopped her.

"Listen, Xen asked if you wouldn't mind staying until this evening. He's under the impression that if you go home you may be placing your aunt in danger, which is exactly what I'm thinking."

"Xen doesn't need to know. And I can handle it. I am a cop, Kane."

"Not happening on my watch." He folded his arms across his chest and parted his legs.

"I could run your ass in."

He raised an eyebrow. "That's not advisable."

She let out an exasperated breath. "Fine."

She'd stay for the moment, then she'd work out a way to get out. He really didn't need to know all her movements. He'd have enough to tend to without watching over her twenty-four seven. The horrid thought of her aunt being unprotected stabbed her in the gut. "You don't think the demons would try something? I mean you've seen your fair share of things. Would they hurt an innocent old lady?" She needed clarification for sanity's sake and her aunt's safety.

He adjusted his stance, dropping his arms from his chest, and looked her square in the eye. "These things don't care for humanity, they feed off it. We are sworn to protect humans from them. Don't challenge Xen on his decision to keep you here. Make a good excuse to your aunt and we will back you up all the way." He paused. "The fact that you didn't go back to your aunt's place last night has more than likely granted her protection. Don't be foolish by going there on your own. They could be watching."

"I'm a good police officer and would never endanger any in-nocent lives—even more so when it comes to family. I will follow through for now." He couldn't possibly expect her to sit around and do nothing all day.

"Understand that not everything is black and white where unearthly creatures are concerned. Their realm has rules and laws much like we have here in the human realm. You have to remember you are a part of both worlds now. You crossed that boundary when you met Xen."

The man in front of her might be big, and could pass for a men-acing brute, but she recognized the compassion in him. She liked him already and felt the connection, as if he were related to her in some way. Sometimes you met people and hit it off immediately, a familiar feeling like you've known the person all your life. That's how it was being around Kane. A natural comfort bubbled inside her chest.

"I understand. It won't be easy and I'll have to deal with it one blow at a time. It's already too much to take in. I still feel like I'm in a dream and I'm going to wake up from it soon." Somehow, she didn't think things would be normal when she got back to Charleston. "How did we all end up at the warehouse if you were supposed to be fighting these things without raising human suspicion? Why did we get the call to be there?" She pulled out the stool from under the kitchen countertop and sat back down.

"We have our theories, but nothing concrete. Perhaps the demons wanted a few humans there to expose us. You realize the detection of our world would lead to chaos? It is a secret we have kept for a long time."

Deepening her voice for effect she sang out, "Like Count Dracula and Wolf Man?"

His laugh rose and echoed in the kitchen. "You watch too much Hollywood crap. The existence of vampires and wolves goes back further than five hundred years. They weren't born. Both vampires and wolves are cursed by the gods, the vampires by Hera and the wolves by Zeus."

She raised an eyebrow. "Wait a minute. So you, Xen, and everyone around you are cursed by the Greek gods?"

"Precisely."

"But those are myths."

"Are they? You're talking to one now." He winked at her.

The coffee cup she lifted from the kitchen countertop shook in her hands.

"You know, the more questions I ask, the crazier this whole thing becomes. All I really want is to find those responsible for putting my partner in hospital."

"As I said before, it's a lot to take in. The best way to understand it is by thinking of it as a whole other structure that sits right alongside the human one, only we are by far the stuff of nightmares." He wasn't wrong—by his own estimation. "And that's putting it lightly."

She studied him for a moment. "How do you fit into the picture? Aren't wolves and vampires enemies or something?"

"Unearthly creatures have always interacted, just on different levels. Sure, we have the good guys and the bad guys, and we take sides in times of need. Much like humans do in time of war—which, I hate to tell you, we have been smack bang in the middle of for a thousand years precisely."

Coffee spluttered out of her mouth. "Did you say a thousand?"

He handed her a napkin to clean the dribble off her chin. "Yes."

"Gee, you really do keep on giving with the surprises, Kane."

"I'm a sharing kind of guy." He winked again.

"So the attack at the warehouse had nothing to do with drug dealers or mafia or anything remotely criminal?"

"No, we don't involve ourselves in human crimes. As you see, we have a bigger and more destructive problem to deal with."

"No doubt about that, but I'm still puzzled as to why my contact tipped me off to be there. I was expecting a meth lab."

"That is puzzling. Maybe your connection wanted you and your partner dead."

"Looks like I'm definitely nailing Tom's balls to the wall when I catch up with him." *Rotten slime.*

"If you need help, you only need to say the word."

"Don't give me ideas."

"Oh, I'm all ideas," he sneered.

Somehow, she didn't doubt he could inflict more damage on Tom than she could ever do. "Thanks, I appreciate you talking to me. You're officially my new bestie."

Laughter ripped from his lips.

"More like beasty," he said, with a grin that could devastate women by the hordes. Mentally, she ran through her list of friends—Ligi and

Kelly—then shook her head. No, she couldn't bring them into this. Not now, not ever.

"Okay, I think it's time to squash my curiosity and see what's in the box." She hopped off the stool and headed to the living room with her cup of lukewarm coffee.

She placed the cup on a coaster and attacked the box like a kid on Christmas morning. "Wow. That man certainly knows how to charm the pants off a girl."

Under the wrapping paper lay two pairs of jeans, two shirts, two lacey bras with matching underwear in turquoise—of all colors—and two pairs of shoes, both flats. *Wow.* How? She checked the sizing. No, they were all her size. Warmth radiated throughout her body. Grabbing the box, she headed upstairs to change.

She spent most of the morning exploring the house. The need to get out overwhelmed her, but she had given her word and would honor it until she'd had a chance to talk to Xen.

Coming around the corner to the dining room, she found Kane and Adam sprawled at the table playing cards.

"Can I join in?"

"Sure," they chorused.

She pulled a chair out and sat down. "What are we playing?"

"Poker," Adam sang.

Looking at the table, she realized these guys were playing with real money. Big money.

"Okay. I don't think I can play. I don't have that kind of money." She rose to her feet.

Adam jumped to his. "No need to leave. We will give you money to play with."

"No, that wouldn't be fair."

Kane pulled the toothpick he had in his mouth out. "It's poker and it's our rules." He shoved the toothpick back between his teeth.

"Come on. Join us." Adam pleaded. "I promise it will be fun." He flashed his eyebrows.

"Okay." She sat back down and watched as Adam pushed a pile of money towards her while Kane dealt a new round of cards.

Her fingers collected the hand she'd been dealt. It took every ounce of her control to slap the euphoria that threatened to break free on her lips back into submission. *Straight flush, what were the chances of that? All hearts.*

Adam and Kane placed money in the middle of the table. She matched them but decided to raise by fifty dollars more.

"You sure you know what you're doing, little lady?" Adam pointed to the money she'd just bet.

She rolled her eyes. "Oh please. I've been playing poker since I could walk."

"That's a long time." Adam interjected.

She laughed. "Okay, maybe I exaggerated. Let's just say, I can play."

"She could be bluffing, Adam," Kane warned. Looking at the curve that turned up at his mouth she realized he didn't believe she'd bluff for one second.

"Okay. I'll call your bluff," Adam teased and added to the pile of money in the middle.

The ruse went on for five minutes before Adam folded. "Okay, Carissa. I'm curious to see what you have," Kane proclaimed as he threw down his cards.

"Straight," Adam chimed at the cards tossed on the table. "Woo."

"Straight flush," she said, smoothing the cards with her hand onto the highly polished table.

Adam's jaw dropped and Kane wore a mildly annoyed look. After a few rounds and a multitude of laughter, tears in her eyes, she'd had enough.

"What time does Xen wake up from rejuvenation?" she asked Kane.

"Around six thirty p.m."

"That late?" She couldn't help the loud pitch in her words.

"Not always. It depends on how much regenerating his body needs." A grin sat firmly etched on Kane's face.

"Oh. Okay. Thanks." She pushed her chair back and stood. "I'll catch you both later."

She made her way upstairs. There wasn't much to do, so she stripped off her clothes and, in her underwear, hopped into bed with Xen. It didn't take her long to fall into a heavy sleep.

"Who are you?"

"I'm your grandmother."

"But that can't be right. I've got my mother's mother, and my father's mother died a long time ago."

"Ochi, paidi mou—no, my child. I am your father's mother, Hera, and I have a gift for you."

She touched her stomach and warmth spread through her body.

"Take care, my child. You'll need your warrior's protection."

Blinding light hit her irises. She squinted, but when she refocused, the scene before her had turned black. Something wet and sticky squished through her toes. She looked down to find herself standing in a pool of blood. A scream tore from her throat.

Heart pounding, Carissa awoke from her dream shivering. Strong arms pulled her into a tight embrace.

"*Koukla*, you were dreaming. It's okay."

"I hate it when they are so strong, you feel as if you are there."

"Your heart is racing. What did you dream?"

"I was standing in a pool of blood." It can't be good. Something was going to happen—something big—she could sense it.

"I've got you. Remember, I will protect you."

Pieces of the dream began to replay in her mind. *"You'll need your warrior's protection."*

"What else do you remember?"

"I don't want to think about it now." Her attention shifted to his broad and naked chest, then to his muscled arms. The temptation to swipe her tongue over his skin beckoned. *I want to lick you.*

His body covered hers before she had a chance to vocalize the words.

"I'd like that very much," he said before his lips descended to hers in a slow and sensual kiss. She moaned when he broke the kiss to lick and kiss his way down to her breasts. "This color suits you." Lazily, he stroked his fingers all the way down to her panties, then he tore them from her body. She gasped and he rewarded her with a wicked gleam in his eyes. He closed his fingers around the straps of her bra. "I also think this needs to go." The garment flew across the room, leaving her bare to his ravenous gaze.

Deliberately, he traced kisses all the way down her body. She moaned when his expert tongue swiped across her core. He bit down on her sensitive flesh, causing a shockwave to pass through her and a lament to sing from her lips. Her sounds elicited a deep groan from him, evidence that her passion fueled his. He lifted his head.

"I will never tire of hearing the cries of passion you make." He traced kisses back up her body. He stopped at her breasts and licked around her areola. Then took a little nip of the nipple before sucking it into his mouth. Her body ignited and she arched her back up off the mattress. Her fingers clasped the bed sheets. When he finished his assault on one breast he started on the other.

If he kept this up she would die a happy woman.

He scraped his fangs over her breast then followed up to her neck where he nipped lightly. The sensation stirred a deep lust within her, making her pant. He retracted his fangs and captured her mouth with a devastating and hungry kiss. The sweet invasion of his tongue short-circuited her senses as it swept and stroked her mouth to rapture. When they were both breathless, he pulled back.

"*Koukla.* I don't think I can hold back anymore. I have to have you." And with one thrust, he entered her swollen sheath. He flipped her so that she sat on top of him.

The position hit every sweet spot. She rocked her hips in a frenzied motion while she ran her fingers across his wide and muscular chest.

He leaned up and caught one of her breasts in his mouth. A deep whimper escaped her lips.

Her lust-filled mind could no longer cope with the building sensations.

"Xen. Please." She pleaded for her release.

He flipped her over then thrust his length in fast movements before pulling out and starting again.

The sensations and crescendo of their bodies gliding together sent her spiraling to a combustible orgasm. It racked every ounce of energy from her body.

Xen followed right behind her with a guttural groan that vibrated through her body. He stayed joined with her while he pressed featherlight kisses all over her face.

"Now that's what I call phenomenal."

"I think I've died and gone to sex heaven," she laughed.

He pulled out from her and pulled her into a spooning position.

"We can shower in a little while and I'll show you what sex heaven is like with water cascading down your beautiful curves."

"You could do this again?"

"With you, all night, *koukla.*"

TEN

"It is possible to provide security against other ills, but as far as death is concerned, we men live in a city without walls." ~ Epicurus

Collecting her bags and car from Aunt Paula's house was like pulling teeth. Carissa glowered at the thought that her aunt assumed she'd share details about her and Xen. The devious glint in her aunt's eyes had been the final straw.

"*Thitsa,* there is no way we are going to have any discussion about whether Xen and I got it on." She slapped her hand on her forehead. "I can't believe you even asked," she gritted out, trying to keep her voice low so that Xen, Kane and Adam couldn't hear their conversation. Her gut told her it would be useless. A flush crept up her throat. They'd heard her screams of pleasure.

"Well, I wanted to know if my *proxy* worked." Her eyes sparkled with excitement and she practically beamed. Honestly, the woman had obsessive matchmaker carved on her face, and those past, failed setup dates were all too fresh and playing back in her mind.

The first guy took her to a bar and bought her a disgusting cocktail. At the end of the night she'd puked on him and he'd never wanted to see her again. The second had taken her to a movie and basically grabbed her breasts a quarter of the way into the movie. She'd jumped up and he'd stood too, giving her the perfect opportunity to punch him. She did, in the face, and then kneed him in the balls. Popcorn went everywhere; she'd left him there in agony. After that episode, she'd refused to entertain any of her aunt's "I-have-a-nice-boy-for-you" ploys.

"Let's just say your *proxy* arrangement is more than fine for now. I promise to clear some days in a month and come visit for longer. It's unfortunate I've been called back," she fibbed and her aunt bought it without too much trouble. She hadn't mentioned that she was unfit for work, nor could she divulge anything about Xen, wolves and demons.

"Promise me you'll keep me updated. I think you have a good catch there." Her aunt emphasized this by sizing Xen up from head to toe and, speaking of the devil, he ceased his conversation with Kane and turned to give them both a dazzling smile that melted her panties. She hugged her aunt then tossed her bags into the trunk of her car.

Xen held out his hand for the keys.

"Oh no. This is mine." Her feet were already moving to the driver's side door, but she didn't stand a chance with his speed. He had her with her back to the door while his muscled arms closed her in. His gaze collided with hers.

"The keys, *koukla*."

"But I like to drive ..." The words died on her lips when Xen's locked with hers.

His tongue swept against hers in a tangling dance, turning her body to soft dough. The sound of someone clearing their throat jarred her to reality. Everyone, including her aunt, had just gotten front row seats to their make-out session. The devious look on her aunt's face said it all. She handed the keys to Xen and scooted around to the passenger side and jumped in.

Xen started the engine, his joy evident.

"What were you thinking? And in front of my *thitsa.*"

"If I'm not mistaken, your *thitsa* approved."

"Oh stop. Just drive."

During the trip back to Charleston, Carissa learned more about Xen and his world, but her bladder and her stomach desperately needed a pit stop.

"I need a rest break and maybe some coffee. I haven't had anything this evening." *Because we were too busy and I missed dinner.*

Xen picked his phone out of his pocket and with lightning speed, sent a text without taking his eyes off the road.

"Now that high speed texting ability could come in handy."

His mouth curved up in amusement. A second later his phone bleeped. "There's a gas station up ahead. We'll stop there."

"Thank you."

"*Tipota,* it's nothing. I probably should have gotten you something the moment I heard your stomach growl.

Heat rose to her cheeks. *Great.* A horrible thought came to her. "So if I let a silent fart go, you would smell it and hear it."

A deep laugh tore from his throat. "Real charming, *koukla.*"

"No seriously, that would be utterly embarrassing."

"Why are you even thinking this?"

"Maybe because when I'm hungry, I get a little deranged."

"Then I'll have to make sure that you eat after our horizontal exercise." He winked at her.

She couldn't help the silly butterflies in her stomach that reminded her of her fifteen-year-old self who had been crushing on a star athlete. Only this was more intense.

A few minutes later, the gas station lights came into view. The road lay deserted.

"It looks too quiet."

"We have Kane and Adam and another vehicle three minutes behind."

His reassurance did nothing to stop the hackles on her neck from jumping up to soldiery attention.

Xen pulled the car up near one of the pumps.

She hesitated a moment before pushing the door open.

"I'll fuel up, you're low."

"Thanks."

She spied Kane and Adam pulling up in one of the parking spaces. The urge to leave ran a marathon through every nerve in her body and only intensified when she saw that the clerk wasn't behind the counter when she walked in.

Okay, let's get the peeing done and get out of here. A spike of unease stabbed her chest and quivered all the way to her stomach.

Strong arms locked around her and dragged her to the back of the store. She tried to scream, but a hand closed around her mouth. Vile-smelling breath fanned her ear. "Stop it, you bitch, or I'll slit your throat here."

Her brain went into instant combat mode. She latched onto the hand that covered her mouth then stomped down hard on her attacker's foot. He loosened his grip and it gave her space to pivot and elbow him in the stomach. She yelled out.

"Xen!"

"Fuckin' stupid bitch," her assailant roared, grabbing her and placing his hand over her mouth again. This time he squeezed her nose, cutting off her air and fogging her senses. He exited through the back door of the service station, dragging her with him.

Her mind screamed. *Stop. Stop. Stop.*

He ceased dragging her for a split second. Seizing the opportunity, she broke free and ran. Her eyes slowly adjusted to the darkness. Spying a dumpster, she headed for it. Crouching, she waited to calculate her next move.

"Come out, bi—" Her attacker's words were silenced. She heard a grunt and a thud, then nothing.

A scream dislodged itself from her throat as arms banded around her.

"Shh, *koukla.*"

Her brain wheeled back into motion. Xen's aftershave wafted past her nose. *Did vampires really shave?* "You scared the shit out of me!"

"It's either me or them, *koukla,* and yes, we do shave."

She was sure he was smirking. "Better you than them," she threw in. Adam appeared beside him.

"How many have you scented?"

"Three rogue vampires including the one you just decapitated. And demon, but the scent seems further away," Adam reported.

"I have the same estimations. We need to hurry. It smells like an ambush."

"Let's play." Adam made it sound more like a game of football than a fight with the bad guys.

"Carissa, stay here."

It was definitely a command. She wasn't given a chance to say anything before they disappeared. Any protest she had been about to voice appeared pointless. She peeked around the dumpster in the direction she assumed they raced toward, her vision adjusting to the darkness.

Adam fought one vampire while Xen fought another. A wolf appeared and went straight for the jugular of one of the rogues. Adam finished him off with his sword. With a flash of steel, the other rogue was eliminated too.

"*Koukla*, come out."

Slowly she stood and walked towards the men, shocked when a very naked Kane stood next to Adam. She slapped her hand over her eyes.

"Kane, you know you can get arrested for indecent exposure? Has no one ever told you this?"

Kane let out a deep and throaty laugh. She still had her hand over her eyes, trying not to look at that perfect body. *Gods, a girl could go blind looking at these guys.*

"Save your vision, *koukla*, you will need it," Xen said through clenched teeth.

Oh, I think I hit a raw nerve there. Possessive. She made a mental push and it was like a door came down inside her mind.

"Carissa, what did you just do?" Xen demanded.

"I'd like my thoughts to myself for a while."

Kane and Adam laughed.

"You can look now. Your eyes are safe," Kane joked.

Carissa dropped her hand from her eyes. Her lips tugged up at the corners in silent satisfaction. The thought of Xen being jealous entertained her, but also made her body tingle.

"Let's move," Xen commanded in a gruff voice.

She wanted to giggle at the exchange, but thought better than to poke at a somewhat proprietorial and adrenaline-fueled Xen-bear. She'd wait until he'd calmed down a little.

Carissa walked around to the passenger side of the car. Her fingers touched the door handle, but she didn't get the opportunity to open it.

Hard, steel-like arms banded around her waist and pulled her back. Her abductor's movements were accelerated, which meant it had to be a vampire. Kane, Adam and Xen made a move, but it was fruitless because they were surrounded by two vampires and four demons. She dropped the wall and opened her mind to him.

Xen, don't. Let them take me. You can follow. You are outnumbered. Do the math.

"NO." Xen's roar split the air.

The clink of metal and crunch of bones were the last impression of Xen that registered in her mind.

Darkness filled her eyes as the arms around her pulled her into a swirling vortex. Intense contractions in her abdominal muscles started and the contents of her stomach rose to her esophagus.

Three demons lay at Xen's feet. One remained only because he allowed it. Adrenaline coursed through his body.

"You too, demon, will meet your demise." He pointed his sword at the demon's head.

The demon growled.

The squeal of tires on the road sounded. Xen didn't need to look in the direction of the slamming doors. Paris appeared alongside him with two other men.

"Sorry I missed the party." He scanned the damage Xen, Adam and Kane had caused. "Might I have the honor of this one, at least." His sword was already unsheathed.

"Not this day, Paris." Metal sliced through the air dislodging the beast's cranium. It did nothing to calm the ferocious typhoon that spiraled out of control within him. Uncontrollable tremors coursed through his body.

Kane sped to his side. "We'll find her, Xen. You know we will."

"Alert. Everyone. Now!" He clutched his sword tightly. Carissa's words still pounded in his ears.

Xen watched as Adam punched numbers into his phone. The grim look Kane and Adam gave him told him his command had veered off-course. He needed to rein in his self-control and not give in to his emotions—something that'd never happened before.

"I've just sent a message to all the *Phi*," Adam said as he put the phone back in the pocket of the black vest he wore.

"Get as many eyes and ears out between here and Charleston as possible. They're bound to exit the portal they used midway. I'd be really surprised if they used more than one portal. Even for a vampire those things can sap the energy out of you," Xen proclaimed.

"If they exited and are in a set of wheels, we will find them," Paris said.

"Adam, take Carissa's car and follow. Paris, you lead in front, and Kane, we'll ride together." Xen's torrid anger had only diluted a fraction when he sat in the passenger side of the SUV. He hummed from the intensity of it.

Time was a critical beast. If they were to have any chance of intercepting Carissa's abductors, they'd need to move fast.

"Would you recognize her scent?" Xen asked as they sped along the highway.

"I got her scent yesterday and I'm sure I can follow if we are near." Kane's power of scent sat equally with his own, but in wolf form it was far superior.

"I'm going to kill the ones responsible."

"Of that I have no doubt." Kane paused. "This isn't about you, is it?"

"No, our suspicions were correct. They had the opportunity to jump any of us, but they didn't. They wanted her. The question is, why?"

Pain laced through his chest, a throb he didn't know he could possess for a female. "*Diki mou*—mine."

"Xen, we will do everything to help you get her back."

"You are a true friend, *lykos*."

"You would do the same for me."

"Unquestionably."

A deep groan escaped Carissa's lips. The pounding of her head intensified when she tried to move and found that her hands were tightly bound, adding a burning layer to her discomfort. They were in a Hummer and speeding along the freeway.

"What do you want with me?" she questioned Goon One. He didn't answer.

"Where are you taking me?" Nothing. So much for throwing questions out there. She wiggled her wrists, but the rope only chafed her skin.

"You guys are very talkative, you know."

"Shut up, bitch, before I cut your tongue out," Goon One said.

"You guys must have taken classes for your manners."

Goon Two just growled.

She rolled her eyes. It would be fruitless to try and obtain details. Her thoughts turned dark, and to Xen and his men. They had been outnumbered when she'd been pulled through some sort of black hole. *What the heck was that and how did people not accidently step through these things?* Questions. She had lots, but no one to give her the answers.

And how had Xen faired? she wondered. *He's a warrior, it's what he does—kills the bad guys. He can handle them and more.* True, she should be thinking about how she would get out of the clutches of these goons. What did they have on the agenda for her?

Judging from their hateful tone, kicking and screaming would be involved.

The sign for Route 501 came into view. A sense of relief washed over her. She knew this road so well. They were approximately two hours out of Charleston. The car veered to the right, gravel skidding under the tires. If they stayed on this road, they'd be headed to Myrtle Beach.

When the car stopped, Goon One moved at lightning speed and pulled her from the car by her hair. Pain stabbed her scalp.

"Let go, you bag of shit!" Her legs refused to work properly as he pulled her along. When she gained a little balance and co-ordination, she shot her leg out in a kick.

"You stupid slut!" he bellowed.

Goon Two gave her a push that sent her tumbling to the pebbled ground. With her hands tied, there was no way she could break the fall. She went down right shoulder first then her face skidded on the ground. Pain speared her skull, the intensity of it shooting through to her body. She rolled over onto her back. The night air blew across her face making the graze sting.

Goon One grabbed her and pulled her to her feet. He shoved her through an open door and forced her to her knees on the floor of the living room. Goon Two pulled her hair as he walked by.

What I wouldn't give to fill you both with lead. "Asshole!" she yelled.

Goon One's eyes turned red. The burning graze on her cheek distorted her clarity. She didn't anticipate the kick that landed in her stomach. She collapsed to the floor in agony. The force of the kick brought thick bile racing up her throat. She retched and vomited on the floor. She wanted nothing more than to close her eyes and welcome the darkness that danced behind her eyelids, but her instinct refused to give in. *Fight it.*

How long she lay in the fetal position staring at the coffee table legs, she didn't know. The sound of a vehicle approaching startled her out of her pain-induced, open-eyed coma. Gravel crunched.

Please let it be Xen.

The front door opened and closed.

No, not Xen. He would have smashed everything.

She heard voices. Footsteps pounded in her direction. She blinked at the pair of caramel-colored shoes that greeted her line of vision. With a slow rotation of her head she looked up to see a tall blond man with piercing blue eyes, dressed in a white suit, staring down at her.

"I said bring her here undamaged. It does not look that way," he said through gritted teeth.

Okay, so this guy doesn't want to hurt me. At least not yet. White Suit crouched down and pulled a knife from his pocket. Okay, maybe he wants to kill me instead.

He leaned over to cut the rope that bound her wrists. She rubbed them to ease the soreness. He helped her into a sitting position and took in her appearance.

"I should slit both your throats," he barked at the goons. "Get out of here—now!" They left without a backward glance.

He turned to her. "It was never my intention to have you harmed. I am sorry if you have suffered at their hands."

She ached and wasn't in the mood for fluff. "What do you want?" she croaked out.

He laughed and ran a finger down her grazed cheek. His palm came up to caress her skin, his thumb rubbed her bottom lip. "I want many things, and some of those things cannot be obtained by conventional methods."

"So, you take them instead, and without permission." She raised her voice.

"Would you have come willingly if I came and asked you?"

She looked at him. Was this bozo serious? She sure as hell didn't know who he was or what he wanted. "I don't understand. Why would you want anything from me? I don't know you and can't say I've ever met you."

"Sometimes we forget."

Her brain did a quick scan of criminals she'd put away over the years. She'd remember someone like the man in front of her. He held an intensity about him she couldn't explain, his eyes mesmerizing blue Aegean pools.

"I think you should clean up while I organize dinner, then we'll talk."

The mention of food reminded her stomach and brain that she had yet to eat. Her stomach growled in approval and hunger.

The corner of his mouth lifted. "Sounds like dinner is a good idea.

Mortified she said nothing.

He held out a hand to her and pulled her to her feet, then indicated the direction of the bathroom. She walked quickly and closed the door with a light click. Inside the room, she scanned the windows. "Bars. Pfft. There goes that idea."

It meant one thing—she'd have to put up an impressive fight to escape. The cabinets were well stocked but lacked any antiseptic to clean the graze on her face. Taking a facecloth, she wet it with warm water and cleaned around the wound, the sting causing her to flinch. When she'd finished, she opened the drawers of the vanity and found a brush. She ran it through her hair.

"Might as well have nice hair as the knife gets wedged in," she mouthed to her reflection. With her needs taken care of and a partial tidy-up done, she made her way back to the living room.

"Come and sit over here," Mr. White Suit instructed. He stood near a dining table off the living room. The design was open plan and very airy. *A negative if I want to get out of here.*

Carissa sat down. "So, I didn't get your name."

"I never gave it to you."

"Well, it would be good manners to at least—"

Muffled voices and a knock on the door interrupted her question. An entourage of people walked through with a chef in tow. *What the—?* Her mouth opened to ask but her words were lodged somewhere in her throat. This was beyond strange. Who kidnaps someone and then throws a party?

"Are you okay?" he said softly.

"I'm perfectly fine and what are we celebrating?"

The melodic tune of pots and pans began to dance in the kitchen. The aroma of garlic assaulted her nostrils and that Benedict Arnold stomach of hers growled.

Before she could summon any words, waiters set cutlery, plates and wine glasses before the two of them.

Through the whole episode, Mr. White Suit eyed her every reaction.

"So, are we going to talk?" she demanded.

"All in good time."

She gave him a hard stare. Where have I seen those eyes before?

Something familiar pinged in the dark recesses of her mind, but she couldn't quite place him. Her recall was interrupted by a plate of scallops that now stared up at her strategically. She'd have to play along to find out what his game was, and there was no point in wasting good food. Right?

Good one, Carissa, always thinking with your stomach.

Taking the first bite, the scallop melted on her tongue. *Delicious.* She realized she must have moaned at the taste because

Mr. White Suit watched with a smirk on his lips. *Good going, Carissa, show how much you're enjoying the charade and the food.*

"So do I get the pleasure of knowing your name?" *What man doesn't tell you his name? One who wants to kill you. IDIOT.* She mentally slapped herself.

He laughed. "In due time."

Her plate disappeared and new a one replaced it, the sinful aromas wafting up to her nose.

"Are you always so mysterious?"

"Actually no, but it's fun watching you stew."

She bit back a retort. No. She would not give him the satisfaction of her anger because he found it amusing. She clammed up for the rest of the meal. She could play his game and beat him at it. Even with his goons that were stationed everywhere, she'd sure as hell go out fighting.

When the last of the plates were removed, she excused herself. "Thank you for the delicious meal, but if you have nothing further to say, I'd like to get some rest. It has been an eventful night."

"I do have something to say, Carissa, and you will listen." *Okay, he knows my name. So maybe he's a stalker or serial killer who likes to know his victims.*

"Firstly, you should make yourself comfortable because you will be my guest for a while. I will bring you fresh clothes in the morning."

"What do you really want? Cops don't make enough money, so I can't help you there." She reached for the glass of wine that hadn't been cleared away.

He laughed. "Money ... no, no. You've got it all wrong. I have more lewd plans and they only require a bed."

The wine left a burning path in her throat, as did his words. Okay, this guy was all levels of psycho. "Why?" The feeble word, barely audible, made its way through her voice box.

"I have always wanted you. I watched you from across the street when we were children."

"Children," she mouthed. Her brain raced through a maze, turning at every corner to find the answer.

The lightbulb turned on and it lit the whole room. Her eyes widened in recognition. *We were friends. We hung out, we played together, we even did the whole Greek Sunday lunch with lamb on the spit.*

Her body tensed as relief and anger washed through every cell of her body.

"Oh gods. Hal."

She dropped the glass of wine back on the table. The contents sloshed out of the glass and onto the tablecloth. "I can't believe you would do this. This is insane. You know there's nothing wrong with looking people up the proper way. Ever heard of reaching people through social media?" A multitude of emotions zigzagged through her body, but the most prominent one—anger—threatened to burn her from the inside out. In her lap, she clenched her fists.

"Carissa, there is no point getting upset. I had no option. You were getting too involved with a vampire, and I couldn't allow that."

She scoffed at the ridiculousness of it all. "Are you serious?"

"Very. They are parasites and must be destroyed. When I have enough men and the power to go with it, you'll want to be on my side."

"You've got it wrong, Hal. They protect innocents. It's you who have sided with the bad apples."

His complexion reddened. "I will not have my plans thwarted by what you believe is right. We can do this the easy way or the hard way." He gulped down the remaining wine and she watched in utter disbelief. "Trevor," he yelled and goon number two appeared. "Take her to the guest room. Goodnight, Carissa. We shall continue our discussion tomorrow."

"I'm not finished, Hal. This is stupid."

"You don't call the shots." He stood. "I do and you'd best remember that."

"Round one to Hal." She got to her feet and let Goon Two lead the way to the guest room. He pushed her in and locked the door. "*Gamoto*," she swore to the empty space.

Walking over to the bed she dropped her ass on it and recalled the young boy she knew from her childhood. What had happened to him? He used to be kind. Not that man out there. No, that man out there had serious twisted and delusional ideas.

"Find me, Xen," she whispered to the walls.

ELEVEN

"Danger can only be overcome by more danger." ~ Greek Proverb

Xen sped out of the car and up the steps of his Charleston mansion. The hinges of the double doors screamed as he ripped them from the door jamb. Splintered wood littered the floor as he spun through the foyer like a tornado. Vases cracked in his wake.

He. Had. Failed.

They'd lost the trail and were unable to intercept Carissa's abductors. With sunrise approaching, his ability to search for her would be null. It ate at him. He did not trust rogue vampires. He'd seen their handiwork on humans far too many times. Desperate, his mind raced with every possible resource he could pull in to help.

"*Skata!*" He slammed his fist on the table and fractured the marble top. "Ares!" he barked.

A blinding light encased the room. He raised his hand to shield his eyes.

Ares stood before him. "You rang?" came a deep, throaty voice that shook everything in the room.

"Cut the crap, Ares. I'm royally pissed."

"Is the bad vampire going to bite me?" Ares liked toying with those around him and did his best to induce anger. He fed off rage. Xen tightened his fists and reigned in some of his fury.

"I have asked you here because I need to know the position of demons. They've involved themselves with rogue vampires and taken a human girl."

"And I should care—why?" He cocked his head and sneered.

Ares' displeasure at Xen's request was evident.

"The human girl they took is mine and does not belong on their menu. I want her back."

"Good for you, Vampire," Ares mocked.

Xen's anger danced up a notch at the jeer. "I repeat, Carissa doesn't deserve to be a delicacy for some demons or rogue vampires."

Ares stepped in front of Xen's desk. He pressed his hands on the expensive wood and came face to face with him.

"What. Is. Her. Name?"

"Carissa," Xen repeated.

"I got that part. The surname?"

Now Xen was intrigued. He narrowed his eyes. "Alkippes," he breathed.

"*No.*" The roar from Ares shook the whole house. Kane burst through the library doors with a sword in his hand, ready for action, but put it down when Xen nodded that everything was alright.

"You will find the girl." Ares spat his order.

Xen raised his eyebrows. "A minute ago, you couldn't have cared less who had her. What and who exactly is she to you?" Xen glanced over at Kane, whose expression mirrored that of his own.

"She is my daughter."

Kane looked at Xen and spoke the words on the tip of his tongue. "You're fucking kidding."

"You have no idea how this complicates things," Xen emphasized. He knew firsthand that there'd be no room for subtlety with Ares. "You see, she's my fated."

"That is not possible," growled Ares.

"Tell that to the Clotho, Lachesis and Atropos." Xen clenched his jaw. Even the gods could not change what the Fates had decreed.

Ares glared at him. His lips curled. In that moment they were equally affected by the circumstances.

"I want my daughter back without a scratch, otherwise it will be your head, Xenocrates."

Xen sped around his desk, coming nose to nose with Ares.

Ares pushed Xen out of his space. The nudge only added to Xen's fury. He ground his teeth together and his muscles quivered. His control slipped from the tightrope he'd walked on since Carissa's abduction. He pushed Ares, sending him flying against a bookcase. The god's retaliation came quickly, fire bursting from his hands. Xen sidestepped and moved in for the mock kill, his fingers around the god's throat and his sword pointed at his neck. They were locked in a mirror hold. Every ounce of Xen's being knew that Ares could not be defeated easily, and he had only gotten this close to the god because Ares had allowed him to. The sword in Ares' hand broke the skin on Xen's throat.

"Control your anger, Xenocrates."

Xen released Ares. A lump formed in his throat. "This situation ..."

"Has clouded your thinking," Ares finished.

He opened his mouth but closed it again.

"And I accept your apology." Ares' voice dripped with sarcasm.

Xen should not have struck him. The god before him was his mentor, his trainer. Ares had saved him from the *Lamiae* and recruited him, persuaded him to swear an oath to protect humans. A surge of air escaped his lungs. "I have every intention of getting her back, but I need your help," he uttered.

"You know I cannot directly intervene, as much as I would like to break the rules. Zeus would not approve, even if she is my daughter. I can only help her if she calls me, and she cannot do that because she does not know I exist, or that I am her father."

"Give me any info on any demon activity and I'll do the rest."

"Tonight. You have my word."

Xen nodded.

"Bring her back." A thin line of silver mist swirled where Ares had stood a moment before.

Xen straightened to his full height and Kane stepped into his space. He spoke before his *lykos* friend could utter a word.

"I guess words escape you, but I am certain they would be along the lines of 'you certainly know how to pick them'."

"Fuckin' A, Xen," Kane admitted. "You read my mind?" His forehead creased.

"You're projecting rather loudly."

"Fuck."

"Yes, we covered that point."

"I can't believe you mated with the daughter of Ares. Of all the women in the world, it had to be her?"

"It's not mine to question. The Fates have chosen." The fact she was the daughter of a god made no difference to him. She belonged by his side.

"I'm just blown away." Bug-eyed, Kane shook his head.

"Noted. Now let's go over how we lost the trail."

Xen was up early the next evening, pacing the library floor. Nothing alleviated the wide-open chasm in his chest. His anger fluctuated from one moment to the next. It took all his restraint to contain the beast that wanted nothing more than to shred every-thing around him.

The doors swung open. Kane walked over to where Xen had worn the hardwood floor out with his restlessness.

"Any news?" he asked.

"We've got a position from an unknown source—Myrtle Beach. Don't have a number on vamps, but we've got about eight demons confirmed as a definite."

"Let's move. I'll be requesting the pleasure of going in first."

"That doesn't surprise me. Just keep your head attached."

"I intend to, *lykos*." He clenched his jaw then took a few long strides over to his bookcase and hit a button. Gears crunched and the sound of a latch opening echoed in the room. He pushed a section of the bookcase and it swiveled inwards. Beyond lay a weapons room.

Combat gear hung at one end of the room—boots, pants, tops and vests. Xen changed quickly, strapping a knife to his leg before walking over to where the swords were stored. He pulled a dou-ble-edged sword and a curved single-edged sword from the shelf.

Kane raised an eyebrow at the selection. "Going for maximum damage."

"They will not live long enough to regret their actions."

"How will we distract the vampires? You know they'll pick up our scent."

"Send in your human team first and we'll use the D-12 spray we developed last month. It will conceal our scent."

His mind drifted back to Carissa. What if they'd hurt her? "And ask the lab if they could give me one of those trial injections for repelling the desire for blood."

Kane tugged on a vest and slid knives into the pockets, then chose his swords. "This is going to be bloody."

"The only way I like it," Xen sneered before sheathing his swords to the back of his vest.

TWELVE

"Faithful earth, unfaithful sea." ~ *Ancient Greek saying*

"*Skata*, what time is it?" She sat up and squinted at the clock on the bedside table. Five p.m., it illuminated.

"Damn. I've overslept." Rising from the bed she noticed fresh clothes laid out on a chair. She made her way to the en suite shower and stopped to look at her reflection in the mirror. Her face looked somewhat better.

"How am I going to get out of this mess?" she whispered to her image.

Realistically, it would be best to just deal with it step by step. Without further contemplation, her feet moved her heavy-from-sleep body into the spray of the shower. The warmth eased some of the tension in her shoulders. Her mind drifted to how her ordinary life had suddenly gone insane, with a side order of Greek gods.

Her fingers had tuned to prunes, which told her she'd been under the water for far too long. Once dry, she slipped on a pair of jeans and a t-shirt, then looked around the room for the millionth time for something to help her escape. The window in the bathroom was too small for her to squeeze through.

"Bars, small windows. This house was built to keep people in." She let out a nervous laugh. What if Crazy Hal kidnapped girls on a regular basis? The guy needed serious help where asking a girl out was concerned. *Psycho stalker.*

Giving in to the growling of her stomach and the desperate need for coffee, she walked to the door and raised a fist to it. She gave it a few hard thumps.

"Nothing." She clenched her fist and repeated the action. "Come on."

Her ears spiked up at the sound of heavy footsteps. She laughed inwardly when the locks clicked, but it was short-lived when she saw who stepped through the door with a tray of food and pot of coffee.

"Good afternoon, Carissa. I hope you enjoyed your sleep."

Oh great, I really didn't want to talk to the nutcase. Don't talk, don't talk, don't talk. The mantra played in her head as she watched him through narrowed eyes.

Carefully he placed her dinner on the lamp table near the door. "I'll be back in a few hours." His parting words were blissful to her ears.

She raced over to the tray, moving everything and praying for a knife. The cloth napkin slid from her fingers and fluttered to the floor. *Aha!* A set of stainless steel cutlery. She let out a slow breath. This she could work with, a small twist of fate to make a break. She'd have to slow them down enough. Maybe she could turn the tables on Hal and use him as her hostage. The knife could be used as leverage.

As she ate the food, she schemed. When she finished eating, she stashed the knife and fork in the back pocket of her jeans. The t-shirt was loose so it hid the bulge.

Time was slow when you were locked up in a room. Bored, she lay down on her stomach only to yield to the tiredness that seized her body, the snug softness of the mattress made it easier to give in.

"Who are you?" she questioned the tall, dark, handsome man who stood before her.

"Someone you haven't seen in a long time." He studied her and she felt heat travel through her body and into her heart. *Love, she thought.*

"What do you want?"

"Only for you to be safe." He reached out and cupped her face. Heat cocooned her body once again. *"Be careful."* The air shimmered around him.

"Wait," she called out, but only the empty space greeted her.

The potent reality of the dream woke her. She jerked up off the bed. Her heart hammered against her chest. She dashed to the bathroom fumbling with the taps to get cold water on her face. The coolness soothed and calmed her.

When the beats in her chest subsided, she took to pacing back and forth in the room. The click of the lock gained her attention. *Not Hal again*, she prayed.

The door flung open with force and her current favorite friend filled the doorway—Goon One. And he wasn't alone, his buddy stood right behind him.

"Hal wants you to wait in the living room for him," he barked.

Wow, I guess they can speak.

Goon Two strutted up to her and closed his fingers around her arm and gave her a hard pull forward to get her moving. *Would love a chance to poke his eyes out.* It hurt, but she swallowed the pain. They ushered her towards the living room, one goon at her front and one at her back, salami-in-a-sandwich style. *Wonder if I stab him in the back of the neck, if I can immobilize him?* No, they were fast, and the goon behind her would block her movement before she had a chance. Plus where would she run? They were in a corridor. Her cutlery-attack fantasies would have to wait.

In the living room she plopped herself on the sofa and tried not to put pressure on her back pockets. She eyed the clock on the wall; it was nearly 8:00 p.m. Time had slipped by and, if she had hopes of getting out tonight, she'd need to move fast. She required an exit strategy, and right now she resembled a sitting duck in a shooting gallery.

Now, how to distract the goons in order to give herself enough time to get to one of the cars? Last night they hadn't pulled the keys out of the ignition. A sliver of hope blossomed that it might mean her escape could be successful. The universal problem with cocky criminals was that they were all the same. Never did they expect to be challenged.

"So what time will Hal be here?"

"Shut up, bitch."

Bingo.

These goons were so predictable. She opted to sit quietly and wait.

Half an hour later her adrenaline had spiked to ridiculous levels. She knew without a doubt that sitting idle and waiting around to see what Hal wanted just didn't cut it. Different scenarios of attack played out in her head. She would strike at any of the most fatal areas— the carotid, axillary or femoral artery. Any one of those would be enough to slow them down, even if it wasn't enough to kill them as it would a human. Still, it could be enough to get her out the door.

Looking over to the goons, she saw they were deeply engrossed in a card game.

She eyed the front door. She. Could. Get. To. It.

Hell, she'd done crazier cop-shit in her career. Time to dance the dance, as her aunt would say.

Carissa knew she would get hurt, but every ounce of self-preservation fled and in place lay a hue of anger she hadn't recognized in herself before. She ran to the door and pulled the handle, throwing it open with as much force as she could muster. *Shit, that was too easy.*

Her relief was short-lived when steel hands pulled her back and the door slammed close to her face. A fist came down and connected with her jaw. Blood oozed in her mouth, the taste metallic. She staggered back towards the living room. Goon One lunged forward. It was the break she'd been waiting for. Quickly she pulled the knife from her back pocket and aimed for his neck. His eyes went wide when he noticed the target of her intended aim. He moved. The knife met the flesh of his shoulder blade.

"Bitch. You'll pay for that." He backhanded her, sending her catapulting into the glass coffee table in the living room. Shards embedded themselves in her soft flesh. Blood stained the cream carpet. A small piece of glass planted itself in her right calf. She yanked it out and warm liquid spilled from the wound.

"*Gamoto.*" She got to her feet and pulled the fork from her pocket. Goon Two sped across to where she stood and grabbed at her right hand to remove the fork. She brought up her left fist and struck him in the throat.

He staggered.

Her vision zeroed in on one spot she hadn't thought to aim. Adrenaline pumped and poured through her veins. She took a clean, forceful shot at his eye. His unhurried response gave her the satisfaction she craved. The fork came down right in his eyeball. Blood gushed. He hollered and pushed her down on the floor.

The front door burst from its hinges. A wolf leaped through the air and latched onto Goon One's neck. She knew what the outcome would be.

Goon Two stepped in her direction. "I'm going to rip your arms off and then I'm going to fucking watch you die slowly." He advanced. "I should have killed you sooner."

A gush of air hit her face. A familiar scent wrapped itself around her and a flutter began in her belly. *Xen.*

Xen struck Goon Two and sent him flying in the air. He landed on his ass.

Man, I so need to learn to punch like that.

He got to his feet and ran towards Xen. In a swift move, Xen unsheathed his *xiphos.* A familiar swish cut through air.

Well, I guess my butter knife would never have successfully executed that move.

Strong, familiar arms picked her up and sped out of the house. Outside, demons, vampires and wolves fought. Even if she had managed to escape, her plan would have been foiled. She never had a chance. Adrenaline and desperation had driven her actions.

Xen sped through the mayhem. When they were clear of danger he put her down on her feet. "Butter knife?" he queried.

With bloodied hands she grabbed his face and pulled him into a kiss, silencing his question. She consumed him like a woman dying of thirst on a hot summer's day. He responded with the same fierceness. She pulled back.

"Efharisto."

He leaned his forehead to hers. "*Koukla*, you have no idea how crazy I've been. We need to clean you up before I devour you."

She'd forgotten that blood and vampires didn't mix too well. "Sorry." She took a step back. "Is it a problem?"

"*Koukla*, I will not harm you. Now isn't the time to explain. Let's get you to safety first."

He tried to lift her in his arms, but when he touched her this time, a spasm of pain slashed along her right side, sending pinpricks hurtling outward. She winced. The titanic adrenaline dump crashed into nothingness, bringing forth only agony. A scream tore from her dry throat.

His expression darkened at her discomfort. She watched as he tapped the earpiece in his ear. "If there are any rogue vampires left, I want the pleasure of decapitation for myself."

Her hand automatically went to her throbbing hip.

"I'm going to hold my arms to the side and you are going to latch on to me as best you can. I don't care in which position, as long as you are not hurting when you do."

Carissa nodded then stepped sideways into his open arms. She lifted her left arm up around his wide shoulder and neck while pushing herself up on her toes. *He has lots of inches in all the right places.* She shook her head to dislodge her wayward thinking. Two seconds with the man—and they weren't even out of danger yet—and her thoughts turned to sex.

"I'm glad you find my proportions an asset." The corners of his mouth quirked up. "Hold on, *koukla.*" He lifted her into his arms and sped away.

They reached a clearing where several SUVs were parked at different angles. Xen slowly put her down behind a black Land Rover. He fished for his keys in a pocket on his vest. She heard the lock on the back door pop before he pulled it open. "Let me help you so that you can sit up here." He patted the trunk area of the Land Rover.

She backed slowly to the spot he indicated and with her left hand she wrapped her fingers around his arm to use for leverage. A small whimper of pain escaped her lips.

"Ouch."

He pulled a bag closer to them and rummaged through it, tossing out bandages, antiseptic and a range of other medical supplies. "Tell me what happened to cause this bleeding."

"One of the goons tossed me onto a glass coffee table."

"And how did you find yourself at the wrong end of the rogues' anger?" he asked, pulling a pair of tweezers out of the bag. "Can you lie on your side? It will make it easier for me to pull out any bits of glass embedded in your skin. I'll need to rip your jeans for access."

"Sure."

He grabbed the waistband, and pulled out the knife strapped to his thigh. In a swift motion, the material fell away from her body. She gasped.

The corners of his mouth turned up into wicked joy. "I have replacement clothes."

"I'm sorry about all the blood. Would it be better if I did it?" she asked.

"At *Phi* Technologies we do other types of work. One project is an injection to repel the desire that awakens when we smell blood. It's in trial stages, but not knowing what we'd be facing tonight, I took it as precaution." He lifted an eyebrow. "But having said that, would I like nothing more than to lick the blood from you?"

Her eyes met his. "Yes," she breathed.

"Don't tempt me, *koukla,* because it would lead to other things."

She swallowed hard as images of his hard body flashed in her mind.

"Hold those thoughts for later. I want to explain, in brief, the difference between rogue vampires and the *Phi*. The *Phi* have been trained to protect and have control of their base urges. Yes, blood calls to us, but not to harm." He paused. "It sings to us to give carnal pleasure. The rogue vampires are what you call loose cannons. They have no restraint over their urges. Their prime objective is to feed and kill. You were very lucky."

She gulped, taking in his words. His fingers moved lightly over her skin, removing shards of glass.

"So how *did* you enrage the vampires?"

"I made a run for it, and then stabbed one goon, but my plan kinda backfired."

"You stabbed them?" he questioned, his tone incredulous.

"Yes, with cutlery."

"Cutlery?" He raised an eyebrow.

"Yep, a knife in one and a fork in the other."

"So that is what was hanging out of his eye when I took his head?"

"Yep, it sure was." She was proud of herself for at least having tried.

Xen stopped working with the tweezers. His features contorted to anguish. "You know, *koukla,* he would have killed you for that."

She swallowed again. "I knew I would die one way or the other. I had no way of knowing what had become of you or whether you would find me."

"*Koukla,* I would have gone to any lengths to get you back." He pulled her upright. His large hand cupped the back of her head hard. His mouth crashed to hers. This wasn't one of his tender moments. No, this kiss spoke of possession. It was open-mouthed and ravenous. He pulled back, breathing as heavily as she was. "You're mine."

Her heart pounded in her ears. The man could reduce her mind to mush with just a kiss.

"Let's bandage you up." He made swift work of disinfecting all the cuts and then bandaging up the bigger wounds. He helped pull the t-shirt over her head and tore the other side of the denim from her body. He handed her a fresh set of clothing and pair of flat shoes. She slipped her feet into the black linen pants and pulled them carefully over her right leg and up to her waist. Xen watched her movements.

"Enjoying the show?"

"Every minute of it." His gaze dipped to her breasts, which were covered with a very dull and plain white bra. Heat rose to her cheeks. With nimble fingers she pulled the berry blouse over her head.

The heat in Xen's eyes had not extinguished. He gave her a probing visual caress from head to toe that left her body tingling and needy for his passion.

"Hold on to those thoughts, *koukla,* because I intend to deliver."

She had no doubt he would.

"Give me the bloodied clothes."

She took a few steps towards him and gave them over without a word.

Xen placed them on the ground, poured fluid over them and took out a match. Flames engulfed the cotton and denim.

"I take it there are reasons for that."

"Many," he said.

She opened her mouth to say something, but a blur of *Phi* and wolves appeared around them. All dressed in black, they looked like Special Ops. Some were armed with guns while others had swords. Kane stepped over to them.

"Carissa, you okay?" he asked, eyeing her from top to bottom, taking in the damage.

"I'm still in disbelief I'm alive. One more second ..."

"I think our timing was perfect, then." He gave her a warm smile.

"In more ways than one. I was close to being beef *stifatho.*" Kane let out a laugh. He reached into the Land Rover and tossed a few bags across to some of the men.

"We should move." Xen motioned towards the open door and held out his hand to help her get in.

She bit back a whimper when she accidently knocked her leg. Her stomach rolled. Nausea and dizziness threatened her but she slapped the effects of both back in place. *Keep it together, Carissa.*

"Here, lie back and put your head on my thigh."

She did as he suggested. Kane and Adam jumped into the front seats of the Land Rover. The last lucid thought she had was of Xen's fingers softly caressing her face. Her eyes fluttered, then closed.

"*Koukla,* time to wake up." The soft words, a gentle caress and a featherlight kiss on her forehead brought her out of her nap. "Don't move too quickly."

Naturally, she did the opposite. Her mouth fell open in a silent scream. "Damn, I forgot about the cuts."

"I'll help you out." He sped around to the other side, helped her out of the seat then hoisted her in his arms and walked into a house. This one was different from the one in Virginia Beach. She tried to take in as much as she could. "Wow."

"My bedroom is the highlight," he teased, his voice low and thick.

"That doesn't surprise me." She bit back a laugh.

He put her on her feet and cupped her cheek. "As much as I'd like to show you, it will have to wait. I need the full story of your abduction, every detail."

Xen directed her to his library, Kane and Adam close behind. She admired the grandness of the handcrafted wooden bookcases that were prominent. Her eyes fixated for a moment on the double glass and timber doors and how they would look with sunlight dancing through them. An identical mezzanine level added to the opulence of the office. To her right stood Xen's desk—magnificent, like the man. Couches in dusky blue, armchairs in mint, and a coffee table between them filled the center of the room. He took his position behind the desk while Kane and Adam made themselves comfortable on the couches.

"Carissa, come here." He patted the chair next to his. "Tell me what happened."

"They pulled me through some vortex and then I woke up in the back seat of a car."

"That vortex is called a portal."

"Why didn't you jump in after me?"

"We can't because we need permission."

"Permission? From who?" she asked. If these goons could get a pass, then surely Xen and his men could.

"Someone in the underworld." He reached for her hands and trapped them in his. "What happened at the house?"

"They beat me up a little and kept telling me to shut up."

A growl left Xen's lips. "Death was too easy for them. I should have made them suffer."

She continued. "Their leader was a friend from my child-hood—Hal Poseidonis—we lived in the same neighborhood until the accident happened. Then I moved in with my grandmother." She closed her eyes and rubbed her forehead, taking a moment to collect herself from the flashback of her parents' deaths. When she opened her eyes, Xen's intense stare reminded her she hadn't finished tell-ing the story. "He acted really strange. Said he wanted me and that I couldn't be involved with a vampire."

Xen let out another snarl.

"What did you say his name was?" Kane asked.

She pulled her hands from Xen and faced Kane. "First name Hal. Surname Poseidonis." She paused. "Do you know him?"

"Let's just say we have a problem." He looked over to Xen. Something silent passed between them.

A cold shiver danced down her spine. "Is he a serial killer?"

Xen reached out to her and pulled her chair closer to him. She gasped. His eyes once again locked with hers. "Carissa, if he touched a hair on your head, I will remove his without a blink of an eye." Emotions flickered across his face. "Did he violate you?" His eyes didn't waver from hers.

She swallowed the lump in her throat. "He didn't touch me, but I won't lie. He made reference to getting me into his bed." She watched the anger fester under Xen's skin.

"So this is about him wanting you?"

"No. It's worse," she uttered.

"How so?" Adam asked.

"He is raising an army to eliminate all the *Phi*. What I don't know is how he plans to do it." Carissa pushed back a few stray locks from her forehead.

Adam whistled. "Now that's a cause for celebration."

Kane cast him a scowl. "This could be the reason why we've had more frequent skirmishes. He's got the demons on his side and he's on a mission."

"The most troubling thing is the fact that he has managed to get permission to open the portals. The only person who can give that is Hekate, and if she is cavorting with demons and Hal, we have an Olympian-sized problem," Xen added.

Kane let out a disappointed growl. "Conflict amongst the gods."

"Exactly," Xen confirmed.

"How do you stop it?" Carissa asked.

"By removing Hal. Even though he is a demi-god and the son of Poseidon, he is still half mortal and of this earth. The demons need someone who is attached to the earth to vouch for them in order to be able walk on it. But they also need the help from the inside. Their prime directive is to bring forth misery and misfortune."

"Okay, rewind. Hal is a demi-god, the son of Poseidon, and is somehow hosting a demon party on earth? I think Adam was right. There's a big celebration happening right here, right now."

"Och aye, lass," Adam replied.

"Since when do you do the Scottish thing?" Kane jabbed.

Flashing his eyebrows, Adam did his best impersonation. "Since the bonny lasses like it."

Kane let out a sigh and shook his head. "Stick with the Greek, *malaka*."

Carissa let out a giggle. "Never a dull moment with you guys."

Xen's angry gaze sliced over to Kane and Adam. "Let's get back on track," he dropped his fangs with a hiss then retracted them. "Gentlemen." He turned to Carissa. "What else happened?"

"There isn't much more to tell. You got there before I was made into a *souvlaki*." Again, she swallowed at the thought. "Putting me in the equation, though, doesn't make sense."

"I've been puzzling over the same thing, especially since he's recruited rogue vampires and demons. You'll need my protection around the clock."

"That's ridiculous. I'll be fine. I'm a cop."

"Yes you are, *koukla*, but you are no match for demons or vampires. He will more than likely strike again."

"Xen has a point, Carissa."

"But won't the fact that you guys made *keftedes* out of his men warn them to stay away?"

"*Keftedes*. Maybe we should bring the *tzatziki* next time," Adam playfully added. "Now I'm hungry."

Xen and Kane gave Adam a glassy stare. Carissa bit back a laugh.

"Shut it, *lykos,*" Kane growled.

Adam put his hands up in surrender.

"*Koukla*, think about it. They kidnapped you while you were with us. They knew exactly who we were. Yet they ambushed us." Xen paused. "You will need round-the-clock protection."

"Xen's right. Until we can gather some intelligence from our sources, you'll need to put up with us." Kane grinned, recognizing how much she'd hate having a babysitter.

There is no way in hell I'm going to have a shadow following me everywhere.

"Yes, you will."

No.

"Yes, and that's final."

Stop that.

"Stop what?" He raised an eyebrow and his mouth twitched.

"That mind-reading mumbo jumbo."

"It's a gift, *koukla,* and one to be taken seriously."

"It's an invasion of privacy, that's what it is."

Kane and Adam let out rich, well-rounded laughs. Xen narrowed his eyes at them both.

"Let's try a little experiment."

She sighed. All she wanted was some rest. "Okay, on one condition." She held up her finger to indicate the number. "You take me home straight after."

"Consider it done." He waited. "I'm going to read you and I want you to block me."

"Xen, I don't know why you think I can do that." She blew out her cheeks. "I can't."

"You can, you've done it to me before. Actually, twice, and willingly."

"I don't know how."

"Just focus. You will feel a small sensation tickling at your mind. When you do, resist. Just try, *koukla.*"

Puffing out a breath, she waited. Tingling pinpricks squeezed and edged around her brain. She could sense the touch of Xen's mind, much like the night at the warehouse when she had been scared. His invasion pushed.

Stop, she yelled and it echoed in her mind. A cocoon wrapped itself around her mind, closing her off to any further intrusion. "Xen?"

He closed the short distance between them and swept her up into his arms.

"*Koukla.*" He nuzzled his nose into her hair. "Trust me when I say it was like a punch to my mind when you refused access and sealed your thoughts from me." He pulled back and searched her face. "Please understand, I know this doesn't even seem like a big deal, but it is. I want you to try something with Kane. I want you to suggest he walk over to the window."

"Now you're being absolutely ludicrous," she scoffed.

"Try it, *koukla,*" he pleaded.

Slow and even, she started her mantra in her head. *Go to the window.* This time the tingling sensations hummed through her body. Every nerve ending sparked and caused a slow burn to flare from her stomach and race through her body. *Go to the window,* she commanded.

Kane got to his feet. His face expressionless as he took long strides to the window and stopped.

Her hand went to her mouth. "Not possible." They were playing a joke on her.

"That was cool, Carissa," Adam said.

"You guys are toying with me." She dropped into the chair behind her. "Kane, you can stop the charade now."

Kane shook his head. "What happened?"

"You went all zombie-like." Adam got to his feet and stretched out his arms, imitating a zombie from a B movie.

Kane looked over to Xen. "It worked? She used *Anagke* to compel me?"

"She did," Xen diagnosed.

"Compel—*Anagke*?" she scrunched up her face.

"*Anagke,* as we call it, is a force that grants you the ability to control every action through persuasion of the mind. Your power is weak, but with a bit of training, you can develop it. Given the circumstances, it might be wise to do so. I'm proud of you, *koukla*."

"Can you do this?"

"No, *koukla*, I can read minds whereas you can control them."

"Sounds like a Jedi trick," she huffed.

"I can assure you that this is the real deal, *koukla. "*

Next he'll want to give me a light saber.

"My tech group has been testing them. I'll put you on the list."

Her eyes widened.

He pursed his lips.

The rascal was toying with her.

"You think Hal wants her for this?" Kane asked.

"I'm certain that it may be one reason. He may have sensed her power when they were children. Don't forget, he's a demi-god and will have his own talent. See what else we can dig up on him. Kane and Adam, organize the twenty-four seven watch."

Both men were moving before Xen finished his sentence. The click of the door echoed in the quiet of the room.

Carissa cracked her head from side to side to release the tension in her neck. Her train of thought derailed. *Don't these guys ever sleep?*

"*Koukla,* don't worry about our sleeping habits."

"Why didn't I feel you probing that time?"

"Because you haven't fully mastered your guard. You let it down, which opens you up and allows me to read you."

"Do all vampires read humans?" she asked, wanting some clarification as to whether she had to guard her thoughts more.

"No, there are very few of us who have the gift. Like everything, it can be godsend or a curse."

"Why do you read me so often?"

He leaned down to where she was seated to whisper in her ear. "Because, I want you ... every inch of you." His voice was breathy against her ear.

"If you weren't in pain, we'd be in my bed right now." His voice low and sexy, he placed a kiss near the pulse of her neck.

She let out a little moan. He pulled back, his eyes were dark, and in them danced desire. *Oh my*.

"You better believe it, *koukla,* and when I enter you, you will scream with pleasure."

Her face heated at his words. He pulled her up off the chair and sat her on his desk, nudging her knees open. He stepped in between her legs, placed one hand at her neck and the other on her back. His lips took hers and then with a delicious swipe of his tongue she opened to him. His taste was pure decadence. Every cell in her body ignited, fire spread through her body, liquefying her senses. *I could eat you up like chocolate.*

He pulled back from the kiss, his forehead resting on hers. "It is I who will be feasting on you."

His lips returned to assaulting hers, a deep tango of tongues. Her pulse spiked as she fell under Xen's spell. The press of his arousal excited her escalating passion. If he kept this pace up she'd be willing to have him take her on the table. *I like the sex-on-a-desk fantasy.*

"Then we will have sex on this very desk," he said between kisses.

She hated to admit it, but in that moment his ability to read her wicked thoughts stirred her passion to unbearable heights. He knew exactly what she wanted. *You promise to deliver?*

"I'll fulfill your fantasy, *koukla*, and do a whole lot more." His warm hands smoothed over her shoulders and down her arms, but the moment his hands found her hips and he squeezed she flinched and pulled back with a painful moan. His hand had accidently swiped her wound.

"*Vlaka*," he swore at himself. "Carissa, forgive me. I should have been gentler. It is pure selfishness and lust driving me." His voice cracked.

She grabbed him by the tight black t-shirt that was doing a good job of showing off his hard muscles. The man depicted the word delicious no matter what he wore. This time she took control and gave him everything in her kiss. Drowning in sensations, she moaned and he responded with a deep groan that rocked all the way down to her belly, causing butterflies to flicker.

He moved his hand to her center, pressed and rubbed. The action sent pleasure cascading, heating her body. *I need you.*

A loud zap sounded in the middle of the library. It startled them both out of their lust-hazed kisses. She jumped off the desk.

Bright light filled the room; the glow made her squint. She raised her hands to shield her eyes. It took a second to focus. A gasp left her lips when she spied a tall man standing in the center of it, dressed in black leather, his expression lethal.

Something about him called to her. He pinned his gaze to her and a smile broke out on his lips. Something about him was familiar. A part of her wanted to run to him, but her brain slammed the brakes and she skidded to a halt.

Her chest tightened. *What's happening?* Maybe he had her under a spell. The boom of Xen's voice brought her out of her momentary lapse.

"Ares!" Xen snarled.

I must be under a spell. I want to run to him.

"There's no spell, *koukla*."

She stood staring at the man with her mouth open.

Xen leaned over and placed a finger under her chin. His eyes crinkled at the corners.

"If you two have finished, I'd like to speak to you both," the dark and dangerous voice interrupted.

"I didn't think inconsequential matters in the human realm were your style." Xen narrowed his eyes at the man standing before them. "Carissa Alkippes, this is Ares." Xen held out his hand and walked with her towards Ares. She winced again from her injuries. "She's hurt, Xenocrates!" Ares spat.

"And I can assure you that I more than hurt the ones who hurt her," Xen nipped back.

Why would her injuries trouble Ares? Here she stood in front of a god, her a nothing. A recollection burst through her memories, a picture book on Greek mythology, her young fingers flicking the pages.

"He's my favorite Greek god, Mommy."

Her mother laughed. "Yes, you and I both do have a soft spot for this bad boy."

She shook her head to clear it.

Xen raised an eyebrow and she knew he was sifting through her thoughts again. A low growl vibrated through his chest.

Ares took her hand in his. Heat shimmered up her arm, comforting her, making her feel safe and loved. It was similar to what she'd experienced when she used to hug her mother.

"There's no easy way to divulge the information I have for you without it being a bomb of epic proportions."

She found her voice. "It can't be that bad. Whatever it is, I'm a big girl. I can handle it."

Ares let out a breath. "Twenty-six years ago I met a wonderful woman by the name of Aggie, a vision so much like you. She and I had a daughter, Alkippe, which I see is now your surname with an s on the end."

Words spilled from his mouth. She was positive they made sense, but somewhere the meaning blurred in her brain and she was still stuck on *daughter*.

His words pounded through her head.

"Are you okay, *kori mou*?"

Her eyebrows drew together and she swallowed hard, shaking her head in disbelief. "You're my father?"

"Yes."

Her hand fell away from his.

"Here, let me show you." He touched two fingers to her head. Current tingled where his fingers touched her skin and hair. A zap of light flashed before her eyes. A movie began to play. Her mother held a small girl, no older than five, crying for her father. That man stood in the same room with her now. The scene faded and another took its place. This time, the girl was laughing and playing with her father. The reel spun, shot after shot, weaving the history that had long been suppressed in the deep recesses of her mind.

Ares removed his hands, but the scenes kept flickering. She shut her eyes, breathing in, but the weight of everything bore down on her like a heavy axe. Her knees buckled as crushing reality rushed to the forefront of her senses. The air left her lungs and her body descended towards the floor. Familiar arms closed around her—Xen.

"This is too much to take in—"

"I know, *koukla.*"

"But it can't ..." Her voice broke.

Ares step forward. "I understand. You need time to digest this. There's more, but it will have to wait."

"I think it's time you left," Xen growled.

"That is not for you to decide."

A nervous laugh left her lips. "Actually, I'd like to go home. To *my* home. Maybe it's all a dream."

"Call me when you're ready to talk more." Ares turned. "As for you, Xenocrates, I leave her in your care and protection."

"I have made my intentions for your daughter clear. I won't change them."

Carissa looked up at Xen. Warmth flickered in his eyes. She looked to the man standing near her.

"Call me, *kori mou*"

Light burst through the room again, illuminating everything. "*Wow* doesn't adequately cover it," she managed when the room returned to its normal hue.

"No, it doesn't. Would you like to stay? You look exhausted, *koukla.*"

"Xen, I promise I will spend some time with you in your home, just not tonight. It's a psychological thing. I really need to be around my things."

He leaned down and gave her a very chaste kiss.

"I understand. Let me get a duffle bag with a few things. I'll be quick."

"I'll wait in the foyer." In a blink, he disappeared. She walked out of the library to the foyer.

"Hey Carissa, how are you holding up?" She turned to see Kane coming down the stairs.

"I'm okay. A bit much to take in, but I'm sure I'll process it after I've had some sleep. My brain is like mashed potatoes at the moment."

He let out a laugh. "I see what Xen likes."

"What my mushy brain?"

Another bark of laughter echoed in the foyer. "No, your quirky humor. He needs that. Trust me when I say I've never seen him this way before, nor has he let any woman this close and into his life. He can read you well."

"Oh yeah. He does read me well. Maybe a little too well. It seems to me he always knows when to listen in."

"He's been around a long time. He can't only read your mind, but your reactions too. Xen can pick up a heartbeat, and the emotions we wear on our faces basically invite him to slip in, as he calls it."

"Thanks, I'm going to have to remember to keep my heartbeat steady around him."

"Easier said than done. I'll see you tomorrow." He winked before heading to the library.

Kane was right. She had no chance of keeping her heartbeat steady, because around Xen, her heart always did a dance of joy and quite a few somersaults.

Five minutes later, a freshly showered Xen appeared at the top of the stairs. Black jeans and black t-shirt, finished off with combat boots. Drool was definitely forming at the corner of her mouth.

He sped to the bottom. "Let's go."

"I seriously need a set of gears in my engine like yours."

THIRTEEN

"Love is composed of a single soul inhabiting two bodies." ~
Aristotle

Relief skittered all along her body and enveloped her in a tight hug when she stepped into her house.

"I need to make a call to my friend Ligi."

He raised an eyebrow at her.

"She'll be worried I haven't spoken to her." It wouldn't have surprised Carissa if Ligi was already sitting on the couch waiting for her to get back to town.

"I have a few to make myself."

"The study is through there." She pointed to the double doors on her left. "I'll chat in the kitchen."

He nodded. She watched as he walked away, admiring his perfect buns, then dialed Ligi's number. The beeps sounded and then Ligi's sexy, breathy voice instructed the caller to leave her a short message.

"Hey Ligi, I know it's late, but I just wanted to call—"

"Carissa, where the hell have you been? I left messages on your cell."

"Oh, you picked up."

"Of course I picked up. You not answering just doesn't happen. I thought the worst."

"I'm sorry. Things kind of got a little crazy."

"That's a poor excuse, girlfriend, and you know it."

She hung her head at her friend's words. How would she explain? Even recalling it all herself sounded ridiculous. Logically, she should skim over it, but one thing she never did with Ligi was leave out details, no matter how crazy. But this was different, and dragging her friend into danger and her nightmare was not an option.

"I'm waiting. Explain!" Her friend's demand ricocheted around her brain.

What to tell, what to tell? Go for safe—Xen is safe. She let out *a* deep breath. "I met someone and I'm kind of stuck on him."

"Hold on. I'm coming right over and I'm bringing a bottle of wine."

"Ligi!"

"Should I get some takeout?"

"Ligi, he's here with me now."

"OMG, you're banging him. My girl has finally done the deed and it looks like she's hooked."

Carissa let out a laugh. "Hooked, yes."

"Tell me, is he hot and sexy, and does he have one of those sex-drenched voices that make you want to fall on your knees and maybe do something for him while you're down there?"

"Ligi." Her face heated at Ligi's words.

"Wait till I tell Kelly."

"*No.* I'll never hear the end of it." She slapped her forehead.

"So does the man have a name?"

"Yes he does. Xen."

"Oooh, that *is* sexy. Sounds familiar though."

She rubbed the back of her neck. It was time to end the call before she spilled everything. "Listen Ligi, I've got to go."

"You owe me dinner, wine and details."

"Soon. I promise."

"Send me a photo."

"No. That's creepy."

"Is not. Get with the times. Everyone's sending selfies with their boyfriends."

"Goodnight, Ligi."

"Spoilsport. Goodnight, girlfriend. Enjoy your sexy tumble."

"You are going to give me grief, aren't you?"

"You better believe it. Mwah."

The kiss through the phone's speaker reverberated in her ear.

"Right back at you," Carissa said and hung up. She rolled her eyes towards the ceiling. *Forgive me for omitting details, girlfriend, but you need to be safe.*

She grabbed a glass of water and drank deeply. She went to the pantry and pulled out some crackers. A few quick bites did nothing to settle the butterflies intensifying in her belly. Xen was here, in her house. Normal didn't belong in this speedy relationship. In fact, it was nowhere near traditional.

"Those other guys I dated never stood a chance—daughter of a god and all that." She let out a laugh. It was time for bed.

She looked for Xen in the study, but he wasn't there. Climbing the stairs, she headed to her room. Sprawled out on her bed lay the man who was fast becoming the center of her new world. A frown sat firmly on his brow as he typed something on his phone.

"You okay?"

He put the phone down and patted the spot beside him. The frown from his features disappeared and was replaced by that heart-stopping smile with its own zip code.

The news that Hal might be well aware of Carissa's parentage had thrown him off-kilter. It meant that these attempts at grabbing Carissa were part of a calculated plan. Obviously, this plan had been festering for some time. The fact that Hal was working with rogue vampires and demons would be a serious problem. Especially since he had someone on the inside allowing him to open portals. Then there was the other little factor that made his blood boil—Hal wanting Carissa. Fury clouded his vision. No man would touch her. Death would be delivered to any who messed with what belonged to him. *Mine*.

Another thought filtered through his mind as she stood in the doorway of her bedroom. If he bonded with her through customary blood exchange and vows, it would be like having a GPS tracking device to help protect her. The problem was, it only worked for close distance. The thought did, however, appeal to him on a higher level. Every unearthly creature would know she was his.

No one would be stupid enough to touch her, although Hal's actions proved to be beyond ignorant.

"Come here."

She took small steps toward him. "I'm glad you're here." She smiled.

He ate up the way her face glowed when she looked at him.

It triggered every cell in his body. "I wouldn't want to be anywhere else."

The bed dipped with her weight, and she lay where he had patted his hand.

He moved closer, taking in her scent deeply.

"I don't want to get too comfortable. I need to shower and change."

"Can I help you?" His eyes twinkled.

She jumped up. "No, that would lead to other things. Not that I don't want that, I do, but I'm dead on my feet.

"I understand, *koukla*, go shower." His phone bleeped. "I've got another call to make." He rose from her bed and walked to the bedroom window. Lifting the curtain, he scanned the street.

"Is everything okay?" she asked.

"Yes. Our extra sets of eyes have arrived."

"You've got men posted out there."

"For the time being, yes."

She nodded. "Okay, I'll take that shower."

He waited until he heard the shower spilling water. His fingers flew over the number pad on the phone. He dialed a number he hadn't thought he'd ever need to call.

A low-pitched, rough voice greeted him. "*Nai.*"

"Lox, it's Xen."

"Well, what do I owe the pleasure to?"

"A demi-god, demons and rogue vampires, all of which have put my intended in danger."

"So you've found ..." Lox paused. "... your fated?"

Xen let out a breath. "I have."

"What do you need to know?"

A flush of adrenaline rushed through Xen. He was astonished that the demon king, Lox, was willing to comply so easily. Extracting information from the demon had always been a challenge because Lox didn't like to give intel on his supposed subjects, even though he despised them and they him.

Lox was no longer bound by the curse that chained demons to live in Hades' realm, a curse that made them ghastly on the earthly plain. Without the curse, they looked like any other human, and the added bonus for Lox was that he held his own powers. What those were, Xen wasn't privy to, but he had felt them when he was captured and thrown in a demon cell along with the king centuries ago.

Xen had saved him. They'd formed a mutual understanding—don't interfere in each other's business. Xen allowed this because Lox wasn't a bad guy. He could count on him when it was crucial, but acting and talking were two separate subspheres for Lox.

"Have you heard any whispers about why they would want her?"

"I've been out of the loop, tending to my own personal matters. Leave it with me. I'll dig up the dirt."

"Efharisto."

"Don't thank me yet."

The line went dead.

Refreshed from her shower, Carissa stepped out of the bathroom to find Xen already under the covers, minus his t-shirt and looking good enough to eat. Any urges would have to wait. Her feet moved and she knew enough to recognize the invisible thread that pulled her to him. They could be in a crowded room and she'd always gravitate towards him.

She slipped into bed and curved into him. "I'm sorry, Xen, but I really need sleep. I don't think I can keep my eyes open any longer."

"Shh, *koukla,* rest."

Her eyes closed and she vaguely recalled Xen whispering something about dinner the following night in her ear. Her eyes flickered and dark, deep slumber wrapped around her. She gave in to it, welcoming it with her tired and aching body.

A wonderful sensation between her legs brought her out of her sleep. *Oh.* Talented fingers stroked sensitive flesh. Heat skittered across her skin, her desire ramped up several notches.

"A girl could get used to that, you know," she mumbled between heavy breaths.

"Then get used to it." His voice was deep and throaty as he kissed and licked her earlobe. His ministrations sped up.

Her body raced to reach the apex of bliss.

"Come for me," he demanded, his breath hot in her ear.

A guttural scream tore from her throat. She blinked back the stars behind her eyelids.

"Perfect."

"Hmmm." The only response she could give.

"Can I bite you?"

"If you want to."

His lips planted soft kisses on her neck. The scrape of his fangs pierced the tender flesh.

Her eyes rolled back in her head, the bite released another wave of pleasure. How was that even possible?

"I'd like to discuss something with you." He lifted his head.

In her euphoric state, she'd probably agree to anything.

"I've been thinking about blood-bonding with you."

She scrunched her nose up at his words.

"It sounds more repulsive than it actually is," he answered. "It's not like you'd be drinking gallons of the stuff. A few drops to create a bond between you and me, more like a joining of minds."

She twisted around and rested her head on the crook of her elbow, allowing her to look openly into those deep green eyes she loved so much. Her mind processed that what he was asking sounded Herculean.

In the physical world she'd known him only for a short time, but in her dreams it had been far longer. She'd never been in a long relationship before, and she wasn't sure she wanted to be joined on the level he was asking.

"Can you tell me what it means? To what degree does it change things? I don't want to do something I'll regret. I mean, I like you a lot, but you are asking me for a big commitment here, after only a short space of time."

He dropped his head back onto the pillow and closed his eyes.

"Xen, I'm not saying no, I'm just saying I need more time. I've been thrown into a whole new world I know very little about and you are asking me to bind myself to you. What if what we have doesn't last more than a few months?"

A tic started at his jaw. He opened his eyes. Within a second he was on top of her, pinning her to the mattress. "This is long term. *Eisai diki mou.*"

His lips crashed to hers. His tongue plundered her mouth with accuracy. It was demanding, possessive and there was no mistaking how much he wanted her. If she doubted any future with him, she was sure he'd remind her not only with kisses, but with his body. His hardness pressed to her core. He moaned, then broke the scorching kiss.

"You are mine. For now I understand, but I will ask you this again soon. Mutual understanding is paramount in any relationship."

"I just need you to understand this is scary for me. I'm not even sure of myself yet. It's daunting, that's all."

"Understood. Now as much as I would like to stay here and devour you, we have to get ready for dinner."

"Dinner, what time is it?" Her brain was slow to catch up.

Surely she hadn't lost a whole day.

"Seven. You slept through the day."

"Argh. Can we just eat in?"

"No, *koukla*, we have reservations. Time for some clean fun before we get ready." He nodded towards the bathroom.

Her eyes raked possessively over him. "How much time do we have?"

Dinner proved to be a provocative lead-up to all the X-rated thoughts that caused a tsunami to crash through her mind. In the shower he teased every inch of her body with kisses and now she was wound tight and ready to explode. In the passenger seat of the car, she smoothed down the tight red dress she'd put on and crossed her legs, squeezing her thighs tight. Her sex pulsed. She craved his touch.

"*Koukla*, if you keep that up, I'm going to have to pull over."

"You should not be reading my thoughts."

"You're basically throwing them at me like a spear." He grinned. "Please don't stop. I rather enjoyed the one of you being tied up."

"Out. Stay out. They are my fantasies."

"They've just become mine."

An engine roared. Xen accelerated. "We have a tail."

"What? Where?" she managed, whipping her head around to look through the rear window.

"Whoever they are, they've pulled over to my side and sped up." She turned back to Xen. She watched his fingers fly over the buttons on the steering wheel with lightning reflexes. A loud voice sounded inside the car.

"What's up?" Kane asked.

"We've got a tail."

Carissa heard the grind of Xen's teeth.

"Where are you?" Kane demanded.

"Four miles out."

"We're not far. I'll be right behind them once you pass."

"Shake them, then kill them."

"With pleasure."

The line went dead. His knuckles were white on the steering wheel.

"It seems you are still wanted."

"I can't be that important." Why on earth would Hal want her this badly? Something was definitely off. He had never seemed obsessed with her when they were growing up. If anything, they'd gotten along well. Then her parents had died and she'd moved in with her grandmother. They'd parted as friends, with the promise to stay in touch.

The car tailing them caught up. "I think your father needs to bring you up to speed on what it means to be his daughter," Xen ground out as he swerved the SUV.

Carissa braced herself for the impact. Xen slammed on the brakes and the other vehicle nipped to the left. He reversed then launched the car into drive. The wheels spun and screeched.

"My gods, you're going to ram them." She swallowed hard.

"I'd say bump." He slammed into the rear of the vehicle then repeated the action a second time. There was no way she could miss the crazy-ass look of satisfaction he wore on his face.

"I don't think this will put us on their popularity list."

"That is where you are wrong, *koukla*. I'd say you're already the star attraction." He had the nerve to wag his eyebrows at her. He reversed again, only this time he drove off.

It didn't take the shell-shocked driver long before they were close on their tail again. Xen pressed the buttons on his steering wheel.

"SPEAK," he yelled.

"We're right behind them and about to introduce them to the ham sandwich," Kane teased.

Carissa turned her head. Three sets of car lights beamed through the rear window. The cars sped up. Xen moved the vehicle to the center of the road. The tail followed his action. The cars that Kane and the other *Phi* were in sped up on either side of the car tailing Xen. "Oh no. Now I know what you mean, Kane."

The two vehicles swerved into the car tailing Xen, then pulled back out only to slam back into it.

"Time to eat the sandwich," Kane exclaimed before the line went dead.

The crash and screeching of cars echoed behind them.

Her chest tightened. Words made their way through her vocal cords. "Will they be alright?"

"I assume you mean Kane, Adam and the other *Phi*?"

She looked at him and nodded.

"This is what they do, Carissa. Don't worry yourself. Let's get you to safety first."

"Is this what it is going to be like for me, Xen? Me on the run ... looking over my shoulder all the time? The *Phi* can't be there every minute of every day." Her voice shook and her muscles tightened, irritation flared. How dare Hal turn her life into one of a fugitive. "I don't know what he thinks he can obtain from me."

"I think your heritage is a contributing factor," Xen supplied.

"Really? I mean what does he stand to gain? I won't join his demented cause. So it's useless. What doesn't he understand?"

"That's something we are both puzzling over."

"I can't live like this, Xen."

"I know, and you won't. We will get to the bottom of it."

The car veered off to a secluded driveway then reached Xen's maximum-secured residence. When the engine died in the garage, the loud banging in her brain increased. Her mind sifted through childhood recollections, her adult life. There had been nothing extraordinary about her then or now. Yes, she worked hard at her job, but so did every other cop.

Xen helped her out of the car and through to his large library office.

"Nice digs."

Xen raised an eyebrow. "Can I get you something to drink first, *koukla*?" His mouth curved in amusement. "Then I can show you around my *digs,* since you didn't get the tour last night."

Her thoughts had been so clouded that her body and brain were on auto pilot and flying at 38,000 feet.

"I'm sorry." She let out a laugh. "That's a bit juvenile of me."

"No need to apologize. I like the constant surprises that come from you."

She watched as Xen moved over to the wet bar and poured liquid into a crystal glass.

"I think water for now," he answered for her.

Frankly, she didn't have the capacity to respond, and this time it had nothing to do with the events of her past swimming around in her cranium. No, it was the way the man walked towards her, all power and strength, purpose in the contour of every stride he took.

"Drink." The word was soft, commanding and pleading at the same time.

She took the glass with shaky hands. "Thank you."

His eyes did not shift from hers.

"Better?" he asked.

"Much." She placed the remainder of the water on the coffee table. "I think it's time we got some inside information."

She uttered the words she hadn't anticipated ever needing.

"Ares? Father?" She waited. Glancing at Xen, she tossed up her palms with a shrug of her shoulders.

She closed her eyes, breathed deeply and pictured her father in her mind's eye.

"Father." This time the words were a quiet breath.

A dazzling light appeared in the center of the library. *Flamboyant.*

"Carissa." In a few short strides, Ares strode over to where she sat and pulled her up and into an embrace. Odd and stiff, her body reluctantly moved into his, but when her nose crushed into the crook of his neck, the floodgates of memory unlocked and washed right through her body. Relaxing her muscles, she curved into the hug like she'd been doing it all her life.

"You used to love hugs when you were a little girl," he stated as he pulled back.

"I didn't think you were around enough for me to remember." It was a cheap shot on her part, but the fact that he walked out and never came back had burned a hole of sadness in her heart.

"Yes, you did, and contrary to what you may believe right now, I visited often."

"How often?"

"Every day until you turned five."

"Then you disappeared until now?" Her tone rang sharp and accusing. A part of her regretted that she sounded harsh.

"No, Carissa, I've watched over you, but time moves differently on Olympus than here. Time is slower there than here."

"So why show up now?"

"It is through a conversation that I was alerted you were in danger. Up to that point, there had been no reason to believe you were in any life-threatening situation. Whatever the reasons and circumstances, I'm here now."

She looked at him for a long hard moment, trying to process. If he hadn't heard, he wouldn't be here and she wouldn't exist to him. Her chest tightened and her breath hitched. Her shoulders sagged and desolation seeped into her body. Xen lifted his hand to hers and tried to pull her back down onto the couch from her standing position.

Her father sensed her despair. "Carissa, it is difficult to understand the way of the gods. We are not simple. We obsess about power, and the gaining and loss of it. Explaining in minutes something that is the core of our existence doesn't work. These things take time to see, adjust to and comprehend."

She understood and saw no reason to argue. "It's just ... everything seems to be happening all at once."

"I never meant for you to be hurt for being my daughter. I would not have intruded and caused you pain if I had known it would."

Shit, I hope he can't read my mind like Xen can.

Xen answered for him. "Yes, *koukla,* he does read your mind, as well as your emotions and aura."

"Well, I'm going to have to start pushing everyone out."

"That's the thing, *koukla*, you can."

"Xen is right, Carissa, you can push people out, and if I'm not mistaken, you also have a little gift of *Anagke,* the ability to use force through your thoughts only—compulsion. You don't even have to utter the words. Alas, your powers have been constrained."

"Constrained? By whom?"

Ares sighed and sat down on the couch. He swung his feet onto the coffee table.

Xen growled.

Her father patted the seat next to him. "Come sit here, *kori*."

She sat next to her father. Xen moved to the opposite armchair.

"When you turned two, odd things started popping up in your playpen—toys, pens, books, pot and pans. Your mother never had any recollection of giving these things to you but I thought nothing of it until I saw it with my own eyes." He inhaled. "Your mother had commissioned some repairs to be done to the house and there were a few workmen at the house on a daily basis. One morning I walked into the room to find one of the handymen standing over you with a television. I caught it before it could crush you. The handyman had a glazed look in his eyes. You somehow compelled him to bring you the TV. You didn't have the vocabulary but you did have the mental pictures of what you wanted. Your mother and I realized that you had the ability to compel people. And that, at such a young age, you could do it without words was astounding, but also concerning."

"So you constrained my powers at that point?"

"No, the deciding factor to bind your powers was when you turned five and inadvertently called Zeus's name, and he appeared. I had to pretend it was I who had summoned him. I bound your powers that night and the hardest week followed." He shifted and turned towards her. "I did not want to leave you or your mother, but I had no choice. It was for your protection. Zeus would have eliminated you both if he thought you to be a threat."

"But why would a child be a threat? That doesn't make sense."

"Mortals or demi-gods do not hold the power of being able to summon a god without some form of magic. That you did it with just a whisper was cause enough to have you killed."

She reached over for her glass of water and took a large gulp. Her hand shook. *Why would they kill me? I'm no one. I'm not that strong.*

"Wrong, *kori mou*. A few years ago I heard Zeus fighting with the Fates—in particular Lachesis—about a demi-god who will lead an uprising to defeat the Olympian gods. Zeus's first reaction was to obliterate every demi-god, even the children, but Lachesis threw him—as you say—a curve ball. If he killed all the demi-gods, he risked executing the one destined to save the Olympian gods from the rebellion—another demi-god." He paused, waiting to see if she followed the story. She nodded.

Xen spoke. "And as we know from repeated history, their demise would not guarantee that all would be eliminated, or which one might survive, the rebel victor or the protector of the gods."

"Exactly. Take the primary example from Kronos, who swallowed all his children—the Olympian gods—so he wouldn't be overthrown. Rhea hid one child, Zeus. He survived and eventually overthrew his father."

"He fears the same?" she asked.

"Every god fears it. It is how it has always been."

"A vicious cycle," she threw in.

"The merry-go-round no one can escape," Xen added.

"Let me finish this prophecy."

She nodded for him to continue.

"Zeus asked if the *moirai*— the Fates—could see the gender of the demi-god that would save them. They told him no, only that the gods would be forever in debt to the one who would destroy the threat. That a demi-god would be their champion."

She opened her mouth to speak, but Ares held up his hand.

"I bound your powers and stayed away for longer periods of time to take away any attention from you and to keep you hidden, safe. Your mother—as much as she did not want to remarry—married the human man you knew as your father. All necessary. All for your protection."

"But they loved each other."

"They did, but not in the way you think."

Her stomach clenched at Ares' words.

"Do you think some of this is why Hal wants me?"

"I doubt it. No one knows about this other than Zeus, the *morai,* and I. Whatever his interest, it's of a different nature, but that doesn't mean he doesn't want collateral damage."

"What if you unbound her powers, Ares? What would happen?" Xen raised an eyebrow in question.

"That is difficult to say, but I will say one thing, if she could summon Zeus at the age of five, I have every confidence the power has multiplied since then. She would need training to harness it, and she will need to learn how to use a sword."

"Hey, I'm right here, and I can defend myself. I'm a cop." She had years of experience and could dish out hurt as good as any bulked-up male.

"Yes, but your human gun can do very little to a god or supernatural entity."

Okay, he had a point. She couldn't argue with that.

Ares stood, as did Xen. They met toe to toe. "There's also the problem that if I unbind her powers, she will be like a satellite signal to every Unearthly till she can mask her power."

From where she sat, Carissa watched the exchange. Something silent passed between them.

"I'm all for *not* being a human glow stick."

Xen and Ares laughed.

"Wise girl," came her father's reply. "Again, as to why you are being targeted, I do not know. You are to stay with Xen for protection until I can get answers."

She stood and walked over to them, breaking their toe-to-toe stance. "Why do I get the feeling you're not telling me something?"

Ares reached over and pulled her in for a hug, muffling the rest of her words.

"Believe in yourself, my daughter."

Light flared, leaving her alone with Xen.

FOURTEEN

*"I am sadly afraid that I must have done
some wicked thing." ~ Antisthenes*

"Wow, I'm dreaming and I'm inside a Greek myth."

Xen let out a bark of laughter then wrapped his arms around her waist and pulled her in. "How about I show you around?"

"That might help get all those psycho images of gods trying to kill me out of my head."

"*Koukla,* no gods are trying to kill you. If you listened carefully, you'd realize that demi-gods are off the menu."

"But Hal ..."

"Wants you, yes. We'll work it out. For now, you have to accept my protection."

She nodded, but was not happy with the way her life had spiraled into something unexplainable. Ares had left her with only more questions. His news wasn't exactly a box of chocolates or that brand spanking new pink bike she'd always wanted as a kid, the one with all the bells and whistles on it she'd wished for every Christmas.

Oh no, instead she got the mother of all packages from her absent father. This one made up for all the missed birthdays, Christmases, Greek name days and other religious festivities she might have missed out on. Yep, she was a demi-god with powers. Powers that were likely to get her killed if he released them.

I've got an invisible target on my back.

At some point her mind registered that she'd been walking around Xen's house. She looked without really seeing any of it; the news had left her numb. She followed Xen up the stairs and down a corridor to his room. He opened the door, and at that moment, the haze lifted and some of those dreams she'd experienced came cascading to the forefront.

Oh, it's just like in my dreams. "Wow!"

He raised an eyebrow at her reaction and declaration.

"What?" she queried.

"*Koukla*, I just showed you half of my house and my bedroom is the only one worthy of a reaction? I'm flattered it means so much."

"I didn't mean to look uninterested. I was in shock. It's a lot to take in." She turned to face him. They were still standing in the doorway.

"You're overthinking it." He moved them into the room and shut the door. He pressed a few buttons on the panel and the door locked. "It's bulletproof."

She stood there with her mouth open. He leaned in and put a finger under her chin. Delight spread across his face, he pushed lightly to close her mouth. *I must look like a dimwit. What could he possibly like about me?*

His hands cupped her cheeks. "*Koukla*, I'm going to show you exactly what I like about you, and after round one, I'm going to show you over and over again."

She gulped. Warm lips crashed to hers, hungry and relentless. Pleasure flooded her body as his tongue moved deeply in her mouth. *This feels so good.*

She moaned.

He growled.

Captivated by the feel of him, she melted into his embrace.

Her hands found his shirt buttons, fingers working, pulling the shirt free. The Greek symbol of the letter *Phi* tattooed on his arm drew her attention. *Sexy.* She ran her fingers over it, tracing the symbol. "Why this symbol?" He grabbed her hand and drew it to his mouth kissing and licking around her fingers.

"That story is not for now."

Desire sizzled over her body. She wanted to lick him everywhere, to give him more.

He was always pleasuring her; it was time to turn the tables. So she took charge and pushed him back towards his bed. He kept kissing her as he turned her and walked her backward towards the bed.

"I want to lead tonight," she said between kisses. He met her gaze, lust pure and raw danced slowly and erotically in his eyes. Uncertain of whether to proceed, she asked, "You don't want me to?"

He licked the base of her ear then nibbled on it, sending shivers over her hot flesh. "*Koukla*, do what pleases you. Don't hold back."

She didn't need more encouragement. She pulled at his pants, got the belt undone while he placed soft kisses around her neck. Unzipping his pants, she pushed them down along with his underwear. *Naked and perfect.*

He stepped out of them, taking his socks off too. *I really hate that naked-man-in-socks look.* He laughed. "Then the socks will be the first to go next time. Turn around, *koukla*".

"I thought I was in control tonight." She gave him a stern reminder.

"You are. I just want to help with that painted-on red dress. I've been thinking countless wicked things all night."

She turned around and let him unzip her. The dress pooled at her feet and she stepped out of it then slowly turned to face him.

His eyes raked over her hungrily. Pleasure speared her. The red lace lingerie was a hit.

"*Carissa.*" He said her name as if he were swearing an oath. She stepped closer and pushed him with the tip of her finger to get him moving to the bed. He complied.

"Move to the middle."

He did as she asked. She climbed onto the bed and positioned herself between his legs then brought her mouth down to his hard erection. She slid her tongue along his silky length. Her hand cupped his lower base.

"God, *koukla*, don't stop." His hands fisted in her hair.

She took the swollen head of his arousal into her mouth. His hips drove up until it met the back of her throat.

A loud growl split from his lips. Her passion heightened at his reaction, becoming more prominent as wetness seeped through her panties.

He raised himself, reaching forward to unclasp her bra, and pulled it off with lightning speed. Her heavy breasts fell loose, stroking his thighs while she continued her ministrations, biting and licking. He hissed, his movements frantic.

"Carissa, slow down. I need to get inside you before I explode."

She stopped and licked her way up to his abdomen and chest, grinning all the way. She was addicted to his taste, to him. She took his nipple in her mouth, suckled it, then increased the pressure.

He growled and she bit down. Her control of the situation was overthrown. He flipped her over and took her breast to his mouth, returning the attention she had just given him. Pleasure speared straight to her core. He stretched his hand down and tore off her panties. She fought back for control, pushing him down and attacking his lips with hunger. Something possessive came over her.

I want to claim you and make you mine.

He pulled back from the kiss and looked up at her, read her thoughts. His eyes searched hers, looking for approval.

"Let me bond with you, Carissa. Be mine."

She kissed him and fed from the decadent taste of his mouth—something she was becoming more and more addicted to. "*Nai*."

At her agreement, he flipped her underneath him and spread her legs with his, lifting her arms over her head.

"Hold the headboard," he instructed in a husky voice. His arousal probed at her entrance and with a devastating kiss that took her breath away, he thrust his hips forward. She lost all coherent thoughts and gave herself completely to the sensual movement of his hips.

"I'm going to open a vein for you, I want you to drink a little of my blood while I draw out some of yours. It has to be done simultaneously."

She nodded as understanding broke through her lust-filled mind.

He pressed a fingernail into his chest and made a small cut. *Wow, that's one powerful fingernail.* He squeezed to get a drop of blood out.

"How can I not want you? You make me laugh at the most unexpected moments. Now, *koukla*, draw out some blood."

She lifted her head and placed her mouth on his chest, sucking the small wound. He moaned and his sharp incisors met her neck, pierced it. Pin pricks jabbed her body as he drew blood. She licked the puncture on his chest. *Divine.*

He thrust his hips hard and her orgasm tore through her, exploding like fireworks. A burst of white light crashed at the back of her eyelids.

"Xen," the primal cry tore from her lips. Her climax burst through her, but it didn't stop. Neither did Xen. He pumped steadily into her heat. She raced towards that spike of ecstasy again. A loud growl ripped from Xen's lips at the same time as hers as they both reached a mountain of pleasure.

That was the most mind-blowing orgasm ever.

They stayed joined, panting and trying to recover from the exhilarating high.

She is divine and beautiful. Mine.

"Xen, I just heard your thoughts." She seized his shoulders and shook. *I can do the mind mumbo jumbo.*

"You can, *koukla,* and you will be able to sense me when I'm close by." He bent his head and thrust his tongue in her mouth, devouring it, then pulling out to bite her lower lip before plunging back in again. The intensity short-circuited her brain. When he broke the kiss, they were both breathing hard. Slowly, he rolled off her and pulled her into a spooning position.

"I want this, Xen. I want to be with you. I'm not the same person anymore. You've changed my life in such a short space of time. I would not have thought it possible."

"And you've changed me, *koukla.*"

"So, this bonding is a deep connection of some sort. Like marriage?"

"Clever girl. Yes, it is, but I understand your need to have a proper wedding with customs you have been raised to value."

"I don't think I'm ready for that part just yet."

"Know one thing, I won't wait indefinitely. I want people to know you are mine, both in my world and yours."

He leaned forward and gave her a light kiss on her swollen lips. *Delicious.*

A giggle left her lips. She could hear him. Now she understood what he must have heard every time she let her guard down.

"Why was your blood tasty to me? I mean, the thought of licking someone else's blood is as appealing as eating cardboard. Yours is better than triple chocolate delight."

His deep laugh echoed around the room. "I'm glad I taste better than ice cream. It's your body's reaction to mine, it understands and senses a connection. We are destined to be together ... two parts to make a whole. That's why you didn't find what you did repulsive. If it was someone you didn't like and you were forced, then you would not like the taste of their blood. A blood bond is supposed to be mutual. If not, it would cause you to be sick because it's against your will. It's not a ritual to be taken lightly."

"So I'm technically a Mrs."

"Yes, you are."

"Welcome to the family and good luck with my aunt. She'll want all your financial figures in the morning."

"Maybe we should send her to Greece?"

It was her turn to laugh. "Now there's an idea."

"But I have a more pleasing one," he said close to her ear. Then kissed a trail down her neck.

Xen waited till Carissa's breaths were deep before he rose to attend to matters. He threw on some sweatpants and a t-shirt, and made his way down to the library. Pushing the door open, he found Kane sitting and staring out the window.

"What are you doing up, Kane?"

"Just double-checking all the men are in position. In case we get a nasty surprise."

"Something tells me they won't be back tonight. Tomorrow, however, is another thing."

"By the way, how is your bonded?" he asked with wolfish smile.

"She is fine and asleep. Your keen sense serves you well, *lykos*."

"My keen sense is going into sensory overload. I can smell her all over you. Just a word of warning, you might want to make sure you are de-scented a little when around the other *lykoi* and *Phi*. Your woman has a sweet scent and you might be fighting off more than demons and Hal."

Confusion marked Xen's face. "I thought it was only I who picked up that scent?"

"It's probably more potent for you, but she does raise attention."

"Well, I don't think Hal picked up her scent."

"No, but she does emit a vibration," Kane added.

"He wants her for something, but I can't imagine how it would benefit him. Besides, her powers aren't developed," Xen said, crossing his arms over his chest. "I'm thinking back to the visit from Ares earlier. He said he constrained her powers."

"What? Ares was here again?" Kane asked.

"Yes, and I'm enlightened to the fact that I have a power-restrained firecracker upstairs."

Satisfaction warmed his chest.

"So share the details already."

"Once he releases her powers, they will be quite strong." Xen dropped his arms and started to paced around the library. He omitted the fact that "quite strong" meant a possible threat to the Olympian gods. No, he'd keep that to himself for now. "The more I think about it, the more I'm led to conclude that Hal might know who Carissa's father is. What he will gain is as much a mystery to me as to you." He stopped and looked over to Kane. "Did you manage to obtain anything further about his younger life?"

"I did, and I can confirm with certainty that, at this stage, there isn't much there. Mother, father—or supposed stand-in father— moved not long after Carissa's family moved. I have them relocating thrice, then the trail goes cold and everyone disappears. Dead end. No financial records. No medical. Not a thing. Zero. I've got men talking to some people who may have interacted with them, see if we can reignite some memories. Might give us some clues. Something tells me they didn't go off the radar voluntarily."

"He's dangerous, and whatever he wants ..." His thoughts drifted. She was his responsibility and he would have to keep her safe. "... I want extra resources on this."

"Consider it done," Kane confirmed.

"Get some rest, *lykos,* you look tired."

"That's because some insane vampire keeps me up at all hours," Kane threw back as he walked through the library door.

Alone with his thoughts, he contemplated his next course of action. The sooner he eliminated Hal the better.

Lox. He'd yet to hear anything from the demon. The longer it took, the deeper the involvement.

He made his way back to his room and a sleeping Carissa. Standing before her, his tender fingers brushed some of her hair away from her face. He inhaled deeply—tuberose, jasmine and sex. Her potent scent lay heavy in the air around his room. He removed his clothing and joined his sleeping beauty, an addiction he knew he would never give up.

His thoughts lingered and then it dawned on him that she might well and truly age slower than humans. Now that he had a taste of her, there could be no other for him. This woman would be his immortal existence or his immortal demise.

Images shifted in his mind. The *lamia* the ghastly creature cursed by Hera for Zeus's infidelity. His life was meant to end in that cave all those years ago. How ironic that Ares would save him and recruit him, and that his daughter would be bonded with him. Ah, the Fates, they truly spun a chaotic thread.

FIFTEEN

*"Love is simply the name for the desire and
the pursuit of the whole." ~ Aristophanes*

Elation filled her when her eyes blinked open to a stunning profile.
The previous night's intimacy replayed in her mind. Her decision
to bond with Xen and form a deeper connection delighted her to
no end. She understood that in his world it meant marriage, but she
was not yet ready to proceed to that level in the world she knew and
grew up in. No, her world consisted of diamond rings and weddings.
And if her Aunt Paula got a whiff of it, it would be the *biggest* obese
Greek wedding on the planet.

Wonder if my father would come to the wedding? Her eyebrows
drew in together. How had her mother met Ares? How did she come
to have a relationship with him? Not that it would've been difficult,
she thought. The man appeared no older than Xen did, and, in a nut-
shell, not only did he *look* like a god, he *was* a god.

Guilt stabbed her thoughts. Thinking about her new father
was not respectful to the mortal man she knew as her father. The
man who'd raised her would always be her father too. Memories
flooded her. There had never been a time when he didn't shower
her with his kindness and love. She had been truly blessed that he
had been a part of her life.

The thought of Hal slammed into the forefront suddenly and obliterated past memories. Her mood darkened. She'd have to talk to her newly found father, Ares, soon. He'd have to unravel her constrained powers. Armor and arsenal were her friends, and with the company that Hal kept she'd need every weapon she could get her hands on.

Leaning over, she placed a kiss on Xen's lips then headed to the shower. She didn't want to be late for her appointment, as much as she would have preferred to stay in bed all day. *Let's see what the psychologist thinks.*

"Hey, Kane."

"Morning to you, Mrs. Lyson."

Her stomach dropped. Mortified, her cheeks heated—no doubt to a lovely shade of dark red. How did he know?

"Did Xen say something?"

"No, I pretty much sniffed it." The corner of his mouth quirked up.

Skata. At this rate she'd be red enough to be a Christmas decoration.

"Oh." She ducked her head. *Do these guys know everything that goes on? Of course, they do, you idiot. They can smell and hear like nobody's business.* "So, you can smell …?"

He nodded his head with a monumental "I know what you did" grin. "Carissa, there's nothing to be embarrassed about."

She swallowed hard. Ears flaming, she cast her eyes to the marble floor.

"How about I pour you a cup of coffee?" he offered.

"That would be nice before I go."

"Oh no, you are not to go anywhere."

"I have to go to my psych appointment."

"Then I will arrange to either take you or have one of the other men take you."

She began to protest, but when Kane crossed his thick muscular arms across his chest and pinned her with a menacing stare, it was plainly obvious she'd have to agree.

The appointment was a total brain sap. She walked out of the psych's office with the notion that she was a basket case. How did they do that? Make you sound worse than you were? Her fingers typed on her smartphone. Kane made it clear that he'd be expecting a text message when she'd finished with the quack. Her fingers failed to hit send because she ran straight into a tree trunk.

Strong arms darted out to intercept her fall.

"Jones," she breathed. "What are you doing here?" They hadn't spoken since that morning at the warehouse. Another stab of guilt tore through her chest. She needed to see Lopez.

"Kane," he answered and removed his hands from their hold. Her mind raced and her eyes widened in comprehension. Ever so slowly, she shook her head. *No. He couldn't be ...*

A grin split his lips. "Whatever it is you're thinking, the answer is yes."

"You're ... you're part of the *Phi*?"

He nodded.

She threw her hands up. Boy, she hadn't seen that one coming. She grunted at him.

"That's my girl." The damn man had the nerve to be entertained by it all.

"Where in our close friendship did you not see it fit to tell me this?"

"Let's talk in the car."

They walked in silence. There were a thousand questions she wanted answered, but knew the impossibility of having them answered all at once.

He unlocked his car and opened the passenger door for her. He eyed her carefully. Why, she had no idea. Maybe he thought she'd run or something. Her brain needed time to process. And food. At the thought, her stomach growled.

"Are you okay, Carissa? You seem miles away."

"I'd like a burger, Jones. Then we can talk about this *skata*." Two minutes later, he pulled up near a diner. The aroma of cooking onions hit her nasal passage as they walked through the door. Her stomach decided to do a little dance in celebration by growling again. She slid into a booth.

"I just can't believe it."

"You should. It's true."

"Duh, but forgive me. We've been like this"—she flicked her index and middle fingers together to show him how close they were—"since our training in the police academy. You could have said something that night at the hospital when you gave me the third degree."

"You know I could not have divulged anything without you thinking I was crazier than you looked after seeing the psych."

She let out a belly laugh. He had a point. "Okay. I'll let it go." She lifted her menu. "For now."

The waitress strode over to their table and took their order. "Any more news on this Hal guy?" Jones asked.

She raised an eyebrow. "Gee, news travels fast in your network."

"What can I say? We're a close-knit organization."

She smiled. "No. Nothing on Hal. It's like he's disappeared into thin air."

"Or through a portal to somewhere else," Jones added. "And those things just can't be detected."

"I just don't understand what he wants with me?" The waitress dropped their orders in front of them. "I mean I'm not powerful, so I can't see what he stands to gain." She took a bite from her burger and moaned. She had skipped breakfast because of her appointment.

The grease from the Angus beef patty tantalized her taste buds.

"Carissa, the thing you have to remember about any unearthly creatures, is that why they do things doesn't always make sense. Being a demi-god, Hal could have ulterior motives that haven't been revealed.

"Demons don't play fair, and their idea of revenge maybe more of what you would call uncanny."

"It's quite possible Hal could want me for something other than being around Xen and taking down the *Phi*?"

"Yes, I heard about that little nugget," he said, looking over his burger. She reached over and pulled the pickle out of it and ate it. He laughed. "It's nice that some things don't change."

"Well, burgers are sane. You know, Jones, from the moment I walked into the warehouse my police mojo disintegrated. I'm like a walking cop bimbo, unable to piece this thing together."

"Carissa, you've just been introduced to another world. The pieces will fall into place."

"You don't think it has anything to do with me being the daughter of Ares, do you?

He dropped the burger on his plate. His blue eyes widened. "Are you serious?" He coughed then reached for his glass of soda.

"Yes. Good ole daddy decided to pay me a visit."

He blew out a breath. "Well, that changes why they might want you." He looked over his shoulder and quickly scanned the restaurant. "I think we should get moving."

His sudden paranoia made her jittery too.

"I've one more stop to make before we head on back to Xen's place."

"Carissa, with what you just admitted, I think it's best to get you back under protection."

And that was the final straw for her. She would not be afraid. Fear didn't make her shrivel up. No. She squashed it before it could rear its ugly head. She would not hide. She'd had a life before all this madness decided to stifle her. She clenched her fists and met his eyes. Through gritted teeth, she spoke, "You will take me to Lopez. You understand this." She did not dare to blink.

"Okay, but we get there, you spend ten minutes tops and then we move. I can't risk it."

"Agreed."

The moment she had stepped into Lopez's room her knees buckled. Seeing him like this ate at her soul. Regret washed over her at her stupid decision to follow a lead from a source that she knew to be unreliable. It burned her heart to monumental degrees, but more than anything, her stupidity irked her.

He would be safe and well if it weren't for me.

Tears clouded her vision. *Yes, that scum Tom.* She'd have to locate him and really pin his balls to the wall, but right now she wanted to go home. Her lunch was doing the tango in her stomach, the contents threatening to rise. Jones's racetrack driving on the way over to the hospital hadn't helped, either. What was it with everyone and their driving lately?

"Can you at least try to take the corners properly? I'm going to hurl."

"I am taking them properly."

"Jones, you have to pull over."

He glanced over at her. "Shit, you don't look so good."

Yep. She was green. Everything in her body told her so.

"Turn here and head to my house."

"We can't and you know that."

"Jones, please. Call Kane and tell him we are taking a detour."

"Okay. I'll take you to your place then call him."

He pulled into her driveway and she bolted up the stairs to the front door. She fumbled with the keys.

"Here let me." Jones took them from her shaking hands.

She raced through the house towards the bathroom. Dropping to her knees everything she ate earlier came back up and into the toilet bowl. When nothing more would come up, she got up and stumbled to the washbasin and splashed water on her face. She headed towards the kitchen for a glass of water. Jones sat at the table with a grim look on his face.

"Carissa, I can't leave you like this. I have to stay until Kane can get someone here to watch over you."

"No, it's okay. I don't need anyone. I'll be okay. I just need to get into bed and sleep. Maybe it's all catching up with me." *Sleep, that's what I need. Sleep.*

"Well, I hate to break it to you, sunshine, but that's not going to happen. I do agree you need to rest though. Let's tuck you in."

He was right of course. She'd caught a glimpse of her face in the mirror. She looked tired, drawn and pale. She got to her feet, the room spun, the dizziness caused her to sway.

"Do you want me to call a doctor?"

"No, I'll be okay. It was the food, that's all. Thank you, Jones." She gave him a hug and made her way up the stairs to her bedroom, unbuckling and unbuttoning as she went.

She climbed into bed in her underwear and bra. Her stomach rolled again and she couldn't bring herself to put any sleepwear on. Her cheek brushed the cool pillowcase as she sought comfort.

"I feel like I'm on a rollercoaster ride that I can't get off from," she mumbled as she pressed her eyelids shut.

Jones grabbed his cell phone and punched the button on speed dial for Kane.

"Kane, I've got a problem. Carissa isn't well, so we're back at her place."

"Why the hell did you take her there? She's to be brought here."

"She's a mess. She threw up all over the place."

There was a pause.

"I'll let Xen know. Give me half an hour."

Jones ended the call and made his way up to help Carissa.

When he entered her room, she was sound asleep. She'd been bombarded with a whole other co-existence, and the knowledge that she was a demi-god wouldn't have been easy on her. She accepted other people for who they were, a highlight that had attracted him to her as a friend. This was evidence that she needed to rest and process. He brushed his knuckles over her cheek then turned to leave her room.

"So how is she?" Kane's words bounced from the walls in the kitchen.

"Out for the count."

"Thanks, pup."

A low growl left Jones's lips. He watched the amusement at his reaction play out on Kane's face. "I'll check in with you in a couple of hours," he snapped then stepped around Kane to exit out of the kitchen door.

"No problem."

Jones stopped with his back to Kane. "You know it's probably all too much for her."

"Even so, there is no going back now. She'll have to adjust."

"At what cost, Kane?"

"How is my bride?" Xen asked Kane, who was lounging on Carissa's couch. He shot to his feet.

"Based on Jones's account, she's been out since he brought her here. I can confirm she hasn't shifted. I would have heard."

"Have we enough men in place?" Xen asked, rubbing the back of his neck.

"You could say we have a small army."

Xen lips lifted in approval. "I'd best see how she is."

"Let me know if you need anything," Kane said as Xen let him out and locked the back door.

He sped up to Carissa's darkened room and made his way over to the bedside lamp, turning it on to get a better look at his woman. She looked pale lying there in the middle of her bed. He toed off his shoes and lay next to her, spooning her.

A million things sifted through his mind. What if the whole ordeal of learning about the co-existence of the Unearthly with the humans had been too much for her, or if his blood had made her sick? As he ticked things off his list, he realized she was stronger than most of the theories he had on his inventory, and that maybe she'd genuinely come down with something. He would insist she see a doctor. He stroked the hair from her face. She stirred.

"Carissa."

He watched her face as she struggled to orient herself.

"How long have I been out?"

"All afternoon from what I'm told. What happened?" he asked her.

"I don't know. It must have been the burger. One minute I'm all good and the next thing I know, everything wanted to come back up." She turned and looked at him. Even in her sick state he wanted her.

"How are you, Xen?"

"Better, now that I know you are okay. Would you like me to order you some dinner?"

Her breath caught, the words she had been about to utter died and her face contorted as she dry-retched. Within seconds he had her in the bathroom, her head over the bowl. She heaved twice and brought up green bile. His hands held her hair out of the way. When it appeared there was no more retching to be done, he helped her over to the sink to wash her face.

"*Koukla*, I'm going to call a doctor for you and I don't want to hear no for an answer." He lifted her in his arms and carried her back to bed, tucking her in. "Sleep. I'll go make the call."

Exhaustion showed on her features. She looked drained and could only manage a small nod to his words. Her eyes fluttered and closed.

A beautiful woman sat in a Grecian garden talking to her. She wore a beautiful crown on her head. Carissa eyed the detail it held. "You are beautiful," Carissa said to the woman.

"As are you, my granddaughter."

"But how can you be my grandmother?" she asked.

"Why are so many things as they are?" replied the woman.

She narrowed her eyes at the question.

"Don't frown. I have given you a gift. I hope you like it." Gentle hands caressing her face woke her from her strange dream, but her eyes were still too heavy to open.

"Carissa." An angelic voice called her name. Her eyes fluttered open to meet very pale blue eyes. The woman looking down at her looked like an angel. Golden hair framed her flawless face.

"That's the girl. I'm Dr. Aci. I need to take your temperature properly. Can you sit up?"

It took her a moment to get the gears working in her head. Xen had called a doctor. The woman in question stood at the end of her bed, looking grim.

"I'm sure it's nothing serious," she said with a shaky voice, more to convince Xen.

"Well, then let's be sure," the doctor broke in.

She sat up for the doctor to take her temperature and proceed with a routine medical examination.

"I have a hunch as to what I think it is, but I'm going to need to take blood," Dr. Aci announced.

"I have a few calls to make so I'll head downstairs." Xen walked around the bed kissed Carissa on the forehead. "Let me know when you are done." He turned to leave the room. He didn't say anything, but turned back at the door to meet her eyes. She tried to focus and projected, *thank you for being here.*

"Where else would I be?" He smiled and she melted on the inside.

The doctor tied the tourniquet around her arm then tapped a vein before piercing a needle into her arm for blood. "I should have some results back for you in the morning."

"Maybe it's food poisoning? Thank you again."

"Perhaps, but let's just wait and see. And you are quite welcome." The doctor paused and the corners of her mouth turned up. "You are one lucky girl to have snagged Xenocrates." A hint of envy laced her words.

"I still can't believe it!" Great. Now you sound like a sixteen-year-old.

"Well, you'd better, because I have known Xen for quite some time and I can tell you with absolute certainty that I've never seen him like this over any woman."

"So you've treated him?" she asked, trying to work out how she knew him.

"No, no." Dr. Aci giggled.

The woman actually giggled. Great, now they were both carrying on like sixteen-year-olds. Her man reduced women to girlish fits of giggles. That thought sent a spike of warmth through her body.

"I've not treated Xen, but some of the *lykoi* have needed healing from time to time. Their skirmishes are happening more frequently these days." She shook her head in disapproval as she packed her instruments in her bag.

"I'd better go. I've got another house call. I'll give Xen some instructions and hopefully we can get something down in your stomach. You are looking a bit pale. Are you not eating well?"

"Define well. Since meeting Xen I think my eating habits have been all over the place."

Eyebrow raised, the doctor pointed out, "You will need to maintain healthy eating habits if you are going to be around Xen."

"I intend to."

The doctor rose from the bed and pulled off her latex gloves and threw them into the wastebasket next to the bed. Carissa noted the graceful exit. *So angelic.* She lay back down. Her eyes were heavy but she lifted her lids when Xen entered with a tray of steaming chamomile tea, and a few dry crackers. She forced her eyes to stay open as she watched him.

"Have these, and if you can keep them down, I'll get you some real food," he said as he placed the tray on the bedside table. She pushed herself upright and he sat on the bed to give her the tea.

"I'm sure it was that burger I ate. That's it, I'm not having one of those again." Annoyance and anger were directed at the culprit—Mr. Hamburger—for spoiling her favorite unhealthy eating habit.

"*Koukla*, whatever it was, I hope it's passed. Have your tea."

She took a few sips and then he handed her the cracker plate. Her shaky hand took a cracker from it. She bit and chewed and swallowed while watching the vision in front of her, and here she was—well, at her worst. Heat crept up her throat and cheeks.

"*Koukla*, don't be embarrassed. Believe it or not, I can still get excited about you even if you think you are not in the best of shape. From where I'm sitting, that white lace bra is doing things to me." His eyebrows danced up and down.

Oh god, I'd forgotten I didn't have any pajamas or a t-shirt on. What an exhibitionist. Oh my, the doctor. The warmth on her face intensified.

He belted out a loud laugh. "Oh, my silly *koukla*. Don't be modest. My plans include having you with less on, and often. As for the doctor, she's seen it all."

She tugged at the covers with her free hand and pulled them up to her chin as best she could. He pulled them back down. His eyes travelled over the lacey bra covering her breasts. He growled.

Admitting a silent defeat, she took another gulp of hot tea. Her stomach seemed to be returning to normal.

"I wouldn't mind a bit of fried rice," she said between gulps of tea.

Xen pulled out his cell phone and typed quickly. "What did you want, *koukla?*"

"Veggie fried rice." His fingers moved quickly to finish the message. He placed his phone and keys on the bedside table, removed his shoes, grabbed her cup, and moved it to where it was safe.

I'm going to need a dining table as a bedside table.

Then we can use the dining table for other things, he projected as he climbed onto the bed.

"Is that all you think of?"

"With you, yes." He reached over and pulled her into a spooning position.

A comforting relief washed over her.

"Just stay with me like this for a little while, that's all I ask."

"*Koukla*, you know I will not leave you unless I have to." He pulled the covers down, got under them, and encircled her in his arms again. She sighed.

"I might fall asleep again. This is cozy."

"Then sleep, *koukla.*"

SIXTEEN

"And a sweet expression spreads over her fair face." ~ *Sappho*

The aroma of coffee tickled her nose, its sweet temptation too much for her to lie around any longer. She dragged her sorry self into the shower. Once done, she threw on some sweatpants and a t-shirt, then headed downstairs.

At the top of the stairs, she could hear Kane talking to someone on the phone. He was giving more orders to the men parked discreetly around her house and street. Her descent was slow and as her foot slid off the last stair, Kane came through from the kitchen.

"Hey, Kane."

"Hey yourself. How are you feeling?" His gaze skittered over the length of her body.

She raised her palms outward. "What?"

"You look pale. Xen wants me to hang around, are you okay with that?"

"Sure. You know, *you* look tired."

"Do you have somewhere for me to crash for a couple of hours? If not, I'll take the couch."

"Dibs on the couch. I'm going to park myself in front of the television. There's a spare bedroom just through the living room. It's all yours."

"I appreciate that, Carissa. A couple of hours would be great. Yell your lungs out if you need anything. I've left some coffee and toast on the counter."

He really was an amazing guy. Wonder if Kelly or Ligi would be interested? Stop it. Now you're trying to do the Greek setup like your Thitsa.

"Thanks, Kane. You didn't have to do that. I can do it myself."

"It's the least I can do. Plus, I heard you ruffling around upstairs."

Damn. I forgot these guys had supersonic hearing.

"Just changing the subject, this 'protecting the fortress' is slightly excessive." She let out a heavy sigh. "It's been a few days and nothing has happened, so maybe they got the message."

"Carissa, demons don't base attacks on time. A strike can happen at any time. Having someone like Hal on their side is even more dangerous." His eyes held hers and for a second, she could swear that she could see his thoughts. He didn't need to elaborate.

"I hear you and I understand, but I think it's safe."

"And that's what they want you to feel, safe. Often, when they return, they do so with a festival crowd."

That was seriously something she did not want to hear.

"Okay, point taken. I guess you'd better get some rest. You're no good to me if you can't fight."

Amusement spread across his face. "Don't go anywhere, otherwise you'll ruin my beauty sleep."

She scoffed under her breath. "Like you guys need help in the beauty department."

She headed to the kitchen and grabbed the cup of coffee that sat waiting for her. Her toast looked undercooked; she'd reheat it. As she moved over to the sink she noticed Kane's previous attempt with the blackened evidence in the trash. The image of Kane cussing over burnt bread caused a bubble of laughter in her chest. When the toast popped, she slathered a good amount of butter on it then padded over to the couch and television.

Clicking the remote, she scanned through the channels and found an old Elvis movie. *Perfect.* It wasn't long before her stomach started to churn. Nausea reared its ugly head again. She lay down to try to keep it at bay. *Food, you're staying in my stomach.*

The ring of the phone startled her into a quick upright position, causing her to fall off the couch and hit her knee on the edge of the coffee table.

"Gamoto!"

Kane came bolting into the room, ready to kill someone or something. Feral was an understatement. And the boxers looked hot.

"Kane, cover up, please. I don't want to go blind."

His mouth twisted into a grin. "I heard you yell and thought something happened."

"I accidently hit the coffee table trying to get to the phone," she said, trying to look everywhere but at him. She took a quick glance. He was still grinning.

"You are a handful, aren't you?" Then he turned to walk away, giving her a good view of his muscular back and a pair of buns that were pretty close to perfect. Xen's, of course, outdid his. But, man, his rear gave Xen's a run for his money.

"What's that supposed to mean?" Just because a girl is clumsy from time to time, doesn't mean she's not capable. "I was better coordinated before I met you lot." She huffed under her breath. "Got my police mojo going haywire." She'd have words with the *lykos* later, when he had put on some clothes.

The phone had stopped ringing, but it clicked over to voice mail. Dr. Aci's voice filled the silent room, asking her to call her back later for her blood test results.

"Doctors!" she scoffed. "Can't they leave a message like everyone else?" She picked up the phone and called the number Dr. Aci had left after her message. An overly friendly receptionist greeted her.

"Carissa Alkippes for Dr. Aci. She just left a message for me."

"I'm sorry, but Dr. Aci is booked solid till five this afternoon. You'll have to call back then, or I can ask her to return your call."

The nerve. Really? Pfft. It was only seconds ago. "She literally just called a minute ago."

"I'm sorry, but she's with someone," the receptionist said in a sing-song voice. "Call back at five."

She hung up and ran a hand through her hair. "Why do they do that?" she said to no one in particular.

"Do what?" Kane's voice startled her. She closed her eyes and let out a deep sigh.

"Doctors, they call you and you miss them, so you call them back and then you can't talk to them until the end of the day, and that's if you don't miss them then, too!"

"I can't understand that either, Carissa, and I've been around a long time. They run on Greek time."

"Greek time?" she repeated.

"Yeah, the concept of time is mashed into everything else they do. They invented the whole thing to look busy. Makes you think you're getting something good because they're unattainable."

"Pfft, and it works."

"Time is not applicable to Greeks. Are you hungry? I'm going to get the boys to go pick up some takeout. Are you up to it?"

"Actually, no, I won't, Kane. I was feeling a little queasy earlier."

Kane nodded and headed for the kitchen.

Rearranging herself on the couch again, she reached for the remote. Before long, her eyelids became weighted and sleep pulled her under.

Darkness surrounded her. The air became cold—freezing— stinging her lungs as she took a look around, only to discover she was standing in a cave. There was a terrible stench. Squinting her eyes again, she tried to get some clarity—nothing. As her eyes adjusted slowly, a hideous face came into view. Her mouth opened wide but her screams were muted.

A cry tore from her throat. Her heart fisted against her breastbone, her body shot up from the couch to a sitting position. Xen and Kane were standing over her, eyebrows drawn together. They mirrored each other.

"*Koukla,* were you having a bad dream?"

She nodded. "Some water," she gasped. A glass appeared before her in a blink. *Damn, that man is fast.*

"How do you do that without spilling the water?"

"What?" came the double replies from Xen and Kane.

"The water. How is it you don't spill it at top speed?"

They looked at each other and laughed.

"Carissa, you really are something!" Kane said shaking his head. "If you don't need me, Xen, I'll be heading off."

"Thank you, *lykos.*"

They nodded to each other. Man language, she thought. Xen moved to the couch so he could sit with her.

"Now, *koukla,* tell me about your day."

She shifted a little before she broke out into a long boring string of her uneventful day. As soon as she mentioned the doctor, Xen's face lit up. He appeared ready to make the call for her, but she jumped into scolding him.

"It's mine to make, since it's my health."

"Since you are mine, it makes no difference, because what affects you, affects me."

She rolled her eyes at him.

"Okay, okay. Now, let me make that call." She rose from the couch, picked up the phone and dialed the number.

"Hello." The doctor's voice filled the earpiece.

"Dr. Aci, it's Carissa. I'm calling about my results."

"Good evening, Carissa. I've got some good news for you."

The tension in her shoulders evaporated. Relief surfed through her body. The doctor, however, sounded a little too excited for comfort. A sour taste skittered on her tongue. Surely her iron and cholesterol levels weren't anything to get excited about. It wasn't like she'd be comparing notes with her Aunt Paula.

"Is Xen with you this evening?" the doctor asked.

A tingling started in her chest. A small voice found its way up her throat. "Yes, he is here." She turned to face him. He looked on and it was evident he could hear every word, but his face revealed no emotion.

"Excellent," she said. "Carissa, I've run all the usual tests on your blood and everything is fine. You are not suffering anything major. But you are expecting a baby!"

Her body began to burn. "Sorry, did you just say what I think you said?"

"Yes, you're pregnant."

The doctor talked on, but she couldn't decipher a single word. Xen picked up on her lack of response and moved over to her, taking the phone from her hand and continuing the conversation with the doctor. She sat there with her mouth open, trying to work out how.

He had clearly told her that it couldn't happen, and to happen so quickly. *Impossible.*

At some point, her legs found the couch again.

Xen hung up, sat down next to her and lifted her onto his lap, her legs on either side of his. His fingers tangled at the back of her hair; gently, he tugged her down to his lips. The kiss was gentle. She broke the contact to look into the pool of those mesmerizing green eyes.

"Xen, don't you want to talk about this?"

"*Koukla,* there is nothing to say. You've given me the most precious gift of all. One that I did not even think would befall my long existence. As to your belief that it is impossible, I can say with certainty that you are a daughter of a god and therefore anything is possible. We will ask your father, but I'm more than happy." He finished with one of those dazzling smiles that showed a little dimple and made her weak at the knees. *Yep, that smile has no business owning a zip code.*

"I am puzzled. I just don't see how it could happen so soon. I guess I don't know enough about my heritage."

"*Koukla*, I sensed something in you from the very beginning. We'll work it out together. I don't want you to stress as to the how of things. Let's talk to Ares first, maybe he can share some knowledge on that one. The gods work with their own agendas in mind." He gave her another soft kiss.

He wasn't upset. The captivating man she straddled wasn't upset, in fact he resembled a man doing a victory dance. She could see it in the depths of his sparkling green eyes.

There was only one thing left to do, her lips crashed over his. She bit his bottom lip then licked it. He growled his satisfaction. He flipped her under him on the couch and took control in ravaging her mouth.

SEVENTEEN

"The bad of the morning becomes
worse by the night." ~ Greek proverb

At four in the morning the pillow had become a slab of concrete. Carissa tossed and turned for an hour and half after Xen left. Sleep became impossible, so she opted for some fresh morning air. Cabin fever had struck. She dressed and placed her feet in her flip-flops then made her descent down the back stairs. A guard stood poised on the porch.

"I don't think you should be out here."

"I need some fresh air. It's getting stale inside."

"Boss's orders are to keep you close."

"Then walk with me."

He eyed her for a moment. "Okay, but only five minutes."

"Fine." If that was all she was going to get, she'd take it.

They walked to the far end of the property and she stood at her favorite spot between the red oak and the willow oak. The willow evoked mixed emotions. Family get-togethers came flooding back. Those long afternoons with lots of food, with her Grandmother Vetta, friends and cousins. Everyone had gone their separate ways, and with Grandma in the nursing home, there were no more visits. Loneliness sucked, but having Xen had filled the void.

She took a deep breath of the morning air, filling her lungs. A slight breeze added to the freshness. It was truly wonderful to take in the crispness and see those first rays of light as they flickered in the east. She turned. Time to go back inside and brew her first cup of coffee.

"Would you like a cup of coffee?" she asked.

"Sure, that would be great."

"What's your name?" She could hardly serve the man coffee and not know his name.

"Philon. Or just Phil."

"Okay, just Phil. Let's get some black poison into us."

He let out a deep laugh.

The morning breeze stirred around them. The hairs on her neck stood to attention as the air tingled, then zapped. She had no time to process or make the connection. Arms tugged at her, pulling her and Phil into some invisible force.

"No!" The word ripped from her throat and reverberated in her ears.

Phil's growl split the morning air. Reinforcements were running to their aid. She watched the grim expressions on their faces. They would not reach them in time.

A full-body shiver ran through her. *Not again.*

Time suspended and everything froze, there was only one sensation—that she was being torn apart from the inside. An invisible arm pushed her, and she lurched forward. With tremendous force, she catapulted to the ground. A pair of shiny black shoes were an inch from her nose. She leaped to her feet and faced the owner with one of her award-winning happy faces.

"Hello, Carissa. We meet again."

"Gee, Hal, if that's happy I'd hate to see when you're really excited," she bit out.

Jaw set, he turned to leave.

"Secure the portal and chain the wolf!" he shouted as he walked off.

Her head snapped around. She met Phil's eyes, pain etched in his features. He mouthed the word, "Sorry."

"You don't need him, Hal. Send him back."

Hal stopped, turned and let out an insane laugh. "That's not going to happen. He stays."

"He is of no use to you. You have enough minions."

"That is where you are wrong. Along with you, he'll be quite a bargaining chip."

Carissa turned to look at Phil again. He shook his head slowly, the silent "stop arguing" evident in his demeanor.

"Bring her," Hal yelled, and two goons came forward to push her in his direction.

She scanned her surroundings. They looked familiar. *Jostlers warehouse, where it all started.*

An ache ignited in her throat. Her tongue soured. She placed her hands in her jeans pockets to stop them shaking. Pieces clicked into place. The portal had been in the warehouse all along. The demons were in this warehouse the night Lopez was left for dead. She'd bet her last dollar that Hal somehow had intricately arranged everything to play out this way. The question on her mind and lips was *why*.

They walked outside. Hal grabbed her and pushed through another portal. This time, she landed on her feet with Hal's arm around her to steady her. She flinched and stepped back. Her eyes darted around the room. They were standing in a large library.

"Sit down, Carissa." Hal's abrupt command startled her out of her roving observation.

A chair seemed just the thing. No need to waste any energy on standing through whatever Hal wanted to say.

"What do you want, Hal?" she demanded.

"Blunt, aren't you?"

"What's the point of pretending we're going to have a friendly chat?"

"There is nothing fictitious here. Every action I take has a purpose."

"Then tell me, for what reason am I here?"

He laughed at her question, and she really wanted to poke him in the eye.

"Oh, we'll get to the core of it, but first breakfast. I'm sure you're dying for a cup of coffee. It is your preferred drink, is it not?" *How would he know I'm addicted to caffeine?*

Her mind flicked through data. She'd never mentioned her dependency on the beverage to him, although her gut told her he was every shade of a psycho stalker and more. The man in front of her clearly wasn't the boy she once knew. This man oozed stranger from his pores. The little boy she knew had been sweet, caring and protective. What made him this creepy? She shook her head. Everybody liked coffee. He was probably making reference to the general population and not just her.

"Yes, I'd love a cup of coffee, and since you don't want to give me any details as to why I am here, I'd like to ask something else." She looked at him, making sure her eyes met his, and yes, there was sadness in them. He cast his eyes down.

"And what could you possibly gain from anything I answer," he said, toying with the letter opener on his desk.

Boy, that thing looks a little too sharp. You could skewer someone with that. "Nothing, Hal, just polite conversation and a cup of coffee." She held her best poker face.

"Ask away, but know this, you only get an answer if the question is worth answering."

"So how does one gauge if you'll answer?"

"I'll answer based on whether it is relevant." He clucked his tongue.

God, this guy was a waste of space. This was kindergarten stuff. *Gamoto.*

"I have no recollection of ever being nasty to you or fighting with you. In fact, we were close friends right up until I lost my parents and moved away. What made you hate me, Hal?" She watched as he struggled to form an answer. A tidal wave of emotions twisted across his face.

He opened his mouth to say something, then closed it, then opened it again. "I don't hate you, Carissa. It's that you are a key to a personal endeavor. A topic I don't wish to discuss right now."

"If it involves me, I should know."

"You will know when needed and not before."

Vlaka. She rolled her eyes. Evasion raised her anger meter. "No, I think ..." The library doors opened and she swallowed her words at the sight before her.

A whole team of waiters scurried in and set up breakfast on a round table, another one of Hal's dramatic displays. He was trying to prove something here, other than the obvious—his wealth. No, this advertised his power.

A waiter walked over to where she sat and placed a coffee cup on the table beside her, then proceeded to pour her coffee. She greedily seized the cup when he walked away and gulped down as much of the black liquid as she could without burning her tongue. Her taste buds soon came to life and wanted more of the full-bodied and tasty beverage. *Damn, that's a good drop. If I wasn't in this predicament, maybe I could enjoy this more.*

Hal motioned for her to serve herself from the assortment now spread on the large table to the side. She stood and helped herself to breakfast. The croissants were the only thing that appealed to her. The moment she placed one on her plate, the hair on her neck picked up. Turning slowly, she met Hal's intense stare. A sneaky suspicion that he wanted to fatten her up jabbed at her brain. An eerie scene seized her imagination and catapulted her into the story of *Hansel and Gretel*. It flashed behind her eyelids for a millisecond. She paused mid-bite.

"Why aren't you eating, Hal?"

"Oh. I've had my breakfast, but seeing you eat is pleasurable." His tone deepened.

Dread spread through her. *Sick and demented bastard!* She put her plate down, appetite fleeing.

"What's the matter, is something wrong with the food?" His eyebrows drew together.

"No Hal, the food is fine, but it's odd that you would go to this much trouble for only one person. Do you have a fetish for fuller women?" *Really*. She let out a frustrated breath.

"I have a fetish for many things, Carissa. You will learn that soon enough. Now, if you are done, I have work to do and you can find some entertainment in the room I have made up for you." He waved a hand to his men signaling her removal.

The goons standing inside the doorway made their way over to her.

"Prisoner, huh?" She narrowed her eyes. "Very original."

"You know, you should be happy to be in my presence."

The man seriously needed a lobotomy. "You're an arrogant fuck!" she yelled.

He sneered. "Oh, I'm arrogant and I fuck quite well." He eyed her from top to bottom, his gaze lingering on her breasts.

Whoa. You aren't getting into my pants buddy. Her brain did a somersault.

"If you think that I would jump into bed with you, think again. You lay a finger on me and I'll beat you to a pulp. Sick bastard." Behind her eyelids splotches of red appeared. Anger.

He stood in front of her before she could say anything further. He pulled her head back by her hair. It hurt, but she refused to give him the satisfaction of making a sound or showing any sign of pain.

"Know this, you will submit." Then he kissed her.

Carissa shoved him off her with extreme force. He tumbled backwards taking some of her hair with him. His goons were on her before she could do any physical damage, and boy, did she want to break this guy. Her rage ebbed up another notch.

She broke free from the vise grip holding her back. Only one thing stood in her path and she used it for leverage. Her feet pounded on the coffee table and she dived towards Hal.

With a loud thud, his head connected to the wooden floor. In seconds, she straddled him. Her anger steered every pulse point and muscle in her body. She swung hard and a loud crack sounded at the connection of her fist to his jaw.

"You. Were. My. Friend," she spat out. She wanted to tear him to shreds. Her hands now pulled on the lapels of his suit.

"How ..." Her words died as Hal's goons peeled her off him. "*Vlaka.*" It appeared useless to scream at him because anything she threw at him ricocheted off.

The goon's hands tightened like a vise as he pushed and shoved her upstairs, then dumped her on her ass in a large room. The doors slammed shut and the click of the lock echoed in the room.

"*Skata.* Doesn't look like I'm going any place anytime soon," she muttered as she pushed herself to her feet.

She shouldn't have been outside, but how did they know she'd be standing near the trees? Her cop instincts kicked in. He had someone on the inside watching. If only she could get word to Xen that he had a mole amongst the *Phi.*

She walked over to the window. "Bars. Shit."

Ocean. She could see the water. They were near a beach, but the question hammered in her head—where?

Glancing over to the bed, she saw a pair of jeans and t-shirt neatly placed on it.

"Way to go Carissa, thanks to your stupidity, you're in a mess again." She should have stayed inside the house.

She placed her hand over her tummy. So much for thinking about her pregnancy. She had been reckless in her actions. One thing she remained certain of—Xen's fury would not be pretty.

EIGHTEEN

"Courage is knowing what not to fear." ~ Plato

One tug from Xen and the bookcase dislodged from its secure fastening to the wall. The crash of books and wood echoed around the house and in his ears. Yet it did not bring satisfaction nor help the anger raging within him to subside. He had awoken to the news of Carissa's abduction and ordered everyone out before he started ripping his library to pieces.

"Gamoto."

He ran his hands through his hair and looked at the pile of books sitting among the torn and shredded furniture that was piled in the middle of the library like a huge pyre, waiting to be set alight. Still, the destruction brought no comfort. Killing Hal, who had just one-upped them, would certainly ebb the fury coursing through his veins.

How? Guilt stabbed him in the gut, his chest tightened. His emotions for Carissa had overridden his ability to foresee the real danger she'd been in.

"Never give a sword to a fool or power to an unjust man." He murmured the Greek proverb. He had just given Hal a sword by allowing him the opportunity to pull Carissa out from under his nose. No one took what was his! Time to reclaim the sword.

"Kane!"

He heard the commotion out in the foyer. Kane appeared in the doorway where once was a hinged door to the library. He let out a whistle.

"Are we barbecuing something?"

"I'd rather make it quick and take his head."

"My preference is torture," Kane snarled.

A sneer broke over Xen's lips. "Perhaps I'll hand him over to you. Have you an update?"

"We've gone through the cameras on the street and there's no movement on those, they're clear. The camera pointing to Carissa's backyard shows them coming through a portal near the oak tree. They nabbed Phil too. Our guys moved, but not fast enough."

"You need to find me a *pharmakeia*. Hal is opening these portals with help."

"You know witches are hard to find."

"Kirke owes me. Find her. It's time to collect."

"I'll get one of the men on it. Meanwhile, I think we need to pay my pal Benny Benitti a visit, since he claims to be a descendant of one of the *Nereides*."

"I'm overdue too—for a drink of someone." Xen's fangs pulsed at the thought of un-leashing vengeance.

"And I haven't had a decent bite out of that weasel for a while. I think it's time for a snack," Kane added.

On the drive to the Vrykos pub, Xen contemplated the idea that Carissa was somewhere near the ocean. The fact that Hal was Poseidon's son pointed to the likelihood he'd be near water. The oceanic gods pulled their strength from the sea, so it made sense that Hal would seek a coastal hideout. Ares, even with his anger, was the god of civil order, so it wasn't difficult to see why Carissa chose to be a cop and stayed in Charleston. The fire god loved the heat.

"Our operatives need to check coastal areas, lakeside and riverside too. I have a hunch our man is somewhere near water." Xen's voice fractured the silence in the SUV.

His fingers were already flying over his smart phone.

"Yello," Adam's voice cheerfully danced in the receiver.

"I need you to go upstairs to my room and grab any clothes that belong to Carissa."

"Oooh, do I get to go through the lingerie too?" he teased. Xen growled into the phone. "Sorry, Xen. I was just kidding."

"Get the clothes and no lingerie."

"Not even a bra?"

"Don't tempt me to break your neck, *lykos.*"

"Okay, I got it. No lingerie."

"Clothes only," Xen bit out.

"Thong?"

"*Adam!*" Xen's voice shook and his fangs elongated. He'd choke him just for the hell of it.

"Touchy. Okay, clothes only."

"Have them ready. Summon the other *lykoi* and *Phi*. I'll explain when I get back."

Kane pulled up at the Vrykos pub as Xen ended the call with Adam. They moved quickly from the vehicle to the door.

"Dean," Kane said.

The bouncer lifted his chin to them both and waved his arm to move aside several patrons waiting to get in.

Inside they split to locate Benny the Snitch faster. The rat had a distinct smell about him. Xen followed the scent that got stronger as he got nearer. He noticed Kane had picked up the eloquent perfume and was zeroing in from the other end.

"Benny," Xen sneered and when his eyes met Benny's, the snitch's face paled, the pink of his cheeks turned a chalky shade of white. "Happy to see me?" Xen said with a smirk. Oh, how he loved the smell of fear. Something his true nature never tired of.

The rat made a move to run but ran right into a six-foot-three brick wall of *lykos* muscle.

"Benny, we should stop meeting like this."

"K-Kane, Xen. What are you guys doing here?" Benny's voice shook.

"I needed a drink and Kane needs a bite of something," Xen replied and watched a shiver rake right through Benny. Oh yes, he understood Xen wasn't talking about a beer and a hamburger.

"Ha, ha. You're so funny, Xen. Can I buy you guys a drink? To quench your thirst and all?" Benny gulped.

"No, we'll do you one better." Xen bit out, then let his fangs descend as he leaned closer to make his point. He caught the rapid movement of Benny's eyes.

"We'll buy you one," Kane's rough voice boomed and blended with the loud music.

They ushered him over to a booth. Xen bent and said something to the young couple sitting in the booth. They moved—fast. He nudged Benny in first then sat opposite him, giving him the advantage if he needed to grab him by the throat to enhance his threat.

"No small talk. We want information."

Benny dropped his eyes to his lap then looked back up. "I don't know anything?"

Xen slammed his fist hard on the table, the surface cracked to where the rat he questioned sat. Benny's eyes widened.

"I'll answer what I can, X-Xen." Sweat beaded on his temples.

"How about we start again. Anything peculiar happening with the demons?" Exposing his fangs once again, Xen leaned across the table to make sure his message hit the target.

"There have been whispers."

"What kind?" The question was a growl from Kane.

"Th-they may have teamed up with some rogue vampires and some other guy."

"Who?" Xen asked as he pondered tapping into Benny's mind and thoughts, but didn't—because if he picked up on something he didn't like, he'd kill him right there and then. So for the sake of Benny's somewhat unglamorous life, he decided to spare him today. Tomorrow would be another story.

"I don't know the guy's name, I swear," he bawled. Defeated he dropped his shoulders.

A muscle jumped in Xen's cheek. His eyes narrowed. "Continue," he commanded through clenched jaws.

"There are whispers flying around that this guy—whoever he is—has a secret weapon. He's going to use it."

"Any idea on what this weapon does?" Kane asked.

"Something about power and unleashing demons." He paused. "Can't wait for that."

Xen's resolved melted. Automatically his arm darted out and his fingers tightened around Benny's neck. "Tell me where and spare me your joy for a death wish." He released his grip.

Benny coughed several times before he spoke. "S-something about palms," he said, waving his chubby arms around.

"Think, Benny, or I'll ram my fist down your throat," Kane snarled.

"Ah." He snapped his fingers. "I got it, I got it—the Isle of Palms, the beach."

"Your usefulness tonight has earned you a reward. We'll let you live." Kane slapped him hard on the back. Benny's head fell forward from the force and hit the table.

"Th-thanks." He gulped in relief and rubbed his head.

A waitress made her way to the booth.

"Give him a bottle of your finest champagne." Xen pulled out a couple of hundred dollar bills and threw them on her tray. "The rest is a tip for you." He winked at her. She bowed her head in thanks.

Then he turned to Benny. "Consider your life span extended."

Xen looked at Kane and dropped his thoughts into his mind. We're wasting time. We have to get to Carissa before Hal moves her again.

They stood and left Benny in the booth. The crowd had thickened but they moved through the throng with ease. Xen pushed open the back door to the Vrykos pub and raced down the stairs with Kane. The sound of their boots on the concrete echoed in the quiet alley.

"This alley is usually busy."

"Something smells off." Xen pulled his *xiphos* from under his trench coat. The joy of a prize unfurled across his lips. The unique scent of demon hit his nostrils. He glanced over at Kane to see his coat on the pavement. He had shifted. The *lykos* by his side snarled.

Four demons jumped out in an attempted ambush.

Xen's fangs extended. "Just the party I'd been looking for."

He ran head-on towards two of the demons. His *xiphos* sliced the air with speed, he found the gap he wanted and slit the throat of one demon then turned to his right and drove his blade deep into the heart of the other.

He raced over to where Kane battled with the other demons. One lay dead, the other was in the process of being extinguished.

He pushed his sword into the demon's back while Kane ripped out his throat.

Xen watched as his friend padded over to where he had dropped his clothes, then shifted back to human form.

"Surprise, surprise. I guess I did get to have that bite." Kane's joy was evident as he threw his clothes on.

"Let's move. It's a twenty-five-minute drive to the Isle of Palms and we need to brief the men first."

At the SUV, Kane took the driver's side and floored it all the way back to Xen's house.

"What are you thinking?" Kane asked as they pulled into the entrance of Xen's property.

"Hal's final breath for taking what is mine. His death will give me ejaculatory satisfaction."

Kane's belly laugh engulfed the interior of the car.

He was definitely a stalker and it was obsessional, and psychopathic. Her mind raced as she pulled snippets from her memory on stalkers. They usually fell into one of five distinct categories, but Hal here was a definite exception. There were two she could pin on his chest on a piece of paper, labeled in big writing with a black marker. The first one didn't bother her so much, but the other equaled problem with a capital P.

Obsessive she could handle, but psychopathic drew an entirely different picture. This type of stalker wanted to induce fear and ultimately kill the victim.

A heavy breath escaped her lips. Her fingertips slid on the silk sheets as she pushed herself up from the bed and dawdled towards the bathroom in half a daze. She was going to have to turn the game around if she was to get out alive. The question was how? Maybe all that compulsion mumbo jumbo would work. She splashed water on her face. No, what she really needed was a sword.

The door opened with a loud click. She walked out of the bathroom to find one of Hal's goons standing near the door. A piece of folded paper twisted in his fingers. She looked at the piece of paper he held out to her.

"Read it," he growled, flashing his fangs for effect. He turned and left.

"Interesting," she said to the large room. This guy seemed different from the goons who took her the first time. *Okay, so we have a different Gumbo. So what? Doesn't change your situation, girl.*

She read the note. Her mouth dropped open in disbelief.

"The nerve of this guy." He wanted her to wear the blue dress, blue lingerie and six-inch heels he had placed in the walk-in closet of the room. She had yet to dig around in there. Apparently he wanted her dressed for dinner.

"Not going to happen," she bit out in anger and scrunched up the note. She would not give in to a madman's request, whatever his reasons. She'd dress how she wanted. Besides you couldn't adequately execute a martial arts kick with a fitted dress. Right now, not only did she want to kick Hal's demented head in, she wanted to kick him where it hurt most—his balls.

She sat back down on the bed and waited.

Twenty minutes later the door opened. She was right. Hal's goon was pissed.

"Why aren't you dressed?"

She looked down at her attire then looked back up to the goon. "Something wrong with your vision? I'm wearing clothes." She gestured up and down with her hands. "See."

The goon took three big strides and pulled her up from the bed. His hands were iron around her arms.

"Don't provoke him," he said, his tone low and warning. This was new. The other goons never spoke to her unless they were swearing at her.

"Hands off, Gumbo, or I'll kick you in the balls." Twisting her body, she tried to break free.

His grip tightened. "You'll regret it," he said in a tight voice, then let his hands fall away from the vise they held her in. He stepped aside. "Ladies first," he said with a sweeping gesture of his arm.

"Really," she huffed. Gumbo did not appear to be what she'd expected.

As they walked out of the room and down the stairs, her mind galloped with a number of scenarios for an escape plan. They were all stupid and pointless and would probably get her killed, but a girl had to try. As part of her ploy she descended the staircase with labored steps, using the time to scan below and take in as much as possible. *Hallelujah!* Long metal candleholders sat on the side table by the front door. *I could whack Gumbo over the head with one of those.*

"Don't get any demented ideas," the low breathy voice said close to her ear. Startled, she grabbed hold of the banister and stopped a few steps from the bottom.

"You scared me." She turned to look up at Gumbo.

"You should pay attention."

"Listen, Gumbo, my attention span is no business of yours."

"Wrong."

"Wrong?"

"Your lack of attention to the obvious will get you killed."

She bit back the bile rising up her throat. He had a point. Her behavior was a little sloppy. *Must be all that hormonal skata.* She turned and her feet tapped down the last few stairs. At the bottom, Gumbo pushed her past the library and to a large dining room.

Seated at the table was Hal.

"Carissa," he said looking up from the smartphone that he held in his hand.

"Evening." Her voice hitched an octave too high. Gumbo pulled out a chair for her. Maybe there was hope for Gumbo. At least his manners were a teensy-weensy bit better.

"Wonder if he has a real name?" she mumbled.

"Gumbo is fine." A glint of humor danced in his eyes. And just like that he was back to the grouchy Gumbo. Her internal radar spiked. *Who is this guy?*

"I hope you're hungry?" Hal asked, breaking her internal inquisition on Gumbo.

"Not overly, but I will pick at something." Going for honesty rather than entertaining Hal's little charade here seemed to be the logical course of action.

She placed her napkin in her lap and looked across the room, avoiding any eye contact with him because looking at him would only anger her more. A plate was placed in front of her. Steak. They ate in silence. As far as she was concerned trying to pry information out of him was a total time-suck.

When the dessert arrived, the temptation to devour the chocolate pudding proved to be a challenge. She feigned indifference and pushed it around her plate. Her instinct screamed that every meal with Hal was the last supper.

"Well, aren't you going to probe tonight?" he said, breaking the silence.

"Actually, no."

She caught him studying her for a minute. "Why the sudden change, Carissa?"

"I've asked you more than once. It's fruitless and I won't waste any more of my energy on you, Hal. It's a dead-end street and let's leave it at that."

"Actually, it's not a dead end, Carissa, because you will give me multiple avenues through your sacrifice."

"Sacrifice?" Baffled she looked at him, willing her brain to understand the meaning. "What do you mean?" she asked, puzzled.

"You will be my sacrifice to the gods. I will use your life to gain power."

She let out a hysterical laugh. A rock settled in the pit of her stomach. She grabbed the glass of water from the table and downed half of it.

"Gods, power ..." She trailed off. "... are you insane, Hal?"

"The demons will have their feast on humanity once I combine my power with yours."

"Now I know you're completely unhinged. I have no power, Hal. Didn't you get that memo?"

"And that is where you are wrong, daughter of Ares."

Gamoto, how did he know? Her head swam in facts, moments, words and conversations. Everything spun as she tried to achieve clarity. None of this was anything to celebrate, but at least it confirmed her suspicion that she wouldn't be walking out of Hal's clutches alive.

"You will be disappointed when you kill me. It will be for nothing." The man was a lunatic. Demons feasting on humanity, when had he started hating the world?

"NO. It is you who will be crestfallen because I know your power. Your foolish father was an idiot to hide you and what you are, but I know and have known for a long time."

Fancy that, this loony knows more about me than I do. How does that work? "You're crazy. And what will you kill me with,

Hal? Some magical dagger on an altar? Sounds like you're out of luck there."

He burst out laughing. The laugh sent a shiver through her body. "You might be partially right—definitely on a Greek altar and definitely with a dagger, but you won't be sacrificed here. I'm moving you to the land of the gods tomorrow."

She stood up, knocking her chair back. Her vision blurred. Red rage filled her eyes. She grabbed the spoon from her discarded dessert and lunged for him. Powerful arms intercepted her attack. "Not a smart move," Gumbo spoke into her ear. She whipped her head back and got him in the nose. The bastard didn't flinch.

"Remove her from here!" Hal yelled.

Gumbo threw her over his shoulder like a caveman and sped her up the stairs. Why didn't she think faster? She should have pocketed a knife during dinner.

"Put me down." Her fists crashed into his back.

"Your wish is my command." Gumbo sat her down on the floor of her temporary room. He crouched in front of her. "You have a strong desire to bring your expiration date forward. What were you thinking?" He stood, turned and walked out, locking her in again.

A lump formed in her throat. She pulled her legs up to her chest and wrapped her arms around them, slowly rocking on the floor. *I'm going to die and so will the life that is inside me.* There would be no way Xen would be able to track her now, not with Hal moving her to Greece.

Her eyes watered and tears burned a path down her face. "I'm sorry, Xen," she choked out in a stutter.

NINETEEN

*"Hunger fights castles and hunger
surrenders castles." ~ Greek proverb*

Carissa sensed Xen's emotions the precise moment a shattering roar reached her ears, startling her out of her sleeping position on the floor.

She heard a voice in her mind. *"Carissa."*

"Xen?"

"Yes, koukla. Where are you?"

"Upstairs."

A tingle of anticipation raced through her body. She took a few quick breaths. He was here. Xen had come for her. There was no time to waste. She lifted herself up off the floor as the door to the room splintered from the hinges.

There, dressed in black, stood one angry immortal. The sword in his hand only added to the menacing look on his face. He looked like an avenging angel.

"Xen, behind you!"

He turned in time. Gumbo's sword never connected.

Recognition flashed on Gumbo's face, and he stopped before he executed his strike.

"Xen," Gumbo said, the corners of his mouth turning up in recognition. He leaned in for a man hug.

"Tithon." Xen slapped Gumbo on the back.

Carissa's feet decided they would unglue from the spot she was frozen in. She raced to Xen in a few steps.

"You know each other?" Her voice shook.

"*Koukla*, yes, but that story is for later. Right now, I have to get you out of here." He sheathed his sword to his back.

She nodded approval and watched as he looked into Gumbo's eyes to communicate telepathically. Xen voiced his last words out loud.

"She's mine, and I won't let anything befall her or my child."

"That's not possible for our kind." Gumbo wasn't buying the baby conception by Xen.

"You wouldn't believe it if I told you." They did the telepathy thing again.

"Then she must be special, so must the life that grows inside her," Gumbo said with a grin. His eyes diverted to her for a second. She didn't know whether to like him or punch him.

"More later." Xen grabbed Carissa around the waist, his lips descended on hers. Her body became soft and relaxed. His tongue probed hers in a scorching kiss. When he broke away, she was sure no bones existed in her body.

Loud grunts echoed from the stairs below.

"Hal has Phil, but I don't know where." She had been too busy having her own pity party to think about where they might have put him.

"Do you know where he's keeping the *lykos* Phil?" Xen asked Tithon.

"There is no wolf on the premises. I would have picked up his scent," Tithon replied. Something passed silently between them.

"Let's move." Xen lifted her in his arms then sped down the stairs. Gumbo was directly behind.

A hoard of demons at the bottom of the stairs blocked their path. Xen's men fought them. A wolf tore at the neck of one.

Tithon forced his way between them, clearing the path. Xen took the small gap afforded to him and raced to the library entrance. In the mayhem Carissa didn't know where to look. The scene had all the makings of a dance party with swords and wolves. Xen put her on her feet and then pushed her behind him.

"Give me a sword," she yelled.

"Cute, *koukla,* but we don't have time for lessons."

A demon came at him. Xen's reflexes were faster. The head of the demon rolled to the ground.

"Okay, I'll leave the head-chopping to you."

"Xen," Tithon called as he cleared the way to the front door.

Xen backed Carissa out the front door. His sword pointed at a few demons in front of him. He swung it and jabbed at them. "Where the hell are they coming from?" she asked.

"That's exactly where they are coming from."

"But ..." Her words disintegrated on her lips. Someone pulled her backwards. One hand covered her mouth. She fought against the grip and sunk her teeth into Gumbo's hand. *Double-crosser.*

She let out a piercing scream. He continued to back away with her and from the corner of her eye, she caught Hal coming for her.

Xen turned and met her eyes. There was sorrow in them. Anger replaced the sorrow when he spotted Hal. He sped towards her, but there was no way he could reach her. She was sucked into another portal.

She managed to yell out, "Sacrifice in Greece."

Blackness danced in her eyes.

Xen pulled back his lips and exposed his fangs. His veins and muscles tightened under his skin. Pressure raced up from the dark fissure of his stomach to his esophagus. The monster inside him released a guttural roar. The control gauge that kept the beast at bay flashed to an unstable and vicious level.

His mind transported him to Ancient Messenia. "*Alala*!" The battle cry vibrated from his chest and rage and adrenaline punched every cell of his body. With his sword unsheathed, he stabbed and slashed, decapitating every demon in a whirl of fury. More heads dropped. Warmth spread through his chest in satisfaction, but this did not give him the retribution he craved.

When he had unburdened the outside of the premises of demon vermin, he proceeded inside where some of his *Phi* fought with demons and rogue vampires. He spotted Adam fighting a rogue vampire in wolf form. He'd taken a couple of bites out of the demon and sat ready to pounce for his jugular. Xen stepped in, and with one swipe, the demon's head rolled to the floor. His ears were met with silence.

He looked around at his men and raised an eyebrow. His lips twitched in gratification.

The wolves shifted back to human form. One of the men sped into the room and threw clothes at the now naked wolves. Even in human form, they were faster than the average man. Adam finished dressing first.

"Fuck Xen, that *malaka* was mine to take down.'"

"Too slow," he growled.

The quietude in the room from the *Phi* told Xen that the savage within him was not contained. He willed his fangs to retract and passed his *xiphos* to Kane. An act to show his men he was still in control and would not harm them in his current state. One they'd never witnessed before. The beast inside subsided to a dark corner. Carissa's abduction pushed his emotions to levels he hadn't endured since he was human.

He watched Kane motion for the men to leave. When they were outside he spoke.

"Xen, I need to know you can see this through."

"I want his head."

"What happened?"

"He pulled her through another portal. She screamed the words sacrifice and Greece. I think you can understand my rage."

"Fuck."

"The only comfort I have is that Tithon was with her."

"Tithon? What the fuck?" Confusion held Kane's face.

"Yes, apparently someone has put a high bounty on Hal and that someone wants him alive. Tithon is waiting for the right opportunity to drag his prize away from the demons."

Kane's eyes widened at his admission. He let out a loud whistle before a smirk lifted at the corner of his mouth. "Well ain't that something? Who would have thought that someone has a price tag on that pesky demi-god's head? And who would have thought that they would call in the best bounty hunter to deliver the goods." He let out a laugh before handing Xen's *xiphos* back.

"I'd say lethal," Xen blew out. His demeanor and rage finally subsided.

"No, you got that wrong. He's professional. You are the one who is death-dealing, especially after what I just witnessed."

Xen flipped the blood-drenched *xiphos* in his hands and let the words of his *lykos* friend sink in.

"They took my woman. No one is going to sacrifice my wife and child."

"Child?" Kane's eyes met Xen's. "How is that possible?"

"She is a daughter of a god. Anything is possible."

"Why didn't you tell the men how much is at stake here, Xen? This changes the game." Kane's voice rose.

"I would have preferred to make the announcement over a celebration of drinks. I had just been given the news myself, only to have them both snatched away." Xen ran his hand through his bloodied and messed-up hair. "The other bad news is that Phil is missing. According to Tithon, Hal either moved or disposed of him."

Kane let out a growl. "Let's roll, boss. We need to find us a lame-assed demi-god and barbecue him Greek style. Like a lamb on the spit with plenty of lemon juice."

"Stop salivating, *lykos*. That would be too good a death. He needs to suffer," he sneered.

Outside, the men were grouped and waiting.

"If you don't mind, Xen, I'll go first." Kane wanted to address the *Phi* first.

"The honors are all yours," he said, as he flipped his *xiphos* in his hand.

"We have a problem and it's bigger than Houston." Kane turned to Xen. "With your permission?" Xen nodded. "The situation is delicate ..."

Xen interrupted Kane. "I probably should have told you when we set out on this little mission, Carissa is pregnant with my child."

A gasp or two came from the men. Urgency filled their features. Every set of eyes bored directly into his as he looked around at his men.

Adam spoke. "I've seen a lot of things—not nearly as much as you, Xen—but this takes the cake." He, too, let out a long whistle. "Okay, we need to get back to base."

"Before we do, you should also know that when they dragged Carissa through the portal, she said something about a sacrifice. Hal, the sick fuck, wants to kill my woman." Postures stiffened, shoulders squared, and jaws tightened. He knew that look too well as he wore it often. His men were readying themselves.

"Let's move out." Kane yelled.

Booted feet took off for their vehicles.

Xen was left standing alone. He tipped his head back and let out a yell that vibrated all around him. The beast in him wanted retribution. No one took what was his.

Blue-grey eyes stared down at her. Carissa's eyes closed, then awareness spiked, shooting adrenaline through every nerve in her body. Recognition dawned. She sat up and delivered her best right hook. Gumbo fell backwards at the surprise punch. Pain raided her fist. She shook it. It hurt, but connecting with Gumbo's face, marble as it was, brought her immense gratification. "Gods and goddesses, that felt fantabulous."

Gumbo found his voice after the unpleasant surprise.

"Well, hello to you, too." He rubbed his jaw.

She could have sworn he was smirking, the *malaka*. Pity it couldn't have been a harder and more damaging punch.

"Why?" She needed to hear why he'd pulled her through the portal when only moments before it looked like he and Xen had some sort of an understanding.

He stood back up and moved closer to where she sat on the bed. "The reasons are many and cannot be discussed here, but I will swear I will do my best to keep you safe until Xen locates us. I don't want to face his wrath, but we do have a conflict of interest where Hal is concerned. I want him alive and Xen wants him dead."

"I see, but I have to say that I'm keen on Xen's idea."

He stuck out his hand. "Friends."

She eyed him for a minute before placing her hand in his to shake. "I'm also not going to apologize for hitting you—that, you deserved."

"I don't expect an apology."

"Good, because it helped me vent some of that frustration I've been holding." A long breath escaped her lips.

His mouth twitched. "You are a bit of a firecracker."

"So why are you here, Gumbo?"

"Much to my dislike, I have to take you to Hal who is waiting in a car outside."

"Where are we, by the way?" she asked.

"Motel near the airport."

"Why not use a portal straight to Greece?" she queried.

"Doesn't work that way. You can only travel in short distances and to move all the way to Greece that way would take over a week and lots of spells and energy. Something that is not easy to come by." He waited. "Sorry about back there, but there's more to this than I can explain."

"I'm sure there is." She got to her feet. "Take me to the great demented pooh-bah."

Gumbo let out a laugh.

Hal didn't only epitomize the characteristics of a madman hell-bent on getting what he wanted, he refined them, so they fitted him like a glove. He had enough manpower to succeed in his pathetic attempt to achieve what he thought would bring him godly power.

With her heart heavy, she wished she had enough knowledge on how to use her own powers. She wondered whether she would be successful in using what Xen had shown her in his library with Kane. Would it work against the demons? If she could compel them, maybe she'd have a fighting chance. By the gods, she would not give up without a fight. All this daughter of Ares, God of War, business was wearing thin on her.

Gumbo stopped at the door. "Word of warning—no jumping across tables or trying to choke him."

"Scout's honor." She raised her hand palm out and held down her little finger with her thumb, showing the universal three-finger salute. He laughed thickly, from deep in his throat.

"Let's see if we can work a way out of this. But first, Hal."

"Showtime," she said as he walked her out to the far end of the motel, to the waiting limo. She climbed in the back with her least favorite person, who was smiling. *Idiot.* The man Hal had become had no resemblance to the echo of the boy she once knew. This man, she loathed. What she wouldn't give to have her gun. Would she shoot? Hell yeah, but not to kill. She'd definitely put him out of action, but Xen would not be as merciful.

"Well hello, Carissa. Glad you could join us in the land of the living on this exciting evening." His voice dripped with sarcasm and she knew why. The cocky asshole thought he'd one-upped Xen.

"How about you let me go home? This is stupid. Surely we can work out something that would benefit both of us."

"There's nothing to work out. I need you, so here you are."

"Hal. You. Are. Not. Listening. Whatever it is you think I have, I don't have it." She lifted her chin and her nostrils flared.

"No, Carissa. It is you who lacks attention. If you believed in yourself, you would know that you have power. All demi-gods have power. Yours is compulsion and I worked that out a long time ago, but you refuse to accept it."

"My father ..."

"Your father was a fool to hide your power, and you were a fool to involve yourself with that parasite, Xen," he spat.

"Who I involve myself with is none of your goddamn business." Her hands clenched on the leather seat.

"Wrong! You were and are my business because your power will be mine." His eyes flashed red and for a split second he reminded her of Judge Doom from *Roger Rabbit*.

"You know, Hal, regardless of how much power you think you're going to wield, you are not exempt from being eliminated. Immortality requires the skill of staying alive without having a blade slice your pathetic throat."

He paused and then in a loud voice, he shot out his words. "Look around you, Carissa. Your lover failed to extract you from my clutches. I have an unlimited supply of demons, therefore it makes getting close to me difficult. Surely you've noticed that. Hasn't the police force taught you to pay closer attention?"

She cracked her neck, pulled her lips back and went straight for his throat. "You"—she'd show him how easily she could get to him—"son of a ...." The door of the limo was yanked open and in seconds, she was pulled out.

"Let me go, Gumbo." The door of the limo slammed shut and the window came down. Hal stuck his head out.

"You can kiss your sweet life goodbye," he sneered at her. "And your precious cargo too."

She fought Tithon, but it was no use, his tight grip held her in place. The limo took off and Gumbo pushed her back towards the motel. She stopped fighting and he let go.

"Didn't we say behave?" he said in a mocking tone.

"With that *vlaka*? Impossible." She cast a thumb over her shoulder in the direction the limo had sped off in. Shooting him would be too good, gutting him would be better, but deep down she knew he'd intentionally provoked her.

A multitude of images flashed in her head, like her shooting Hal, but it would be over too soon. Making him suffer tasted more inviting. She wanted to kick Hal's ass.

"Carissa, Xen will find you. Trust me, I've known the man a long time. He has never, and I repeat, *never* considered any woman his. Besides, you carry his child, so he will raise Hell on Earth to get to you. We vampires are possessive, and we don't like it when someone tries to harm what is ours."

"Can't you just, you know, sneak out and call him, and tell him where we are?"

"I'm afraid, I can't. You see, the thing about working with Hal means no outside communication. That way there's less chance of anyone betraying him."

She digested that for a minute or two.

"I will do whatever I can to stall him," he said.

"Thank you, Gumbo or Tithon?"

"Tithon, but if you prefer Gumbo to keep the charade up, that's fine." He paused. "Why Gumbo?" he asked.

"I don't know. It just sort of popped into my head. I thought you were one of Hal's rogue goons. The last lot were vermin. I even managed to stab Tweedledee in the eye with a fork."

He let out a loud laugh. "Nice, but a definite suicide move."

"Well, if Xen doesn't ...." She swallowed. "You think he'll find me?"

"Xen's been around a mighty long time and so have his men. They will find you."

"Thanks, Tithon. I guess you will be standing guard for what's left of this evening. I promise to let you know if I'm planning to stab you or make a run for it."

His mouth turned up and in a flash she was left in the shabby room. She headed straight for the bed and dropped onto it, face first. *This whole situation sucks. MEGA.*

TWENTY

"When you do what you can,
you do what you must." ~ Greek Proverb

"Where do you want to start, Xen?" Adam threw the question out when they were all assembled in the living room. The library remained a pile of wood and books from Xen's earlier outburst.

Xen lifted his chin in acknowledgement to Jones when he walked through to the living area. The young *lykos* returned the gesture. Most of the men stood, save for Kane and Adam who were stretched out on the couch. Time to get on with business.

"I need some of the *Phi* at the airport. As I said earlier, Hal plans to move Carissa to Greece where he will sacrifice her and my child."

"Wait, did you just say child?" Jones inquired.

"Yes."

"How?" Jones asked.

Xen let out a long breath. Time to spill the rest about his bride, not something he liked to do. "For those of you who don't know, Carissa is a demi-god and the daughter of Ares."

Silence followed. All the sound in the room had been sucked out and with it all the air. They all stood in what appeared to be a vacuum. And then Xen spoke and blew air and sound back into the room.

"She has powers, but they have been bound by Ares. With them, she could probably defend herself; without them ..." A grim darkness settled into his bones. "... I fear the worst."

"Then why are we wasting valuable time?" Jones challenged.

"The *lykoi* will need rest. That includes you, Jones. I can't expect you all to keep going around the clock. The rest of the *Phi* will move out with Paris." He looked over to see if his soldier was clear. "Anything that moves in or out of the public and private airports, I want to know. Give me a complete list of flights to Greece. Get our technical eyes onto every network. Notify me when you have the men in place."

"I will report as soon as we are in position." Paris confirmed. The men filed out of the lounge, leaving Kane and Jones behind.

"Jones, we need your inside intelligence," Xen said.

"I'm onto it. I've just texted two detective vamp boys to make their way to Charleston International. Better to have them scouting the passengers at close range."

"Fast thinking, pup," Kane remarked from where he sat.

Jones let out a little growl. Xen understood that Kane's jibes always got the young *lykos* aggravated. "If that's all." He was already moving through the door.

"So where in Greece do you think this vermin will do the deed?"

"The only place an Ancient Greek sacrifice can bear any significance whatsoever is in a *naos*. Everything leads me to believe he is headed to the Temple of Poseidon at Sounion."

"What do you think he will gain out of this?"

"Your guess is as good as mine, because sacrifice in Ancient Greece had always been about appeasing the gods. The question is, why does he need to satisfy any of the Olympian gods with Carissa's life?"

Xen walked over to a tray with scotch and glasses. A small bar fridge sat under the side table. He pulled it open and dug out some ice. "Drink?" he asked.

"I'd say we need one."

The amber liquid splashed over the ice. He placed both glasses on a tray that contained an oval dish then walked over to Kane and handed him his glass.

Kane lifted one eyebrow as he eyed the volume in the glass. "Now you're thinking along my lines when it comes to drinking."

Xen took his glass in hand and placed the oval bowl on the coffee table. Then dropped his weight on the couch opposite Kane. They held out their glasses over the oval dish.

"*Stous theous*—to the gods," they said, then poured some of the scotch into the oval dish as libation to the gods.

"What now?" Kane queried as he pulled the glass from his lips.

"Now we prepare for Greece on the assumption that they've slipped through our fingers. The Temple of Poseidon at Sounion is our first stop. See if we can get the *Phi* and *lykoi* in Greece to start surveillance."

"Are you sure that's where he'll be?"

"Poseidon's son can only gain more attention and power if he sacrifices on the altar of his father's temple."

"Then we have to make sure he doesn't make that flight," Kane added.

"That's what I'm aiming for." Xen's jaw clenched. Hal would die by his sword, this he promised himself.

His phone beeped with an incoming text message. He set his glass on the coffee table and stood. His fingers tugged at the phone in his back pocket, pulling it out. The message was from Paris.

> Paris: Men in position at all locations. Hacking into their security system as we speak. Will update you when I have something.

"Paris and his men are in place," he advised Kane, then leaned over, grabbed his scotch, and threw it back in one go.

The amber liquid slid down his throat in a quick burn. It wasn't enough. Even if he downed the whole bottle, it would not burn enough to stay the guilt that coursed through him. He'd let Carissa down, and he'd also let down the little life growing inside her—his unborn child.

He stood and paced back and forth while Kane watched him from his seat on the couch.

"We'll get them, Xen. Stop worrying. You know he can't travel via portal to Greece. Once there, it's a different story, but it's a no-go from here. The only way he can get there is by plane."

"Any news on the witch Kirke?"

"Nothing. No one has seen or heard from her in months. You know what witches are like, if they don't want to be found, they stay invisible."

"Not this one. She likes to live on the edge."

"I'll chase the boys in the morning. See if they can trace any communication."

"I think you should rest for a few hours."

"I might take you up on that offer. Wake me if anything urgent comes through." Kane stood and headed to the door.

Best that his *lykos* friend sleep. Tomorrow, he was betting, things would definitely escalate to unimaginable proportions. They'd have to fight more demons. Hal had an endless supply and the only way they could plug the portals would be with magic.

"Kane," he said as the *lykos* reached the door.

"Yeah?"

"Thanks."

"You'd do the same for me."

"Of that, there is no question." He stopped pacing and dropped to the couch.

What would Hal gain by sacrificing Carissa to the gods? Human sacrifices were a rare thing. Animals were customarily used in sacrifice in Ancient Greece. He should know because he'd lived it. His life and home stemmed from there before his immortality. He pulled his phone out of his pocket again. His fingers flew over the buttons.

Xen: Lox. Any news?

Lox: It's complicated at my end, but you should know portals are being opened with the aid of a witch.

Xen: I've discovered this already. Any idea on their current location and where they might have popped out?

Lox: Negative. Trying some other sources.

Xen: Grateful.

Why was it so hard to track down one demi-god? He stared down at his phone, raised his arm, and threw it across the room. It splintered against the plaster on the wall.

TWENTY-ONE

"The secret of happiness is freedom.
The secret of freedom is courage." ~ Thucydides

The carpet in the dingy motel room was worn down to its base yellow thread. The appalling shade did nothing to enhance the seventies-looking furniture. She scrutinized the peeling lacquer on the armchairs. The bed looked no better.

"Probably full of bedbugs and dust mites and who knows what else," she muttered.

A light tapping noise at the door startled her out of her disgust. Her spine straightened. She took a step forward, the urge to investigate rushing through her veins. She was a police officer first, after all. Curiosity slapped her hard. Her feet began to move towards the door, but she didn't reach it because it exploded from its hinges and came down with a loud crash. And there sprawled on his back was Tithon. She ran to his side.

"What happened?"

"Attacked by some fairy," he answered.

Astonished, her brain churned the information as coherent words failed to form.

"You can't be serious. You're a badass vampire."

"I would not kid you about something like this," he said through gritted teeth.

"Okay, the fairy kicked your ass. Why?"

"She was angry at me." He paused, closing his eyes. "I stood her up."

Carissa looked down at him in disbelief. "A fairy attacked you because you stood her up. One for the lady. Wouldn't mind a chat with her. I like that she kicked your sorry ass."

Tithon let out a laugh. "Trust me, you don't want to mess with a pissed-off fairy."

"I never said I'd mess with her. I said I'd chat with her."

"No ... don't think that would work."

"Well, are you hurt?" She looked for any visible stab wounds. He didn't appear to have any blood on him.

"No, I'm fine. Trust her to fucking turn up here."

"And who exactly is she?"

"A double-crossing, two-faced, money-hungry fairy. She's not even worthy of a name."

She eyed him suspiciously. "Uh-huh. Look who's calling the kettle black."

"I am not like her. I at least deliver on all my promises, unless of course something goes sour. Fucking fairies!"

"Hmm looks like 'sour' is the key word here. So we have a very pissed-off fairy." She gave him her hand to help him up off his back.

"Thanks." He took the offered help. Not that he needed it. She knew he could spring to his feet without assistance. "Oh, and let's keep this incident between the two of us."

"My lips are sealed, Gumbo."

He let out a laugh as he walked over to salvage what was left of the door. "You really do like that name, don't you?"

"I think it suits you."

She watched him try and put the door back. A spark of an idea travelled through her body. She clasped her hands. Maybe she could convince him to help her get away.

"I've been thinking," he said.

Damn right, so had she. Music to her ears at last.

"They are going to move you in an hour. By then it will be almost time for rejuvenation for me, so I'm going to try and get a message across to Xen. No promises of delivery because I'm not Mr. Popular, as you have noticed." The corners of his mouth turned up.

"No, I guess the fairies missed the memo about your fame. Besides, the getting thrown through the door business just proves your lack of awesomeness." Her gut instinct told her that the fairy didn't want to get all hot and heavy with him. On the contrary, she was certain that his lack of popularity extended to other creatures too, not just the said fairy. "So how do you propose to get word?"

"Not by any conventional methods, if you get my drift." He waggled his eyebrows and gave her a lopsided grin.

"Actually no, I don't get your drift." She frowned, her mind racing, trying to work out what he meant. "What method?"

His lips quirked up cheerfully. He, too, had that twist-your-panties-in-a-knot smile, like both Kane and Xen. The fairy must have been pissed about something more than Tithon standing her up. Men, whether mortal or immortal, didn't get why women occasionally lost their heads over little things. Tithon didn't work with Xen, but she would bet a fair bit of moola that he'd been wronged somewhere and preferred his own brand of justice—whatever that involved. She speculated, but had nothing solid.

"Darlin', you need to reconsider what you know about pre-technology methods. Did anyone ever teach you how the ancients communicated?" He gave her a penetrating stare.

"Come to think of it, my uncle Greg believes the Greeks invented everything." A recollection of past images flashed through her head. Every Sunday she'd been subjected to long and torturous hours of his drivel. "I give credit where credit is due, but my uncle was very biased." One particular story rushed to the forefront. "I remember something about giving a guy a verbal message and making him run somewhere to deliver it. Didn't someone die doing that?" she asked, scrunching her eyebrows together.

"Phidippides—he ran all the way from Athens to Sparta then back again in two days, then from Marathon to Athens to announce victory over the Persians at Marathon. The marathon run is held in his honor," Tithon supplied.

She pondered what he'd said, then shook her head.

"No, no, no. You can't possibly mean ..."

Tithon was nodding in approval.

She squealed at the ridiculous suggestion.

He stuck a finger to his lips to shush her. "Yes," he said quietly.

"Silly Greek immortals." They could certainly get with the times. "Can't you send a text? I mean that's normal, it's speedier."

"No can do, sweetheart. Told you that before. No phones allowed around Hal. He's got everyone watching like a hawk, and the fact that I've been in here talking with you this long, isn't good either. So, it's been fun, but I must shoot. See you tomorrow." He winked, moved the door, and then sped out of the room.

She laughed at his feeble attempt to put the door back. "Like that's really going to help."

Pity the fairy didn't hang around for introductions. Carissa believed the said fairy would have been able to get a message to Xen a lot faster than Gumbo's marathon runner.

She'd take what help she could, in any shape or form. It was pointless arguing or killing the help—even if she thought it ridiculous and outdated. "Next thing they'd be sending up smoke signals." She laughed at her own joke.

Walking to the bathroom, she eyed the ghastly shade of pink tiles on the wall. At least there appeared to be no mold in the shower; she had her limits. She opted out of a shower and splashed some water on her face to freshen up a little. Then waited for Hal to make an appearance.

Her predicament and the whole demi-god nonsense irked her every time her thoughts slipped into that whole otherworld existence. She'd been brave so far but, heck, inside she clawed at her fear, trying to keep it from bursting out and making her a sobbing mess.

Calling her father wasn't an option. Zeus had forbidden them from visiting the mortal realm. She clenched her jaw as annoyance bubbled up to the surface. If it had not been for her accidental encounter with Xen and demons, she would still be clueless. She stood and walked over to the window and threw out a one-two punch to soothe her anger.

Looking out, she mumbled, "Rosy-fingered Eos in all her brightly colored hues." Dawn, with all its brightness, gave her hope. "Maybe I could try some of that compulsion mumbo jumbo when they come to move me."

Xen was pleased when she'd compelled Kane. So why not practice her newly discovered skill? Hal would not spare her, no matter how much she begged or tried to reason. Actually, trying to talk to him only resulted in her wanting to throttle him every time. No, she needed a plan. An idea started to formulate in her mind.

The door came flying down for the second time that morning and brought her out of her muddled musings. Hal strutted in with takeaway coffee and a bag of donuts. His ugly goons walked in after him. One took his position near the door, the other walking deep into the room so he was behind her as she faced Hal.

Wow, this is different for him. He usually travelled with his chef, largely because of his arrogance and his need to prove something. The smell of coffee hit her nose, making her taste buds water.

"Well, well, what happened here?" he asked.

She had forgotten to get a story together with Gumbo so she opted for what was safest, a clumsy lie.

"Gumbo tripped over a mop bucket and came hurtling through the door. Your cronies are built like a block of apartments and those doors are paper thin."

Hal looked at her like she had grown another head. Yeah, it sounded ridiculous, but hey, things like that happened all the time.

"If you don't believe me, ask Gumbo when you see him next." She shrugged her shoulders.

Hal gave her another look. "Oh, I intend to, and let's hope you haven't attacked another of my vampires."

"I swear I didn't stab him or gouge his eyes out, although I would have loved to. Seeing that vampires can recover from such small hurts, it would have been fun just for the hell of it," she added smugly.

"Very well." He handed her a cup of coffee and the bag of donuts then sat on the bed.

Hope you get fleas or something, she thought when he sat down. She wasn't game enough to try the bed. She was famished and didn't waste any time diving in for a donut. She devoured the first one without breathing, only managing a slight pause to take a sip of coffee.

"Thanks, Hal." Manners were manners, right? And you didn't bite the hand that fed you till after you ate. "Coffee is good. So are the donuts," she managed between bites and gulps of coffee. *May be my last so I might as well savor it.*

"It's time for a trip back to the motherland, Carissa. Have you ever visited Greece?"

"No." The muffled answer escaped behind the last piece of donut she shoved into her mouth.

"Well, then you will be pleasantly surprised. It's beautiful. Pity I won't have time to show you all the ancient sites."

"I don't really need a holiday, Hal. I was having one when you decided to kidnap me the first time."

"Those pesky police wolves made it difficult."

Her posture stiffened. The first person that popped into her head was Jones. She hoped he wasn't in any danger from Hal's cronies.

"Thank you for the coffee and donuts. Best I've ever had."

Walking over to the trash can, she dumped the empty bag and coffee cup.

"We have a flight to catch." He stood and made his way to the door.

"Before we go, Hal ... one more question?"

"Make it quick," he snapped, turning at the door.

"How do your demon goons not attract attention in broad daylight?"

"You're a smart girl. I'm sure you'll work it out."

"What I would give to use some of that compulsion hocus-pocus on you," she breathed to herself.

One of Hal's ugly goons stepped up behind her and tied her hands behind her back. She didn't know which was worse, the sight of him or the fact he'd touched her hands. She swallowed back the bile that threatened to rise. No, she'd stay calm and in control. That way she could assess the best time to try some hocus-pocus on these demons. Her bindings were rope. A bonus. A memory flashed from when she was a kid; she used to get her cousins to tie her hands and see if she could get out of it. She called herself little Houdini. *This should be a piece of cake.*

The goon pushed her toward the waiting vehicles. The door opened and her body hit the back seat. Hal rode in the vehicle in front. Her chest expanded as relief washed over her that she'd be alone and wouldn't have to endure his weird conversations. Silently, she uttered a thank-you to the gods.

The two goons rode in the front. *Showtime.* She tried not to wince as she struggled against her bound wrists. The rope chafed her skin. It would be raw by the time she'd done her Houdini trick. By the time the vehicles hit the main road she'd pulled her hands free. To keep the goons from noticing, she kept her hands behind her back.

Carissa had no real way of knowing whether her attempt at compulsion would work on these ghastly goons, but it was worth a try. She waited for the signs indicating the turn for the airport then started her mental chant. *You will keep going, you will not turn. You will keep going, you will not turn.* She kept the chant up for a few seconds.

To her complete surprise, the goon drove past the exit for the airport. They were no longer following Hal's car. The compulsion had worked. They turned onto Dorchester Road, away from Charleston International Airport. Her chant changed to Xen's address. Once she had them there, Kane could deal with the goons.

The car was heading towards the turnoff for Xen's house, when the game changed. The CB radio installed in the car went off like an alarm bell, breaking the compulsion she had the goons under. Seeing it as an opportunity, in a rush she leaned over and tried to snatch the gun from Goon Two's hands. Her fingers wrapped around the gun. They struggled as the car swerved when Goon One tried to shake her off Goon Two. The gun went off and Goon Two roared as the bullet tore through the skin on his thigh.

He turned. She saw his fist coming, but her body did not react in time. His punch landed directly on her nose. She fell back in her seat as pain tore through her head. A swish sounded and thick glass went up between her and the goons. They looked back at her. *Assholes.* Her nose throbbed and her eyes watered. Dizziness loomed, but she leaned back and tried to ride the wave of it.

Guess a trip to Greece is in my horoscope after all.

Fifteen minutes later, they were at the airport and she was being torn out of the car and pushed towards what looked like a private plane. It would be a hell of a ride with Hal. She folded her arms across her stomach. A tingling started in her chest. She sent a silent prayer to the universe. *Find me Xen.*

TWENTY-TWO

"Hide nothing, for time, which sees all and hears all, exposes all." ~ Sophocles

Kane stood drinking his coffee on the lower balcony of Xen's house as the first rays of light hit. He enjoyed this time of the morning. The quiet and the freshness of the morning air stirred the beast in him. They had a fight on their hands and so it would be until Xen got his fated back.

He took a long sip of the hot brew and looked to the distance. His *lykos* vision caught a glimpse of a man running towards the house. He put his cup down on a nearby table, sniffing the air to see if he recognized the runner who approached the house at a measured pace.

"Friend or foe?" He spoke to the wind, prepared to shift and tear at the man, until he heard him shout.

"Tithon! Message from Tithon."

"Well, isn't this a fucking surprise."

The man ran right up to where Kane stood. Kane's cell phone rang. He fished it out of his pocket just as the runner spoke. "Tithon ..." he panted, "... said they are moving Carissa this morning ... via plane to Greece. They've got a private plane. You need to move fast if you want to stop them." The man dropped to his knees.

"Kane!" Adam yelled out from the phone in his hand. "I was ringing to tell you the same."

"Fuck!" Kane yelled. This bordered on a "fucked if you do, fucked if you don't" moment. The mother of all scenarios. How to get there fast enough? "Adam, grab whoever you have near you and just go. Intercept. You hear me? Intercept! I'm on my way." He turned to the runner. "Leave your details with one of the men. You will be properly rewarded. And thanks."

The man looked up and nodded, still panting.

Kane moved on autopilot as he sped through the foyer of Xen's house and out to the SUVs. Two men were already having a cigarette nearby.

"In," he growled.

One thing his *lykos* sense craved in this moment was the possibility of retrieval. The fact Tithon had risked sending someone meant they had a small chance to get Carissa before Hal whisked her away again. Kane drove like a man possessed. The drive from Xen's to the airport—twenty minutes tops. He looked at the clock on the dash. Tithon would have sent the runner ahead of time. *Smart boy*, he thought.

He hit some buttons on the SUV steering wheel.

"Adam. Update. How many men are with you?"

"There are four of us. How many do you have?"

"Two with me."

"What's your plan of action?"

"You rip them to bloody shreds and then get Carissa out." His voice was steel.

His foot pressed harder on the accelerator. At the speed he was driving, he would be there in ten minutes. He'd join Adam in slashing Hal and his demons with pleasure. The only downside was they'd be fighting in broad daylight. Up until this point, that had never happened. Something had changed. The demons never fought in daylight hours. Someone yanked some serious chain to get them to do that, but who?

"You'd better hurry your ass up, I'm not saving any of them for you," Adam threw back at him.

"I'm eating up the road as we speak. If you see a window of opportunity to get her out, you do it!" He stabbed the air with his finger for emphasis. "Let the men worry about getting their own hides out. I'm sure that won't be a problem." Sarcasm seeped through with his last words.

The men in the car with Adam all answered.

"No problem, Kane."

"No problem."

"Got you, no problem."

"Loud and clear, Alpha. Seek, extract and abort," Adam vocalized.

"Don't fail me," he bit out and ended the call.

There was one more call to make. His police beta needed to pull some strings or they would risk discovery.

Carissa's eyes zeroed in on the black SUV that sped towards them on the tarmac. Her feet wanted to move, but a strong hand banded around her arm and held her tightly in place. Hal's goons had pulled her out of the vehicle and now the idiots stood and stared at the car that would collide with them if they didn't move soon.

A flutter started in her chest as a sense of calm washed over her. Could this be the work of Tithon? Had he got the message to Xen's men?

In seconds, events unfurled with such momentum it resembled a blockbuster action movie, where everything happened all at once.

A woman with flame-red hair exited Hal's vehicle. She stood to the side as Hal climbed out.

"Who the hell is she?" Carissa asked, knowing there would be no answer from the goons at her side.

The woman cast a seething glare at Hal. He barked something to her ... about an illusion. She stepped aside and raised her arms. A silver cuff bracelet shone on her left hand.

"Witch. She's a witch?" Carissa mumbled to herself.

The realization sent a wave of tingles through her skin. Her muscles went rigid. How did she know that? She didn't have an immediate answer, but something stabbed at the dark recesses of her mind. She could sense it, but she couldn't bring the recollection to the forefront. The perfect opportunity for escape stared at her right between the eyes ... the car she'd just gotten out of.

The witch continued her arm-waving. Her lips were moving. *A spell.* Then it dawned on her—a magical shield. Heck, what would human eyes think if they saw Hal's goons? Security would have the whole area in lockdown and there'd be police everywhere.

She looked back in the SUV's direction. It had pulled to a stop and the men who flew out of it were Xen's. "Adam," she whispered. A sight for sore eyes. Never had that cliché sounded so right in her life.

The extra men Hal had placed around the plane did battle with Adam and his men. Three lay at their feet, only two remained. Feet pounded on the tarmac. Adam came straight for them. One of the goons who held her let out a growl and bolted toward Adam. She had her money on the man with the sword, the one she trusted to get her back to Xen.

Carissa counted down to the point of impact between Adam and the demon.

Three.

Two.

One.

Adam sidestepped to the left and with skilled speed, sliced the demon through his midsection. The demon dropped to his knees. Adam turned and brought his sword down executioner style, severing the demon's head.

The chaperone goon standing next to her tightened his grip and let out a roar. Adam locked eyes with Carissa. In that moment, she read his intentions. She'd have to try and break out of the demon's grip.

The goon beside her, for some reason, didn't have the gumption to move. Adam came straight for them. She tugged against the goon's hold, trying to break free from his vise grip. Her skin tore and she didn't need to look to know her arm bled. Adam had reached them, pulled her behind him then lunged forward with his sword, skewering the demon in his throat.

"Carissa, we don't have time—" He didn't finish his sentence because another demon appeared and Adam got stuck into him.

She looked back towards Hal and the witch. They were heading for the plane.

Swords clashed and clanged. She did what she thought would work. She ran for the car. Her feet pounded on the ground. The light sole on the flats had not been designed for the hell she inflicted on them. Jumping back into the car, her hands frantically pushed down the visor in case they'd stashed the keys there. Nothing. She looked at the ignition. *Well, hello.*

"Woohoo!" she squealed, thankful Hal's goons weren't the sharpest tools in the shed. Bringing the car to life, she saw one clear way out—reverse first, then drive towards Adam's SUV.

Another of Hal's cronies came running towards her and flung himself onto the car. "Oh no you don't. This is my round now."

She shifted the car from reverse to drive and sped towards her target like a maniac. A couple of demons jumped out of the way. The goon on the hood hung on. She swerved, trying to dislodge him and then she slammed down hard on the brakes. The wheels locked and screeched. Her uninvited passenger went flying off.

"Talk about burning some rubber." She threw the car into reverse again, foot to the floor. She turned to look over her shoulder. Adam had just slain another demon, but more had popped up. They were coming out of thin air.

"Portal again, but how does he summon them?" Another question that remained un-answered.

Adam ran in her direction but another goon intercepted him. Her clean getaway in reverse was thwarted when something hit her on the left side tail end. A blind spot when she'd been looking over her shoulder to the right.

"Come on." She hit her hands on the steering wheel and shoved the car into drive. Something ripped the door open like a sardine can and pulled her out.

In the distance, she saw another car arriving on the scene. It pulled to an abrupt stop near Adam's vehicle and three men got out.

"Kane," she whispered. For the second time that day her breath caught in her chest as she watched Kane shift to wolf form. Maybe they'd get her out of this mess. Hope fluttered in her chest.

The demon pushed her in the direction of Hal and the witch.

"Ouch, that hurts," she yelled, then elbowed him in the face. His hand came down and heat flared on her cheek as he slapped her. A loud growl came from the wolf sprinting towards them.

Carissa moved out of the way as Kane pounced on the demon, knocking him to the ground. Razor-sharp incisors tore into the demon's neck. Adam's sword finished the job. Their actions were so fluid and well-timed, it looked like they had choreographed the whole thing. Blood splattered. The demon's head dropped to the ground.

Her legs wobbled, relief washed right through her. She owed them her life.

"Thank you," she choked out, looking at Adam, his sword dripping blood, still poised at the ready. Then her eyes met the huge wolf's. He padded over to her and nudged her on the arm with his muzzle. She grabbed the massive wolf by the neck and hugged him.

"Quick, we have to move." Adam steered her back towards Kane's car. There were already more men fighting, but as she surveyed the scene more demons were materializing.

"There are too many," she shouted.

"Keep running," Adam replied.

They dodged around decapitated bodies and Kane's men, with Kane still in wolf form. Just as they were about to enter Kane's waiting car, Hal appeared with his lovely witch.

"Lock the car," he commanded Kirke.

She raised her hands, mouthed some words, and locked the vehicle so they couldn't get in. Carissa had to admit it ticked all the boxes as an impressive trick.

Adam pulled out a dagger and threw it towards Hal's chest but it froze in midair away from the target. No doubt the witch again. Three more demons appeared behind Adam and Kane. Then everything went to Hades in mythical proportions.

Growls, heads dropping—everything spun so fast. Hal grabbed her and pulled her backwards.

"*Gamoto*, not the portal again."

TWENTY-THREE

"Friendship is a single soul dwelling in two bodies." ~ Aristotle

The moment her feet connected with Greek soil, her body began to tingle. The hair on her arms and neck stood. *What the hell is that?* Startled, she took quick gliding steps towards the waiting cars. She didn't want to contemplate anything hopeful. Her *hope* button had been disconnected.

A small spark of joy ignited within her when Hal went to the other vehicle, but it was short-lived when she saw the witch getting in the car and sliding into the seat opposite her. This was one of those welcome and not so welcome prospects. Carissa noticed there were only two demons around today—the two that never left Hal's side. Obviously bewitched with some witch ju-ju juice—complements of Ms. Magic, parked elegantly across from her.

Carissa scrutinized the look the witch gave her. Thinking there wasn't much to lose in an already lost battle, she decided she'd be a little bold and vocal.

"So what's your name?" she blurted out.

"Kirke, and I already know yours," she said dryly.

Isn't she happy? Not!

Kirke ... she played around with the name in her head. The information hit her mind like a browser bar upload. Kirke, the goddess of *pharmakeia*, a sorceress proficient in the magic of metamorphosis, illusion, and, to top it off nicely, necromancy—a dark art. *Why do I even know this?* A chill ran through her body. She bit her lip and straightened in her seat.

"You're obviously thrilled to bits to be on this pleasure trip," she announced to the witch.

"No more than you," Kirke replied flatly.

Carissa observed her for a second and thought a different line of questioning might get the witch to open up.

"Tell me, what do you think about Hal getting his thirteenth god status? I have my assumptions, but I would like to hear yours."

Kirke's eyebrows rose at the question. She was an attractive woman and Carissa placed her at no more than thirty.

"I think he is insane and wasting my valuable time on nonsense. If it were not for his taking my man hostage, I would not be entertaining such ridiculous notions."

Whoa, this was deep. The witch sat here against her will. Blackmail. That, she wasn't expecting. She wondered which demon head honcho Hal was bribing in regard to the portals. Her gut told her that Hal would get his just desserts when Kirke was no longer bound to him.

"Gods, Carissa, are born, not made. There is no power that can give one godly status, in spite of what Hal believes." She paused. "Immortal yes, but god, no."

"So if there's no chance of this being a success, why haven't you talked him out of it?" Carissa said, with a touch of hysteria.

"Contrary to what you may believe, I have tried to talk him out of it, but it's fruitless because Hal is full of hatred and wants vengeance against the gods. He's having his own pity party and wants to make them pay."

"So let me get this. Hal's pissed because he's stuck down here with mortals and not up there where the big guys and gals reside? And he thinks killing me will give him power to leave Earth?"

"Pretty much, yes." Kirke let out a breath.

Carissa let out a puff, too. Yep, he was a madman. Confirmation, yet again. She rubbed her tummy absentmindedly. Kirke caught her hand movement.

"You're pregnant?" she asked, eyes wide in shock.

"Yes, and I didn't have time to enjoy the news. I was snatched from my own backyard hours later."

By the look on Kirke's face, Carissa gathered Hal hadn't told her that little nugget of news.

"Your partner, is he mortal?"

"No, he is a vampire."

Carissa almost laughed at Kirke's saucer-wide eyes.

"But they can't reproduce. How is this so?"

"I don't know." It sounded lame, but it was the truth. "Why, and why me? Again, I don't know. I only have wacky assumptions and those are not strong enough."

"And what is your 'wacky' assumption?" Kirke asked, doing air quotes.

"That I am the daughter of Ares may have something to do with it. I can think of no other reason why Xen and I were able to conceive."

Kirke's demeanor changed. She paled at Carissa's words. "Daughter of Ares." Kirke's face looked ashen.

"Xen ... Xenocrates. You carry his child?" she asked. Shock etched thunderstruck surprise all over her features. Carissa didn't miss it.

"Yes. Xen," she confirmed.

"I apologize, I didn't mean to be rude, but you see, vampires do not normally reproduce. The fact you were able to do so with one makes it all the more extraordinary. You have bonded, haven't you?" Her eyes flickered for a second.

"We have bonded," she replied.

Kirke's features finally softened. "You know that your child will forever be a target, and you more so than the child. Thank the stars Xenocrates bonded with you. Otherwise you'd have every supernatural after you." She fiddled with her emerald green dress. She looked like something out of Camelot. Carissa thought it wise not to ask if it was her usual attire.

"Why would they want me?"

"Think, Carissa. If you were the only being a vampire could reproduce with, do you not think there would be others out there wanting to get to you for various selfish reasons? That you are the daughter of Ares, even more so."

"Well, not many people know Ares is my father." Hal did, though, and that couldn't be good for her. "I still don't see how my lineage can benefit anyone." The moment those words were spoken, she realized they were not true.

Kirke laughed. "My dear, think about the dual advantage. One, control of the daughter of Ares allows you to call him forth for anyone wishing to go to war. Always an advantage to have your father on side. Two, your child will be born with Ares' warlike abilities and Xenocrates' powerful vampire talents, a child who possesses not only the mother's talents but the father's too. How many people would love to manipulate your child in their power plays?"

"I see your point. So I'm pretty much damned whichever way you look at it." Nausea threatened her. She closed her eyes and took a deep breath.

"I wouldn't say damned, Carissa. You've just made the Most Wanted list in the other world."

"Great, just great!" Carissa didn't want any of this, but here she was right in the middle of it all. Her relationship with Xen was a definite health hazard, but the thought of not being with him pierced her heart. She would not live long enough to tell him the depth of what made her heart flutter.

"I will do what I can to help deflect Hal. Xenocrates has helped me more than once over the years."

Carissa's eyes lit up. She reached across and hugged Kirke then pulled back into her seat.

"Wow, what a small world it is, and right at this moment, I can't tell you how grateful I am to hear that you know Xen." Excitement laced her voice.

"We're slowing down so I take it we are almost at our destination, so let's continue the charade." Kirke winked.

Carissa saw a sign that read Aegeon Beach Hotel.

"Wonder if I'll be allowed a cocktail by the pool? As a dying wish and all."

Kirke let out a laugh. "Good attitude to have."

TWENTY-FOUR

"Success is dependent on effort." ~ *Sophocles*

The room Carissa had been tossed into had all the comfort she could desire and, she hated to admit, the view of the ocean from the double sliding doors looked magical. When she nudged the latch it didn't budge. "*Gamoto.*" No relaxation would be had on this insane journey that screamed of her imminent demise. Her former childhood friend wanted her dead.

The door swung open. "Nice of you to knock," she said to the goon standing with a tray in his hand. He walked into the room and placed it on the coffee table. Carissa watched him closely, another new face. *Wonder how many rogue men Hal brought on the trip?* This one was not a demon. The way he moved reminded her of Kane and Adam, a distinct fluid movement. Lethal in Kane and Adam. This guy possessed that identical danger. He gave her a sideways glance on the way out. "Great, he's recruited every species to help in his make-me-a-god scheme."

She made her way to the coffee table and uncovered the dishes on the tray. The aroma of roast chicken and potatoes hit her nose as she lifted the lids. There was a salad, Greek style of course, and dessert, baklava, something she hadn't had in a while. The heavy cinnamon scent wafted in the air. Grabbing the fork, she speared a potato with it and brought it to her lips. The flavors burst on her tongue, eliciting a small moan of satisfaction.

When her hunger subsided, the idea of an afternoon siesta appealed in more ways than one. She lay on the bed with a groan. She fluffed a pillow and lay her head down. Her eyes fluttered closed, but the kaleidoscope of color at the base of the bed had her sitting up. Someone appeared—Kirke.

"Wow. Now that would be handy."

"Keep it down." She motioned to the door. "I wanted to see how you were."

"Thank you, Kirke." Her favorite witch. Move over Samantha and Sabrina. Kirke, my new favorite witch, just outdid you.

"I can't stay for long."

Carissa moved over and Kirke sat down on the bed. Wherever Xen was at the moment, she silently thanked him a million times over for helping this woman.

"If you can do that, why don't you leave here?" she asked. With her power, getting away should be easy.

"Well, I could, but I can't."

Carissa's thoughts froze. "Why?"

"Ah, that. Well, as you know, Hal has my man, but I don't know where, and if I don't comply, he will issue an order to eliminate him. In short, I'm Hal's latest party trick."

"Bastard!" Carissa said. "I'd love to give him a good kick in the balls." She meant it too. "Maybe stab him in the balls. That would be better."

Kirke let out a laugh, then put her hand over her mouth. She waved her other hand and music sounded.

"Clever," Carissa mouthed.

Kirke's lips broke into a half smile. "I just wanted to tell you that I don't think the sacrifice will be taking place in the next day or so. I heard some of the men talking about a sacred knife and they can't seem to locate it. So we've got a little time to do some planning."

Now this woman she liked.

"What have you got in mind for the knife of doom? What's so special about it?" Now that she knew a whole other world resided right alongside the human one, she wanted to know more.

"At the moment nothing extraordinary, other than the fact it is ancient. I don't think he understands that what he is trying to achieve is not possible. Even if I were to pour magical energy or a spell on the knife, it can't possibly aid him in the way he thinks.

"Truth is, Hal doesn't realize all his actions are pointless," Kirke said.

"So what exactly did you have in mind as far as a plan goes?" Even a slight chance of getting away would be worth taking. Having Kirke here gave her a new strength, one she thought she'd lost. Her cop instincts, though, wanted to know why Kirke put her herself at risk to help her.

"Don't fear me, Carissa. I wish you no harm. I explained that your bonded has helped me in the past. Consider me a friend amongst foes." She looked genuine.

"You can't blame me, Kirke. This hasn't been a smooth ride. Believe me, I am grateful Xen has helped you and I'll have to give him many kisses of gratitude when and if we get out of this jam." She let out a deep breath.

"I'm sure Xenocrates won't say no to any kisses. Mind you, there have been many women lining up to get kisses from him."

A little pang of jealousy speared Carissa in the gut. She smothered it. Of course, Xen would have had plenty of women wanting him. She'd seen it firsthand, and for the first time, she actually felt a little smug that she had, after all, managed to snag such a catch. Especially considering her past experiences had all been flops.

"Now," Kirke said. "Let's get on with our options."

After a few minutes of debating when the best time to break free would be, they came to the conclusion it would have to be pretty close to her sacrificial demise. It would be the only time where Kirke could "accidently" throw in some magical mayhem to allow Carissa to get out of there. In the meantime, they had to be cunning enough to extract the information on where Hal had Kirke's lover holed up.

"Well, then it's settled," Kirke announced.

"Whatever way you look at it, I'm toast," Carissa murmured. Their plan had many flaws, but Carissa was willing to trust that Kirke was on her side, and the only thing that made escape even thinkable was Kirke's ability of illusion.

Kirke stood. "Let's hope the delay with the dagger buys us a little more time to fine tune things." The air stirred and with a shimmer, she disappeared.

Carissa bit her lip. The reality of her situation clawed at her throat, constricting her breathing. It would not be easy, but she had to keep up a pretense. Maybe Xen would find her. She had to keep that hope alive.

The door opened with a quiet whoosh.

"Oh, glory be. It's Hal," she wheezed.

"What a damn good evening it is, Carissa." Nothing genuine came from his words.

Ugly as they were, she understood immediately. How she would love to punch his pathetic face.

"Good evening, Hal." It took every ounce of control to even spit out the simple words. She'd much rather ignore him.

"I hope you are enjoying your room. I own it, of course."

Of course he did. She rolled her eyes. "I don't find that surprising." He was a first class jerk. *Malaka.*

He strode into the room and dropped onto one of the lounge chairs near the coffee table.

"So Hal, to what do I owe the pleasure?" His goons weren't with him. Maybe now that he'd touched Greek soil and sat not far from his father's temple, he considered himself ballsier.

"I wanted to talk," he drawled.

"O-kay." Her mouth set in a hard line. Up until now he'd spent his energy being cryptic or evasive and not answering her questions, but here he sat wanting conversation. How ironic that it would be just before he killed her.

"You know, if you side with me, we would be unstoppable."

Her stomach heaved, but she regained control before he could pick up on the fact that his words were not only knives to her gut, but they made her skin crawl in repulsion.

"Hal, I was on your side. We were friends and you ruined it with your stupid kidnapping fiasco. Did it ever occur to you that everything you've done so far is not at all how friends act or treat each other?" She watched him through narrowed eyes.

He waited a moment before he spoke. "Actually, I've thought of a lot of things, but the key is that you ruined it with that vampire."

"Hal, we don't pick who we fall in love with. It happens." Her tone was controlled.

"Pity you think that way, because I would have picked you."

A dull ache started in her temple. She rubbed it. This man was impossible on a gargantuan scale. "So, killing me will give you what, Hal?"

He tsked. "Ah, Carissa, you fail to see the magnitude of Olympus and residing there with the gods."

She let out a choked laugh. "What, sitting around all day, drinking ambrosia? If that's magnitude, I'd rather watch paint dry," she spat.

"Your ignorance keeps you blind." He stood up and clenched his fists. "It's not immortality I seek. As a friend, I thought you'd understand that. I guess I was wrong."

"Friends. Do. Not. Kidnap. Friends!" Even slowing it down to make the point had been fruitless on Hal. His arrogance superseded any rational and logical thought.

He walked to the door, pausing to add, "Your sacrifice will be held in two nights. Pity your blood-sucking vermin won't be present to watch."

His insult split open a nerve. A pounding began in her ears. "You could never be half the man Xen is. *Eisai tipota*—you are nothing." More words would be wasted on him. She'd be better off reserving her energy for when she needed it most. "I'd like you to leave."

She turned and walked towards the double sliding doors that led to a balcony. The click of the door told her what she wanted to know. Hal was gone, for now at least.

The whole interlude with Hal had unnerved her. He had gotten under her skin yet again. It had taken every ounce of self-restraint to stop from lunging for Hal's throat. Her temper had been escalating to a degree that was foreign to her, whether it was the pregnancy or something else, she didn't know. Her hand automatically went to her belly.

"I hope I can get us out of this."

TWENTY-FIVE

"Why, I'd like nothing better than to achieve some bold adventure, worthy of our trip." ~ Aristophanes

Xen's team touched down at a secret location in Athens. He moved out of his seat with the plane still in motion. When Kane and Adam had briefed him on what had transpired at the airport, they'd had to hold him down before he ripped the rest of the house apart.

"Hal has the witch you seek." Kane's words now echoed loudly in his head. He knew enough about Kirke to piece together that Hal had something considerable over her. She did not, by principal, work with anyone. Alone had been the witch's motto for the thousands of years he had known her.

He grabbed his bag from the overhead compartment and headed to the exit. His phone buzzed.

"Xen, Benny here. Just thought you'd want to know that Sounion in Greece is a hotspot for non-mortals at the moment"

"Thanks."

Four SUVs waited. *Phi's* organization was global, so when Xen announced he'd be landing back on Greek soil, his men in Athens had jumped at the opportunity to join in on the fight to get his woman back.

Many of his men were hardened by war. Fighting had always been a way of life and they reveled in the bloodbath created by it. To their disappointment, they didn't get enough action these days, they'd said when he enquired about equipment for his mission. He might not live in Greece anymore, but he still ran a tight ship.

"Update," he said as he slid into one of the SUVs with Kane and Adam.

The driver, from his Athenian team, spoke quickly.

"We believe she's in Sounion. One of our men has spotted some unusual demon activity."

"Head there," Xen commanded. It tied in with what Benny had said.

"What if it's a trap?" Kane threw in.

"Then we strategize so we are not ambushed." Xen paused. "Adam."

"I'm on it, boss." He took out his phone. Xen watched as his fingers flew over the screen. A few seconds later Adam's phone beeped. "All set," he confirmed.

Behind the tough walls he had spent endless years of his immortality building, little fragments of his heart splintered. Steady cracks opened, something he could not afford to let happen. One name danced in his thoughts on repeat. *Carissa.*

The ways he'd love to carve up Hal were endless, though none seemed to satisfy him. He would have to draw out Hal's death so as to please the beast within him. Exasperated, he let out a low growl.

"We'll get her back," Kane said, his voice tight.

Xen had taken Kane aside on the flight and told him sternly that if they failed to retrieve Carissa, Kane was to take his head because failure would render his status as the *Phi* leader meaningless. If he could not save his own woman, he would no longer stand as the man who gave the orders. Death would be welcomed.

Kane had been furious at his words. He'd grabbed him by the throat and threatened him with the removal of all *lykoi* from the *Phi* cause. "We. Are. In. This. Together." He had spat out the words through gritted teeth. Xen understood after the exchange on the plane that the only acceptable outcome was to beat Hal at his own game.

"There is no other option," he finally managed.

"Two minutes before we reach impact point," the driver announced.

Xen reached out with his mind. *Carissa.*

Xen's voice sounded in Carissa's mind. A dream. There was no way that Xen could be here for her. She sat up on the couch and rubbed the stiffness in her neck. Doubt stabbed her in the chest. Why couldn't she do better with her mumbo-jumbo talents? She glanced at the digital clock on the bedside table—two in the morning. She heard doors being opened and closed. What were Hal's goons doing?

The air around her shimmered. She recognized the witch's power this time. "You make a good entrance."

Carissa, can you hear me? Xen's voice spoke in her head. "Xen?" She looked at Kirke. Her face was a wall of confusion, and then Kirke's eyes grew wide in comprehension at the same time as hers.

You're here? Her hands came up to her chest. She pressed her palms to her heart, relief washing through her.

Koukla, can you tell me how many men Hal has guarding you? And where in the hotel is he keeping you?

She looked at Kirke. "He wants to know how many men are guarding, inside and out."

Kirke did the math. "Nine."

Nine and Hal, she projected to Xen. Oh, and he's keeping me in the rooms to the right wing of the Aegeon Beach Hotel.

See you soon, koukla.

You're not here yet?

Kirke looked at Carissa for more information.

No, koukla, only a minute away.

She gave Kirke what she been waiting to hear. "They're a minute away. I guess we should brace ourselves because the impact isn't going to be friendly." She wanted to scream in joy. Xen would get her out of Hal's psychotic clutches.

"I hope he nails Hal's ass. I'd have to say, I want him equally as dead as Xen wants him," Kirke bit out.

"This may be our lucky night," Carissa said. "But what about your man?"

"Leave that to me. I overheard Hal talking to his men. I have a hunch where he might be holding him."

"What if you're guessing the wrong location? He'll kill him the moment you disappear."

"I'm going to have to take a chance and hope my hunch is right."

"I hope so ..."

Outside, the noise level amplified. Carissa looked to Kirke. "They're here." They raced to the sliding doors.

Carissa gasped the same moment Kirke did. Something flew straight for the sliding doors. Her arm darted out and she pulled Kirke with her, out of the way. Glass flew in all directions. Kirke threw out her hands and suspended the fragments that would have hit them.

"Neat trick. You'll have to teach me," Carissa marveled.

"Magic lies in belief, that's where the power comes from," Kirke replied. She raised her hand and the suspended glass landed on the floor with the headless demon body that had been catapulted through the doors.

Carissa opened her mouth to say something, but Tithon's voice stopped her question. He stepped through the shattered frame.

He looked over at Carissa and Kirke. Surprise sparked on his face when he saw the witch. Something silent passed between the two. She would have to ask him later.

"Let's move. Xen's already at the front of the building. You too, Witch," he added.

Xen, we're on the move with Tithon, and I have Kirke with me. Kirke—what's Hal got on her?

Apparently, Hal has her man hostage and she's as much a victim as I am.

I will not harm Kirke. We have a history of favors. Now, enough talk, I have demons to kill.

They followed Tithon at a half-jog pace.

"You okay, Carissa?" Tithon questioned.

"Yeah, I'm good. I just find it weird that Hal hasn't got anyone back here."

"I took their heads. Cleared the path," he said casually.

"Now that, Vampire, is the best thing I've heard all evening," Kirke said.

"Hopefully, we can make it good for everyone this evening." Carissa turned to glance behind her to Kirke. She was feeling unexpectedly happy. Here were two people willing to help her and she was nothing to them.

"I owe both of you for this, and if I have my way, I'll be paying you both back. Maybe with lots of baklava and frappé." They both let out a stifled laugh.

The soft tread of grass under her feet turned to sand, giving them the stealth to get around to the front of the hotel. It was dark so she followed close to Tithon, waiting for her eyes to adjust.

"You ladies lay low here. I have to switch sides now and make it look like I'm on Team Hal."

"Vampire, do as you must," Kirke answered.

He began to walk away.

"Tithon," Carissa called.

"Yes."

"Thanks. I owe you, Gumbo."

The corners of his mouth quirked up, then he was gone.

"What now?" Kirke queried in her squatted position.

"We wait a little, then we sneak closer," Carissa answered. She turned her head. Booted feet lined her vision. Her eyes moved up till they met the owner. The face looking down at them looked extremely pleased. "Adam," she whispered.

"Didn't they tell you that you can't work on your tan at night?" Carissa jumped up into Adam's arms, giving him a tight hug. "Easy girl, you don't want to make your vampire jealous."

"I didn't think you'd find me."

"Are you kidding? Xen would have ripped Earth apart to get to you." He pointed in Xen's direction. "That man is insane for you."

Warmth spread through her body and her heart pounded at his words. She loved Xen and wanted nothing more than to be in his arms and away from Hal's demented scheme.

"It means the world you would all risk your lives to help save mine."

"We would do this for any of our men or women. It's who we are." He gave her one of his cheeky grins. "Let's move, ladies."

"You are lucky to have them at your back," Kirke said.

"Don't I know it."

They followed Adam.

"Kirke, can you see anything?" Carissa whispered from behind her.

"I'm still trying to get my bearings. I may be a witch but I don't have night vision like the wolf does."

Adam laughed. "Night vision is not all it's cut out to be, it's overrated. There are times I wish I didn't have it."

"That's nonsense," Kirke spat out.

"Why?" Carissa asked. She, for one, would kill to be able to see as if it were daylight.

"Well, you've never seen some go skinny-dipping. I tell you, you'd go blind, especially since we pick up even the smallest of details."

Kirke stopped and Carissa smashed into her back. She straightened up and stood shoulder to shoulder with the witch. Adam turned to look at them. They looked at each other, then at Adam. Loud laughs split the air. Simultaneously, they both slapped a hand over their mouths.

"Adam, stop it! We don't want any nasty surprises," Carissa whispered.

They pressed on until they were close to the front of the hotel. Light illuminated the area. SUVs were parked around it. Her head darted from left to right trying to locate her warrior. *Xen, where are you?* Her feet moved forward faster trying to overtake Adam. He pulled her back behind him.

Then she caught sight of him. He was fighting with a demon. She saw him duck then move behind the demon before taking his head. His fangs were visible, and he looked lethal and beautiful. His head snapped to her direction. And then he blurred and she knew that he was headed her way with that impossible speed of his.

One of his arms snaked around her waist and pulled her to him. She gasped. His lips crushed hers. She opened without hesitation. One calloused palm snaked up to the nape of her neck and held her tight. Every nerve awoke and fired in her body. Euphoria charged every cell. His overwhelming need filled her, the bond between them fueling their desire. They mirrored each other, like two parts of a puzzle fused together again.

You feel so good, koukla. He spoke to her mind as his tongue ravished her mouth.

"If you two are finished, I'd like to get out of here." Kirke broke the spell

She pulled away from Xen's embrace, embarrassed by her shameless reaction to him. Xen saw her withdrawal and looked annoyed. Adam's wolfish grin spoke volumes. He winked at her. She wanted to slap him.

"Witch, you understand the situation. Don't embarrass my bonded. There is nothing wrong with sharing a kiss," he finished, then flashed that gorgeous smile of his down at Carissa, turning her into a pile of goo.

"I did not mean to cause your bonded distress. I was merely pointing out that we should get out of here before more demons arrive."

"I won't argue with that." Xen looked at Carissa and Adam. "Kirke is right."

Xen grabbed her hand and they moved to where the rest of the men were assembled. Kane stood with them. She automatically gave him a hug.

"Good to see you too, but we need to be out of here ASAP."

"Get the men to comb the place as planned," Xen instructed Adam.

Adam spoke into a device attached to his ear. She watched as the men moved in all directions.

"Xen, doesn't it all seem a little too easy? Where is Hal with the other demons?"

No sooner had the words left her mouth than a huge group of demons surround them. *Maybe he's got these guys on speed dial.*

"We expected his ambush." Xen finished the rambling in her head.

He was listening in. He grasped the back of her neck. Before she could register anything, she was in his arms and melting into another one of his scorching kisses. He pulled his head back, still holding her steady.

Wow, I think I'm going to faint.

Xen laughed. Koukla, you are my heart and soul. I will protect you till my last breath.

Her eyes misted at his words. She pushed a thought back to him. *And you are mine.*

Xen turned to Kane. "You know what to do."

They beamed at each other like silly school boys. The men formed a circle with Carissa and Kirke in the middle. Mayhem was too simple a word for the slashing and slaying taking place before her eyes.

"Kirke," Xen growled. "Get to one of the cars."

The circle surrounding them broke and Kirke pushed Carissa in the direction of the vehicles.

"We need to get you out of here."

"What about Xen and the others?" Concern stabbed her voice.

"Don't worry they can look after themselves," Kirke replied.

"But … but ..." A swooshing sound came through the air. Instinct kicked in, and she ducked. A demon stood too close for comfort.

Kirke blasted him back with magic. He fell to the ground groaning. "He won't be out for long. We need to hurry."

"Lead the way. Maybe we should stay low in case another demon decides to take our heads."

Kirke nodded in agreement. Crouching low, they proceeded to make their way to the cars. Grunts from Xen and his men ricocheted all around them. A headless body landed in front of Kirke.

Carissa looked in the direction the body had come flying from and saw it was Xen, slicing and tossing. His back was to her and, boy, he was gorgeous even from the rear. His sword drawn, he was every bit a warrior.

Koukla, I'm flattered you think my behind looks good.

Xen, get out of my head.

Koukla, I'm going to ask you to move fast. When you get to the car, make sure you head to the airport. The navigation is set in all the vehicles. Board the plane. The Phi have been briefed. They are to get you out, you understand?

But what about you and the other men.

Don't worry about us, koukla, we love a good fight.

Okay.

Be safe, koukla. Now stop talking.

Hey, you started.

Rich laughter sounded in her head. *My koukla.*

"A little more, Kirke. I see one of Xen's men near that furthest SUV. He told me to basically get out of here. You were right."

"Trust them, Carissa. They've been around for eons, they know their stuff. What does worry me is Hal. You can't trust that man, he's very devious."

"You are not wrong. He's managed all this, and one has to wonder how? How does he know everything that's going on?" The notion that he had eyes at the back of his head began to cement itself in her head.

"Maybe he's got surveillance cameras everywhere," Kirke offered.

Carissa stopped in her tracks. Kirke turned and waved at her to keep moving.

"You are absolutely right. That's how he's staying a step ahead." Her feet began to move and she prepared to voice her thoughts to Xen when two demons jumped them.

Kirke managed to get herself loose and knee the demon, giving her split seconds to blast him with some of her power. Carissa used that to her advantage to wiggle free from the demon trying to drag her back towards the beach and away from the action. *Hal, the bastard, is probably watching from there somewhere.* She made a dead run for the car. This felt just like *Ground Hog Day* and Bill Murray had nothing on her. The sound of Kirke's footsteps behind her sent a wash of relief over her.

"Carissa, if I don't make it to the car, you get out of here," Kirke yelled.

"You're coming with me, no matter what." She couldn't leave Kirke, not after she had risked so much to help her.

Carissa skidded around to the driver's side and Kirke to the passenger's. The *Phi* near the car were fighting off demons.

They were going to have to make the break on their own. As she opened the door, a demon skidded over the hood. *I wish I had a weapon.* She turned and another demon approached Kirke. She did the only thing she could think of. She ran towards Xen.

Xen, I'm coming up behind you. I was surrounded. I wish I had a weapon.

Xen and Kane finished off the demons they were fighting. Carissa flew into Xen's arms. Quickly, he pulled her behind him, sandwiching her between himself and Kane. Five demons surrounded them.

"Where the fuck do these things keep coming from? I can't see." Exasperation filled her voice.

Xen gave his theory. "Hal is holding a portal open and they are coming through there."

"Can we block it or something?" she asked between swords swinging and synchronized forward-backward movements from the men.

If we can get Kirke to cast an illusion through it, we might be able to block them, Xen communicated silently.

Carissa scanned for Kirke. She stood near the car with the *Phi* minus the demons. She'd have to get to her so she could tell her. Carissa guessed that the portal was somewhere on the beach, since the last few seemed to ambush them when they were closest to the sand leading to the beach.

"I'm going to have to get to her, so that I can tell her."

"No, Carissa. There are too many of them and I can't risk it. Not again, *koukla*." She understood the pain in his voice.

"But Xen you can't outfight that many. I mean, I know you guys are bad asses and all, but really, how long can you hold them off for? You are the ones running out of steam, not the other way around."

"Your brainy beauty has a valid point," grunted Kane as he swung his sword.

"She does, but she is my bonded and carrying my child. I do not want her in Hal's clutches again, nor do I want to see harm come to either of them."

"Please," she begged. "We have to stop them coming through." Blood splattered as Xen and Kane finished off the demons that surrounded them.

Xen grabbed Carissa's hand and took off towards Kirke who had had a small company of demons surrounding her. Relief washed over Kirke's face the minute Xen and Kane jumped in and fought the demons back. Carissa took that opportunity to give Kirke the rundown on what they wanted her to do with the portal.

"I have a good idea where the portal is. I felt the energy earlier."

A head rolled near Carissa and Kirke's feet.

"Vampire, come with me."

Xen finished the demon he was fighting, turned, grabbed Carissa's hand, and they followed the witch.

Kirke took them close to where the portal energy vibrated. She pointed. "Over there by the large olive tree."

Carissa squinted, trying to see. For a split second, she thought she saw a pale blue light. She shook her head.

"Do you think you could effectively block it to stop them coming through?" Xen asked, checking left to right for any surprises.

"I can do it, but I don't know how much time it will give us. He's definitely got someone on the other end opening it up with a spell." Kirke cast out her hands and chanted quickly.

Carissa felt a tingling and knew that Kirke's illusion spell was taking effect in the portal. She swore the portal glowed pink before the witch put her hands down.

Xen leaned over to Carissa. "She is the strongest at casting illusion. You'd never want her on your bad side. She can make you imagine your worst nightmares."

"You mean, live them," Kirke said with sly amusement.

"Well, I'm on your side, girl," Carissa threw back.

Xen's arm darted out, grabbing her around the waist and drawing her in. He pinned her to him.

"Okay, Witch, let's move." They raced back towards the action. "I expect the two of you to take one of the cars and head to the airport," he commanded.

"I can't, Xen. Hal has someone I care deeply about," Kirke admitted.

"And I will make a solemn vow to do whatever it takes to help you."

"I respect your offer, Vampire, but I fear I must decline."

"You said you had an idea where he might be," Carissa reminded her.

"You were right earlier, I can't risk it. What if I've got the location wrong, or I misheard?" Her fingers tugged on the lace of her sleeve. Carissa recognized Kirke's doubt.

"You know I will help you, Witch," Xen said.

"I know and I am grateful. Now, let's get your Carissa out of here."

"*Koukla*, you get to that plane. I can't lose you again."

She nodded at his request. Then he sped to where the other *Phi* and *lykoi* were fighting. With the illusion cast through the portal, no more demons were coming through. Xen's men had a tiny window of time to wrap up the skirmish. A small comfort of hope buzzed over her, but her heart sank at the thought that Kirke would not share her joy in getting away from that lunatic Hal.

"Come on," she said to Kirke. They moved to one of the SUVs. "Kirke, what will Hal do to you when he realizes you've helped me escape?"

"I can cast an illusion faster than he can blink, so if he tries to hurt me, he doesn't stand a chance. I don't fear for my life ..." She trailed off.

Carissa understood that her concern rested with her man. "Let Xen help you."

"Normally I would, but not today." Sadness broke at the corners of her lips. "Now quit talking to me and get in the car."

Carissa obeyed. She threw open the door to the driver's side. Something grabbed her from behind and flung her into the nearby bushes. Twigs snapped beneath her body. Her arms felt like they'd been hacked by rose thorns. They would sting later. Pushing up, she got to her feet feeling a little dazed. "Xen," she mouthed.

He must have been in tune with her thoughts because his primal roar caused the hair on her nape to rise. She glanced up to see his face in the distance, the look of pure horror. Her eyebrows drew together. She didn't have time to register why he wore that expression. Arms seized her and an all-too-familiar feeling of dread choked her voice.

"Koukla! No!" The last thing she heard before being encased in blackness.

TWENTY-SIX

"Appearances are a glimpse of the unseen." ~ Anaxagoras

"Gamoto." She heaved again. Having her face planted in the toilet bowl had never been her idea of a wakeup call. Rolling away from the bowl, she lay on the marble mosaic floor. *Back to square one and sick as a dog. What a royal mess.* The coolness ebbed its way through her, her skin breaking out in goosebumps.

She forced herself up and into the shower. The scratches on her forearms stung. Little moans of discomfort escaped her lips. Her muscles were weak, making her tremble. She rinsed off and made her way out of the bathroom in slow steps. Beat. Depleted. Exhausted. She needed a few hours of sleep.

Her head hit the pillow, its softness providing the comfort she craved. She tried to think what had gone wrong, but all she could see behind her closed eyelids was Xen's face.

Loud banging woke her later; her heart raced as disorientation swept through her. She tried to focus her vision towards the door. Nothing moved or sounded from beyond the door. A moment later, the thumping began again. She sat up and strained her ears to get the direction of the noise. Next door. Someone banged on the wall. Then it dawned on her what that noise had been and continued to be—the consequence of someone engaged in carnal acrobatics.

"Way to go, Hal." Her feet landed on the plush rug as she pushed herself up from the bed. She paced around the room. Anger raced through her body. She should be with Xen, not here and not in this room. Glancing over at the digital clock, the soft glow read 9:00 p.m. She gasped and her hands flew to her face.

"No way!" She had slept the whole day and then some. A loud groan escaped her lips.

The banging next door increased to a louder tempo. She stifled a laugh.

She paced back and forth. Losing a day did not bode well for her because it meant one moment closer to being beef *stifatho* on a temple altar. She had no idea where they were or whether Xen knew her location.

Back and forth, she paced in the room.

The moans and tempo increased a decibel. Someone was definitely having monkey sex and didn't care who knew.

"Damned exhibitionists."

She'd worn out the rug near the bed with her pacing. Escape, she decided, had become the new search for the Holy Grail.

"*Gamoto*, all I need is my gun. Then I can put a hole in Hal and move on," she mumbled.

So simple, yet here she was with no weapon and no way of getting one. She rolled her neck from side to side, her hand massaging the tension that had built up in it. Then, without further thought, she grabbed for the door handle. It moved. Someone pushed it forward the same time she pulled it open. Her jaw tightened.

"Hal," she gritted out.

"Get dressed," he bellowed, his appearance disheveled. Clearly her speculation had been correct. He had been one of the parties who contributed to the wall drumming. He held out a blue dress on a coat hanger. She nabbed it and stalked to the bathroom.

Pulling the dress over her head, anxiety punctured her lungs. She blew out a few short breaths to regain control. This. Was It. The moment of her impending doom had arrived. Sacrifice time. The plain blue dress fell to her feet. It was Grecian in style. *Who am I to question a madman's taste?*

Walking out of the bathroom, she held her head high. She would not shatter or break for Hal, she had been created of sterner stuff. *Oh, I will have the last strike, but not yet.*

Years in the police force had taught her to be patient, too. She'd learned the hard way. Her Greek temper had often gotten her into hot water in the early years. No, she would wait, then she would hit her target with as much force as she could gather. She had one last card up her sleeve and she would play it at the right moment. At least she would go down knowing she'd done her best.

"You seem relaxed, given you are being led to your death."

She looked Hal in the eyes, remembering something from Socrates she had read in her youth. She bit out with vehement words, "The gods will not forsake me. I am innocent in all this and I have nothing to fear from you nor death."

A flicker of something stirred in Hal's eyes, but he turned his head so as not to look at her. Regret, fear, or something more? Whatever lay hidden in the depth of his soul did not, however, change his mind. It didn't matter to her anymore. This man, who she once called a friend, would not ever be redeemable. His goons pushed her toward the door.

She was placed in a car on her own. A takeaway coffee cup was placed in her hands. This time it contained tea. On the seat beside her sat a bag with a cheese pie in it. When she pulled the *tiropita* all the way out, the smell made her stomach growl. She had missed an entire day and was famished. She welcomed the food and the quiet ride.

"I'm sorry, Xen," she breathed.

Absentmindedly, she rubbed her abdomen. She had let down her unborn child. Hot tears ran down her face. Her lungs squeezed in restriction. She gulped air to ease the pressure. Nausea threatened, but she pushed it back down. And then a flicker of hope spread in her heart. She was the daughter of Ares. If she could channel her supposed powers maybe she had a fighting chance. She wiped the tears from her face and downed the rest of the tea. A peculiar metal taste lingered on her tongue. Her tea was drugged. Dizziness and heavy lids disabled her lucidity.

"Hal, you *malaka*, I'm not going out without a fight," she mumbled.

Xen gathered his men and Kirke aboard his luxury superyacht. They were bound for Poros. One of his men stationed there had tipped them off that Hal had arrived. They wasted no time getting there. The bitter pill of his stupidity ate him up. What had he been thinking letting Carissa get to the car alone? He should have jumped in the car with her. She had rattled his entire logic. Every plan he'd put in place had fallen to pieces.

"Shutting down the portals is the key to disabling Hal's plans, but how do we put a lid on them?" Xen mused as he looked out to the sea from the opulent yacht.

"What are the chances of succeeding?" Kane queried.

Adam had dropped into the seat opposite Kane. "We still have a chance, and you know it. Maybe the witch can help with her hocus pocus and zap Hal into a toad."

Kirke shot up from where she sat, "Witches don't turn people into toads, but we do turn wolves into cats."

Kane let out a laugh. Adam's face soured. Xen's mouth turned up at the exchange.

Adam stabbed a finger in the air at her. "You. Are. Not. A. Nice. Witch!"

Kirke winked at Adam.

Xen turned. "Kirke, if we locate the portals, is there a way to seal them? I know the illusion you cast back at Sounion didn't hold for long. We need something stronger. Any suggestions?

Kirke ran through a multitude of spells she could cast, but none would hold long enough. No, they needed a powerful spell that would lock the door from directly inside the demon realm.

One name danced in her mind over and over—Hekate. Hekate had resided from time to time with Persephone in Hades. As the goddess of witchcraft, necromancy and crossroads, she'd be the best bet in casting a strong spell in the portal.

"Hekate," came Kirke's one-word reply.

"Hekate?" Adam and Kane both uttered, confused.

"Hekate!" said Xen with a smirk, catching on.

"Yes, Hekate. Her power is much greater than mine and what I can't do, she can. But summoning her is no easy feat."

"What do we need to do to get her help?" Xen asked.

"You, Xenocrates, do not need to do anything. I will summon her and ask if she will cast the spell I think will be vital to the next phase of the mission."

Adam and Kane had stilled to listen to Kirke. Xen let out a breath. "So let it be done."

They mapped out the logistics. They threw in a handful of "what if" scenarios and hoped this time they could kick Hal's ass.

"We cannot fail her this time," Xen said. Kirke knew that those words ate at him. He had already failed in rescuing his bonded because his emotions were running rabid.

Once they reached the island, Kirke went ashore first. There wasn't time to spare; they were working in the dark and she needed every ticking minute that passed. A prickle of awareness alerted Kirke that Carissa was already being prepared for the sacrifice—if not already on the altar, knowing Hal's urgency in wanting to complete the sacrifice.

"Hekate, great goddess, answer my plea for help."

The air around Kirke began to crackle and shift. Mist formed and through it, stepped Hekate.

"Daughter."

"You answered."

"I always do, if you ask."

A range of emotions speed through Kirke's veins. Even though Hekate was her mother, it wasn't like they were going to go on a shopping spree anytime soon.

"Mother, I need your help."

"This better be worth my time, daughter."

Kirke caught her mother's narrow-eyed look. Her mother detested anyone sucking up her time with trivial requests, so she had to coat her words a little.

Kirke broke down the enormity of the situation with the demons. She did, however, leave out the vital piece about Carissa's parentage. For some strange reason she figured that it was not pertinent to the perplexity of the situation.

"Someone is using your gateways to let demons through." Kirke let out a deep breath. It had been a marathon run to dump all that info.

"I will help," her mother announced.

Dizziness mixed with euphoria mingled in Kirke's body. Her mother's simple answer was the gods' ambrosia in itself. She had been prepared to beg, grovel and argue until her face had turned blue. Her mother had been known for giving her children a lot of tough love. But not this time. She stood with her mouth agape, just staring at the goddess in front of her.

"Don't look at me like I've grown a third head, child." Her mouth curved at the corners.

"My apologies, Mother." She stifled a small laugh at her mother's third head reference. She'd been depicted throughout Greek art with three heads. "I didn't mean to gape. It has been a long and exhausting exercise, and I do wish to help my friends."

"So let us set the wheels in motion, child."

She'd bring up the "child" thing another time. Right now a sense of gratitude warmed her.

Hekate's nostrils flared. "No one uses my gateways without my permission."

TWENTY-SEVEN

*"Deliberate violence is more to be
quenched than a fire." ~ Heraclitus*

When the fog in Carissa's head cleared, her predicament wasn't one she would gloat about. She'd been laid on a makeshift table and chained down in a rather compromising position. *Okay, maybe not so makeshift, but more like a slab of stone.* She lifted her head and looked around. Hal had the ancient ruins illuminated like a football oval. "Great sacrifice under the stars." Over to her right, a sheep was tied down, and near it a girl dressed all in white with a basket in hand, terror evident in her eyes and on her face. *This is so not good. Demented, Hal, why bring in an innocent girl?*

It was not so much her predicament that hurt, but the poor young girl dragged into Hal's lunacy.

Shifting her wrists from side to side, she tested the bonds. The limited movement told her they would not budge anytime soon. Her buttocks were at the end of the table and her legs hung over the side. They were spread and tied down to the legs of the table. She had to give it to Hal, he had the whole "stab the girl and get what I want" ritual down pat.

"No use, you won't be breaking through your shackles anytime soon." The voice of her favorite person filtered down from the top of her head as he looked at her upside down.

"Hal, what a lovely surprise. Nothing like a pleasant evening to butcher a few innocent women, all on the presumption that you may become some divine being with oodles of power to boot," she sneered, a growl threatening to come through. She wanted to roar, scream, break the bonds and rip the piece of shit standing over her to small bits of scrap.

"Ah Carissa, there will be no butchering, sweet. I'll make sure you die quickly with a swift slice of the blade to your throat."

"Gee, Hal, how romantic. You really know how to woo a girl." She paused. "I only pray that the gods take a swift blade to your throat once they know what you've done." *A donkey is what you are!*

"They won't have a chance. I'll be like them—a god," he sneered. "Their ambrosia will be mine."

She scoffed at his pathetic immortality fantasy.

"Let the girl go, she doesn't belong here. I'm what you want and I'm willing to die for your crazy plan, but the girl doesn't deserve any of this," she shouted.

"If she dies, it would be from her own hand and not mine. Her job is to perform the ritual of old. After that, she's food for the demons." He shrugged.

"Okay, me, I understand. You don't need the girl. I can double up and do both." *Who am I kidding? He's not going to buy any of it.*

He inched closer to her face.

"You take me for a fool," he hissed directly at her.

"No, I don't. I'm trying to save the life of an innocent before you begin your act of idiocy." She had to try for the girl's sake.

"Nice try, but the girl stays."

"Why won't you reconsider? I'll follow your commands. Just let her go. If there is an ounce of good left in you, release her. She is human, of no consequence, of no royal blood nor a descendant of the Olympian gods." There she was, on a roll now. She hoped the last bit helped the poor girl's situation. Looking over, the child trembled like a leaf. The girl looked no older than ten.

A scene flashed through her mind. A young girl in a 7-Eleven holdup, gun to her head. The burglar tells the cashier he wants all the money from the register in a brown bag. Jones and Carissa are there, but they can't do anything because he's got the gun to her head. The cashier does as he's told and tosses the bag to him. Then he shoots the girl. Naturally, that was the perfect excuse for Jones. Jones shot him but didn't kill him. There was an all-too-common outcome in these types of scenes—innocents often ended up dead. The robber doesn't always have a conscience, and in Hal's case, Carissa knew he was born without one. He would take what he wanted and leave a pile of bodies in his wake.

"Nice try, but no. She stays," he gritted out.

"What made you this way, Hal? The boy I remember was good and kind."

"Good and kind gets you nowhere, and in the end everyone pisses on you. Being an asshole, however, gets you everywhere, and earns you respect."

"Respect?" she shouted. "I don't think any lucid person would even consider the notion that they could respect you. Your lovely *Kakodaimones* don't count, since they have no thoughts of their own. They are zombies to the one who commands them."

"Don't be so quick to judge."

"You are a fool, Hal," she said through gritted teeth.

"And you are in no position to lecture me," he screamed.

She made one last plea. "Just consider it, Hal. Let the girl go. She isn't made like you and I." Carissa watched as doubt schooled his features for a split second, but then all hope died when he spoke his final words.

"She has a part to play and play she will." He walked away.

Carissa tugged at the chains, they merely rattled. *Nope not budging.* Internally, she screamed out for Xen, Kane, Adam, Kirke or Tithon—for anyone—and then she remembered her little gift of compulsion. But even if she could compel the young girl, there were still too many demons around for her to make a clean getaway. Maybe if she sent her towards the trees she might have a chance.

She pondered a few scenarios. The basket the girl carried held barley and a sacrificial knife. The knife would come in handy. If she compelled the girl to take the knife and stab one of the demons, she would meet her death. The demons would not spare her. They didn't have the capacity to distinguish who served what purpose in Hal's mad plan. *The whole thing was mental, in virtually all senses of the word.*

Hal returned with vials of liquid in his hands.

"Why?" she asked.

"Those cursed gods who dabble with mere mortals are to blame."

"But you seemed happier when I knew you as a kid."

"Happier because my talents had not shone through, made their presence known to unbalance me."

"So why not use them for a better purpose?"

"Better purpose!" he spat. "So people can take advantage of you and mock you? Face it, Carissa, humankind does not like freaks!"

"What if you met more people like us? Would that help you deal with it?"

"I don't wish to entangle myself amongst half-breeds. I want what those pesky gods on Olympus have."

She motioned her head to the vials still clutched in his hands. "What's with the vials?"

"Ah, a little something to help you along."

Her mouth went dry as understanding pierced through her gut. He was going to drug her again. Anger rose quickly. "You asshole, as bad as all this is, you want to drug me!"

He laughed. "It will make it easier for you, and how should I put this, more enjoyable." He enunciated every syllable of his last word.

"*Bastardos*," she yelled, trying to reach up through the shackles to throttle him.

A loud roar split the air.

Hal's eyes opened wide like saucers, then he moved out of her line of sight.

"Coward," she screamed.

Blood splattered around her.

A familiar voice sounded in her mind.

Koukla.

TWENTY-EIGHT

"Death does not concern us, because as long as we exist, death is not here. And when it does come, we no longer exist" ~ Epicurus

Xen, you're here?

> *I'll have you out of your shackles soon.*
>
> *Thick chains.*
>
> *Let me worry about that, koukla.*

Hope ignited in her body and soul. Her man had made it to her and she had every intention of going home with him this time. No more portal abductions. She was seriously going to stab the next person or thing to drag her through one. She lifted her head and turned it left and right to see where Xen fought, but something—or rather *someone* else—caught her eye. Phil. He was chained to an olive tree. She reached out with her mind.

> *Xen, you have to get to Phil, and there's an innocent girl right in the middle of this skata. You have to get her out of here.*
>
> *On it, koukla.*

Carissa tugged at her chains again. She focused on the young girl. *Move away from the sheep and demons. Go hide behind the trees. Leave the basket on the ground.*

She could use the sacrificial knife that lay at the base of the basket. She repeated her command. It worked. The girl moved away. The demons were now preoccupied with Xen's men.

She lifted her head again. Finally, she caught a glimpse of Xen. Her heart sped into a gallop. She wished she could contribute in some way, rather than lie there on the slab like a piece of *gyros* meat.

Rogue vampires joined the demons in the fight against the *Phi*. She rattled the chains again, but it was no use. Pain shot from her elbows to her fingertips. She winced and swallowed hard. She'd relaxed her body for a moment when she saw a familiar shimmer.

Kirke appeared, and next to her, a beautiful woman. She looked every bit a goddess with her Grecian dress and snake bangles wrapped around her arms.

"Kirke, you're here too," she blurted out.

"This is Hekate. The portals Hal is using are her gateways."

"Someone is in a lot of trouble then," she said, amused that Hal was moving up on the Most Wanted list.

"Let me help you out of your bonds."

"No, Kirke. Go cut off Hal's supply of demons."

"That's not all I'd like to cut off," Kirke said.

"I'll gladly help you," she breathed. "Now go. Let's get this over with."

Kirke waved her arms and disappeared with Hekate.

She lifted her head and was shocked to see the number of demons fighting against Xen's men. The *Phi* looked outnumbered.

"Please let Kirke and Hekate succeed."

Again she lifted her head. *Go the neck exercise.* She spied them in the distance next to the tree Phil had been chained to. Xen must have freed him. Relief washed over her.

She saw Hekate wave her hand once. Her lips moved. Hope flared in Carissa's stomach.

Blood dripped from Xen's sword. For every one he took down, two more appeared. The rogue vampires weren't helping things either. Unlike the demons, they had speed on their side, like Xen and his *Phi*.

A familiar scent tickled his nose. Tithon appeared at his side, sword ready.

"Come to join the fun?" Xen queried in the middle of taking a demon head.

"Looks like you could use some help with the rogue vampires," Tithon said as he speared a demon with his claymore. Tithon's use of sword choice did not puzzle Xen. The vampire had lived through some of the most brutal Scottish wars. Yes, he was another old boy.

"I would be grateful, Tithon, and you know it."

With that, Tithon sped to where two rogue vampires were attacking Adam.

Tithon speared one vampire through his back and straight into his undead heart. A second later, Adam ran his sword through the other vampire's heart and with his second sword, took his head.

"Glad to have you at my back," Adam said.

"Let's move. Looks like there are more demons coming through."

Xen heard the exchange and a sense of relief filled him. He'd have to talk to Tithon about a possible work proposition.

His sword sliced the air and severed another demon head. He had to get to Carissa, but the demons kept blocking his path. He looked around for the witch and saw her directly across from where he was fighting. A glow of pink shone to their right. A portal. No demons were coming out of it. The witches had it under control. He did a double take. Next to the portal were *phantasmata.*

"Ghosts."

His temporary distraction cost him. Silver chained nets were tossed over him. He made a futile attempt to move. He winced when the silver began to burn the flesh on his arms, neck and face. It had been bespelled. He dropped his sword, he fell to the ground, withering in pain. From his position, he watched Kane turn and pounce at one of the demons in wolf form. His effort was extinguished with the same means that brought Xen to his current predicament. One he hadn't made allowance for.

"*Gamoto,*" Xen yelled, biting back his agony. He needed to communicate to his men. He lifted his hand up as best he could, swallowing hard as it moved under the silver. He tapped the device attached to his ear. "Kane and I are down." He paused, taking breath. "Move the men back and recon the situation. Now." He gave his orders.

Xen wouldn't risk any more of his men. He ground his teeth and his muscles tensed. Anger coursed through him. His momentary lapse had given Hal the upper hand, a game changer he did not welcome.

"Ten minutes max as a recon then I'm coming back in, guns blazing." Adam's voice was loud.

"Old dog just got himself caught," Adam bellowed into his communicator. "Retreat!"

Even in pain, Xen stifled a laugh at Adam's reference to Kane being an old dog. Lucky he had shifted to wolf form and didn't have a communicator. He'd hate to see the consequences later when they were free.

"Adam, don't risk the men. Do you understand?" Xen couldn't allow his best men to fall.

"I hear you, Xen, but I can't just leave you and Kane ..." His voice trailed off.

"You assess the situation first. If it looks bad, you abandon the mission. We need you and the *Phi,* don't forget that. If this turns sour, give me your word you will abort."

"You have it, but I don't like it."

"It's not a question of like." Xen paused. "It's about living to fight another day, especially if you are outnumbered."

"Point made."

Xen ripped the communicator from his ear, replaying that scene over in his head. Frustration blurred his vision.

"Fuck!" yelled Kane when he shifted back to human form.

"Absolutely," came Hal's voice from behind them. "Now, isn't this a plus in driving the stakes home." He glared at Xen. "Literally speaking, that is."

Xen growled at him. The parasite had the audacity to make puns. Kane on the other hand let out an earsplitting wolf call. Hal startled at it.

"Careful, dog. You're not in any position to be barking your tune."

Xen would bet good money that Kane would take a nice chunk out of Hal if he got loose.

"Bring them to the sacrificial table," Hal ordered.

Xen dragged his sword with him. The demons pushed them both towards the table Carissa was bound on. When his eyes traveled over her position, his throat went dry and his fists clenched under the net. He reached out to her through his mind.

"Koukla."

"Xen. Just know that whichever way it ends, I love you."

"Koukla ..."

"Now," Hal said, snapping Xen's attention back to him. "It's time for a once in a lifetime experience and show. We seem to have lost our virgin with the sacrificial dagger, but no biggie. I'll just have to do it myself."

He walked over to where the basket lay on the ground. The dagger was nested between leaves. He pulled it out and walked over to the sheep which was still tied up. Sensing its doom, the sheep kicked when Hal tried to grab it. He managed to still the lamb, and in one clean sweep, he slit its throat. Blood poured on the ground. He caught some in a libation bowl. He took the bowl over to where Carissa lay then took the bloody knife and slit his wrist—but not deep, only enough to draw some blood.

He approached the table and ripped Carissa's underwear from her. Xen and Kane simultaneously growled. Pulling his pants down, he made himself ready by stroking his length. Xen growled again and pulled against the bewitched silver net to free himself.

"STOP. Hal, you don't know if this will work. I'm not that special." Carissa tried to move but it was fruitless.

"Oh, but you are! You see, when that filthy vampire impregnated you, he added to your potency with the new life that grows in your womb. Your lover over there stands for all things that are life-giving and nurturing. He and his *Phi* are the embodiment of life and the universe. The fact that you are pregnant by him fortifies that the gods have touched you. So you see, it's not really you I need, but rather the life that grows in you. Your baby's life is my pass to Olympus.

An inhuman roar from Xen split the air. This could not be happening. He had failed his fated and his unborn child.

Hal raised his dagger directly over her womb.

"*ARES.*" The name coursed up from her belly to her throat and tore out from her lips. While she screamed, she dove into the deepest, darkest recess of her mind and unlocked a part of herself that had been pushed into a corner. She was the daughter of Ares and she could summon any god to her. Her skin tingled and she called again.

"*ARES*"

Bright light circled Carissa. Ares appeared by her side. He took in Hal's form and state of undress and without a second thought, blasted him with his power and sent him flying through the air. Her father stalked over to the spot where Hal was splayed.

Kirke appeared near Kane. She muttered a spell in both Kane and Xen's direction. Kane threw off his net and moved fast to free Xen. Xen got to his feet then raced towards Carissa. He lifted his sword and smashed the chains that held her in place on the altar.

"Hey, that's some sword."

"Only you, *koukla,* would say something like that at moment like this!" He gave her his hand to help her up off the sacrificial table. She righted her dress.

In the distance, Hal got to his feet and started yelling instructions to his demons. The demons moved to attack Ares.

"Oh, you want to play," Ares leered. His battle armor appeared out of thin air.

Demons ran at him and Carissa winced. Not for her father, but rather that he took several heads in one go.

Carissa saw Hal making a beeline for her and Xen.

"Xen, we have to—" The words died on her lips because Hal jumped up in the air and lunged straight for her with the knife in his hand. Xen turned her with his vampire speed. Hal's sacrificial knife pierced Xen's shoulder blade. Xen twisted around and grabbed Hal by the throat. He squeezed his larynx and tossed him to the ground.

Carissa watched Hal stumble to his feet, choking, then her eyes met Xen's and she recognized that glassy look in his eyes.

"No," she screamed as he wobbled then dropped his sword. She helped him down to the ground.

Fury. Red in the deepest shade danced behind her eyelids. She lunged at Hal in martial arts mode, beyond sensible reproach. Anger on another level ignited and flared within her. She kicked him in the abs and sent him flying back, enraging him to all hades. She was at the end of her rope, and it had frayed. The damage she wanted to inflict on Hal had become far too great.

Hal tried to get up, but she was there faster than he could regain his footing. She threw a roundhouse kick which connected to his face. He went down. She raced back to Xen.

"You're bleeding a fair bit. I need to get you out of here."

"*Koukla*, I'm the one that's supposed to be getting you out of here."

"It doesn't matter who gets who out. All that matters is that we get out of here. I'm sick of Hal and these demons."

"In that case, *koukla,* it would be faster if I did this." Xen grabbed her and pulled her to him. His lips came down on hers and he planted a swift kiss on them.

You're bleeding to death and you want to kiss me, she projected to his mind.

There's never a bad time to kiss you, koukla. I'll have you know that I'd take every opportunity. " He waggled his eyebrows. She was starting to think the whole demon/Hal thing had sent them right over the edge.

They stumbled to their feet. Carissa was ready to go at Hal again.

Two demons sprang up behind Xen, grabbing him and yanking him away from her. She was left to face off with Hal. He gave her his best kick to her stomach and sent her flying backwards. Her head hit something solid. Her eyelids fluttered and she welcomed the darkness she swam in.

Xen's muscles tightened. He'd lost a lot of blood and needed healing from the burns on his skin, but when Carissa hit the ground, adrenaline spiked and he tore into the demons—literally ripped the demons' heads off their shoulders with his hands.

He let out a roar. He could no longer feel anything. Blood pooled around Carissa's dress.

He saw Ares turn and watched his demeanor change at the sight of his daughter unconscious on the ground. Hal stood over Carissa. Xen watched as he raised the dagger to bring it down on her heart. A loud war cry from Ares vibrated in Xen's ears. Blinding light hit every demon standing. The *Phi* understood that cry and ducked in time to escape the wrath of Ares. Xen was proud of his men in that moment, but as luck would have it, Hal had ducked too.

A low continuous growl emanated from his lips. He pushed to his feet then raced to retrieve his sword, but by the time he headed towards Hal, Ares had appeared behind him. Xen whistled and tossed his sword to Ares. Before Hal could turn around, Ares swung the sword, taking the head of the man who'd brought Xen nothing but grief. Watching Hal's headless body hit the ground sent a bucket of adrenaline rushing through Xen's body. The sweetest revenge he'd witnessed in many millennia. Hal's head and body exploded into dust.

Xen sped to Carissa's side and dropped to his knees. He could hear her heartbeat and thanked the gods she wasn't taken from him this day. Sharp pain skewered him in the heart, a vise squeezed his lungs. The baby's heartbeat was no more. Hal's death, although satisfying in the rush of the moment, was too quick. He would have made him suffer over and over and over.

Xen's head snapped up to a flash of bright light. Standing to the left of Ares was Poseidon. Outrage carved on his face. Water swirled behind him, suspended in midair—an unusual sight since they were inland on Poros.

"Nephew, you dare take the life of Hal, my son?" His voice boomed.

"The seed you sowed was not worth the life it became ... Uncle." Ares clearly didn't fear Poseidon. That much was evident to Xen. "Take your complaints to my father!"

"You will pay for this dearly, nephew." The body of water manifested behind him rose up and grew to a giant wave. Poseidon disappeared and the giant suspended wave came crashing down.

Xen covered Carissa's body. Bright light cocooned them. He looked up to see light around all the *Phi*, protecting them from the impact of the water.

Xen lifted Carissa into his arms. Out of nowhere a chariot with four horses appeared. Its golden form gleamed. Large wings sprung from the horses' backs much like Pegasus. Never had Xen glimpsed such beauty, and he had seen and ridden many horses. He recognized at once they were the horses of Ares—*Aithon, Phlogios, Konabos* and *Phobos.*

His recollection also clued him in to the fact that these were more than ordinary *hippoi*; these four could breathe fire and bring destruction in mere seconds.

Ares jumped onto the chariot and motioned for Xen to join him. His arms laced around Carissa's body and carefully, he lifted her into his arms.

Xen looked around at his men. His eyes met Kane's and he sent his thoughts to his loyal friend. *Get the men back to Athens.*

Kane nodded in understanding.

Ares roared and the horses moved. The *hippoi* let out a breath of fire before taking to the sky. Large wings flapped as the horses drew the chariot higher and higher. Xen had no idea where they were going or what intentions Ares had, but from the way he looked over Carissa, there was genuine concern.

"How serious are you about my daughter, Vampire?"

"She is my fated."

Ares let out a laugh at his words. "Ironic, don't you think?"

"No one does irony better than the Greeks."

"I am your maker. She is the life you protect first and foremost. I do not ever want to see another hair on her head out of place again. If I do, I will take your head myself."

"If she is harmed ever again, I'll let you take it."

He watched as a sneer broke out on Ares' lips.

TWENTY-NINE

"In a just cause the weak will beat the strong." ~ Sophocles

Featherlight kisses brushed her cheek and brought her out of her heavy slumber.

"*Koukla.*"

That one word almost started an avalanche of tears. She tried to move but realized her head was lead and wanted to tip forward. Battered and bruised, her midsection ached, but she couldn't yet recall the why of it.

"Don't move, you've suffered some very bad injuries. I have given you some of my blood to heal you faster. You didn't fair too well, *koukla.*"

Her hand jerked immediately to her abdomen. Xen turned her head to him. His fingers brushed her cheek. The look in his green eyes told her what she feared, she was no longer with child. A thousand images swam through her head, trying to grasp at what point it must have all happened. She remembered fighting Hal. A kick had sent her flying into a hard wall, the pain harrowing. She remembered when her head connected with the wall, then someone turned out the lights. She watched as Xen saw all her recollections. There was a deep sadness in his eyes. She knew he had been reading her.

"*Koukla.*"

And then that one word succeeded in breaking the dam. Hot tears spilled, causing every fiber in her body to spasm and shake. She was so overwrought with grief, her lungs tightened. It was so hard to breathe. Xen pulled her close. He whispered to her, only endearing words. Words which her brain memorized because she needed to anchor to something in order to get through this, and Xen and his soothing voice were the only thing she could hold onto without losing her mind completely.

Hours later when the rivers ran dry and she could not shed another tear, she stood in her zombie state. Her legs felt weak and numb, and her body was not responding to her commands. She was somewhere else. Xen rose from his position and wrapped his arms around her, firmly holding her up.

"Can you help me take a shower?" Her voice cracked.

"You need only ask, *koukla*."

What would she do without this man? He had changed her whole life. He'd given her a gift and she'd lost that precious gift. Guilt punctured her heart.

"*Koukla*, this is no fault of yours, and I will not have you blame yourself for it. The man who did this to you is dead, and I for one wish he weren't, so that I could watch him die slowly and savor it."

Turning her head, she saw the rage in his eyes. He looked at her and she noticed his eyes were puffy and red. He was crying too. Her immortal warrior had been shedding tears over their loss.

She wobbled but managed to grab him in an embrace. They stood there, not saying another word, just holding on to each other for dear life.

She pulled back a little and looked him in the eyes.

"I want to speak to Ares."

"Ask. He will answer you."

"Father," she said in a whisper.

The air sizzled and crackled. A flash of bright light bounced off the wall in their room. Ares stood before them. She let go of Xen, feeling somewhat better.

"*Kori mou,* how are you feeling?" he asked as he reached out to smooth her hair from her face.

"I'm dry from crying. I'm deeply scarred and wounded by this outcome, and above all I'm pissed to high Hades."

"Careful, *kori mou,* don't ever mention my uncle Hades. You don't know what he is capable of." His voice dripped with calm, but a warning came with it.

"But why would he answer me?" The thought that Hades would answer sent a sharp spike of fear down her spine. She'd suffered enough and didn't need more.

"As to the why, I cannot answer, but know this, Daughter ... if you call, they will come. You are the only demi-god on this mortal plain with the power to do that." He paused. "You seem to have unlocked that talent."

Carissa stood with her mouth open. Her father leaned over, placed a finger under her chin and pushed it up. She felt color shading her cheeks. Xen let out a laugh and that was the first time since she woke that she'd heard him laugh. She'd missed it.

"What other fancy little talents do I possess that I should know about?"

"Well, that's a good question. You showed remarkable talents early—a new one every six months to be precise. I don't know the extent of them because I had to bind your powers. I just know they must have stopped because your mother stopped calling me. I figured you were done, but one can never know, Carissa."

Xen spoke before she could ask the same thing. "What you're saying is that, unbound, she could be a live wire, so to speak."

"*Exactly!*"

Carissa took a minute to digest the enormity of what her powers might be and realized there was no going back. If she was born with these talents, as well as any that might pop up in the future, then she would have to deal with them. Ironically, her one-God belief system echoed in her head: *"God would not give you something if he thought you couldn't handle it."*

Xen tilted his head at her thought. His lips curved.

"I want you to unbind my powers, Father, and then I want you teach me how to use them, but it doesn't end there. I want retribution for my loss. Hal's death does not soothe me enough, as he didn't die by my hand. I need to voice my anger to the gods."

Ares laughed. "Daughter, no one voices their opinion to the gods. It's just not permitted."

"I don't really give a damn what is permitted." She bit back the anger rising to the surface.

"Those gods sit up wherever they are and pay no attention to the progeny they so carelessly leave in the human realm. Someone needs to be responsible. I want my say, one way or another. If you don't help me, Father, I will find my own way. And I assure you, I may be battered and bruised right now, but I will recover, and when I do, I'm going to want heads just as much as Xen does."

A loud laugh echoed around the room. Ares thought it was funny.

"This isn't a joke."

"I didn't say it was. I was admiring how brilliant my daughter is that she wants to fight. Just like her father." Ares walked over and embraced her. She hugged him back. Before she could say anything else, he whispered a few words over the top of her head. She felt his breath.

"Apolyo," he spoke the ancient Greek word.

She didn't understand the word but Xen projected a multitude of meanings to her mind. *Unbind, release, set free.*

The air shifted. Ares tightened his embrace. Light tingles started at the top of her head and worked their way down her body. It felt like thousands of pinpricks; it intensified and her body burned from the inside out. It happened quickly and she could see Xen standing closer, his face frozen with concern.

I'm okay, she projected.

He let out a breath.

"You are now unbound, Daughter. Be ready in three days. I will come for you." He pointed to Xen. "He stays here."

"She will not be going alone, Ares," Xen gritted out.

"She won't be alone. She will be with me," Ares bit back.

They stood nose-to-nose, toe-to-toe.

"Can you two quit talking as if I'm not here? Oh, and *she* as you both put it, can make up her own mind."

"*Koukla,* I'm so—" Xen didn't finish his sentence because Carissa cut him off.

"In three days, Father and you will agree to whatever I decide at the time." He gave her a knowing look, but she pushed on. "Audience with all the gods, and I won't take no for an answer."

"You'll have your audience because I will be on trial for Hal's murder. You aren't the only one who wants retribution," Ares responded. "Oh, you should also know that if they give you an audience, it is because you are not only my daughter, but the descendant of the great Cecrops. He was the founder and first king of Athens."

"He was half man, half serpent. A myth."

"Daughter, so am I," he said, giving her a subtle wink.

Bright light engulfed the room. Her mouth hung open and so did Xen's. She put a finger under his chin and pushed it closed. He pulled her into an embrace.

She had three days to learn the extent of her powers as well as how to control and use them. She would not be unprepared or underprivileged when she stood before the Greek gods on Olympus.

Xen's phone rang. He fished it out of his pocket and answered. "Yes she's here. Who's this?" Carissa could hear a frantic woman on the other end.

"For you," he said and handed her the phone.

She took the phone from Xen and put it to her ear.

"Carissa, where the hell have you been?"

"It's a long story. What's up?" What on earth would she tell Ligi without bringing her into all the madness?

"Kelly."

"What's happened? Is she hurt?"

"No, she's been kidnapped by some badass named Lox."

"Lox who ...?" The words died on her lips when her eyes met Xen's and saw his paled complexion.

"Gamoto."

GLOSSARY OF GREEK TERMINOLOGY

Alala	Ancient battle cry.
Aletheia	Truth.
Anagke	Force.
Bastardos	Bastard.
Charis	Grace, boon, favour, forgive.
Diki mou	Mine.
Doxa	Honor.
Efharisto	Thank you.
Eftychos	Fortunately.
Eisai	You are.
Entaxei	Okay.

Gamiseta	It's all fucked.
Gamoto	Swear word for fuck.
Gyros	Grilled meat on pita bread with salad.
Kori mou	Daughter mine.
Hippoi Areioi	The four fire-breathing horses that draw the chariot of Ares.
Hypnosi	Spell of hypnosis.
Kakodaimones	Demons.
Keftedes	Meatballs.
Kori	Daughter.
Koukla	Greek endearment meaning doll. Used in the same context as saying babe.
Lamia	Vampiric demon, which preys on young men in guise of a beautiful woman.
Lycanthrope	Werewolves that shift to human form and vice versa.
Lykos	Wolf.
Lykoi	Wolves.
Malaka	Greek swear word for asshole.
Mnemoneuo	Remember, memory.
Mou	My, mine.

Nai	Yes.
Nereides	Sea Nymphs.
Paidia	Kids, children.
Pantote	Always, forever.
Phantasia	Fantasy, dream
Phantasma	Ghosts or phantoms which haunt the living. Some are corporeal in form. A term often used by Greeks for any supernatural form, activity or manifestation.
Pharmakeia	A witch or sorceress.
Phi Athanatoi	Immortals protecting mankind. Also known as the Athanatoi or just Phi.
Skata	Shit.
Souvlaki	Small pieces of meat skewered on a stick.
Stifado	Beef stew.
Ta leme	We will speak later.
Thitsa	Endearment for auntie.
Tipota	Nothing.
Tzatziki	Sauce made of yogurt with shredded cucumber and garlic.
Xiphos	Double edged sword.
Vlaka	Idiot.

www.ingramcontent.com/pod-product-compliance
Lightning Source LLC
Chambersburg PA
CBHW050008120726
47903CB00006B/1686